Hebron Public Library
W Sigler St.
Hebron, IN 46341

Dead Water

Also by Barbara Hambly

A Free Man of Color

Fever Season

Graveyard Dust

Sold Down the River

Die Upon a Kiss

Wet Grave

Days of the Dead

BANTAM BOOKS

New York

Toronto

London

Sydney

Auckland

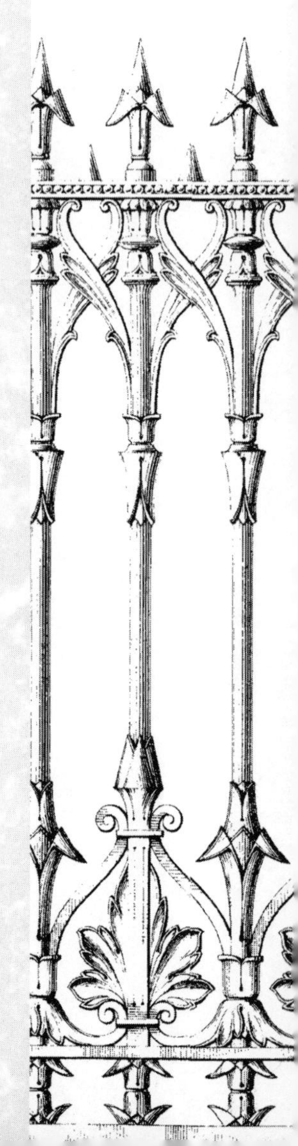

Dead Water

Barbara Hambly

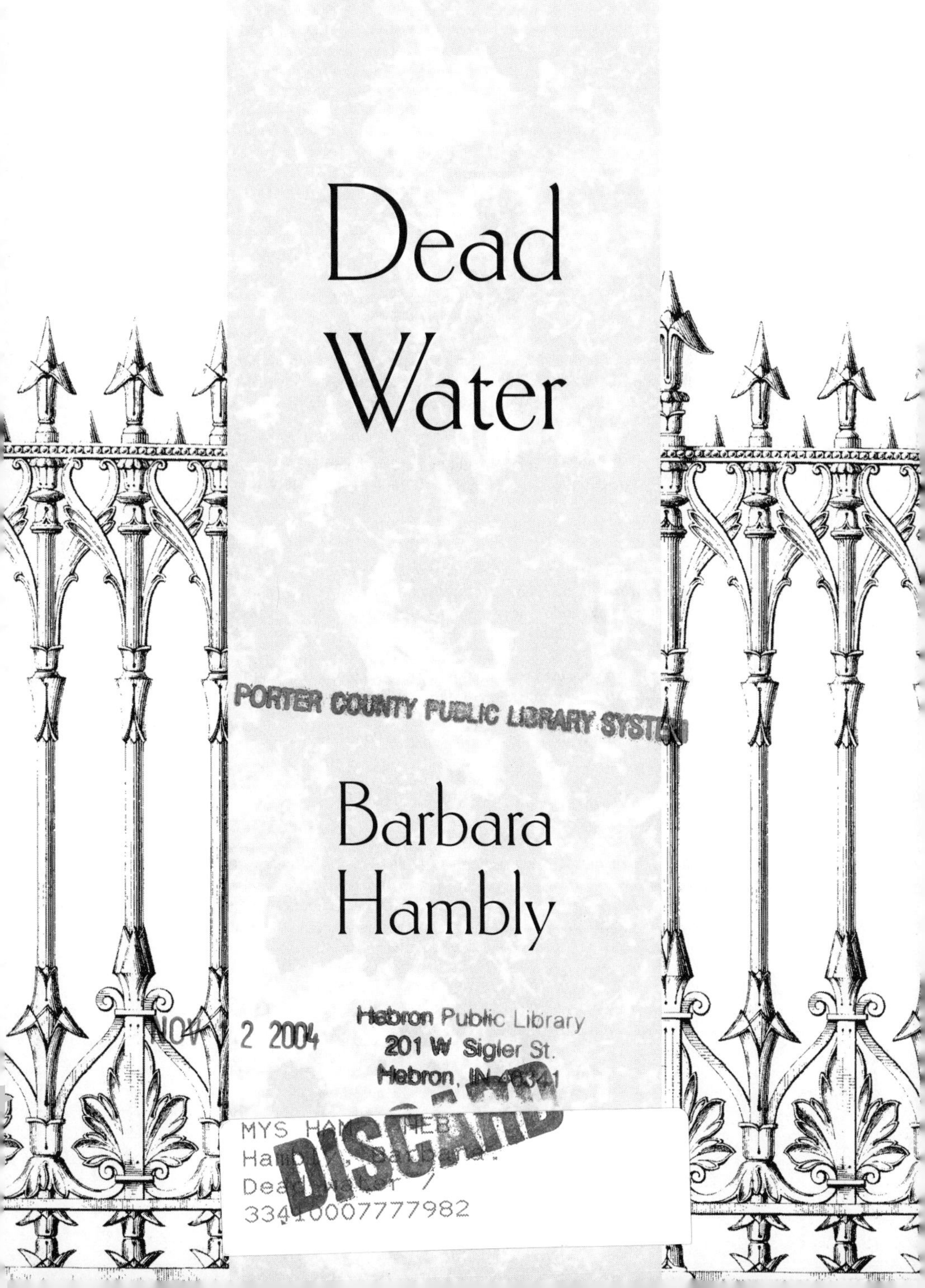

DEAD WATER
A Bantam Book / August 2004

Published by Bantam Dell
A Division of Random House, Inc.
New York, New York

This is a work of fiction. Names, characters, places, and incidents either are the product of the author's imagination or are used fictitiously. Any resemblance to actual persons, living or dead, events, or locales is entirely coincidental.

Book design by Laurie Jewell

Library of Congress Cataloging in Publication Data

Hambly, Barbara.
Dead water / Barbara Hambly.
p. cm.
ISBN 0-553-10964-2
1. January, Benjamin (Fictitious character)—Fiction. 2. Private investigators—Louisiana—New Orleans—Fiction. 3. Natchez-under-the-Hill (Natchez, Miss.)—Fiction. 4. Free African Americans—Fiction. 5. African American men—Fiction. 6. New Orleans (La.)—Fiction. 7. Embezzlement—Fiction. 8. Steamboats—Fiction. I. Title.

PS3558.A4215D43 2004
813'.54—dc22
2004040766

Manufactured in the United States of America
Published simultaneously in Canada

BVG 10 9 8 7 6 5 4 3 2 1

For Yeoman Mel

A PORTION OF THE RIVER

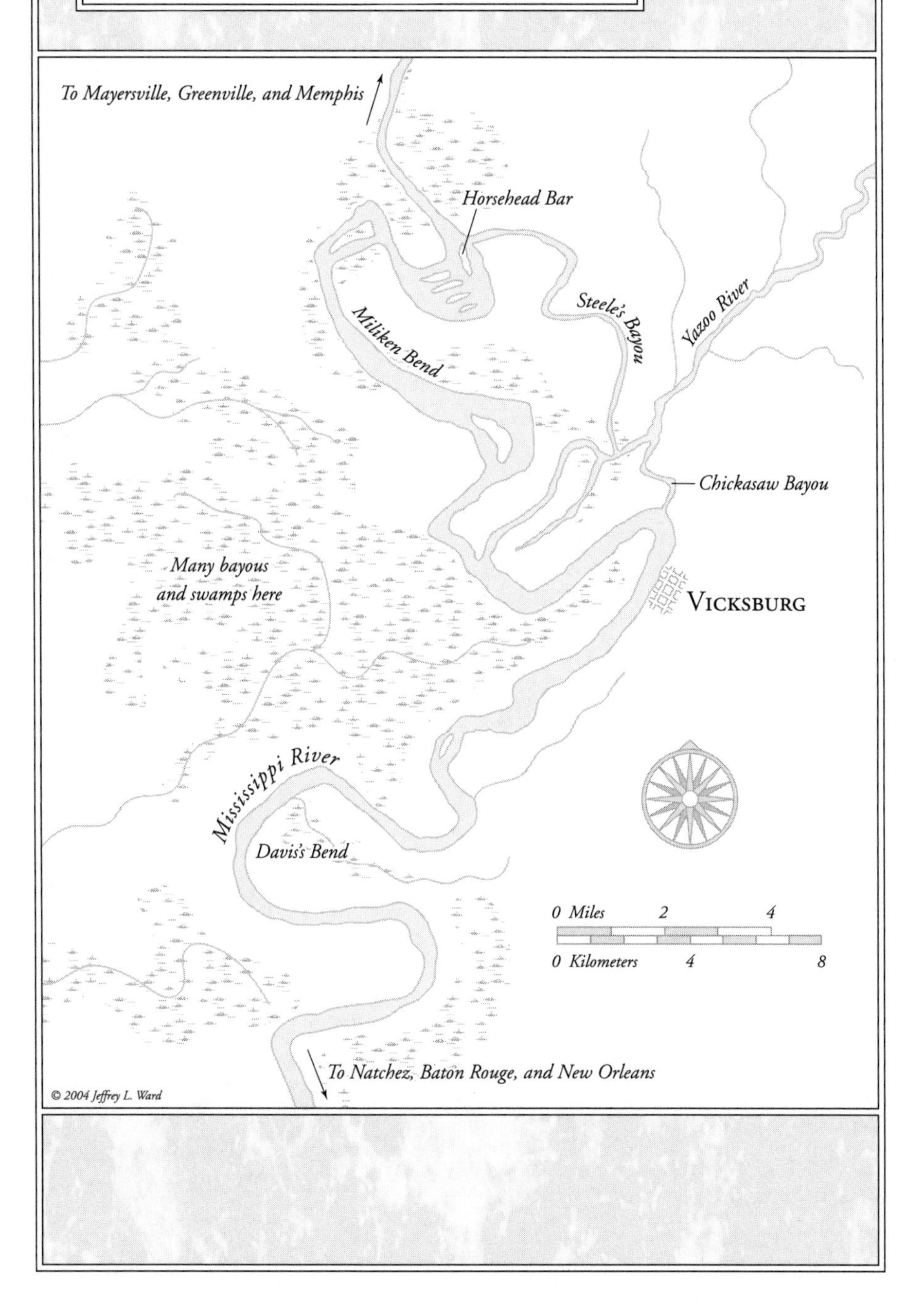

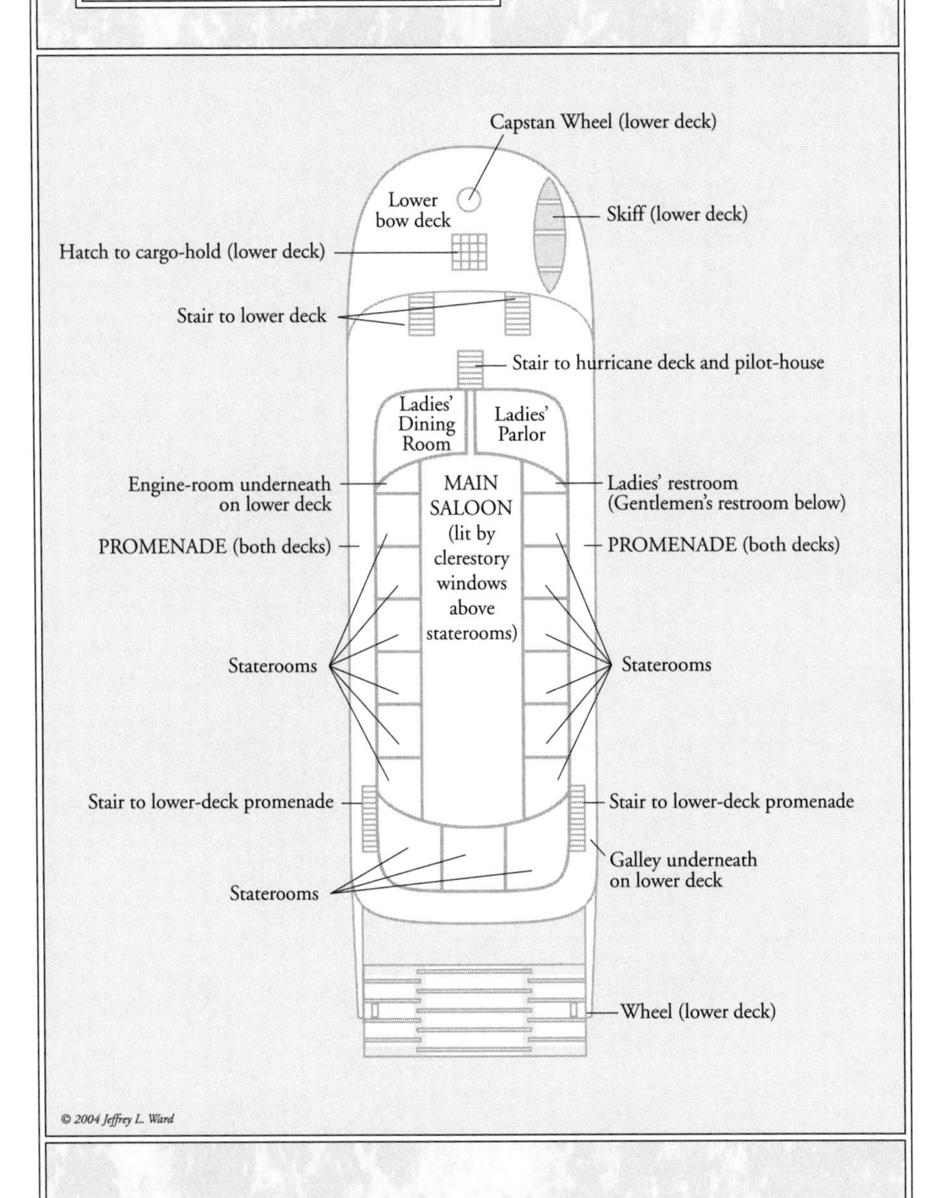
THE SILVER MOON
Capstan Wheel (lower deck)
Lower bow deck
Skiff (lower deck)
Hatch to cargo-hold (lower deck)
Stair to lower deck
Stair to hurricane deck and pilot-house
Ladies' Dining Room
Ladies' Parlor
Engine-room underneath on lower deck
MAIN SALOON (lit by clerestory windows above staterooms)
Ladies' restroom (Gentlemen's restroom below)
PROMENADE (both decks)
PROMENADE (both decks)
Staterooms
Staterooms
Stair to lower-deck promenade
Stair to lower-deck promenade
Galley underneath on lower deck
Staterooms
Wheel (lower deck)
© 2004 Jeffrey L. Ward

Dead Water

ONE

Six days out of seven, the ten thousand or so people in the city of New Orleans whose bodies were the property of other people were kept pretty busy. Having no legal right to choose what they'd rather be doing, they tended to get the dirty jobs, like mucking out stables, cleaning the always-horrifying three-foot gutters that rimmed the downtown streets, cooking everybody's food in sweltering kitchens, and washing everybody's clothing, and getting damn little thanks for any of it—they were better off doing white people's chores than living in heathen villages in Africa like their ancestors (said the white people).

Sunday afternoons, the slaves got together in what was officially called Circus Square—unofficially, Congo Square—next to the turning basin where the canal-boats maneuvered, and close by the old St. Louis Cemetery. Those who had garden plots sold their surplus produce: tomatoes and corn, this time of year, and peaches whose scent turned the thick hot air around them to molten gold. Old women peddled gumbo for a penny or two a bowl, or bread, or pralines: brown, pink, or white. Old men sat under the plane-trees around the square's edge and told stories to the children, about Compair Lapin the rabbit and ugly stupid Bouki the Hyena, and High John the Conqueror, who always got the better of the whites.

Always, someone played the drums. Ancient rhythms flowed and leaped through the American dust, rhythms passed down from mothers or fathers or grandparents who'd been taken from African shores—even the modern tunes were quirked into African syncopation.

Always there was dancing, the men turning the women under their arms, leaping and slapping their feet, wriggling in doubled and quadrupled rhythms, styling to show off what they could do. Ankle-bells jangled, hands clapped. Voices shouted encouragement, and when the sun glanced low over the slate roofs of the pastel town and flashed like a burning sword blade on the river, then Mamzelle Marie would come—Marie Laveau, the Queen of all the voodoos—and dance with her snake, and sing the songs of her power and her triumph.

At the gates of the paling fence that circled Congo Square, Benjamin January stood watching the voodoo queen dance in the twilight.

I walk on pins,
I walk on needles,
I walk on gilded splinters;
I want to see what they can do. . . .

January had met the voodoo queen soon after he'd returned to New Orleans from France, where he'd lived for sixteen years. Then, as now—three years ago, that was—the summer heat had lain on the town like a damp and itchy blanket, but in that summer three years ago had come not only the usual yellow fever, but the cholera, too. It was the cholera that had brought January back to New Orleans, the cholera that had taken the life of his wife in Paris, that had driven him, half-crazy with grief, home to this city of his birth. When he'd gone to France in 1817 to study surgery, he had vowed he'd never return to the land where he'd been born a slave, where, despite his freedom, the color of his skin still dictated what he could and could not do.

Yet here he was, he thought as he watched Mamzelle Marie raise the seven-foot kingsnake high above her head—as he watched the reptile slip and coil down her arms to wrap around her bronze throat and the bosom half-covered by her red cotton blouse.

Back in New Orleans.

Back with his family—with the mother who strove to pretend she'd never been a slave herself, or borne two children to a slave. With the one sister who was a rich white man's mistress, and the other sister whom he now hoped to find here, somewhere, in this moving mass of dancers.

Back home. And married again—the thought still filled him with wonderment—to a lady named Rose, who'd been no more than a gawky, nearsighted schoolgirl when he'd left New Orleans all those years ago.

He slipped his hand into the pocket of his scruffy corduroy jacket, touched the thing Rose had handed him that morning, bony and nasty even through wrappings of bandanna and newspaper.

The gallery where they customarily had breakfast overlooked the narrow courtyard of that creaky old Spanish house on Rue Esplanade that for eight and a half months now had been their home. Rose had been upstairs, helping Cosette pack—Cosette, who had boarded with them for four of those eight months as a pupil in the school Rose had established. So far they'd had only three pupils. One—Marie-Anne—had departed a few days previously, to join her mother in a cottage by the lake rented by her mother's white protector. The youngest, Germaine, shared bread and coffee with January on the gallery. Ten years old and a fragile little miracle of ladylike deportment, she had a creamy dark complexion and African eyes that made her look like some ancient Pharaoh's daughter inexplicably masquerading in ruffles and lace. Germaine's mother, also a rich white man's plaçée, was coming for her that afternoon. The morning air was silky, before the day's brutal heat began, and scented with café au lait.

"I found this in Cosette's room," Rose had said, coming out onto the gallery, and handed January the thing that was now in his pocket.

It was a rooster's head, the eyes and much of the flesh gone, but black wax still visible clotting its bill.

And so he had come here.

He-ron mandé,
He-ron mandé,
Tiqui li papa. . . .

Men sang as they heaped wood in pits gouged in the dust, kindled fires to light the shadows that gathered thick beneath the trees. A few of the stinking little saloons on the other side of the turning-basin had lit their lanterns; smoke from the gumbo-lady's fire scratched January's eyes. Someone jostled him from behind, and glancing back, he saw a couple of young white ladies, with an elderly female servant in tow to lend them respectability, staring through the fence with avid eyes. One of them whispered, "Which one is her?" in English.

They weren't the only ones staring. Looking away from the firelight, January saw white idlers strung all along the fence, peering in: Creole French and Creole Spanish in starched collars and well-cut coats of Bath superfine; Americans from the other side of Canal Street, with the greedy, restless eyes of those who view everything as a potential source of income. In the winter Carnival season, and on up through late spring, young ladies in their bell-shaped skirts and wide sleeves would come to gaze, though by this time of year most of them had left town. The two young women who whispered behind him were clearly of the class that didn't have summer houses by the lake.

January went back to scanning the faces of the dancers in the leaping yellow firelight. Men and women who had to return the next day to being what the whites wanted them to be: stablemen and laundresses, stevedores on the wharves or milliners in the tiny shops on Rue Chartres. People who had to pretend to be white in their hearts if they wanted to get money from the whites who were its only source.

Beyond them in the shadows beneath the plane-trees January picked out others, though it was rapidly becoming too dark to see clearly. After three and a half years back, he knew most of the voodoos, the root-doctors and ouangas and the lesser queens with their bright-colored headwraps worked up into five points, like gaudy flame around their faces. Some he knew from before he'd left, all those years ago. He saw withered old Dr. Brimstone, and John Bayou with his expressionless reptile eyes. Saw hugely fat Queen Lala, and Queen Régine like a dessicated black ant, strings of peeling glass pearls rattling around her withered neck.

Behind him he heard the young women still whispering, wondering if, later, they dared to go to Mamzelle for a love-ouanga or a spell to drive a rival away.

Roaches the size of a child's hand dove on roaring wings at the fires. A shift of air too sluggish to be termed a breeze filled the hot night with the sewage stink of the basin, and smell of the cemetery beyond it.

In the shadows near Mamzelle Marie, January glimpsed the woman he'd come looking for.

She was called Olympia Snakebones among the voodoos, a tall woman and thin. She swayed with half-shut eyes, and sweat shone on her dark African features: strong wide cheekbones and firm mouth, and despite one white grandparent, that glossy darkness the slave dealers called *le beau noir lustré*.

January edged past the two white girls and into the torchlight. His clothes weren't fancy—rough wool trousers, good boots, a blue calico shirt, and a short corduroy jacket—and many of the slaves were dressed far better than he. The men wore their best liveries if they were butlers or valets, the girls, bright dresses or satin skirts if they'd saved up the money from tips and gardening sales. Many greeted him, recognizing him from the wintertime Carnival season, when he'd play piano for the white folks' balls and parties, or knowing him as the man they'd call in for a difficult childbirth, or an injury they didn't want their masters to know about. Even in France he'd been unable to make more than a bare living as a surgeon, and had had to return to his first love—music—when he wanted to earn enough money to marry. In

New Orleans the *libres*—the free people of color—followed white society in preferring professionals of lighter skin and more European features than he.

Even his mother, January reflected wryly, sometimes passed him on the street without acknowledgment if she was with someone she wanted to impress. God forbid she should admit that a man who looked every inch of his enormous height to be a full-blooded African (not to mention being forty-three years old) was her son. He sometimes wondered with amusement what she'd do if she needed a surgeon: call in one of the lighter-skinned *libres* as all her friends did, or send for her son because he'd work for free.

Like a chameleon set down on plaid, he supposed she'd simply die of vexation.

"Olympe," he said, and Olympia Snakebones turned and smiled up at him with a white slash of protuberant teeth.

"Brother," she greeted him.

They drew a little aside to one of the fires, and January dug out the bandanna with its ugly secret.

Olympe flicked a corner of the cloth aside with the back of her fingernail, and made a face. Above her glittering forehead the tignon she wore—the headscarf mandated for all women of color, *libre* or slave—was dark with moisture: Olympe loved to dance and would have done so in the heat of noon-day, let alone the sticky magical warmth of evening. Her great dark eyes rose again to his.

"Somebody good and mad at you." Like January, when their mother had been bought and freed by St. Denis Janvier, Olympe had been given a tutor to eradicate the casual African sloppiness from her speech. It hadn't worked, of course. Nobody could teach Olympe a thing she didn't want to learn. Having discovered early in life that she could annoy her mother by saying "tote" for "carry" or "niame-niame" for "food," Olympe still spoke like she'd been cutting cane all her life.

"Not at me," said January. "Rose found this in the room of one of the girls at the school. The girl's been sick, on and off, for weeks."

"That's no surprise." Olympe pulled a pin out of her tignon and used it to turn over the half-rotted head in its crumple of newspaper and cloth. "When Queen Régine puts a cross on somebody, she follows up with poison if she can."

January's face hardened. "I thought it was something like that."

"Who is it?"

"Cosette Gardinier."

Olympe nodded. Voodoos dealt in secrets, and the free colored community of New Orleans throve on gossip and the intimate knowledge of everybody else's business. "That mother of hers been takin' her older girl, Fantine, to the Blue Ribbon balls all last winter an' this one," she said. "And she ain't got a place yet."

January nodded. The information wasn't new to him. White men would come to the Blue Ribbon balls—the quadroon balls—to dance with their free colored mistresses, their plaçées, and to gamble and chat with their friends away from their wives. Fathers would bring sons there to meet the young ladies of the free colored demimonde, quadroons or octoroons sometimes as fair-skinned as white girls themselves, carefully educated in fashionable accomplishments but, unlike the white girls, educated also in the techniques of pleasing men.

The men sought mistresses, not whores, quasi-wives who would live in their shadow for years, sometimes decades. A woman like Cosette's mother—or January's, for that matter—could parlay the house and housekeeping money that were part of the arrangement into serious investments and a good living even after the protector was long gone.

Most plaçées taught their daughters to follow in their footsteps, a necessary education when the alternative was a life of sewing other people's clothes or doing other people's laundry to put food on the table. It was sheer Quixoticism for January's wife, Rose, to open a school for girls of color that taught science, mathematics, Latin, and literature, as well as music, drawing, and just enough poetry to be able to converse with men, and Cosette Gardinier had wolfed down this heftier intellectual fare with the hasty guilt of one who knows she'll be forced into a more acceptable feminine mold on the morrow.

He said, "Fantine is how old?"

"Nineteen."

January pressed his sister's shoulder. "Thanks."

There was no sign now of Queen Régine's bright red bodice and red-striped tignon in the groups beneath the trees. The gate on the up-stream side of the square opened into a muddy lane that ran past the basin and on beside a high brick wall whose top was a fringed jungle of resurrection fern. The smell of the basin was bad, with the privies of its plank-built saloons draining into it, but the stench from beyond the wall was infinitely worse.

January saw the flicker of Queen Régine's striped tignon as she turned a corner of an even muddier lane—the municipal gutters didn't extend farther inland than Rue des Ramparts, and it had rained that afternoon, as it did nearly every afternoon in summer. He followed cautiously, boots slurping in the ooze. The iron-barred gate that led into the cemetery stood ajar.

Once inside the cemetery, visibility dropped to two feet. Though light lingered in the sky, January knew it would fade fast. The ground was even wetter here, and sent up, with each step, a ghastly reek of mortality. Around him tombs rose like little brick houses in some silent, horrible city. Because the ground-water in south Louisiana lay so close to the surface, even a shallow hole would fill, and corpses buried in New Orleans earth had a way of working to the surface in the winter. After the first flood or two brought coffins bobbing down the streets—giving a new meaning to the phrase "Grandma's coming to visit"—tombs began to be built above the ground.

Some were only brick benches barely knee-high and stuccoed to protect the soft local brick from crumbling away. Others stood as tall as a man, with marble slabs on the front inscribed with the names of their occupants. Some had little railings before them of wrought iron, like yards before the houses of the dead; others were fronted with locked and gated grilles. Nearly all sported spikes or brackets, so that family members could hang wreaths of zinc or jet-bead flowers on the

Feast of All Saints, when they came to patch the stucco, renew the whitewash, and picnic among the graves.

It had been seven months and a half since the Feast of All Saints, and even on tombs newly furbished up, resurrection fern had begun to sprout in crannies. Those tombs that hadn't been repaired for a year, or two, or ten, were gay little islands of greenery, with the stucco rotting away and the bricks crumbling within. Crayfish crept in and out of the cracks of such tombs, breeding it seemed by spontaneous generation in the pools where the ground lay low; three-inch roaches and palmetto bugs emerged from crevices almost visibly picking their teeth.

The smell was what one could expect. After passing through two cholera epidemics and any number of fever summers, January was only glad it was no worse. He'd heard rumors that in the rear parts of the cemetery, not only crayfish but small alligators lived in the swampy puddles, and was half inclined to believe it.

Queen Régine, of course, could be six feet from him among the tombs and he'd never see her.

He knelt almost the moment he was through the gate, picking out the tracks of her small, narrow shoes in the mud. There was barely enough light left for that.

They led away to his right, between two high sepulchres that surrounded the still-taller edifice of one of the burial-society group tombs. January followed cautiously. Once the woman he tracked guessed his presence, she would take pains to hide. With night coming on fast, he'd never find her.

Movement caught his eye and he turned. But it was only an undertaker wheeling a black-draped barrow with a little coffin. A solitary mourner followed, a woman. Not the baby's mother, January guessed, for she did not wear black, but a moss-green gown whose figurings of rust and cream blended in the twilight like the pelt of an animal half-hidden in leaves. An old family, he thought, for the pair halted at an unkept tomb whose name had been eradicated by time. The woman unlocked the grille that surrounded it; the faint scrape of metal sounded loud in the cicada-rattling dark.

Was everyone but the child's mother, and this woman, away in some summer home by the lake?

Or was there some other story there, one that nobody would ever know, in the half-secret burial of a child's coffin in the gathering dusk?

January slipped around the corner of a marble-fronted mausoleum inscribed with the name DUFRESNE, and saw Queen Régine.

She was on her knees between the two-story tomb of the Blanque family and a low bench surmounted by the statue of a sleeping baby. She dug in the earth with a stick, like a fierce child making mud-pies in the dark. But it was a deadly serious occupation, for graveyard earth, January knew, was the chief component of death-spells, of the jujus of ruin and fear. She worked furtively, glancing around her, pausing now and then to scoop up handfuls of the wet black earth and scrape them into the gourd bottle she carried tied to her belt.

January used the DuFresne tomb to shield him as he edged nearer. He could hear her voice now, a high-pitched jumble of whispered nonsense words, some garbled African, others broken bits of Spanish or Chickasaw, memorized from someone who'd memorized them herself long ago. He heard the name of the demon Ozoncaire, a favorite of the voodoos: "Hex him good, Ozoncaire, don't let him sleep nor eat till he decide this case for Bernadette Metoyer. . . ."

As he emerged around the other side of the tomb, January saw that she was burying something—a split beef tongue was what Olympe used, with the name of the judge in the court case her client wanted to win sewed up in it. He waited and watched as she lit a black wax candle and dripped some of the wax on the newly-turned earth and while she worked a few coins down into the soil.

The Queen buried the candle-stump, corked the gourd, worked a few bricks loose from the near-by tomb to cover the place so the priest of St. Jude's wouldn't see that the earth had been turned. Then she got to her feet to find January standing mere inches away.

She turned to bolt and January caught her by the arm. Her hand whipped to her tignon, and he grabbed her other wrist before she could stab him with the pin she held. She spit in his face, but he was ready for that, too, and didn't loosen his grip as many men would have. "I got a warning for you," he said.

She froze, seeming to get smaller in his hands, like a rat pulling itself together before it bites. Her lifted lip showed sharp teeth, and gaps where the bearing of children had lost her some of them. "What I need a warning for, me?" she asked. "Ain't nobody can take me on and win, piano-player."

"They know it's you who was hired to cross Cosette Gardinier. If ill befalls her, they'll know whose door to come knocking on."

"And who's 'they'?"

"Those that have her good at heart."

The voodoo spit again, this time on the ground. "You dreamin', piano-player. There's none got that girl's good at heart."

"*I* have Cosette's good at heart," replied January quietly. "And if she dies, you think anyone's going to listen when you say it was someone in the girl's own family behind it?"

Queen Régine tried to pull her arm away; anger blazing in her hot little eyes. "The poison won't kill her. Her mama just want her sickly, to stay out of the way when Yves LaBranche come around courtin' the older girl. LaBranche been lookin' on that Cosette a little too close."

"That's what they tell you," retorted January. "Cosette was like to die two nights ago. So maybe somebody else added a bit to what you gave the candy-lady on Rue Burgundy, thinkin' if the girl does die it'll be easy for you to take the blame."

The accusation of the old woman who sold pralines along the Rue Burgundy was a shot in the dark—January only knew Cosette was deeply fond of the pink-dyed coconut candles—but he saw the anger and alarm flare in the mambo's eyes. Then rage took their place, and she jerked on her hands again, her little wrists like sticks, lost in January's vast grip.

"You lyin', piano-player," she snarled. "You take your hand off me! No man lay a hand on Queen Régine!"

"Let the girl alone. I'm warning you."

"*You* warning *me*? *I* warning *you,* piano-player!" And she pulled hard at his grip, so that when he opened his hands suddenly she staggered back, and fell over the low tomb with its chipped marble child. Furious, she sprang to her feet, no more now than a shadow in the darkness, a shadow from which one single skinny finger, clotted with graveyard dirt, stabbed out at him.

"You keep your silence, and you stay out of this matter if you know what's good for you! You think 'cause your sister a voodoo you got a suit of armor, but you don't! I curse you! In the name of the Baron Cemetery, in the name of the Guédé, in the name of the Grand Zombi, I curse you, to the ruin of all you touch, and the destruction of all you hope!"

In the blackness her eyes had a slick silver gleam, like a demon's eyes in shadow. Her voice turned shrill and nasal, like the voices of those ridden by the Guédé spirits in the voodoo ceremonies along Bayou St. John.

"Guédé-vi, take the gold from out of his hands! Guédé-Five-Days-Unhappy, tear the roof away from over his head! Marinette-of-the-Dry-Arms, take his wife from him and let him walk the roads of the earth to search for her, and men hunting behind him and even the priests of God raising their hands against him!"

She stepped back into the darkness, and her voice came to him, normal again. "You leave me alone, piano-player! You will curse your own hands that you raised against me!"

He heard the slop and squeak of her feet, running away into darkness.

Far off a cannon sounded, signaling curfew for all people of color, slave or free—except, of course, those whose professions made life more convenient for white men, like hack-drivers and musicians and waiters and the stevedores who unloaded cargoes on the levee, even at this slow season, far into the sweltering nights.

The drums in the square had ceased. Like the voice of angels rebuking some pagan chant, churchbells floated out over the lamplit town, calling the faithful to evening Mass. January, who had gone to early Mass that morning, wiped the old woman's spit from his cheek with his bandanna and resisted the urge to head straight for the mortuary chapel of St. Jude that stood at the corner of the cemetery, to confess and take Communion again.

Confess what? That he believed that the name of the Guédé spirits had the power to harm him?

Oh, God will appreciate hearing that.

He made his way out of the graveyard, walking carefully, for it was well and truly dark now and he had no desire to stumble into the brimming brown fluids of the gutter of the Rue des Ramparts.

Along that street, lamps had been lit in a few of the small pastel cottages, where plaçées would be setting tables for a light supper for when their protectors dropped by, seeking quiet and relief after the inevitable and interminable Sunday-dinner gatherings of French Creole families. Most of those houses were dark. Plaçées, protectors, and families alike had retreated to the cooler precincts of Milneburgh or Spanish Fort, or Mandeville on the other side of the lake, leaving the city to the mosquitoes and to the sweltering poor. The Americans, in their own faubourg of big wooden houses and wide yards on the other side of Canal Street, had retreated to such northern resorts as White Sulfur Springs or to the White Mountains of New England. Along the levee the river was low. Most of the big side-wheel steamboats lay drawn up at the wharves to wait until autumn brought higher water and the successive harvests of corn, cotton, and sugar to turn a profit again.

January looked for Olympe as he passed Congo Square, but only a few market-women remained, gathering the last of their produce into baskets and folding up the blankets on which it had been spread. The smell of ashes vied with the stink of sewage and the cemetery reek in the air.

Except for the gambling-parlors along Rue Orleans and Rue

Royale—which never closed and never emptied—New Orleans was dark, and quiet save for the roar of the cicadas and the incessant whine of mosquitoes in January's ears.

No, he admitted to himself, he didn't think Queen Régine's curse, or the power of the Guédé spirits, would be able to harm him.

But poison, and surreptitious fires set in the kitchen while he and Rose slept, were another matter. They had bought their house from the French Creoles who owned it for nine thousand dollars, of which half had been paid immediately and another twenty-five percent was due in September, three months away. January didn't think the DeLaHaye family would remit a penny—or allow more time on the loan—should the house itself burn down one night.

He found himself listening behind him, all the way down the breathless street, for the whisper of the voodoo's feet and the rustle of her skirt. He heard nothing.

But he knew she was there.

TWO

The house January and Rose bought when they married the previous October stood on Rue Esplanade, and before this corner of the old French town had been built up, it had been surrounded by extensive grounds. January recalled the place from his childhood, a Spanish house of the kind usually seen on the smaller plantations, two rows of five rooms each with galleries front and behind, built high off the ground to avoid the Mississippi floods. It was angled on its lot so that it wouldn't face directly into the dilapidated old city wall that had still stood at that time—the "Rampart" of Rue des Ramparts—but would instead catch the river breezes.

As a result, the courtyard behind it was an awkward, narrow triangle. A poor man couldn't afford to keep up a house of that size, and a rich one would purchase a regular town-house on one of the more fashionable streets of the French town, Rue Royale or Rue Bourbon, not back here, where these days mostly artisans and free colored plaçées lived. But when, as the result of a singular chain of circumstances, January and Rose had unearthed a small pirate-cache of gold coins in the bayou country, they had bought this place to establish Rose's long-held dream of a school for young girls of color.

Coming around the corner of Rue des Ramparts, seeing the

crooked angle of the slate roof, the amber glow of the dining-room window in the sticky cobalt velvet of the evening, January felt his heart lift.

His place. His home.

Rose.

The fear of Queen Régine's silently dogging tread melted in familiar joy. Sometimes he felt he could just stretch out his arms the way he did in dreams and lift off from the dirty brick banquette, and fly to Rose and to that crooked old Spanish house as lightly as a bird. Germaine's mother would have come and gotten her already, he thought as he climbed the tall front steps. He entered the French door of the bedroom—like a civilized person, his mother would have said: only American animals came straight into the parlor, like burglars, like thieves. If Cosette's mother was paying a voodoo to make her sick, he'd have to . . .

Rose was waiting for him in the parlor.

With her was a white man he recognized as Hubert Granville, President of the Bank of Louisiana.

The bank where their money was.

Before a word was spoken—before Rose even could draw breath—January saw her face in the candle-light, and Granville's, and felt as if he'd ducked around a corner to escape a knife in the back, only to take a spear through the heart.

It didn't even hurt.

Yet.

Just the cold of shock.

"What's happened?" His voice sounded astonishingly normal in his own ears.

Your house will be ripped from over your head. . . .

He had not the slightest doubt as to what Granville was going to say.

And he thought: *I'm going to kill my mother.*

Granville was an old crony of his mother's. It was on her urging—as well as because January himself had known the banker for three years—that he'd put the money left after the initial payment on the house into the Bank of Louisiana.

He took a deep breath while Granville tried to find a way to say *Your money is gone.* For months January had been reading about bank failures in the newspapers, the messy aftermath of President Jackson's fiscal policies. All over New Orleans, merchants consulted Bank Note Reporters before any major purchase, to learn how much the notes of any particular bank were being discounted that month, and Bank Note Detectors, in a vain effort to learn if the notes they were being offered were counterfeit. There was no way of telling when any of the state-chartered—or frankly private—banks would collapse, leaving depositors with handfuls of worthless paper.

All this went through January's mind in the seconds between his question and the banker's reply.

"I'm empowered to offer you three hundred dollars."

"Considering we have over four thousand in your bank," said January, remembering to add—because he was addressing a white man—". . . sir. Or we *did.*"

"I have strong reasons to believe that the bank's specie and note reserves were cleaned out by a man named Oliver Weems." Granville's small hazel eyes were sunk in pouches of fat, their watchful expression like an intelligent pig's. "Weems was—is still, officially—the manager of the bank. He came to us with the highest recommendations. . . ."

"I expect Iago had them, too," said January in a level voice. "Sir. And the reason you're not going to the City Guards is . . . ?"

"Good God, man!" The banker's square, heavy face puckered with alarm. "All that would do is bring the bank crashing down around our ears! Weems didn't take the silver reserves—about thirty thousand dollars. We can keep going for a few weeks on those, since it's the slow season of the year. But if the police get word of it, that word will spread like fire in a hayloft. If you—or anyone—demand their money in full, our doors will close and no one will get anything."

You bastard. January felt the heat of rage sweep through him. *You robbing, irresponsible bastard. . . .*

The school was nowhere near self-supporting, and might not be for years. The gold they'd held out from paying for the house in full had been to support them until it could take hold. At this time of the year there wasn't even work as a musician, since anyone with the money to hire musicians for a party was using that money to rent quarters someplace other than New Orleans. His dozen or so piano students had left town, too, with their various parents. The money he'd saved from the winter's lessons, and the winter's work at subscription balls and Mardi Gras parties and the opera, had all been banked with Granville as well.

Because Granville was white and January black, January held his silence, and the scorching wave passed through him and away, leaving its throbbing glow behind. But looking down at the white man's face, he saw, behind the calculation in the piggy eyes, the wariness of a man who has to get himself through a painful and humiliating situation.

And, thought January, Granville was here, at ten o'clock on a Sunday evening. From what January knew of the man, he wasn't going around town informing every one of his clients that they were now as poor as the wretchedest of the derelicts on the levee.

He'd sought January for a reason.

January brought up a chair and sat—the gesture seemed to reassure the banker. Granville's massive shoulders relaxed in the expensive linen jacket, and when he spoke, his voice had lost some of its cautious hardness. "Your mother tells me you're good at finding things, and finding things out. You were the one who solved Simon Fourchet's murder the winter before last, weren't you?"

January nodded. He'd hated Simon Fourchet, the man who had once been his mother's master and his own. Only his mother's blackmail had sufficed to make him work to save the man's life and bring the murder home. "I take it that's what you're offering me three hundred dollars for?" he asked. "To find Weems?"

"To find the money," said Granville. "I know where Weems is."

The candles on the small table—one of the few pieces of furniture in that darkly cavernous room—began to gutter. Silently Rose took candle-scissors from the table's drawer and mended the drooping wick. The reviving glow flickered across plastered walls painted yellow, touched the keys of January's beloved Austrian piano, and warmed color from the faded upholstery of the chairs. The light creak of footfalls overhead marked where Cosette was getting ready for bed in her attic bedroom.

January wondered what she prayed, on this night before she was going back to a mother who held her in such contempt.

The oval lenses of Rose's spectacles picked up the candles' orange gleam. It had been January's idea to bank with Granville. Her silence now was like broken glass.

"And where," January asked, "is Weems?"

"At his lodgings, recuperating from the shock of the theft," said the banker grimly. "The day watchman went in this morning and found the night man unconscious—the man still hasn't woken up. God knows what happened to him. Sometime last night—Saturday night—all the strongboxes were opened and everything but the silver taken. When I broke the news to Weems this afternoon he collapsed; I could barely get any sense out of him. He couldn't accompany me to the night guard's lodgings, where I had a devil of a time keeping the doctor in attendance from suspecting anything. Afterwards I went for a cup of cocoa at Madame Metoyer's shop in the Place des Armes. . . ."

. . . *Which belongs to your free colored mistress,* January mentally added. *Or one of your several ex-mistresses* . . . He'd never been able to keep track of his mother's accounts of the banker's squadron of ladyfriends.

". . . and Madame Metoyer happened to mention to me that she'd seen Weems only this morning in the steamboat office, making arrangements to leave town on the steamboat *Silver Moon* first thing tomorrow."

"*Only this morning,*" repeated January thoughtfully. "Before he'd 'heard' about the theft."

"Exactly. And he told me straight out that he'd been in all morning."

"So the trunk with the money in it—or trunks—will be on board by this time."

"If he's smart, they will be," agreed Granville. "And not marked with his name."

"No." January stared into the shadows for a time, while Rose got to her feet and slipped quietly through the gap in the sliding-doors to the dark cave of the dining-room, and the pantry that lay beyond.

Seeing in his mind the levee that lay at the foot of the Place des Armes, the bustling offices of the steamboat companies that crowded one side of it, the boxes and bales of goods that even at this slow season piled the waterfront: packets of skins from the mountains of the Mexican territories, bolts of cloth from England and New York. Corn and pumpkins from the river valley to the north, hay and fodder, squealing hogs and chickens in coops. Tools and machinery, plows and harness. Coming down-river or heading up. Quiet at this hour, probably, whereas during the business season, the winter season, the time when the river was high and the cotton and sugar crops coming in, men would be loading and unloading, dragging and rolling and cursing and sweating, throughout the torch-lit nights.

And among the noise and confusion, quiet lines of men and women would be loaded, the chains that linked them together clinking softly in the juddering glare. Slaves bound north for the markets in the new cotton lands of Missouri and Mississippi.

Even through the wooden shutters that closed most of the French doors of the big house, it seemed to January that he could hear the far-off sounds of the levee, the shouting of the gang-bosses, the clank of steamboat bells.

He had been to Europe, to London and Paris, but he had not been farther than St. John's Parish, thirty miles up-river from the city. Even that had scared him.

In New Orleans, he was known. If anything happened to destroy the "freedom papers" that he was required by law to show anyone who asked, there were prominent shopkeepers, merchants, even a lawyer or two who could point to him and say, *That is Benjamin January, the piano teacher. He's a free man, and not a slave.*

Once out of town, on the river, that would not be the case.

"And you want me to find the trunks with the money in them, and bring them back?" he asked at last. "Without letting anyone know what happened?"

"Yes," said Granville. "I'll have a notarized letter of introduction to you by midnight, authorizing you to act as my agent in this matter and requesting the captain of the *Silver Moon*—and whatever law enforcement officials you need—to assist you. But I promise you, if you play that trump-card without having the money right under your hand, all you'll do is lose everything, destroy the bank, and ruin every depositor we have."

"Ourselves included." The incomparable smell of coffee filled the quiet gloom as Rose returned with a tray. The coffee would have been warming in the pantry, awaiting his return from Congo Square—it seemed like another lifetime. Rose made excellent coffee, though she was an otherwise execrable cook. It crossed January's mind that without the assistance of the hired freedwoman Abigail and Abigail's daughter, Rose would be quickly swallowed up by the drudgery of cleaning, cooking, and endless sewing that occupied the time of most women who kept house.

Until, of course, the house itself was foreclosed.

His hand shook a little as he took the coffee cup she offered. One bite told him that the sweet biscuits that accompanied it had been made by Abigail, not Rose.

"How much money are we talking about?" Rose seated herself again. "And in what form? How many trunks are we looking for?"

"Three or four at least," said Granville, turning a little to speak to her. "Maybe as many as ten." *Having set up four of his former free colored mistresses in business,* reflected January, *at least Granville didn't suffer from the common white man's delusion that women of color—or women in general—were slightly incompetent.* "He stole nearly four million dollars, of which about a hundred thousand was in gold."

Rose's eyebrows shot up. "That's a *lot* of gold."

"About six hundred pounds of it," Granville replied. "The rest is in notes and drafts on other banks—including the Bank of Pennsylvania, which as you know received a great deal of the Federal gold—and the Bank of England. There are also sight-drafts on a number of the plantations hereabouts against next winter's crop. Any single trunk containing the gold would be too heavy to lift, so it has to be spread out among several, padded up with the paper."

"You say Weems came to you with the highest recommendations," said January. "From whom? What do you know about the man? Where is he from?"

"Philadelphia," said Granville like a New Yorker: *Philadelphier,* a trick of speech that made January wonder whether there was a still-more-brotherly town of *Philadelphiest* somewhere even farther north. "He was a clerk when I was vice-president of the Broadway Bank and Trust, and worked his way up after I was sent down here. Everyone spoke highly of his abilities."

Granville scowled, as if everyone had conspired to lie and would, if he had anything to say in the matter, suffer the consequences.

"It probably paid him to have abilities when the whole country's economic system wasn't being run by wildcat private banks," remarked January dryly. Granville opened his mouth to protest—the Bank of Louisiana, though private, had been chartered by the State—and January asked, "Drink?"

Granville's square face darkened, and he looked as if he were about to demand what the hell business it was of January's. Then he subsided a little, like porridge coming off the boil, and sipped his coffee. "I've seen Weems look down his nose at drunkards on the street," he answered. "I've never seen him go into a public house. But I don't keep company with the man, so in fact I don't know whether he drinks or not."

"Women?"

Again Granville's beady eyes flashed at the suggestion that an employee of his bank would chase trollops up and down Gallatin Street, but since that employee had almost certainly walked off with large sums of the bank's money, there wasn't a great deal he could be self-righteous about. "He was engaged to the daughter of the President of the Jersey Trust Bank," he said slowly. "She married someone else. That's when he came here. He looks down upon women as he looks down upon drunkards. Looks down on a great many things, for a man who's only five feet five inches tall himself." Granville gave out a bear-like rumbling guffaw. "Nor does he gamble, beyond a hand or two of whist. He often said how he despised waste and wastrels."

"Which must have made it easier," remarked Rose, "for him to walk off with the money—if he gave the matter a second thought at all. I'm sure he considers he has better uses for the money than its legal owners." She folded her long-fingered hands on her knee, a tall, angular woman who moved as if she were perpetually about to trip. She had the light medium-brown hair of her white father and grandfather, worn in a neat chignon as long as she was out of sight of the laws that required her to cover it in a slave's headcloth. Behind the gold reflections of candle-light on her spectacles, her eyes were gray-green. "What does he look like? How will we know him?"

Granville raised his eyebrows a bit at the "we," but January—though he experienced his usual sense of protesting shock at the thought of Rose sharing his danger—felt no surprise. A spinster into her late twenties and a woman who had operated her own school for several years, Rose was not one to watch knight-errantry from the dull safety of a bower window.

He knew, too, that there were things a woman could learn in conversation with other women, that would be hidden from a man.

But he felt sick inside at the thought of her taking the steamboat north into territory where she'd fetch seven or eight hundred dollars on the auction-block, if she happened to lose her freedom papers or have them taken from her.

"I'll take you to the wharf when you get your tickets, and point him out as he gets on board," promised the banker.

"The *Silver Moon*'s an American boat, isn't it?" asked January.

"Will they even hire a stateroom to a man and woman of color? Or are we going to have to take deck-passage? In which case," he added, "we're not going to be in much of a position to observe whatever Weems is doing."

"You'll do it, then?" The hope gleaming in Granville's eyes, and the lightening of his voice, made him seem younger, like a child suddenly relieved of terrible fear. January realized then that the man must have been as sick with dread as he was himself.

"I'll do it for five hundred," replied January. "In advance, whether we succeed or fail—plus the expenses of the journey. And I want your word as a gentleman"—he tried to keep the irony out of his voice—"that if either of us gets into trouble, you'll get us out of it."

The banker's sandy-red brows pulled together in momentary puzzlement. *Of course a white man wouldn't understand,* thought January. Certainly not a New Yorker, coming from a town that had a thriving free black population that didn't live looking over their shoulders, worrying about whether they'd be kidnapped into slavery.

"We'll be traveling through cotton territory," January illuminated for him grimly. "We'll be in country where nobody's even *heard* that there are free colored people or that there *can be* black people who aren't somebody's property. Where nobody's going to look too closely at a black man's ownership papers if he turns up on some auction-block for cheap, and where no local sheriff is going to go against one of his constituents if that constituent has a newly-bought slave who claims he's a kidnapped freeman.

"If we get in trouble," January concluded, "I'm trusting you to buy us free. Just as you're trusting me not to breathe a word about your bank having eight million banknotes in circulation backed up by the change in your pockets. Sir."

He didn't even mention the problems he would face, in the event of "trouble," in getting word back to Granville that he or Rose needed help. In the low water of summer, it could take nearly a week for a letter to get to New Orleans from Vicksburg, two weeks from Memphis—longer, if the boat got tangled up on a bar or tore out its paddle on a snag. A week in the hands of slave-dealers or professional kidnappers could be an eternity, and once in the deep heartland of Missouri or Tennessee, it was almost unbelievably difficult for a black who didn't know the area to travel.

But he said nothing about that. Only watched Granville's eyes, counting the seconds of silence before the banker replied. An immediate *Of course, that goes without saying!* would have been his signal to renege at once and to get Hubert Granville the hell out of his parlor as quickly as he could. A reply that unthinking meant that Granville had no intention of laying out so much as ten cents to purchase his freedom, much less the fourteen hundred dollars a prime cotton-hand, six feet three inches tall and massively built, would fetch on the open market.

But Granville thought about it, asking himself—January could see the infinitesimal movement of his kid-gloved fingers as he toted up estimates—if it was something he could actually afford. "How much danger is there of that?" he asked finally.

"Some," said January. "We'll be safer on the boat than ashore. But if Weems off-loads those trunks somewhere along the way, we'll have to follow. I won't know how much danger there'll be until we see what we're faced with on board. Some of it depends on how desperate Weems is, or will become if he realizes he's being dogged. We need to know that you'll stand by us."

Granville rose, massive and only inches shorter than January himself, and held out his hand. "I'll stand by you," he pledged. "And in addition to the thanks of the bank officers—most of whom don't know and won't know that there's a problem—you have my personal thanks. I won't let you down."

"And if you believe that," remarked Rose, standing on the front gallery minutes later as they watched the banker disappear down the darkness of Rue Esplanade, "as your sister Olympe would say, you and I both deserve to spend the rest of our lives picking cotton in Tennessee."

Her voice was light, but he could tell she was still furiously angry, and he knew he could not say to her, *I won't let you come.*

Behind those words, if only in their hearts, lurked the reply: *It's your fault we're in this mess.*

Besides, he knew he'd need all the help he could get.

Far off, thunder rumbled in the tar-black darkness and flashes of heat-lightning flickered over the lake. Here beyond the range of the French town's iron street-lanterns, the blackness was absolute. Across Rue Esplanade, where the small houses of Faubourg Marigny lay hidden among the trees, the roar of cicadas beat like a metallic sea.

January took a deep breath. "Rose, I'm sorry."

"You're sorry that you disregarded me when I pointed a pistol at your head and said, *Put it in the Commerce Bank or I'll shoot*? We both made the decision, Ben." She sighed, and put her arm around his waist. "It will, however, be some time before I can bring myself to be polite to your mother again."

Soft laughter shook him, and he cupped her face in his hands, kissed her gratefully, then again with slow, deep enjoyment of her lips. In the darkness she had an animal sensuality completely at odds with her daylight persona of a schoolmistress and scholar.

A mosquito whined in his ear, and they parted while he slapped at it. "Will you do me a favor, Rose?" he asked as they retreated into their bedroom from the gallery and so through to the parlor. One of the candles had gone out, and the other was guttering again. Rose fetched the candle-scissors and January cracked his shins against Cosette's small trunk, waiting by the door.

"Write to Dominique." He named his sweet-natured younger sister who was so often in and out of the house. "Ask her if she'll take Cosette for a few days. You know they get along well, and that maid of Dominique's has her hands full with the new baby. Then write to Cosette's grandmother, Serafine Poucet, in Spanish Fort."

Taking the candle, he walked through to the dining-room and into the pantry, where a supper of cold chicken and bread waited for him in covered dishes. He ate a few hasty bites standing, knowing that it was nearly midnight already, and the later it got, the less safe he'd be in accomplishing his next mission that night.

Safe being, of course, a completely relative term when applied to a black man venturing into the rough dives and grubby gin-palaces that straggled out into the swamp at the back of town.

"Tell her Cosette hasn't been well, and hint—without saying anything so vulgar—that you don't think she'll get particularly good care spending the summer at her mother's house."

"What, that awful old lady Poucet is Cosette's grandmother?" Rose leaned her shoulder in the pantry doorway. The daughter of a plaçée herself, she knew just about everyone in the free colored demimonde, by reputation if not by actual acquaintance.

"Yes, and according to Dominique, Poucet hates Cosette's mother."

Rose began to chuckle, and followed January back out to the parlor again, where he collected his jacket, the disreputable old cap he'd worn to Congo Square, and a tin lantern. "God help the voodoo who tries to trespass on old lady Serafine's yard. She'll take Cosette in just to show up her daughter, won't she?"

"It's what I'm hoping." He bent again to kiss her lips, standing in the dark of the bedroom, whose French door was the only one in the house unshuttered, and entertained a momentary question about how much time it would take to fling Rose down on the bed before he proceeded with his next task. . . . "I should be back in two hours."

Rose nodded, not needing him to explain where he was going, or whom he was seeking, or why. That was one of the things he most loved about Rose. She knew already that they'd need a third member of the party if they were going on board the *Silver Moon,* and knew exactly who that had to be.

"Go carefully," she told him, although she was perfectly well aware that the City Guards who enforced the ten o'clock curfew on blacks never went anywhere *near* the Swamp.

I've already had the roof torn away from my head, reflected January as he descended the steps, *and the gold dissolve from my hand, and the curse hasn't been on me two hours yet. What further could go wrong tonight?*

He looked around him, right and left in the darkness. But the lantern he held gave no more than the dimmest flicker, barely enough to keep him from falling into the gutter as he set off along Rue des Ramparts. If anyone followed him, they were cloaked utterly in the night.

THREE

If a stranger to New Orleans were to follow the street called Perdidio back from the handsome American mansions of St. Charles Avenue, he would be struck, almost certainly, by the rapidity with which those imposing houses gave way to the humbler dwellings of shopkeepers and artisans, to red-brick boardinghouses and then to brickyards, cotton-presses, livery stables. The gaps between buildings grew wider, yielding to undeveloped lots of rank weeds or stands of trees that had seen the Houmas and the Natchez Indians camp beneath them. The pavement failed, the roadbed narrowed to a path which in turn became a slot of gumbo-thick mud. Among the trees, the buildings dwindled to shacks and sheds, nailed together from the planks of the flatboats that came down-river filled with Ohio corn, Indiana hogs, Iowa pumpkins, and illiterate Kentucky ruffians in Conestoga boots, spitting tobacco in all directions. At night, cicada-roaring darkness lay between the trees like God's curse upon Egypt, broken only by the feeblest splodges of lantern-light from makeshift taverns that bore names like The Rough and Ready and The Nantucket Virgin. From those dim doorways hoarse shouts and curses resounded, the crash of breaking benches punctuating the tinny laughter of whores.

This was the part of town called the Swamp. It was here that the half-savage Kaintuck keelboat crews took refuge, and the gamblers, publicans, and harlots who fleeced them. It was here that the runaway slaves hid out, in sheds and tents far back in the trees; here that gaggles of snarly-haired prostitutes hunted, giving themselves to forty men a night in rooms barely wider than the beds they contained or on shuck mattresses on the floors of tents; here that the poorest of the city's poor squatted in squalid cabins among the marshy pools.

The hypothetical visiting stranger would have, by this time, learned how Perdidio Street acquired its name: attenuated to a mucky track, it finally lost itself—*elle se perdre,* the French would say—in the soggy ground.

That is, if the hypothetical visiting stranger even made it this far, and hadn't been knocked on the head in the dark beneath the trees and relieved of his watch, his purse, his boots, and possibly his clothes as well.

Only strangers in town ever wandered into the Swamp. The local inhabitants knew better.

All except Benjamin January, January reflected as he made his wary way through the darkness toward the shouting and the grimy dots of light. *Benjamin January doesn't have the sense to stay where he isn't going to get his head broken for going into the Swamp at this time of night.*

He'd come, not up from St. Charles Avenue as a white man would have, but around through the literal swamps at the back of New Orleans, his head wrapped in a length of mosquito-netting against the insects that made the soggy ground nearly uninhabitable in summertime. He listened behind him in the moonless dark, less because he thought Queen Régine might be still on his heels than because slave-stealers sometimes haunted these inky woods, looking to kidnap runaways for resale. For this reason, too, he kept the slide over his lantern, leaving only the barest whisper of light to illuminate the path.

It was a good thing he did, for its stray gleam caught the round gold eye of an alligator lying in the path—a big one, to judge by the glint of teeth as it opened its mouth and lunged at him—and January got soaked to the thighs in water that smelled like a cesspool, stumbling into a bog as he circled wide to avoid it.

Queen Régine must be losing her touch, he thought sourly as he tripped over tangles of elephant-ear, seeking the elusive path again. *There weren't any water-moccasins in that pool.*

A deadfall log seemed to materialize underfoot, and he banged his shins.

When I find Hannibal Sefton, I'm going to wring his neck for him.

Ahead on his right he could see lights: the long, ramshackle shed known locally as The Rough and Ready. Lantern-light glowed ruby through the cheap calico that comprised one wall, and like a shadow-play January saw men leap up from the makeshift card-table, cursing like the Devils in Hell. The next moment one man was hurled through the fabric wall, bringing the whole of it down with him.

Women screamed. A large gentleman in buckskins collided with the bar, which, being only planks laid over barrels, collapsed, and the barkeep rushed into the crowd laying about him right and left with a nail-studded mahogany club. A squad of hairy Kaintuck boatmen charged the barkeep with fragments of the benches, and January silently moved on.

The Keelboat Saloon lay to his left, on the edge of a vile-smelling bayou. Its customers nearly trampled January as they rushed toward The Rough and Ready to take part in the fight—it was a slow night, and he supposed one had to take one's entertainment where one found it. The Keelboat was even less salubrious-looking than The Rough and Ready, a dirty wooden box with lines of orange light leaking through its sides. A good kick would bring it down. But January kept on his course for the place, for he heard in the blackness of the steamy night what he'd been seeking: the wild skirl of fiddle music, like a drunken Irish angel embroidering golden fantasias on a Mozart ballet.

January closed the lantern-slide and waited in the trees, knowing that in time someone would come out to whom—if he was careful—he could speak. A black man who walked into a saloon anywhere in town risked being beaten up. Even in the elegant establishments of Rue Royale, he would not dare to be seen to raise a hand against a white man in his own defense; here, such an action would no doubt result in an unpleasant and messy death.

So all he could do was wait, the mosquitoes whining as they tangled up in the veils around his hat and the occasional cicada or palmetto bug blundering into the lantern on roaring wings. He wondered if the gator was still around.

Three burly shapes crashed through The Keelboat's door and ran past January in a reeking backwash of chewing tobacco and clothing months unlaundered; one of the local girls was with them, holding up her skirts to her knees and laughing.

The music stopped mid-bar.

A moment later Hannibal Sefton appeared silhouetted in the weak orange rectangle of the doorway, violin in one hand and a brown bottle of whiskey in the other.

"*They flee from me, that sometime did me seek,*" he quoted plaintively, and took a long pull from the bottle. *"But I have seen them, gentle, tame and meek / That now are wild. . . ."*

He looked at the bottle, sighed, and turned back into the building.

January emerged from behind his tree and crossed to the shack, sprang up the steps to the door.

As he'd suspected, the saloon was empty.

"Don't tell me you actually drink the liquor this place serves."

Hannibal was in back of the bar, replacing the bottle behind a loose board in the wall. "Good God, no! I may be a sot, but I'm not a fool. Old Hunks was charging a Santa Fe trapper fifty cents a shot for this on the grounds that it was Scots single-malt."

He straightened up in the grimy lamplight, resembling a disheveled elf with his long hair straggling out of its old-fashioned pigtail over his back, and his eyebrows standing out dark against his thin white face. "*Thou shalt not muzzle the ox that treadeth out the corn.* . . . But of course it's just the same bilgewater Hunks dips out of the barrel for a picayune a cup. . . . What *are* you doing here, *amicus meus*? If you're seriously looking to get yourself killed, I'll offer you a drink. . . ."

"There are better ways to die," responded January with an exaggerated shudder.

"And being in this room when the refined clientele returns is one of them," retorted Hannibal. "Let us retire to my quarters. Nothing amiss with the owl-eyed Athene, I hope?"

And as Hannibal limped over to the shaggy, out-of-fashion beaver hat that stood by his chair to receive whatever contributions his audience cared to give, January grinned at the nickname his friend had given the bespectacled Rose.

"I must say I am cut to the quick to find my art playing second fiddle, as it were, to a bout of not-very-efficient fisticuffs," Hannibal added as he dumped a few Spanish reales, a British shilling, two American half-dimes, and three eleven-penny bits into his hand. "But at least I can get out of here with all my takings this evening instead of having one of the customers relieve me of them ten feet from the door."

Small heaps of money lay on the room's single table amid a scattering of cards, and presumably there was a cashbox in the same cache as the so-called "single-malt Scotch." But these Hannibal ignored as he wrapped his violin in its usual swaddling of faded silk scarves and tucked it into its case.

"If you're getting robbed every night, why do you stay?" January glanced right and left as they emerged from the saloon's rear door, though in the pitch-black night a platoon of club-wielding Kaintucks could have stood within four feet of The Keelboat unseen. Undetected by any other sense as well, for that matter, for the ambient stench of privies would have covered the collective tobacco-reek of the average boatman, and the combined roar of the cicadas and the hollers of the fight still in progress at The Rough and Ready would have masked any sound.

The ground squished under January's boots, and something

moved—cat, rat, or gator—in the tangle of hackberry that surrounded the building's rear.

"Old Hunks lets me sleep in one of the cribs." Hannibal led the way to a sort of long shed that stood behind the saloon, three of its four French doors open into mephitic blackness. The usual inhabitants of the rooms—and their customers—were presumably at the fight as well.

"It's exceedingly generous of him, considering how much he makes per night out of each room. He's from Dublin, and so regards me as a brother. He worked for years as a doorkeeper at the Covent Garden Opera in London. Sometimes after the place closes down for the night, I'll play on for him for hours."

He opened the door of the fourth crib—none of them had locks—and held January's lantern inside for a moment before entering. Two rats retreated unhurriedly through a crack in the wall. The room was windowless but so rudely put together that in daylight there would have been plenty of light, ventilation, and—to judge by the careful arrangement of old tin pots and broken jars about the floor—almost certainly rain.

"Besides," the fiddler went on, flicking a roach the size of a small mouse from the candle-holder and angling the candle to the lantern's flame, "I defy you to name an establishment in town this summer where you wouldn't be robbed. Everything respectable has closed down. Even the folks out in Milneburgh aren't holding many cotillions this year."

January, settling himself on the goods-box that held most of Hannibal's books, had to agree. In former years, summers had been slow times, but every week or so there would be some banker or sugar-broker or town *rentier* hosting a ball in one of the big hotels by the lake. This year so far they had been few.

"You're lucky that you haven't had to rely on your music this year to butter your bread." Hannibal produced from another goods-box a small bottle of sherry and a square black one of laudanum. He measured a tiny amount of the one and a tinier dose of the other into a tin cup and drank it down. *"In honored poverty thy voice did weave / Songs consecrate to truth and liberty . . ."* After a moment's thought he took another fast sip of the laudanum alone, then stoppered both bottles and put them away. "What's happened? And how can I help?"

"I'm glad you asked." January outlined for him what Hubert Granville had said about the absconding manager of the Bank of Louisiana, and about the need for secrecy that precluded enlisting the City Guards until hard evidence was secured.

"What I need," said January, "is a master aboard the *Silver Moon.* A free black man traveling by himself draws comment. A slave is invisible, and I need to be invisible. In some circumstances a slave is safer than a free black man," he added with a bitterness that had turned to irony over the years. "At least someone's going to complain if a slave disappears. And having a white man along to deal with the local authorities when we do find which trunks contain the money will be a help, too. Granville's paying us five hundred dollars."

"In Bank of Louisiana notes?"

January laughed curtly. "Dryden says that when a man takes a wife and fathers children, he gives hostages to fortune. Disaster falls, not only on his head alone, but on the heads of those he loves. Rose and I have the chance to be something, to have something, to make something, rather than scraping along on what I can earn playing the piano for quadroon balls and what she gets translating Greek texts for booksellers. You can't go on all your life that way. It does something to you, as time wears on."

He stopped, looking around the seedy darkness of the room, with weeds growing up through the cracks in the board floor and roaches spotting the wall behind the candle flame. Looking at Hannibal's face, thin with a lifetime of illness and pain, and at the long, sensitive hands in the frayed cuffs.

The fiddler's grin was wry under his graying mustache. "To save you and Athene from the life I daily live, *amicus meus,* I will gladly play the despot and spend my days in the company of tobacco-spitting

Americans in a steamboat saloon—particularly at the Bank of Louisiana's expense. I think I have a shirt in here somewhere that will not violate the personation of a man with enough money to own a slave."

On the other side of the thin partition wall, January heard a man curse in English, followed by a woman's protesting drawl, "Just gimme a minute. . . ." Bedropes creaked mightily.

"The fight must be over," January opined.

A huge and comprehensively drunk boatman loomed suddenly in the doorway. "Look out, beautiful, 'cause here comes the very child that coined the name of Thunder! Cock-a-doodle-do!" He let fall his trousers, at which Hannibal promptly began to applaud.

The boatman retreated in confusion.

"Happens every week," sighed the fiddler, pulling his valise from under the bed. "I've tried chalking NO GIRLS HERE on the door, but that doesn't seem to work either . . . and it doesn't help that occasionally one of the girls will entertain a customer here while I'm playing up front. . . ."

Shouts of laughter outside. "You done *already*, Kyle? I got me a pet jack-rabbit takes more time than *that*!"

"A man can live in this fashion for a time." Hannibal sighed, fishing in yet another goods-box for his few shirts of threadbare linen. "A long time, in my case. And a strong woman can endure it for a few years. But as the playwright says, *Money is the sinews of love, as of war.* Poverty can break a marriage, and I love you and Rose too much to want to see you turn on each other, as the poor so often do, and your happiness vanish for want of hope."

He tossed in his shaving tackle and three half-empty bottles of opium and sherry. "So it remains only to arm myself, like Prince Achilles before the walls of Troy. *The silver cuishes first his thighs infold; Then o'er his breast was braced the hollow gold. . . .*"

Hannibal held up a much-frayed and slightly too large silk waistcoat, which must have been expensive when it was new, with a triple-notched collar some twenty years out of style. "*The brazen sword a various baldric tied / That, starred with gems, hung glittering at his side. . . .* Should I bring along a brazen sword, *amicus meus*?" He snapped shut his valise. "Or the *great paternal spear* the poet speaks of? How dangerous is Weems?"

"I have no idea." January pinched out the candle, which Hannibal slipped into his pocket as the two men stood listening beside the door, waiting for the customers at the other cribs to go inside. "Nor who his accomplices are, if he has any, or how many of them there are."

The flimsy walls shuddered with the slamming of a door. A woman's voice purred, "Well, hello, handsome," from the next room, and January and Hannibal stepped out into the muggy heat of the June night.

Hannibal pulled shut the door behind him, and gestured extravagantly with his free hand.

> *"So let it be!*
> *Portents and prodigies are lost on me.*
> *I know my fate: to die, to see no more*
> *My much-loved parents and my native shore—*
> *Enough—when Heaven ordains, I sink in night:*
> *"Now perish Troy!" he said, and rushed to fight."*

Even in summer's doldrums, the levee at New Orleans never really slept. In winter, when boats came down-river with their decks stacked so deep in cotton that it blacked out the windows of the engine-room on the main deck and the staterooms above, they'd be lined up three and four deep at the wharves, so that passengers would have to walk across the sterns of several other boats to get to shore, and the shifting of barrels, hogsheads, bales, and crates would go on all night. In summer, when the river sagged twenty feet below its high-water mark and the big side-wheelers lay in their berths, goods still arrived from Europe and New York. Planters up-river still demanded delivery on bolts of silk and crates of crystal goblets packed in straw, and passengers still journeyed in the smaller stern-wheelers, which could travel where and when the larger craft could not.

By the glare of armloads of wood burning aloft in iron cressets, January watched stevedores heave the last of the luggage on board, and stack cords of logs for the ever-hungry furnaces. Soot from the tall chimney stacks gushed into the sullen sky above the levee. Now and then showers of sparks would whirl upward, only the height of the stacks preventing them from igniting the boats themselves. On the deck of the *Silver Moon* a nervous little gentleman with a pot belly and octagonal spectacles fussily marshalled the deck-hands—the owner, January guessed. Beside him, a tall, slim young man in a steward's white coat read from a notebook and called out to the porters: "Leave that trunk on the deck, Mr. Purlie gettin' off at Donaldsonville. Those go in the hold, Colonel Davis goin' on with us to Memphis this time. . . ."

January shifted Hannibal's valise, and his own small satchel, in his hand.

"All the way through to Memphis," requested Hannibal of the clerk at the steamboat office window. The man took the Bank of Louisiana notes without question. January had to admit he'd been holding his breath.

"Hell, don't you piss around sellin' your niggers here and there along the river," boomed a voice near-by. "Niggers are sky-high in St. Louis, fourteen hundred, fifteen hundred for prime bucks. . . ."

January turned and saw the speaker, bow-legged and broad-shouldered, his shortness making him look like an animate barrel, with tobacco-stains in his yellow mustache and a mouth like the hack of an ax. He jabbed a finger at another man, then gestured back to the line behind him: five men, four women, linked together by hanks of chain.

Scared, some of them, looking around in the sickly yellow of the smoke-fouled dawn. In Virginia and Kentucky, January knew, sluggards and troublemakers were threatened by their masters with being "sold down the river" to the cane plantations—and, he reflected, remembering his own childhood, they were right to fear. Three of the men clutched little bundles of clothing done up in bandannas, all they'd been able to carry from Baltimore, Charleston, Savannah, still seasick from the voyage and aching with grief for friends and family they'd never see again. One woman clutched a small child to her side. Another, a girl with the fair-skinned quadroon beauty prized by so many white men, stared at the slave-dealer with naked hatred in her eyes.

"They got more and more land goin' for cotton up there, and they'll pay damn near anythin' for hands to work it. You can't go wrong with St. Louis, or my name ain't Ned Gleet!"

January turned away, sick with the sickness of helplessness, rage, and disgust, and looked around for Rose. He glimpsed her between the brick arches of the market buildings that stretched along the levee downstream of the Place des Armes, nearly out of sight in the shadows. She was dressed like the market-women who were just beginning to make their appearance, with their baskets of roses and oranges: a short red skirt and a petticoat of blue-and-orange calico, a white blouse and a short red corduroy jacket, a gay bandanna hiding her hair. With her spectacles she looked like an intellectual gypsy. With a glance back at Hannibal, who was still chatting with the clerk, January crossed to her, and as he drew close he saw Hubert Granville half-concealed behind the pillar, looking out into the square.

"That's Weems." Granville pointed, and January turned to see a small, dapper gentleman in a full-skirted coat of rust-colored wool and a very unfortunate silk waistcoat of purple and mustard. The bank manager was arguing about something with the pot-bellied owner. The slender steward intervened, consulting his notebook, pointing up at the staterooms that ranged both sides of the upper, or boiler, deck. "Here's the sample of his handwriting you asked for," Granville told January.

January pocketed the folded note the banker offered him, to

compare against the labels of every trunk and box in the hold, if and when he could manage to sneak down there. That this would be difficult, he guessed—that sleek, efficient young steward might prove to be either venal or careless or both, but somehow January doubted it. Nor would he know until he was on board how many ways there were into the cargo-hold, and whose work-stations overlooked them. Through hard experience he had learned that trying to plan ahead without information led only to madness, especially in a situation with so many tiny variables.

He could only take his ticket, get on board, and see what the situation was.

"As I suspected," sighed Rose, "they don't have cabins for colored. I expect I'll have some company on the deck." She nodded as a Junoesque matron in severe dark bombazine ascended the gangplank, a diminutive maid in tow, and behind them a train of trunks that would have embarrassed Marie Antoinette. "Unless of course she's the sort who likes to have her maid sleep on the floor beside her bed."

January gritted his teeth at the thought of Rose sleeping on the deck with the servants. "I'll come down and join you whenever I can."

"Bring food," said Rose unsentimentally, and raised her face to kiss him. "Oh, good Heavens," she added, cutting in over Granville's embarrassed apologies and effusive thanks, "Hannibal's found a girlfriend already. . . ."

January rolled his eyes, snatched up his and Hannibal's luggage, and strode to intercept his friend, who had indeed entered into what appeared to be a flirtation with a dainty blonde in a fantasia of silk rosebuds and lace. The young lady flung up her hands and trilled with silvery laughter: "Oh, Mr. Sefton, you will turn my poor little head!"

"My dearest Miss Skippen, how could Paris hold himself back from complimenting Helen?" Hannibal offered his hand to help her around the two massive crates that were just being off-loaded from a dray. She leaned on his arm, blond curls brushing the shoulder of his coat. "How could Petrarch remain silent when Laura passed him by? *Nymph of the downward smile and sidelong glance / in what diviner mo-*

ments of the day / art thou most lovely? A man would have to be more, or less, than man, to—"

"You get your hands away from her, pig of an Orangeman!" bellowed a voice just as January reached them. A man came storming down the gangplank of the *Silver Moon,* nearly January's height and, like January, massive through the shoulders beneath the blue pea-jacket of the vessel's pilot. "I know your like!" The red ruff of his side-whiskers bristled almost straight out from the flushed red moon of his face. "Sneerin' bastards—and you!" he added, whirling on the blond lady, who had both lace-gloved hands pressed to her rosebud mouth in guilty shock. "Onto the boat with ye, and don't you go believin' the likes of a cozening Orangeman who'd rob old women of their bread, an' turn orphan children out into the road! You keep away from her." He thrust a savage finger almost into Hannibal's face. "You keep away from her or, Kevin Molloy's tellin' you now, it'll be the worse for you!"

The bespectacled owner of the boat had already leaped down from the deck and was hurrying to break up what looked like a serious affray, but the pilot turned on his heel, seized the blond girl by the arm, and shoved her away in the direction of the boat, followed by three porters hauling trunks, hatboxes, and valises, with a sullen slave-girl bringing up the rear.

"Well," said January, coming up beside the still-shaken Hannibal, "getting the pilot of the boat set against you: that'll help things."

"And as sterling an example of bog-Irish manhood as ever graced my homeland by his departure." Hannibal picked up his violin-case, which had been dropped when Molloy had shoved him. "I understand pilots are the true rulers of the steamboats—I hope this isn't going to get me dropped overboard some night." He waited until Molloy had hustled Miss Skippen up the stairway that led from the wide bow-deck up to the boiler-deck above before venturing up the gangway himself, January at his heels.

Because the deck-hands were lowering the last of the cargo—including Miss Skippen's trunks—into the hold, a small crowd had gathered on the apron of the boat at the bow, waiting to pass and go up the stairs. The slave-dealer Ned Gleet was just chaining his four female slaves to rings set in the wall of what was called the promenade, the narrow outside corridor that ran down both sides of the 'tweendecks housing from bow to stern. The men were chained starboard, the women along the port, and one of the young planters who was traveling up-river had stopped to watch. Gleet caught his eye and winked: "She's a beauty, ain't she?" And he tweaked the chin of the girl he was chaining, the beautiful girl January had noticed before, who had stared at Gleet with such loathing. "She's yours for a thousand dollars."

The young man flushed in the paling torchlight and looked hastily aside. But he didn't move off. Gleet's sly smile widened.

"Worth every dime of it," he coaxed. "Sixteen years old . . ." His big hand tugged off her tignon, releasing a soft cloud of dark-brown hair over her shoulders. "Come up closer and have a look. She's a prime one." And he dragged her head back around when she would have turned her face away, her expression wooden but for the tears of shame in her eyes. "Now, you tell me if you've ever seen one half so sweet, for a thousand or fifteen hundred."

The young planter stammered, "I— She's very lovely, of course, sir, but . . ."

"But you got your daddy's money, and can't spend it?" Gleet nodded understandingly, his sharp blue glance taking in the sweat that stood out on the youth's forehead. "But that's the great thing about a gal like this, you see. You don't like her, you can sell her again, and not a penny the worse. Here—feel of her if you don't believe me." With a quick move he tore open the front of the girl's dress and pulled it back over her shoulders, leaving her breasts bare in the torchlight. "Go ahead, feel of her. Tell me if you ain't felt titties as hard as those in all your born days."

Hannibal slipped through the crowd like a ferret and climbed the stair. January followed. The two men were silent as they walked down the long upper promenade on the starboard side of the boiler-deck, past the shut doors of the staterooms to the one Hannibal had been given, three from the stern. The young steward in his white coat was there, setting out a carafe of water and a glass: "Let me know if there's anything you need, sir. My name's Thu; I been with Mr. Tredgold on the *Silver Moon* three-four years now. You're on a good boat."

"I'm sure of it," returned Hannibal, slipping him one of the eleven-penny bits he'd acquired earlier in the night.

"Luncheon is served in the Main Saloon at noon, dinner at six. I see you have a fiddle with you, sir. If it isn't an imposition, if you'd care to favor the company with a little playing after supper, it's often done on board that there's playing and dancing in the evenings. . . ."

"As it happens, my man Ben is also quite accomplished. . . ."

It is only a game, thought January. Only the masque of despotism, necessary to their disguise. But after the scene on the deck below, he felt disgusted and angry, and walked to the end of the promenade, where the most fashionable of the staterooms overlooked the giant wheel. Narrow stairways ran down to the lower promenades, where the valets and maids of the cabin passengers were already staking out their tiny niches among the heaped baggage and piles of cordwood stacked along the walls of the 'tween-decks: maids on the portside, valets on the starboard, at least those who weren't required to sleep on the floors of their masters' staterooms. The doors to the galley and the engine-room opened into this part of the promenade, screened almost completely from the chained line of slaves by head-high piles of wood. Market-women in bright skirts and tignons swarmed in and out of the galley door, with last-minute offers of tomatoes and melons; two white children on the upper promenade dragged their nurse's hands and screamed, reaching toward a pralinière who hawked her wares to the stevedores. None of the market-women, January observed, would go around the piled wood to where Ned Gleet was checking the chains on his slaves; nor would the deck-hands, as they readied their long poles to shove the *Silver Moon* away from the wharf.

Close by the rear corner of the 'tween-decks, where a narrow walkway crossed behind the wheel, Miss Skippen's maid leaned on the rail, gazing at the Cathedral's towers with a face of stone, tears running in silence down her cheeks.

The huge black wheel at the back of the boat began to turn.

A flash of red among the wood-piles drew January's eye. But when he looked, it wasn't Rose's red jacket, but a red-striped tignon worked into five points, and a red-striped skirt, dirty around the hem with smears of earth, and the flash of cheap glass pearls.

For one moment the woman raised her head, and January looked into the eyes of Queen Régine.

FOUR

"Are you sure?" asked Rose worriedly. "Because I haven't seen her."

"Positive. I think she was carrying a bundle of some kind, though I can't swear to it."

Rose said, "Hmmn."

They sat together on a couple of logs, in a sort of niche among the cordwood. Though the steam engine wasn't noisy, its action vibrated the entire boat, and, beyond the corner of the 'tween-decks, if he stood up, January could catch a glimpse of the black monster of the turning-wheel. The stair to the upper promenade threw barred sun and shadow over them; beyond the rails, the brown-green chop of the river widened between them and the dreary tangle of dessicated snags, withered debris, and mud that stretched below the levees.

Smoke-smell drifted through the galley door, as well as the sound of Eli the cook cursing at the open fire in its huge box of sand. The purser's office was a flimsy cubicle off the galley passageway, and Hannibal's only comment on its lock was "Makes me glad I haven't any valuables stored there." There was a door to the boiler-room there, too, and deck-hands carried wood in that way from the supplies on the promenades. It would be tricky, January realized, to get at the locked door of the purser's office—and the record of who owned which trunks—within.

If, that is, he reflected, *by tonight we're not at the center of an uproar brought on by Queen Régine unmasking Hannibal and me as partners rather than master and slave.*

In which case she'll be right, with a vengeance, about the gold dissolving from my hand.

Rose asked, "So what do we do?"

"Warn Hannibal," said January. "I'll stay on the upper deck as much as possible. If she's traveling deck-passage, she has to show up here sometime. . . ."

"In which case she'll recognize me, if she knew you as Cosette's schoolmaster." Rose tucked her small bedroll like a pillow behind her back where she leaned against the wall. "She may have come on board for some other reason that has nothing to do with you and me, and gotten off again, you know. Up until the boat was shoved away from the wharf, market-women were coming on and off. She has to do *something* for a living other than put hexes on schoolgirls, and it isn't as if there were a lot of boats leaving this morning."

But January still felt profoundly uneasy as the *Silver Moon* thrashed its way past the river-side plantations that lay north of New Orleans, and the long, low green mound of the levee that hid the dark oceans of cane-field beyond. From the boiler-deck above, white passengers—and their servants as they came and went—could look over the levee at the great houses they passed, white-pillared American mansions in the latest pseudo-Greek style, or the long, brightly-painted French Creole dwellings, wrapped in their galleries that channeled the river breeze. From the main deck, all that could be seen was the levee, the batture below it, and the dark bobbing snags that pierced the shining brown water as it shelved down to the channel.

The boat hugged the bank as close as it dared, so that the probing black branches stabbed up through the water only six or seven feet from the rail. Now and then January could hear Kevin Molloy's booming Irish voice hurling instructions to the deck-hands, or the clanging of the bells that communicated from the pilot's cupola up on the hurricane deck down to the engine-room. A good pilot, January knew, kept his boat as close to the shore as possible, to avoid burning up excessive wood fighting the current mid-channel. It was a narrow margin to walk, between the force of the river and the perils close to the banks.

Some of them he could see—the snags that could tear the bucket-boards out of a paddle or the bottom out of a boat, or the long fringes of ripples that ran over sand-bars that stretched out from every point of land on the bank. Others, he knew, were visible only to the man in that high pilot-house, and some only to a man who knew this stretch of river in high water and low, who knew what to look for and what to expect.

"Are they taking soundings?" he asked a moment later as two of the deck-hands dropped the *Silver Moon*'s skiff into the water from the bow-deck and began to row over to the nearer shore. Rose shook her head uncertainly, and one of the planters' valets, pausing for air in the galley passageway, said helpfully, "Looks like they're picking up word about the river."

January had heard the skinny, sharp-voiced young Colonel Davis call this man Jim. "See there where he's gone up to that tree on the levee? There'll be a box nailed to it. Pilots comin' down the river sometimes leave word for each other if there's somethin' like a caved-in bank or somethin' big that others need to know about. In high water they'll just yell to each other, but you see there ain't much traffic now the river's so low."

"Couldn't the pilot get the same information from one of the flat-boats?" asked Rose as she and January followed Jim to the rail for a better look.

The older man, gray-haired and with a manner of friendly gentleness, grinned. "A steamboat pilot ask the time of day from one of them bumpkins on a flatboat? You'll see pigs flyin' on angel wings before you'll see that." He nodded toward the main channel, where from time to time that day they'd passed those hundred-foot rafts with their pens of hogs and mountains of corn and pumpkins. "Wouldn't be no use anyway, 'cause they didn't know the river. And Mr. Molloy wouldn't ask a keelboat crew, 'less'n he knew 'em, 'cause river-pirates often use keelboats. Pirates'd have you runnin' your boat up onto a bar, where they'd be waitin' for you, like as not."

"Even a small boat like this?" asked January.

Jim raised his grizzled eyebrows and glanced at the stacked wood that hid Ned Gleet's chained slaves from view. "There's enough cargo on this boat that'd be worth some outlaw's time. There's not near as much piratin' as there was, even a few years ago, and not many gangs on the river that'd take on a steamboat. But you look in the purser's office, an' you'll see we're carryin' a dozen guns, just in case."

"Ben?"

The three looked up as Thu the steward came down the stair.

"Excuse me interrupting," said the young man, "but they're asking for you in the Saloon." He said it without expression, but as he stepped aside to let January precede him up the stair, January guessed, with sinking heart, what that phrase meant.

With half a dozen planters on board—not to mention Ned Gleet—what was coming was probably inevitable.

At least, he reflected as he passed along the promenade to the door that led to the Main Saloon, he hoped that what awaited him was some white slave-owner offering Hannibal money for him, and not a spiteful Queen Régine demanding what he was doing on the *Silver Moon* disguised as someone's valet.

The Main Saloon was a tremendously long, narrow room that ran most of the length of the so-called boiler-deck. Hemmed in on all sides by passenger staterooms and, at the bow end, by the daytime accommodations for the ladies, it was lighted by clerestory windows, above the level of the lower stateroom roofs, and as a result was always rather gloomy, the diffuse light being helped along by two oil chandeliers. These factors combined to give the room the air of a cathedral nave, one furnished with a suite of worn walnut furniture in red velvet, and two or three card-tables. Though the high windows were open, the stench of tobacco—both smoked and spit—pervaded the room, along with the male smells of boot-leather and pomade.

January paused in the doorway, blinking to adjust his eyes to the dimness, as Colonel Davis's high, sharp laugh barked out. "So what I get instead of proper soldiers to hunt down Chief Black Hawk and his braves are the so-called State Militia—farm-boys who can't tell their right foot from their left. I remember once when one of the companies was approaching a fence with a narrow gate in it, this beanpole captain—who obviously couldn't remember the command to form a column—shouting out, 'Company to fall out for two minutes and re-assemble on the other side of that fence!' I nearly fell off my horse laughing, but it's no wonder poor General Taylor was never able to accomplish much."

There was boisterous laughter although personally January would have bet his money, in single combat, on his quiet-voiced Kentucky farm-boy friend Abishag Shaw against the cocky young planter, Colonel or no. Looking around the room, he spotted Hannibal at one of the tables with Oliver Weems, a cribbage-board laid out between them. At the other table Davis and one of the several planters on board—Roberson, January recalled his name was—had a game of whist in progress with a stout gray-haired Northerner whose French valet was sleeping on deck, the fourth player being a smooth, dark-haired man of undistinguished appearance whom January guessed was a professional cardsharp.

Ned Gleet—sitting next to Hannibal—boomed genially as January entered, "Now, *there's* a boy does any man's heart good to see!" Despite the cheer in his voice, his eyes were as expressionless as a china doll's. "Look at those shoulders on him, gentlemen, and tell me it isn't a crime to waste a boy like that folding cravats when he could be working in the fields with the best of them!"

The young planter—Purlie, January recalled his name was—to whom Gleet had shown the slave-girl that morning was absent; January had not seen him all morning. As he'd come up he'd seen that the girl, too, was gone from the promenade, where she had been chained.

Hannibal replied very mildly, "At least it isn't a crime in the State of Louisiana, and I happen to like the way Ben folds my cravats."

Weems said nothing, but looked at Gleet as if a cat had deposited a long-dead gopher on the chair where the slave-dealer sat.

"Hell!" Gleet spit a long streak of brown juice at the cuspidor. "If it's a valet you want, my friend, they're a dime a dozen in Louisville!" He draped a friendly arm around Hannibal's thin shoulders, and with the other hand poured three generous fingers of whiskey from his flask into the fiddler's empty glass with the clear intention of loosening up his mark's sales resistance, not having the slightest notion of how much liquor Hannibal could put away. "Kentucky's creeping with 'em! You can pick one up for six hundred dollars, and you'll have made a clear three hundred profit with that boy of yours."

"Sir, I find your manner of speech completely offensive!" A young gentleman rose from the armchair, where he'd been reading, dark-haired, blue-eyed, and strikingly handsome, with skin as flawless as a girl's. "Have you no shame? You are a kidnapper, sir, a vile trafficker in human souls and human bodies, and you, sir"—he rounded on Hannibal—"are as morally degenerate as he, for participating in the putrid institution of human slavery!"

Whipping a sheaf of folded broadsides from his coat pocket, he thrust one into Hannibal's hands, and another into Gleet's. "How can you face your wife and your dear little children with the moral slime of bondage dripping from your hands?"

"Now, Mr. Quince . . ." A cadaverously thin gentleman in a faded-blue pilot's jacket detached himself from the bar and moved to intercept the indignant speaker even as the handsome young Mr. Quince was digging in his pockets for more tracts.

Gleet bellowed with laughter, and plucked the cigar from Weems's fingers to light the tract he'd been given. January hardly needed to see the masthead, *The Liberator,* to know what it was. "You know what I have to say to you, Quince, and to all Abolitionists like you?"

Quince, with an indignant gasp, tried to snatch the burning tract from Gleet's hands. The slave-dealer whooped harder and held it away from him, like a man teasing a child, which, despite his square-chinned handsomeness, the abolitionist Quince somehow resembled. "Let it be," said the thin gentleman in the oddly rangeless voice that January identified at once as one symptom of chronic palsy.

"What's the matter?" Kevin Molloy appeared in the doorway, crossed the room to the bar. "You're never an Abolitionist, too, Lundy? A bit of the water of life, Nick," he added to the barkeep. And to the emaciated, faintly-trembling Lundy, "I guess you've got to have *something* to keep your mind occupied, now that you're not up to runnin' a boat anymore."

"When I was piloting, Mr. Molloy," responded Lundy, "it wasn't my custom to spend my time in the Saloon."

"What, on this stretch of the river?" Molloy hooted. " 'Tis twenty feet of bottom we've got and not a bar in sight till we get to Red Church. I could take a wee nap and nothing would come of it! You're an old woman, Lundy," he added. " 'Tis a damn shame. You used to be good."

And he swaggered from the room, even as Mr. Quince took the glass from Hannibal's hand and replaced it with another tract, entitled "The Devil's Brew."

"I'm afraid my manservant is not for sale, Mr. Gleet," said Hannibal as Quince poured the contents of the glass into the spittoon near the table. "Although I do appreciate your offer."

"A thousand, then." Gleet waved to January, signaling him over. "A thousand, and that leaves me with barely any profit. What the hell you need a big buck like that for a valet for, anyway? He's got field-hand written all over him."

"He has suffering written all over him," thundered young Quince, stepping between Gleet and January without so much as a glance at January, all his attention on Gleet. "Suffering, and the crying injustices of the system!"

"Get him out of here," sighed Gleet, " 'fore I swat him like a fly."

And as the former pilot Lundy, moving with painful and shaky step, urged the fulminating young Abolitionist toward the door, Gleet looked around at the other men in the Saloon. "What's the matter, Weems?" he demanded. "You an Abolitionist, too? A man's got a right to make a living. You can't tell me a boy like that"—he waved in January's direction—"would have the slightest idea what to do with freedom if he had it."

"Good Heavens, no!" spoke up the stout Northerner in the nasal English of Massachusetts. "Until such time as the government is able to re-settle the Negroes in Africa, where they are best suited to live, it would be an act of cruelty to turn them loose—not to speak of the effect it would have on honest white workingmen in the East." He belched, and bit with great satisfaction into the oyster sandwich in his other hand. Butter glistened as it ran down his chin.

"Gleet spent the rest of the afternoon trying to get me sufficiently foxed to agree to sell." Hannibal sank unsteadily onto the bunk of his stateroom a few hours later and closed his eyes. "Thank God there was a spittoon under the table. It broke my heart to dump that much good whiskey—I must have poured off a pint of it, besides all I drank—but enough is enough. I beg you, if you love me, get me a cup of coffee . . . *quietly.*"

"Yes, sir." January threw his humblest accents into his voice as he rose from the chair in the stateroom, where he'd taken refuge. He'd dozed a little, and listened to the voices of the cabin passengers and their servants as they passed on the promenade, in between perusal of the assorted vegetarian, Abolitionist, temperance, Thompsonian, women's suffrage, and Swedenborgian tracts that someone—presumably Mr. Quince—had thrust under the stateroom door. "Shall I bring you some supper with that, sir? Pickled pork and cabbage, maybe, with some good fortifying gravy . . . ?"

The pillow smacked against the doorframe as January ducked outside.

The coffee seemed to revive Hannibal, however, and he listened with interest to January's account of Queen Régine. "If Her Majesty's on board, she'll be restricted to the main deck," pointed out the fiddler. "And of that, pretty much, to the stern, if not by the deck-hands themselves, by that squad of Kentucky ruffians that's taking deck-passage on the bow-deck. If she wants to expose you as a fraud—does she even speak English?—she may have a hard time finding anyone to believe her. As for getting in to see the purser's records, that may prove impossible to do unseen. The office door is right on the path of the wood-crews, and the steps down to the hold are right beside it. By all accounts the steward Thucydides is as incorruptible as they come. . . ."

"I was afraid of that."

"But all is not lost, nor even mislaid. I've had a word with Byrne, the genial stone-faced gentleman you saw playing whist with Messrs. Davis, Roberson, and that Massachusetts oyster-fiend Dodd."

"Byrne knows you?" asked January, alarmed.

"He knows me, but he'll keep his mouth shut, the same way I'll keep my mouth shut about him being a professional cardsharp and not a dry-goods importer, as he's told all those respectable and well-heeled gentlemen he is." Hannibal drained his coffee-cup and leaned back on the bunk, still looking rather greenish around the edges. "He certainly has no idea you are anyone but who I say you are—a slave I managed to buy with some windfall cash. If he had any suspicion, he'd consider it not his business anyway—he's a remarkably single-minded man about anything that doesn't concern cards. But Byrne and I have worked together before. Now that Weems has accepted me as a reliable partner—it went to my heart to let him win at cribbage—I should be able to draw him into a game of whist tonight. Between the two of us, Byrne and I should be able to strip him of whatever cash he has in hand for the journey. If Weems wants more, he'll have to get it from his trunk in the hold."

"Will he play?" January recalled Granville's words on the subject, but Hannibal only raised his eyebrows.

"My dear Benjamin, the man spent two hours this afternoon practically hugging himself for taking thirty dollars off me at cribbage." He closed his eyes and settled back on his bunk again. "Even splitting the take with Byrne, I think we both deserve more than what Granville's paying us. And as I said last night, there are specific instructions in the Bible about oxen, muzzles, and corn."

Luncheon on the *Silver Moon* was laid out for the gentlemen as a buffet in the Main Saloon—cold meats, cheeses, bread, and fruit—and served to the ladies in their own small dining-room at the bow. The sexes joined for dinner, however, at trestle tables set up in the Main Saloon and presided over by the owner Mr. Tredgold and his stout, raucous-voiced wife. Afterwards, under Thu's efficient supervision, waiters and porters cleared the tables away, and as the steward had urged, Hannibal played his violin for the company and January a guitar, and there was dancing and parlor-games.

Needless to say, neither the immigrant families who were dossing down on the bow-deck nor the wild Kentucky rivermen who shared the space with them were invited to join in the revels. Mrs. Tredgold insisted on singing and required her two children, eight-year-old Melissa and six-year-old Neil, also to sing duets ("Now, aren't they the *most* adorable children you've *ever* seen?") Mrs. Roberson and her younger daughter, sixteen-year-old Dorothea, read a scene from *Much Ado About Nothing,* which the extremely elegant Mrs. Fischer declared compared favorably to the version she had seen at Covent Garden in London.

"And if you'll believe that," murmured Hannibal, eyeing the majestic brunette, "might I interest you in some stock I have in a diamond-mine in the Nebraska Territory?"

It was Mrs. Fischer, January noticed, who took it on herself to draw pretty Dorothea Roberson away from Molloy's fair-haired inamorata Miss Skippen, and to whisper something to Mrs. Roberson and Mrs. Tredgold that apparently sealed that sprightly young lady's fate. By the time the ladies retreated to their own parlor again at ten—

accompanied by Mr. Quince, who proceeded to lecture them on the Grecian System of Round Dancing and the evils of alcohol—there was a decided space between Miss Skippen and all the rest.

After their departure, the men settled down to cards again. Davis, Molloy, Gleet, and a bachelor planter named Lockhart made up one table of whist and—January never quite saw how this was maneuvered—Hannibal and Byrne formed up a set against the Massachusetts mill-owner Dodd and Weems.

They were still at it two hours later when January put up his borrowed guitar, finished the coffee Thu had quietly brought him, and nodded good-night to the impassive steward. Weems was winning, and played his cards with an air of cocky excitement and new-found delight. January saw the glance of almost sleepy amusement that passed between Hannibal and the gambler Byrne, and could have pitied Weems if the man hadn't effectively ruined him and Rose. It was fascinating to see them set him up, playing as much on his greed and vanity as on his inexperience: "Lord, you're hot tonight," murmured Hannibal approvingly, and Byrne shook his head, adding, "Look like it's not going to be my evening."

January was reminded of those farm-wives who made pets of their rabbits so the little creatures wouldn't run away when it came time to knock their heads off for the pot.

Dodd, of course, simply chomped and slurped his way through the "little after-dinner snack" he'd ordered of pickled eggs and crullers, seeming barely to notice how much he lost.

The night was close and hot when January emerged onto the upper deck promenade. The hard silvery light of the quarter-moon sparked on the paddle where it threshed at the water, and from above him he heard Molloy's voice calling jovial insults at his assistant pilot, a gangling and talkative young man named Souter. From the other side of the boat as he descended the steps to the lower promenade, he heard the slave men singing: *"I'm goin' away to New Orleans. . . ."*

And like the sweet breath of evening wind, the voices of the chained women rose in the response, *"Good-by, my love, good-by. . . ."*

Closer, below him in the well of darkness, a woman's voice gasped, "Let go!"

"S'matter, honey, you too fond of them Frenchies to want a *real* man?" The voice was drunken, the accent from up-river somewhere, Kentucky or Tennessee.

Another voice giggled, "Can't tell us a pretty yeller gal like you, you ruther have one a' them black bucks over there, 'stead of Kyle an' me."

"No—"

"You hear somethin', Kyle?"

"Not me. 'Fraid she must be speakin' Frenchy. . . ."

January had already started down the stair—wondering what the hell he could say to an unknown number of intoxicated white boatmen that wouldn't get him beaten up—when he heard Rose's voice: "Allow me to translate for you gentlemen."

She spoke in the carrying steely tone of a schoolmistress, and as he sprang down from the stairs he saw the little group by the thin reflected glow of the engine-room door. There were three of them, shaggy-haired, dirty, and bearded, in faded shirts and Conestoga boots, hemming in the fairy-like little maidservant he'd seen following Mrs. Fischer on board. One of the boatmen had pulled off her headscarf, her thick hair hanging in a dark coil to her waist. She was pressed against the piled wood, arms folded tight over her breasts while the men tried to pull her hands away.

Rose stood in front of them, spectacles flashing.

"Git on outa here, bitch."

Rose didn't move. Only looked at the men with calm disdain.

"Git on outa here," said another. " 'Fore we take a switch to you, too—or some other rod you won't like so well."

Rose stood her ground. From the darkness behind her emerged Miss Skippen's tall, lush-breasted young maid, and the stout nursemaid who'd chased the Tredgold children around the deck, and a little white-haired woman whom January recognized as the mother of Eli the cook . . . all standing with their arms folded, simply watching the men with jeering eyes. Behind them in the dark the deck-hands began to emerge from the engine-room door, not offering any word or deed that could be termed as insolence, or punished as rebellion. Just simply staring.

That ring of watching eyes, January reflected, would be enough to make any man's drink-induced interest in rape stand down.

Mrs. Fischer's maid twisted free of the men's grips and ran to join the little group of women.

"Goddam bitches!" yelled the taller of the boatmen. "I got me a mind to buy the goddam lot of you, fuck the lot of you till you begs me for mercy!"

But the women merely turned away from them and faded into the darkness.

"Bitches!" yelled the tall man. *"Hoors!"* And his shorter companion, who had a yellow beard like a louse-ranch, took his arm and tugged him toward the piled wood that separated them from the chained slave women. "C'mon, Sam, somebody gonna be down here in a minute. . . ."

As the three men vanished through the gap between wood and rails, January heard one of them snarl, "What *you* lookin' at, bitch?" The words were followed by the meaty thud of a kick, a woman's stifled gasp, and the jingle of chains.

"Are you all right, honey?" Rose asked the maid in French as January came to join the women near the stern rail. They were little more than shapes in the dense shadows of the 'tween-decks, save for the flash of Rose's spectacles. Beyond them, moonlight flickered terrifyingly on the shapes of snags and towheads, bobbing in the water nearer shore.

"Thank you, yes, I'm fine. Thank you so much, Madame. . . ."

"Vitrac." Rose used the name under which she'd bought her ticket. "Rose Vitrac."

"I am Sophie Vannure." The girl's voice shook with sobs she couldn't control. January wondered whether the little maid had been so well-treated all her life that this was her first experience with molestation, or whether some earlier wound had been opened. In either case, he saw Rose put her arm around the girl, supporting her lest she fall.

"These yours, honey?" The stout Tredgold nursemaid Cissy came over from the wood-piles, carrying a couple of big shawls that had been dropped there. Sophie held out her arms.

"Thank you, yes. My mistress . . ."

"She turn you out to sleep down here?"

"I know why *my* missus turn *me* out," sniffed Miss Skippen's maid in the rough cane-patch French of one who'd probably cost a good deal less than the refined little Sophie. "With no more than 'Julie, I'll want coffee in the morning.' Don't tell me m'am high-and-mighty Fischer got a gentleman friend comin' to visit her, like my Miss Theodora does?"

Sophie Vannure pulled the shawl tighter around her shoulders, still shaking with fear and humiliation. When she spoke, her voice dripped resentment and betrayal. "What other reason would *Madame* have, to tell me to go sleep outside on the deck like an animal?"

"Could be worse." Julie's tone quirked with a bitter knowledge. "She could keep you in there to make up a three."

Sophie's laugh was a spiteful sob. "Not with Mr. Weems," she said. "Madame, she's not about to let anyone think she so much as knows what a man *is,* but she wouldn't share him—or anything else—with any other."

"You mean Mr. Weems, the little man in the check trousers that looks like a weasel?" Julie hooted with laughter. "He don't look like he got the red blood in him to kiss the parlormaid!"

"He does not," retorted Sophie, clearly steadied by the sympathy of new-found allies. "At the least he has never kissed me, though he looks, out of the corners of his eyes. He's too scared of Madame. He bought her house in New Orleans, and pays all her bills; yet it's *she* who says, 'We will come here, we will go there.' Mr. Weems, he follows, like a little dog."

"Well, think of that," murmured Rose as she and January settled into the dark niche among the wood-piles, where they could watch the passway to the engine-room, and the purser's door. "A respectable lady like that, and a thief underneath."

"What about a respectable schoolmistress like yourself," replied January softly, his arm sliding around Rose's waist, "who is a wanton underneath?"

"I fear," said Rose loftily, "that you have me mistaken for someone else—perhaps my wicked twin sister Elena." And they laughed at the old joke—the twin sister was completely fictitious—and settled themselves to watch the comings and goings of the wood crew, for the chance to slip into either the office or the hold.

But Hannibal had been right in his observation that there was never a time when the passageway was completely empty. While the *Silver Moon* churned its heavy way upstream through the darkness, and Rose and January watched and slept in turns, they never saw either a sign of Queen Régine or of a moment when it would have been feasible to enter the office or the hold.

FIVE

In the pre-dawn dark of the following morning, talk around the water-barrel beside the galley door was all about how old Fussy-Pants Weems had had seven hundred and seventy-five dollars taken off him last night at whist, and serve him right. "Lord, I thought he's gonna shrivel up into a pile of dust when Byrne brought out that trump card, an' we'd have to sweep him off the floor in the mornin'!"

"They had three hundred dollars extra on the rubber—you think a man that won't tip the porter who brings up his luggage would know better than that!"

Fog lay on the river, but the sky overhead was hot and clear. A thousand birds cried their territories in the green wall of willows that grew along the batture, audible even over the splashing of the paddle. "How the devil can the pilot steer if he can't even see the surface of the water?" January asked Jim, who sat on a coil of rope at the far end of the starboard promenade, shaving by lantern-light and a hand-mirror he'd drawn from his pocket.

"By the shape of the banks," replied the valet promptly. "Pilot sights on big trees, or houses on the banks, and knows the river—like knowin' there's a bar just above Houmas plantation, where the current sets around the point. Like walkin' around a chair in your massa's parlor in the dark. I been up and down this stretch of river, between Colonel Davis's place at Brierwood and New Orleans, a dozen times now with him, and even *I'm* startin' to recognize where there's a bar last time we passed."

"I'll keep an eye on the passway here, between the galley and the engine-room," said Rose when January returned to her, bringing wash-water and the gossip. "Thank goodness it's wide—I can see all the way through without being obvious about it." She nibbled on a pear and some cheese, and a little of the bread she'd brought, and scanned the promenade as he spoke, as those deck-hands who'd worked through the night dossed among the wood and others rose and washed, and got their rations from Eli at the galley door.

"I'll come down and spell you when I can." Though Rose had reported last night that she'd seen no sign of Queen Régine, whenever January had dropped off into sleep she was there, stealing up softly just behind the piles of wood that flanked them, or floating in the dark air just above the moonlit water, watching them with flaming eyes. In another dream he was haled before a drumhead court of planters, where Queen Régine accused him of being a free man: he was thrown into the river and had to swim to shore, with the dark snags underwater clawing at his legs, and Ned Gleet waiting on the bank with his chains.

They put in at Donaldsonville as the sky was turning bright, and stayed at the landing there until mid-morning while Mr. Tredgold inquired about the town for a passenger who was supposed to be waiting and wasn't. Molloy cursed mightily at the delay, because it meant drawing the fires out of his engines so that the boilers wouldn't run dry—the water-pumps operated only when the wheel was turning—but Ned Gleet took advantage of the occasion to ensconce himself on the gallery of the biggest of the waterfront taverns, alert for anyone who possessed a slave and who might be talked into selling.

At five in the morning there wasn't much hope of this, and from the upper deck promenade—where he kept a discreet eye on passengers and luggage leaving the boat—January could see the dealer getting himself into a fouler and fouler mood. When Molloy went into the selfsame tavern ("Even *I* don't start drinking at five in the morning!" exclaimed Hannibal self-righteously when January told him about this several hours later) Gleet shouted something at him about staying longer: Molloy didn't even break stride, just turned and backhanded the slave-dealer off the porch, threw the chair after him, and was stopped from following him down into the street and continuing the fight only by Mr. Tredgold and the young junior pilot Mr. Souter.

"There's no man tells Kevin Molloy what he's to do and not to do!"

Gleet's discouragement and chagrin were completed by the arrival of another slave-dealer with a coffle of some fifteen men and women, and by the fact that this dealer, a man named Cain with the coldest yellow eyes January had ever seen, refused to sell any of his stock. "I can get a better price for 'em in Louisville," Cain said in his quiet voice, and crossed the gangplank to see to chaining them along the lower promenade beside Gleet's.

All this January saw from the bow end of the boiler-deck, where he idled most of the morning, trying not to look like he was keeping watch. He didn't actually think Weems would try to desert the boat here—it was far too close to New Orleans—but it was just possible he would off-load one or more of his (or Mrs. Fischer's) trunks of money there, to be left in storage and picked up later. From this position January was able to observe the comings and goings of most of the passengers that morning: to witness the departure of the young planter Mr. Purlie with the slave-girl in tow he'd bought from Ned Gleet; to note how artfully Molloy's fair Miss Skippen, a vision in lavender ruffles, dropped her handkerchief *just* as Colonel Davis turned the corner of the upper promenade deck—and to hear the word she muttered to herself when Davis simply walked past and let it lie; to overhear a fragment of what appeared to be a vicious argument between Mrs. Fischer and Mr. Weems.

"—but what do you want me to *do,* Diana?"

"I want you to get yourself out of a situation you were too stupid to avoid, is what I want you to do." As they passed, January pretended to be absorbed in the spectacle of Molloy, down on the bow-deck, striking a porter with the back of his hand and sending the poor man sprawling into the coils of rope; January slipped his eye sidelong to glimpse the pair as they passed him, and saw that they were still pretending to be strangers, walking well apart and speaking in tones of quiet conversation, until you heard the words.

"But I tell you one thing, you're not touching a dime of . . ."

They passed out of hearing, and Melissa and Neil Tredgold came racing around the corner of the 'tween-decks, shrieking like banshees, followed by their nursemaid Cissy's shouts: "You children get back here!" On the deck below, Mr. Purlie's trunks were unloaded, and a merchant came down to take consignment for several bales of the rough osnaberg "nigger-cloth" and a crated plow. Deck passengers milled about, mostly rough waterfront types or the crews of flatboats making their way north again, with occasional families of Irish or Germans too poor to pay for cabins. Andy, the planter Lockhart's valet, passed January with a tray of coffee in his hands and asked, "Mr. Sefton not an early riser, I take it?"

"Not as of ten minutes ago," replied January good-humoredly. "I expect he'll be stirrin' soon."

"I thought he'd have more wits than to play cards with that Byrne feller in the Saloon." The valet shook his head. "When Mr. Lockhart come down the river last week, that Mr. Byrne was on the same boat, all friendly as can be—stayed at the same hotel as Mr. Lockhart, too. 'Course, Mr. Lockhart don't see a thing funny in Mr. Byrne seekin' him out, but if a man's that friendly for no reason, I always wonder if there's somethin' behind it."

He passed on, and January glanced down at the bow-deck again, wondering if he could relax his guard long enough to make sure Hannibal didn't arouse comment by making his own way down to the galley for coffee. The big bow hatch was open down to the hold, but the deck-hands were stowing the pulley-ropes of the crane on the jack-staff; no other trunks lay on the deck.

Deserting his post seemed safe enough. January passed down the starboard promenade side and rapped gently on Hannibal's door, receiving no answer, not much to his surprise. From there he descended the stair to the lower promenade, looking around him for Rose. A moment later he saw her come through the narrow space between a wood-pile and the starboard rails, encountering, as she did so, Cain the slave-dealer. They stopped, facing one another, for only an instant. Then Cain stepped back and aside to let her pass, and proceeded around her into the promenade where the female slaves were chained. Rose looked back over her shoulder at him, as if something in the meeting troubled her, then turned her head and saw January.

Relief swept her face and she quickened her step toward him, dodging two deck-hands piling still more wood near the galley door and stepping past the two maidservants Sophie and Julie, who were snatching a hasty cup of coffee between fixing their mistresses' hair and tidying up their mistresses' cabins and wardrobes. "My God, I'm glad I caught you," breathed Rose. "Queen Régine *is* on the boat. I've found where she's hiding."

"Sophie got me a sample of Mrs. Fischer's handwriting," whispered Rose as she and January walked, as swiftly and unobtrusively as possible, past the chained coffles of slaves along the starboard promenade. "The doorway from the galley passway to the hold is padlocked, but there's a door at the bow as well. . . ."

"I've seen it," said January. "The white deck-passengers sleep all around it."

"Reason enough to keep it locked." Rose grimaced at the recollection of Kyle and Sam. "There's no one near it now, though, and they've piled luggage in front of it, waiting to be lowered down the hatch."

The slaves in Cain's coffle moved aside to let them pass, chained already to rings along the wall and some of them settling down, to sit where they would sit for the coming days of the voyage, their little bandannas of possessions tucked at their sides. A tall, slim young man chained closest to the engine-room door was saying reassuringly to the man chained beside him, ". . . mostly the ones that blow up are 'cause somebody does somethin' stupid in the engine-room. These things go up an' down the river all the time, with no more danger than ridin' a horse."

"You know how many folks get killed ridin' horses, 'Rodus?"

Rose went on as they reached the corner of the 'tween-decks, "I marked with chalk the trunks and crates whose labels I checked—and there were several of the dozen I checked addressed to people who aren't on the boat, leaving aside entirely the crates and bales that are obviously commercial. I didn't see any of Mrs. Fischer's or Mr. Weems's, but I only had time to . . ." She paused, putting her head around the corner, watching the men on the deck.

Most of these were gathered around the door of the engine-room that opened onto the bow-deck, from which could be heard Molloy's bellowing voice. "Well, damn it, how long are we to kick our heels in this cursed place? It'll take us an hour to get up steam yet, and if you're still pussyfootin' about the town lookin' for passengers, then the back of both me hands to you! You can get that worthless old man Lundy to pilot you . . . !"

Rose and January slipped quickly around the corner, behind the heap of trunks, and down the ladder-like steps to the unlocked door of the hold.

January slipped the padlock out of its hasp and dropped it into his jacket pocket as they ducked through the door, which he closed behind them. In the remaining slit of light he fished a candle-stub and match-box from his pocket, scraped the match in the striking-paper, and looked around.

Rose whispered, in the softest audible breath, "Even if she does see us down here, what can Régine say that won't have her thrown off the boat as a stowaway?"

"She may not care," January replied. The thought of being dumped ashore seventy-five miles from New Orleans, in territory largely American and heavily committed to finding as many field-slaves as possible, was enough to daunt anyone—it frankly terrified him—but he wasn't entirely certain Queen Régine was sane. Most voodoos, including his own sister, didn't think like other people anyway.

Before them, the hold stretched away, a hundred feet into wet darkness. Trunks, crates, and boxes loomed, waking in January uncomfortable echoes of Sunday evening's excursion to the cemetery: the same sense of being hemmed in, of his field of vision being ruthlessly cut. He realized almost at once the difficulty of inspecting any of the luggage stowed aboard—Rose and Hannibal might be adept at the use of pick-locks, but the trunks and crates were piled two and three deep, and many of the crates, even those addressed to individuals, were nailed shut. Some could be discounted—Robert Lockhart, Greenville, Miss.; Col. Jefferson Davis, Brierfield Plantation, Miss.; Mr. Joseph Davis, Aurora Plantation, Miss., addressed in Colonel Davis's spiky hand.

But who was Althea Fitzsimmonds of Memphis, Tennessee? Or Mr. Robert S. Todd of Lexington? The handwriting on both of those labels was nothing like Weems's or Fischer's, but who was to say that the two thieves didn't have other confederates? Or that one or the other of them wasn't as skilled at alternative forms of handwriting as Hannibal?

And as Rose led him deep into the blackness of the hold, January was filled with the sense of being watched from out of that blackness by angry eyes that he could not see.

Rose murmured, "Back here." The candle's light touched a blanket folded in a little niche between two crates of FINEST CHINA——STAFFORDSHIRE——ENGLAND——FRAGILE. A leather valise lay near it; kneeling, January opened it with a fast-beating heart, as if he expected to find a rattlesnake inside. But within, thickly wrapped in sacking, he found a hunk of cheese the size of his own enormous fist, a sack of cornmeal and another of peanuts, and a half-dozen dried apples.

A smaller bundle yielded a juju-bag: black flannel, ashes, the burnt claw of a wren, pins. With it were packets of herbs—holding the candle close, he identified the brittle, half-crushed leaves and roots in one twist of newspaper as Jack-in-the-Pulpit, and in the other as Christmas rose.

Both deadly poisons.

He looked at the newspaper. The French edition of the *New Orleans Bee*. Saturday's.

The darkness seemed to be breathing down his back. The thought of coming back here tonight—picking the locks on the passway door if he could manage to get five minutes alone in the busy passway and trying to search what trunks they could open—filled him with queasy dread. Around him in the dark he seemed to feel the water pressing against the frail tarred wood of the hold, the weight of the boat towering over his head. He felt reminded that the steamboats were nothing more than barns on rafts with furnaces in their bellies; he couldn't imagine how anyone could sleep in this darkness, under the water, listening to the current of the mightiest river in the world surging by.

He backed away from the cubby-hole, signed to Rose silently to show him the trunks she hadn't so far had time to see. They moved from one to the next, January noting addresses and names, comparing the handwritting with the letter Granville had given him, and the shopping-list—*15 yd pink lustring, 60 yds blond lace, 4 pr silk stockings, soap*—that Sophie had let Rose take to make a note of something to herself on the back. "Sophie's already contrite over her outburst against Madame last night," whispered Rose. "She begged me this morning not to repeat any of what she said, about Mr. Weems. She was angry, she said, but of course Madame has had so difficult and painful a life, and Mr. Weems treats her so kindly—I take it Madame expressed proper shock and sympathy over Sophie's experience last night. The world is terribly unkind to women who must fend for themselves."

"I'll put my money on Mrs. Fischer against the world any day of the week," muttered January, remembering the hard glint in the woman's dark eye, as she'd strolled the deck with Weems, and the masterful set of her red mouth. "Which," he added bitterly, "I seem to have done. Here, you were a schoolmistress, you must have learned all the ways girls fake handwriting. Does this look like . . . ?"

Daylight spilled briefly across the ceiling of the hold, vanished again with the shutting of the door.

Silence, then the cautious creak of footsteps on the deck.

January blew out the candle in that first instant, drew Rose behind a stack of crates. Threads of gold light outlined a trunk, glinted on the brasswork of a box-corner, then vanished suddenly. But the darkness was full of another living presence, watching and waiting. Listening. January felt that his own breathing, and the thudding of his heart, were audible for the length of the hold. Something scraped behind him, a furtive skittering—rats, probably, but he startled nearly out of his skin.

Anyone with any business in the hold would have called out, *Who's there?*

But only silence met him, silence that waited for him to make the first sound.

January touched Rose's shoulder, eased gently behind the crates, moving in the direction of the bow-deck door. The light he'd seen had been to the left of the door, and he edged right, feeling the wood of crates, the leather of trunks. Circling around the unseen intruder and hoping she—or he—wasn't doing the same. They'd gone what felt like miles when the door opened again and daylight streamed into the hold, daylight and the yellow glare of a lantern as the steward Thucydides came down the steps. "Who's in there?" he called out, holding the lantern high, and January, not wanting to have questions asked and attention brought to him, crouched behind the canvas bales of osnaberg cloth and waited until the steward had advanced into the darkness.

"Who's there?"

From the back of the hold came a sudden sharp clank. Thu turned in that direction and January caught Rose's wrist to make a dash for the door, only to be forestalled by another dark form breaking from cover, pelting behind Thu and up the steps to the deck. From where he and Rose crouched, January could see nothing besides that it was a woman, a frothy white flash of petticoat under pale, vanishing skirts. Thu cursed and followed, and January drew Rose quickly to the doorway, opening it and slipping out, listening for a moment before scrambling up the steep steps to the deck. He held his breath, waiting for someone to call out, *What you doin' down there, nigger?* But nobody did. Looking neither to the right nor the left, he led the way around the corner and down the promenade deck again, and back to the stern.

Rose gasped, "Whew!" as they dropped into their niche among the wood-piles. Then she giggled like a schoolgirl who's gotten away with a prank, and January, too, was overcome with the exhilarating urge to laugh.

"It isn't funny," he told her. "We could have been put off the boat—they'd never think we weren't down there to steal, especially since *someone* I could mention still has pick-locks in her pocket."

"Did you get a look at her?"

January shook his head. "I was too busy trying to crawl under the floorboards. She was white, though—I don't think there's a black woman on this boat wears that many petticoats. . . ."

Sabrine, the ladies'-maid to Mrs. Roberson and her daughters, passed across the front of their niche, stepping daintily aside to avoid puddled water and showing half a dozen foamy petticoats handed down from her mistresses. January and Rose had to press their hands over their mouths to keep from laughing out loud, and clung to each other in a paroxsym of near-suffocation with mirth.

"It isn't funny," January repeated when he could manage to speak again. "Now they'll keep a tight watch on the hold, and we're never going to get down there. . . ."

"*And the gates of Hell shall not prevail against us*. . . . I'm sorry," added Rose. "I'm obviously not taking this seriously enough. But if . . ."

Footsteps creaked on the stair above them, and a quiet voice called out, "Mr. Bredon . . ."

And past the wood-pile, January saw the slave-dealer Jubal Cain flinch and turn, as if he had been shot.

The promenade was quiet, and nearly empty; Cain reached the bottom of the stairs in two long strides, as the speaker came down. From their place of concealment under the stair and behind the wood, January could see the mustard-colored check of Oliver Weems's trouser-leg—all that he could see, now, of either man.

"It is Judas Bredon, isn't it?" asked Weems, his voice very quiet now. "From the . . ."

"I don't know what the hell you're talking about." Cain's deep voice was like iron. "Or who the hell you are."

"Probably not." Weems continued his descent, out of January's sight. "But *I* know who *you* are. Or who you *were* before you started running slaves for a living." And January thought—though over the throb of the engines, and the voices of the men on the bow-deck, poling the *Silver Moon* away from the levee, it was difficult to tell—that he heard the rustle of paper, passed perhaps from hand to hand.

Cain said in a low, tight whisper, "How much do you want?"

"Four hundred. Tonight."

"Where the hell am I supposed to get . . . ?"

"You might try selling one of your slaves. I'm sure Ned Gleet would pay you that much for a good field-hand."

The stairs above them creaked sharply again as Weems sprang up them. A moment later Cain came into view, his back to Rose and January as he walked to the stern rail. The great paddlewheel had begun to turn at last, silver rivers of water pouring down off it flashing in the morning light. Molloy's voice could be heard from the bow-deck, bellowing profanity at the deck-hands. But Cain stood motionless, holding what looked like a crumpled ball of paper in his hand.

Then, as the boat began to move forward up the river, the slave-dealer clenched the paper in his fist and hurled it out into the churning wake of the boat.

SIX

"Oh, Mr. Sefton, you have no idea how unkind people can be to girls of quite good family who find themselves all alone in the world." The low, sweet voice met January's ears as he mounted the steps. Emerging onto the upper promenade, the first sight that met his eyes was Hannibal, standing with Miss Skippen by the stern railing, his arm protectively around her and his head bowed in an attitude of sympathetic attention. When her rosebud lips trembled, the fiddler immediately proffered a handkerchief, and dried the tears on the long lashes—a shift of wind brought January the reek of very expensive French perfume.

> *"I saw my lady weep,*
> *And Sorrow proud to be exalted so*
> *In those fair eyes where all perfections keep."*

"You say such beautiful things," whispered Theodora, resting her lace-mitted fingers lightly on Hannibal's lapel and gazing up into his eyes. "Not like . . . Well, not like some others I have encountered. Oh, Mr. Sefton"—her small hands turned, and gripped the cloth in a convulsion of feeling—"I declare I am sometimes so afraid of him! He is so rough, so uncouth! Thank God I have *you* to turn to, in my misery . . . you are the only one I can trust!"

"My dearest," murmured Hannibal, "I am hardly the most trustworthy man in the world. . . ."

"Ah, but you are!" Theodora insisted, like every other woman to whom Hannibal told the honest truth about himself—after three and a half years January was still trying to figure out how he did that. "And who else can I trust? You are so sweet. . . . And he's become so capricious, I scarcely know what to believe anymore! If he turned away a good job to take a poorer one, all at a whim, how do I know that his next whim will not be to forsake me for another, prettier perhaps, or more endowed with the world's goods? For though my family is a fine and an old one, we are, alas, fallen upon poverty!"

Her accent alone was enough to convince January that her family was probably not as fine or old as all that—after one generation of wealth, Americans tended to ship their daughters off to schools where refinement of speech was a part of the curriculum—but Hannibal only passed his palm gently over her cheek.

"For the world's goods I care naught, my Angelflower, and as for beauty, how could any man turn his eyes from what I see before me here? *Eyes as soft as honey / and a face / that Love has lighted / with his own beauty. . . .*"

"Michie Hannibal, sir?" Dalliance was one thing, but January had witnessed two examples already that morning of Kevin Molloy's propensity for casual violence. He had no desire to see his friend beaten up over a blue-eyed tart in pink ruffles. The junior pilot Mr. Souter passed him on the stair, on his way to the pilot-house to change over watches—at a guess, once his watch was up Molloy wouldn't linger. No sane man would, in a ten-by-ten-foot pilot-house with Mark Souter droning on relentlessly about his great-uncle's contribution to the Battle of Blue Lick in 1782 and the precise degree to which the Souters were related to the Wickliffes of Glendower, whose

Logan cousins had married into the Todhunter family through a connection who was a first *and* a second cousin, once removed either way. . . .

Hannibal raised a hand to sign January over, and Miss Skippen caught his wrist. "Oh, send him away, do!" There was a slight desperation in her face—January wondered how many others she'd attempted to attach herself to since Colonel Davis had passed by her dropped handkerchief a few hours ago.

"My sweet, I dare not snub Ben, even for the felicity of your violet eyes. It's he who makes my coffee in the mornings." He bent to kiss her hands. "Until tonight."

Her parting from him would have done credit to the great tragedienne Sarah Siddons as Juliet. January half expected her to stab herself on her way through the door of the Ladies' Parlor, where Mr. Quince was holding forth on the subject of the need for the immediate re-colonization of all slaves to Africa.

"Tonight?" January raised his brows as he and Hannibal entered the stateroom.

"We have a tryst on the starboard promenade after dinner, and I rely upon you to be sleeping on the floor here in case she feels faint and demands a place to lie down. Considering the amount of information I've gleaned from her so far, I can hardly cut the poor girl now. God knows she's been cut enough by La Fischer and her co-harpies in the Parlor—not that I'd want *my* sixteen-year-old daughter associating with her, if I had one, mind you. I rescued her while on my quest there for coffee, which I didn't get, by the way. . . ."

"I'll get you some. How long were you with her?" January wasn't certain, but he'd thought Miss Skippen's pink muslin skirts, with their ruffles of blond lace and their silk roses, looked wet and dirty along the hems—they were light-colored, too, as had been those he'd glimpsed in the dark of the hold.

"Twenty minutes or so. Just before we pushed away from the landing. I'm not sure what she'd been up to—mischief, I think. She was breathless and trembling, anyway, and practically fell into my arms. Is all well with you, *amicus meus*? I feared something had happened when you didn't make an appearance. . . ."

"Rose went down into the hold while they were loading and found evidence that Queen Régine is on board, and is hiding down there. I went back down with her to see, with the result," January added grimly, "that Thucydides may very well be keeping a sharper eye on the hold in future. I'll tell you when I get back."

Mrs. Tredgold, who presided over the Ladies' Parlor, only smiled benevolently at January's comicly mock-timid request to "thieve some of your coffee, M'am, for Michie Hannibal," leading him to guess that his friend had exercised his customary charm even over the boat-owner's formidable spouse. Miss Skippen occupied a chair in the corner of the Parlor, nibbling a biscuit and being pointedly ignored by Mrs. Roberson and her elder daughter, Emily—a diminutive widow—and by Mrs. Fischer, whose own comprehensively glass dwelling should have endowed her with a little more charity about casting the first stone. Beside Mrs. Fischer, Mr. Quince continued earnestly on his lecture:

". . . alternative to pushing them into a society in which, in their savage innocence, they will never be able to make a living . . ."

Not with gentlemen like our Massachusetts friend Dodd running the factories, we won't, thought January, pouring coffee from the larger pot into a smaller water-carafe and trusting that Hannibal had a spare cup in his room.

"This way, we will obviate the burden of the government and the tax-payer, and at the same time enable the freedmen to improve the lot of their savage brethren in Africa by their own industrious example. . . ."

January wondered if any of the members of the American Colonization Society had ever actually *asked* any man of African descent—slave or free—if he wanted to go back and live in Africa. At meetings of the Faubourg Tremé Militia and Burial Society—of which January was a member despite his mother's derisive insistence that most of the members were "dark as a pack of field-hands" (*On the subject of glass houses and stone-throwing* . . . he reflected)—not once had a meeting ended with all those *libre* artisans and businessmen leaping to their feet and shouting. *Let's take the Society funds and all relocate to Africa!*

Quince didn't even look at him as he collected the coffee-tray and left the room.

Hannibal duly produced a second china cup from his luggage, and listened while January poured out coffee for them both and related the events of the morning. "Queen Régine obviously has a confederate on the boat—if that *is* her food down there and not someone else's. . . ."

"Someone else's food and someone else's poison?"

"*A hit, a palpable hit.* Hers, then. And just as obviously it isn't Thucydides, if he called out, *Who's there?* As for who was *actually* there . . . What time did all this take place?"

"Shortly before the boat left the landing, which makes me fairly certain that was the lovely Miss Skippen investigating the hold. Eight-thirty? Nine o'clock?"

"According to the lovely Miss Skippen, Mr. Molloy—apparently on a whim and at a few hours' notice—abandoned the pilot's berth on the *Emperor Napoleon* to Memphis, to take considerably less pay piloting the *Silver Moon.*"

"A few hours before departure, the *Silver Moon* didn't already *have* a pilot?" January paused in the act of buttering a roll, with a slight twinge of guilt that he hadn't taken a few more from the Parlor to save for Rose.

"Molloy undercut the original pilot's fee, evidently, and sought out Mr. Tredgold at the steamboat offices to convince him that his original head pilot was incompetent." Hannibal gestured with his open hand, as if inviting January to take this explanation from his palm if he wanted it. "Miss Skippen is most annoyed, because this lesser pay means Mr. Molloy has reneged on several promised gifts—including a purple silk bonnet with pink plumes at La Violette on Rue Chartres that Miss Skippen had her poor little heart set on."

January said, "Hmmn."

"I'd say it sounds like your Mr. Granville's lady-friend at the cocoa-shop wasn't the only person who saw Mr. Weems at the steamboat office and put two and two together. It isn't unreasonable. Even riverboat pilots have to bank their money somewhere, though after a few weeks of providing lodging and apparel for Miss Skippen in New Orleans, I wonder that Molloy had any money left to bank, let alone lose. As for Jubal Cain . . ."

"Clearly Weems took the first chance he could to recoup some of his money without opening one of the trunks in the hold," said January. "Mrs. Fischer at least suspects the hold's being watched. She seems to be the brains of the outfit. And if that was Miss Skippen I saw down there, Fischer has reason to be watchful. . . . How much was your share of the whist takings, by the way?"

"Two hundred and fifty. It grieved me, to mis-lead Weems with our bids so that we lost, instead of cleaning out Dodd, who's a shockingly bad player." Hannibal set his cup aside and drew a roll of bills from his breast-pocket, and counted out a hundred and sixty-six onto the counterpane between them as he spoke—the tiny cabin boasted only a single chair, at present doing service as a table for the coffee-tray.

"But Byrne was as close to singing and dancing as I've ever seen him," added Hannibal thoughtfully, "since Dodd now trusts him and is ripe for a good plucking. Bank of Louisiana notes, you'll observe." He held the last one up, then handed it to January. "With luck this will buy you and owl-eyed Athene a little more maneuvering-room in an emergency. I wonder if La Pécheresse"—he twisted the French word for "fisher-woman" into its sound-alike, "sinner"—"is aware of her partner's efforts to raise extra cash?"

"I wouldn't think so." January recalled the calculating intelligence in Mrs. Fischer's chill, dark eyes, the hardness of her voice. As a black man, he was forbidden by convention to look a white woman in the face, but even a quick glance had shown hers to be a study in wary strength.

An adventuress, like her sister-in-greed Theodora Skippen, but with education and sophistication that put her as far beyond the blond girl as a tigress is beyond a kitten. "Mrs. Fischer's not a woman I'd care to cross, no matter who's paying the bills."

"As you say," said Hannibal thoughtfully. "It would take someone very desperate—or very stupid—to blackmail a man with eyes like Jubal Cain's."

Watching Cain throughout the day, as the *Silver Moon* steamed north—or in fact mostly west and then east again around the Mississippi's huge bends—January was inclined to agree with his friend. Though taller than Gleet, and built heavy, like an overweight bull-mastiff, Cain wasn't a blusterer like Gleet. His eyes—yellow as a wolf's, in a pock-marked, bearded face—were the eyes of an infinitely dangerous man.

The men of Gleet's coffle were cowed by the slave-dealer, but when he was up in the Saloon—as he was during most of the day—they relaxed, and talked and told stories among themselves and with the deck-hands, as men with nothing left to lose will come to do under nearly any circumstances. The men in Cain's coffle were afraid, even in their owner's absence. They talked when they had to, but they kept quiet for the most part, the uneasy quiet of fear. The only one of them who would actually stand up and speak to Cain when he came down was the tall, slim young man—'Rodus, the others called him—chained next to the engine-room door.

January had many chances to observe them that day, for he spent a good part of it down on the stern end of the starboard promenade, while Hannibal amused himself by gossiping with the ladies or playing cribbage with the shaky-handed Mr. Lundy in a corner of the

Saloon. The open passway between the engine-room and the galley, which connected the rear ends of the promenades on either side of the lower deck, was a sort of village square for such of the colored population of the boat as were able to walk around, and a clearing-house for gossip. January heard, on one occasion, Sophie Vannure's warmly sympathetic account of Mrs. Fischer's tribulations with a cruel and domineering husband in Cincinnati—an account he believed in no more than he did in Miss Skippen's "fine old family"—and somewhat later in the day, Julie's bitter animadversions against Miss Skippen herself.

"She call herself a lady, an' go on about how great her family is," muttered the girl, settling herself by the rail beside Rose and January so that January could look at her bruised and bleeding ear. "Maybe Michie Binoche, that owns my mama, ain't no more than a contractor, but I seen decent white folks in my time, an' Miss Skippen ain't one of 'em, no matter what she say. When Michie Molloy buy me for her, an' bring me home to that house he got for her, I could see she didn't have a thing but what he buy her. Every one of them dresses she got is spang new, some of 'em just delivered by the dressmaker that week. . . ."

"That doesn't mean she isn't respectable," objected Sophie, who'd come down to fetch water from the galley to rinse a coffee-stain from her mistress's cuff. "When poor Madame fled from her husband in Cincinnati, she tells me she had to escape with only the clothing she stood up in, lest he pursue her and force her to live with him and endure his abuse again. I am myself a good Catholic," she added, crossing herself, "and of course I believe that divorce is wrong, but in cases like that . . . But what I mean is, Madame is a most respectable woman, even if she is . . . even if she has found a man who loves and cherishes her."

"Oh, Mr. Molloy love an' cherish Miss Skippen, all right, with her hangin' on his arm, an' feelin' faint, an' goin' on about her finishin'-school, an' how she ain't never been with a big, strong gentleman like him before." Julie's lips tightened, and she gazed out over the rail at the brown water, prickled and studded with the groping black fingers of snags, and the tangled gray wilderness of the banks. "He should see her when he ain't there, an' she got a couple glasses of plum brandy in her, singin' about the three old whores from Winnipeg. He'd wonder what finishin'-school she went to, to learn *that.*"

"And I suppose that if she *did* go to a finishing-school," sighed Rose later, after January had ascertained that no more damage had been done to Julie's ear by her mistress's blow than nail-scratches, "she still would not be able to support herself in anything but poverty or prostitution. For Miss Skippen was right, you know, when she said that the world is unkind to girls who find themselves alone in it."

She settled herself against the heaped cordwood in the shade, watching the deck-hands as they walked along the rail, long poles in their hands. As the river shallowed with summer, the bars that the current laid down before every point, on every bend, went from annoyances to be edged around to outright perils. Though noon was far past, Kevin Molloy remained in the pilot-house, and January could hear his voice bellowing curse-riddled instructions to the little crew of leadsmen who had rowed ahead of the *Silver Moon* in the skiff.

Their shouts echoed over the flat brown water, above the engine's slow throb: *"Half one . . . half one . . . quarter one . . ."*

"Move along port there, y'idjits! Is it blind y'are?"

"Half one."

And ahead of the boat—January could see it when he walked to the rail and squinted along the 'tween-decks at the glaring water—the water lay glassy over the bar. Behind it was the dead water, where no current stirred the stagnation, like the poverty that trapped him in New Orleans, when there was not enough money to float him over the bar.

In the low water of summer, even the smallest logs and drifts and reefs became objects of endless slow negotiation, of wearily muscling through, as the deck-hands even now were readying themselves for the chancy prospect of "walking" the boat over the submerged wall of gravel and mud that blocked further passage up-river. And he shivered at the thought of years ahead of doing just that: laboriously pushing through small illnesses, minor catastrophes that even a few dollars in the bank would solve.

People lived like that, he knew. Some even held on to their joy while they did it.

He walked back to Rose. "Do you think Miss Skippen would have appreciated a chance to learn Greek and mathematics, instead of fancy sewing and dancing, at your school?"

Rose sighed. "Probably not. And I suspect our pupil Cosette's mother, and Germaine's, are right, too, when they say they'd rather their daughters learned something that will be 'of use' to them, to make them more 'fascinating' to men."

"You," said January, "are fascinating to *this* man, Greek and mathematics and all. And I can tell you Cosette and Germaine love what you teach them, even if it is difficult. At least I found someone had taken the French copy of the *Iliad* from the study, and is reading ahead of where you're taking them through the Greek." He sat beside her again, gathered her into his arm. "I'd like to take that knot-head Quince to your school, and let him preach there about sending 'savages' who will 'never be able to make a living' back to Africa because it's all they're mentally fit for."

In the end, unable to find any place on the bar that had twelve feet of water, Molloy ordered the engineers to build up steam and rammed the bar head-on, the bottom scraping on the soft sand while the deckhands heaved and shoved with their poles, to literally flounder the *Silver Moon* to the other side. Then the slow process was all to do again, with the leadsmen rowing ahead in the skiff, and the monotonous calls ringing over the water: *"Half one . . . half one . . . quarter less twain . . . mark twain."*

Mark Twain was the magic word, *safe water* . . . barely . . . enough for the boat to get over the next bar. They stopped at Futch's Wood-Yard, and at Home Plantation to drop off bolts of cheap calico and osnaberg and some New Orleans newspapers, after making a wide detour around Claiborne Island—the chute behind the island, navigable in high water, was nothing but a slot of mud now—and reached Baton Rouge slightly after nine that night.

The entire population of the Grand Saloon, who'd been listening to January and Hannibal play, streamed out en masse in the humid night air to look at the torches and movement on the landing. Though he didn't think Weems would disembark here any more than he'd get off in Donaldsonville, still January kept watch, while Tredgold had another quarrel with Molloy over damping the fires long enough to collect passengers.

"Who the bloody hell will be about at this time of the night fixin' to go up-river?" bellowed the pilot, and Mrs. Tredgold sailed into the argument with: "As long as you're in the pay of this boat, you'll do as my husband orders. . . ."

Most riverboat pilots January had ever met would have walked off at that point, with some choice curse shouted over the shoulder. That Molloy didn't confirmed in January's mind that the pilot was, in fact, a fellow depositor in the Bank of Louisiana and suspected Weems of absconding with some or all of its funds.

"But whether the man intends to return the portion of them that aren't his, if he manages to locate Weems's trunks before we do," said Hannibal, leaning his bony elbows on the rail and looking down at the landing in the torchlight, "is, as they say, another story."

After a screaming-match of Olympian proportions between Molloy and Mrs. Tredgold, the *Silver Moon* remained in Baton Rouge until midnight. Tredgold went ashore—propelled by his wife—as did Ned Gleet, to prowl the barrooms of the waterfront district in quest of human bargains. He came back empty-handed and angry, and tried again to talk Jubal Cain into selling some of his slaves to him. This provoked a scene that was discussed in whispers on the stern deck the following day—since every body-servant on the boat had a wholly understandable loathing for both dealers.

"I never heard one man, black or white, lay out another so flat without raising his voice," whispered Jim at the water-butts in the morning, as the *Silver Moon* steamed away from a brief stop at the sordid little settlement of Bayou Sara. "He called him a pusillanimous slime-trail an' I don't know what-all else, and Gleet backed down from it." The gray-haired Davis valet glanced in the direction of the piled wood that hid the male slaves from the servants' end of the promenade. "And I tell you, if I was a white man and he called me that, I'd just say 'Yes, sir' too."

January nodded, and rubbed his eyes, gritty with the exhaustion of having stayed up most of the night watching for another chance to break into the hold. But either because of yesterday's incident, or because Thucydides had discovered the evidence of Queen Régine's presence on the boat, both the bow and the stern doors down into the hold were not only double-locked but, January suspected, unobtrusively watched as well.

Through the day the steamboat pecked and slogged and struggled its way upstream, sometimes seeming to become mired in sunken forests of flotsam and snags. They bulled their way over bars below Dead Man's Bend and Esperance Point, and for a time hung up on a bar below Palmetto Point so badly that it looked as if every male on the boat would be required to help "spar" over—literally lever the boat by means of mast-like poles chained to the capstans on the bow, like a wingless locust shoving itself along the ground. When they entered the horrendous mat of snags and driftwood around the mouth of the Red River, in the final slanting light of the hot evening, it seemed to January that they would be trapped there forever.

"Goddam snaggiest stretch of the river, bar the reach below Vicksburg," panted the old pilot Lundy, whom January found at the bottom of the stern-promenade stairway, clinging to the bannister in exhaustion. "It's like they got a patent snag-makin' factory up at the top of the Red River, and they just dump 'em in and let 'em float down. Never seen the like."

January watched a second night, to try to slip into the hold, but Thucydides seemed always to be walking around the decks with a lantern. In the end, in exhaustion, he bade Rose good-night and returned to Hannibal's stateroom to sleep on the floor. Since discovering the poison and the juju-bag in the hold, he had felt uneasy anywhere on the lower deck at night.

He dreamed of poverty, of sharing a single room with Rose in the house of some aging former plaçée, and teaching piano lessons in the parlor to pay the rent. In his dream it was night, and Rose sat in silence by the window, a book open on her lap and her long brown hair lying in soft curls down her back, but no lamp beside her. January kept asking her in his dream, over and over, *What is it? What's wrong?*

And she would neither look at him nor reply.

Then he dreamed that the *Silver Moon* was sinking, that the juju-bag hidden deep in the hold was burning a hole in the bottom of the boat, was calling out into the darkness of the waters. And from the darkness of the waters great twisted hands reached up, snagging at the paddles, tearing at the fragile boards. He and Rose were in the dark of the hold as the planks began to break apart, she much farther in than he, and running away from him, running into that dark nightmare corridor. Running in the wrong direction, away from the safety of the door. He shouted her name, tried frantically to catch up with her, to pull her back to safety, but her hand slipped out of his, and the water took her. He groped for her in the darkness, holding his breath, fighting the dark water that closed over his head, while huge floating trunks and boxes slid and nudged at him in the blackness, and he heard Queen Régine laughing.

Your woman will be torn from your arms. . . .

He woke panting, drenched in sweat, to find Hannibal kneeling beside him on the straw matting, his long hair hanging down around his face by the light of the single candle.

"Are you all right?" asked the fiddler softly.

Night was black outside the windows. The *Silver Moon* could have been steaming through the depths of interstellar space for all that could be seen.

January sank back down on his rolled-up coat that he was using for a pillow; he was shaking.

"Or I suppose I should ask, is Rose all right?" Hannibal settled with his back against the bunk and his skinny knees drawn up under his immense white linen nightshirt. "You were calling her name."

January shook his head. "It's the same dream," he said wearily, and ran his hand over his face. "Always the same dream, since before we were married. I want to save her, and I can't. Sometimes it's from one thing, sometimes another—once I dreamed she was being carried off by a Roman legion, God knows where I got that idea from. . . ."

"Was she grading Latin papers that week?"

And January laughed. The iron reality of the fear retreated a little. But it watched him like a rat from the shadows.

"I suppose I should be grateful it's Rose I'm trying to save," he said. "I can wake up, and there she is, sleeping beside me and dreaming about planting sweet-peas. Sometimes I used to dream about running through the streets of Paris, knowing Ayasha was dying of the cholera, back in our rooms. . . ." He flinched at the memory of those dreams. Of the way the streets of the river-side district lengthened and tangled into bizarre labyrinths, turned back on themselves, while he could hear his first wife's desperate breathing, her sobs as she lay on the bed. Could hear her calling his name.

"And I'd wake up," he said softly, "and know that she actually did die." He didn't add that sometimes it was Rose dying while he ran through the streets of Paris in that sweltering cholera summer, trying to find the way to her. To save her.

So that he would not have to face the rest of his life alone.

"I suppose that is what it is," said Hannibal, "to be a knight-errant at heart. God knows what Sir Galahad dreamed about. It couldn't have been terribly interesting, fighting to rescue a cup. And an empty cup, at that. I think the worst part of trying to give up opium was the dreams—although mind you, I wasn't terribly keen on the throwing-up part either."

Or the ghastly blackness of depression that had followed hard upon the physical symptoms, January reflected, considering his friend's gaunt face in the tiny seed of orange light. That Hannibal had, with an improvement in his health last winter, actually attempted to break his opium habit had astonished January; that he had ultimately been unable to do so surprised him not at all. To the girls among whom Hannibal lived, in the attics and back-sheds of the whorehouses and saloons of the Swamp, his resolve to give up laudanum and liquor had appeared merely quixotic in the face of the devastating symptoms of withdrawal: "Just have a bit until you're feeling better" had quickly collapsed the whole effort, leaving him, January thought, more fragile than before.

"Does Rose want to be rescued?" asked Hannibal now. "In your dreams, I mean?"

"I don't know," said January. "God knows I've never had any luck with rescuing her in real life. And it may not be Rose I'm seeking to rescue at all, or not Rose only, but my sisters, my mother . . . my father. . . ."

When he slept again he dreamed of the slaves chained along the promenade, sleeping in their chains, while Rose lay curled on her blanket with her head on her satchel, beside Julia, as the huge paddle thrashed and glittered in the darkness. And in his dream he saw the faces of the men and women in the coffle, and knew them: his sister Olympe and her husband, Paul, his sister Dominique with her tiny daughter Charmian in her arms. For some reason his mother wasn't there—probably because she would never permit herself to be perceived as a slave, even in her son's dreams. But his father was, the father he had not seen since he was eight, since his mother was sold to a white man and went to New Orleans to live as his free mistress with her children.

And his father's face was his own.

All in chains. All being taken to someplace they did not know, to be separated forever. All trapped on the wet planks of the steamboat, churning up-river through the night.

Then he woke with the pale light trickling through the shut curtains of the stateroom, to the sounds of horns blowing, of cannon firing in the distance. And coming out on deck minutes later, he saw the town of Natchez-On-The-Hill lying before them in the hot light of morning.

SEVEN

Natchez-On-The-Hill was a handsome town of some four thousand souls, its tree-bordered square looking down on the river from the top of a high bluff and its shady streets lined with the Spanish galleries and graceful brick English houses of its original builders. It was the center of the richest cotton land in the South: even in the hush of summer, the landing at the bottom of the bluff was busy with keelboats, flatboats, and the small stern-wheelers that were the only steamboats that could navigate the low river. Merchants and planters bustled about the levee, seeing to the receipt of goods ordered from Paris and New York; draymen shouted at the deck-hands who loaded up their wagons, river-traders dickered for bargains with one eye open for pickpockets and thieves.

Along the foot of the bluff, between the steep brown cliff of clay and the brown waters of the river, lay Natchez-Under-The-Hill.

"Whatever you do, stay on the boat." From behind the corner of the 'tween-decks, January watched Mr. Weems fussing about the bow-deck, like an animate marigold in his mustard-colored frock-coat, as he supervised the raising of two trunks from the hold. "My guess is, they're off-loading part of the loot for storage here, to be picked up later when the search dies down. I think they'll be back."

In the wide space of mud and gravel that lay between the water's edge and the first row of rickety warehouses and taverns at the foot of the bluff, a dozen drivers waited with carriages of various sorts, now and then hopping down from their boxes to bargain with passengers from the boats. Oliver Weems strode briskly across the landing-stage to the bank, signaled to one of the drivers. Just beyond him, a bearded white man dashed naked from one of the filthy alleyways, howling that he'd been robbed.

In the windows of a dozen ramshackle sheds, women of every shade from alabaster to ebony leaned out and shrieked with laughter; a man in a saloon doorway yelled, "Still got the family jewels, Bert?" The smell of the tangled criss-cross of streets under the summer heat was like the Swamp in New Orleans, and the feel of the place—of casual violence and uncaring vice—was, if anything, worse.

"Be in town awhile, Henry?" yelled a red-haired strumpet from a second-floor window, causing Mr. Tredgold to jump as if scalded; three other girls poked their heads through the same window and blew kisses.

Resplendent in his shabby coat and chimneypot hat, Hannibal paused on the landing-stage and stretched out a hand:

> *"But soft, what light through yonder window breaks?*
> *It is the East, and Juliet is the sun. . . ."*

"And if they don't return?" asked Rose softly as January stepped back into concealment at her side.

"We'll get you word."

In the engine-room, the stokers were drawing the fires from the furnaces, or damping them with ashes, to keep a low level of steam seething in the boilers without running them dry. The engines were silent, the black monster of the paddlewheel still; in the relative quiet, the shrill screams of Miss Melissa and young Master Tredgold could be heard: *"We want to get off the boat! Let us get off the boat! Mama said we could get off the boat, Cissy! We'll tell Papa to beat you unless you let us . . . !"*

The denizens of Natchez-Under, January reflected, would chop those two children up for breakfast and serve them with grits.

Early as it was, the deck of the *Silver Moon* bustled with life. The planter Roberson handed his wife and daughters down the main stairway—as far as January had seen, the first time any of the Roberson females had descended to water-level since New Orleans—and conducted them across the landing-stage to where the brightly-polished black landaulet of family friends waited to take them visiting while the boat lay in port. The deck-passengers hastened ashore as well, the immigrant families to replenish their provisions from the town markets, the Sams and Kyles and their ilk to get drunk and laid and, January earnestly hoped, if possible, killed as well. Thucydides stood beside the hatch, tallying something in his notebook. Mrs. Tredgold screamed orders. Mr. Tredgold wrung his hands.

"Well, if you miss the boat," said Rose, who always had a backup plan, "I'll leave you reports at General Delivery, left till called for, in Vicksburg, Mayersville, and Greenville, and I'll wait for you at the best free colored boardinghouse in Memphis. I'm not sure I'll be able to pursue our friends beyond Memphis alone. . . ."

"You're not going to have to pursue our friends anywhere," insisted January, more to reassure himself than her. He pulled her into his arms, kissed her hard. The thought of Rose alone in a strange city—much less a hub of the slave trade like Memphis—made him shudder, even without the added complication of her trying to convince white American police that a respectable white banker was a thief. . . .

"I won't miss the boat."

"Of course not," agreed Rose far too promptly.

Why do I dream about rescuing this woman? If she ever dreamed about anything more disturbing than conjugating Latin verbs, she'd dream about rescuing ME.

"There," said January softly. "Only one valise. They'll be back."

Mrs. Fischer descended the stair, paused to gaze down her nose at Ned Gleet as he thrust and drove his slave-gang ashore, then swept to the landing-stage, where Weems waited by the cab. Sophie followed meekly, carrying a green-striped canvas valise. Across the landing, Hannibal wandered vaguely toward the insalubrious alleyways of Natchez-Under, gazing about him as if he'd never seen such a place before in his life. It was time to go.

"Take care," Rose whispered.

Convinced that the boat would in fact leave, that Rose would in fact be carried off to Memphis alone with Ned Gleet, January fought not to hand her his half of Hubert Granville's traveling expenses. God knew which of them was actually going to need the money more, in the next few hours . . . or the next few days. . . .

And as he strode across the landing-stage, and through the trampled muck to Hannibal's side, he cursed the desperate necessity of money, that could make the difference between a life that was bearable and one that brought nothing but friction and grief. That could make the difference, for those of the wrong shade of skin, between freedom and a lifetime in bondage.

Especially in the American lands.

He glanced back, and saw Jubal Cain standing on the bow end of the boiler-deck, gazing after Weems and Mrs. Fischer as the pair of them climbed into their cab.

Though the river was low, the usual summer rain of the Mississippi Valley had briefly drenched Natchez the previous night, leaving the landing area, and the ascending mud-wallow of Silver Street, ankle-deep in red-gold ooze. January and Hannibal would have been hard-pressed to remain behind Weems's cab, and the dray with the trunks that followed it, as the horses leaned and slithered in the mud. Fortunately, Silver Street was the only road up the bluff, so they walked up with the air of innocent tourists, passing the vehicles with barely a glance. Above the level of the riverbank willows, the Mississippi unreeled northward, like a skein of silver yarn played with by a particularly mischievous kitten. It was cooler up here, too; the baking heat of the morning was mitigated by the winds breathing over the bluff.

The mosquitoes seemed to have been left behind in Natchez-Under as well.

"Fit penalty, a Protestant preacher would say, for those who linger in the dens of vice," remarked January as they emerged onto the long green space of the Spanish plaza that rimmed the bluff.

"Hard lines on the poor insects, though." Hannibal paused to lean against an oak that had probably been old when LaSalle and his explorers camped under it. "Unless they're fond of cocktails that consist of two parts clap and three parts whiskey. But I suppose that, being inventions of the Devil, the mosquitoes deserve it themselves." He was gasping from the climb, years of consumption having left him, January knew, with lesions and scar-tissue of every kind in his lungs. He fished in his pocket for his opium-bottle and took a drink. "Care to take bets on how many of those poor immigrant deck-passengers make it back on board? I went down last night and tried to warn them—the Germans listened, but the Irish seemed to regard me in the same light that our friend Molloy does, as an Orangeman and a fiend."

"How can they tell?" January kept an eye on the top of Silver Street, where a cluster of the immigrant women made their timid appearance, looking around for the town market at the far end of the plaza. "You sound Irish only when you're drunk."

"Good God, the average Paddy can smell an Orangeman even when he's addressing them—as I was—in purest poacher's Gaelic. It's an instinct. Like you being able to look at Jim Pemberton and say, *Oh, his grandmother was Senegalese,* or at Thucydides and say, *Oh, yes, mostly Fulani*. I can't imagine how you do that."

"And for me it's like telling an Italian from a Swede." January shrugged. "The dealers do that, too, you know. Gleet could probably tell you how much European blood each of his slaves has, and what tribe the African ancestors came from."

"Remind me never to ask him." Hannibal shivered. "There are men who strike one as throwbacks straight to Sodom and Gomorrah;

they make one understand God's use of fire and brimstone. There they go," he added, touching January's sleeve. Horses blowing and sweating, the cab and the dray emerged from the top of Silver Street and swung around the edge of the plaza toward Main Street. January and Hannibal loafed purposefully behind.

Unlike New Orleans, Natchez was a town where a wealthy man could live quite comfortably all year round. The Spanish had done so, as had the English Tories who had fled there rather than remain with the rebellious Atlantic seaboard colonies forty-five years before. Across the river, the rich black delta soil grew the finest cotton in the New World, with the cotton-lands in back of the bluffs on the Mississippi side almost as fertile. The houses here were big, lush, and surrounded by gardens and orchards; the hotels gracious, welcoming the merchants who came to partake of the wealth. The handsome white edifice into whose driveway the cab turned would not have been out of place in London, except for its wider yard and more opulent greenery. The dray entered a side-street, January and Hannibal crossing to follow.

"You think they saw us?" Hannibal glanced back at the mustard-colored figure helping the tall, brown-clothed lady down from the cab.

"They might have. But everyone from the boat, almost, is ashore. We're hardly the only ones."

"Yes, but we're probably the only ones who followed them to this hotel."

"Since I never set eyes on Weems in New Orleans before Monday morning—and since you have no connection with the Bank of Louisiana at all—there's no reason he should take any notice of us."

Through the yard gates January could see the draymen unloading the two trunks, handling them as if they were, indeed, heavy with gold. By the kitchen door—which was in the rear of the hotel building itself, American fashion, and not in separate quarters at the far end of the yard, a practice that always struck January as both unsanitary and dangerous—a laundress and a cook sat in the shade, smoking pipes and talking in a leisurely manner that made him want to send the manager out to thrash them both back to work.

"They look settled for the day," whispered Hannibal as he and January ducked back out of sight around the fence.

"Let's give them fifteen minutes," replied January—a remark he later heartily regretted. For fifteen minutes by January's silver French watch they listened to the account of the family argument that had surrounded the deathbed of the cook's grandmother, which rivaled any stage melodrama January had ever witnessed in violence, greed, and sheer bad taste. When at the end of that time the tale hadn't even reached Grandma's death ("*. . . so she said, What's more, you wasn't even* my *son, let alone* his; *I borrowed you from this friend of mine when you was a baby to get your grandpa to marry me . . .*") Hannibal fished through his pockets for his card-case, from which he extracted a neat slip of pasteboard:

Mr. Oliver Weems
Brinton House——New Orleans

Hannibal had a fine collection of other people's cards, and never wasted the opportunity to add to it.

"They're probably gone by this time," he said. He briefly jingled the pick-locks in his coat pocket, then led the way around to the front of the Imperial Hotel again, January falling respectfully into step behind. The cab that had brought Weems and Mrs. Fischer certainly no longer stood in the drive; January ventured to hope that they could simply cross through the lobby and into the yard, where the porters, seeing the card, would allow Hannibal to open the trunks on pretext of needing something inside.

And then, with luck, thought January, *we can find an officer of the law, present Granville's documents, and head back to New Orleans by the next boat. . . .*

Only one of his three wishes was granted.

"Are you Mr. Hannibal Sefton of New Orleans?"

Hannibal stopped in surprise at the question, asked by a youngish, squint-eyed man in a rough woolen coat who stepped from the hotel doors as he and January mounted the steps.

"I am." The information was readily checkable on the boat, though January later realized that at this point either Hannibal should have lied or the two of them should have immediately turned tail and dashed in opposite directions to divide pursuit. . . .

"And is this your man Ben?"

"Yes."

"Then I place you under arrest," said the newcomer, opening his lapel to reveal the badge of a deputy sheriff of Adams County. "For slave-stealing."

"This is absurd." Hannibal tugged his arm protestingly from Deputy Rees's grip as the deputy escorted him down Commerce Street toward the jail. "I demand to be confronted by my accuser!"

"You will be." The deputy's grip on his arm didn't slack, though the man didn't spare more than a glance back at January to see that he was following. A reasonable assumption of docility, January reflected bitterly, given a fugitive black man's chances if an alarm was raised, in the upper town at least. "That feller Granville said he'd be back here at two, to meet with Sheriff Gridley and give evidence."

Weems, January reflected dourly, seemed to have made as free about lifting Hubert Granville's cards as Hannibal had about helping himself to one of Weems's. The deputy thrust Hannibal through the gate of a dusty yard behind a brick building. In the middle of the yard a hard-jawed young man was chaining a slave to the six-foot timber in the center of the yard that served as a whipping-post. "Tom, lock up Sambo here," Rees ordered with a jerk of his head, and Tom fastened the final manacle to the chained slave's wrist and came to grab January's arm.

"This way, Chimney-Chops." Tom thrust January toward the

slave jail at the back of the yard, a brick building whose only windows were a frieze of gaps in the brickwork up under the eaves.

"And I demand to see the warrant issued for my arrest," added Hannibal as Rees pushed him toward the rear door of the police station. He didn't trade so much as a nod with January, but January knew his friend had the wits to realize that the deputy was not the person to be shown Granville's letter demanding cooperation—not until they knew beyond the shadow of a doubt what was in those trunks.

Even in that event, January would have been unwilling to risk it: no judge could have been found to issue a warrant in the fifteen minutes between Weems's arrival at the Imperial Hotel and Hannibal's arrest. Therefore, Deputy Rees had almost certainly been bribed.

Undoubtedly with Jubal Cain's four hundred blackmailed dollars—with enough left over for lunch.

"You'll see it when the sheriff gets here," said Rees as they vanished inside, confirming January's guess. January himself, he was well aware, was only an adjunct to the whole process—merely stolen property to be secured until those who were legally human determined guilt or innocence.

So he had to force himself silent as he was walked across the yard, past the man chained at the whipping-post, to the door of the slave-jail. Tom keyed open the padlock. Trapped heat, a cloud of flies, and the stench of a latrine-bucket rolled out like the breath of Hell.

The padlock clunked against the wood of the door as the bolt was secured again behind him.

A man got to his feet in the corner, held out his hand. "I'm Bobby," he said in the just-broken voice of a youth.

"Ben," January introduced himself.

Outside came the heavy crack of a whip, and a man's stifled sob of pain. Bobby flinched, too. In the fragments of daylight that seeped through the brick-holes up under the eaves, his face was downy with the first beard of adolescence. "They charges fifty cents a stroke," provided Bobby, trying to sound casual about it. "They whipped a woman this mornin' an' all the men over in the jail back of the courthouse crowded up to the window to watch. You a house-nigger?" He was looking with respectful shyness at January's clean linen and well-cut jacket.

"Manservant," replied January.

"You run away?"

January shook his head, and pressed his eye to the Judas in the door. "That damn deputy Rees arrested both me and my master, on a lie."

"Somebody paid him." Bobby flinched again at the next whip-crack, the next gasping scream. "That Rees'd arrest his own mama, somebody pay him. Least that's what Cuth said." The young man's eyes moved to indicate the man outside at the whipping-post. "He from town here, belong to Marse Simms the blacksmith. Marse Simms say he was stealin', but it's really Young Marse that's takin' iron an' nails an' that an' sellin' 'em, Cuth says. I coulda told him ain't no good to say so."

He shivered a little at the sound of a more desperate cry. "I runned away," he added softly.

Silence outside, then a man's truculent voice: "All right, then, Cuth. You gonna be a good darky now?"

Whatever Cuth said, it was too muffled to hear, but a moment later there was the clank of chain against wood, the crunch of boots on gravel. The soft thunk of the closing station-house door.

Flies, wasps, and bees roared in circles in the blue-brown shadows of the slave-jail's rafters. Far off in the silence January heard a cannon fire, announcing another steamboat coming into the landing.

A few hours, Rose had guessed. Long enough for Mr. Roberson and his family to have luncheon with some friend in Natchez-Over, for Colonel Davis to pay a social call, for half the crew to get robbed and stripped in Natchez-Under. . . .

Had Weems's promise to return at two been based on information La Pécheresse had gleaned from Ladies' Parlor gossip? Was two when the *Silver Moon* would be steaming away upstream, to leave Hannibal and January stranded in the Natchez jail until Sheriff Gridley finally let them out for lack of evidence?

I'll leave you reports at General Delivery, left till called for, in Vicksburg, Mayersville, and Greenville, and I'll wait for you at the best free colored boardinghouse in Memphis, Rose had said as calmly as if she'd been making arrangements to meet him at his mother's house after Mass. *I'm not sure I'll be able to pursue them beyond Memphis alone. . . .*

And if she wasn't in Memphis when he got there? Dear God, how would he ever find her, with the whole length of the river to search? With scoundrels like Gleet and Cain on the boat, eyeing every man and woman of color with cold calculation, resenting the freedom that took seven to fourteen hundred dollars out of his, Gleet's, pocket . . . ?

Despite the oven-like heat of the brick jail, January felt cold through to his marrow.

Blessed Virgin, he prayed, sliding his hand into his jacket pocket to touch the blue glass beads of his rosary, *take care of her. Watch over her.*

In his mind he pictured the serene face of the Mother of God as he'd seen it on the statues in the cathedrals here and in Paris . . . as he sometimes saw it in his dreams. That star-crowned woman in the sky-blue veil, smiling as she watched over the world.

Get me the hell out of here. . . .

The key rattled in the padlock. January and the boy Bobby turned, startled—January noting that whoever had crossed the graveled yard must have done so with conscious silence. A young man who looked like a slave janitor stood in the doorway with a pitcher of water: "I brung this for you," he informed them unnecessarily, and set it down. He closed the door, and January heard his bare feet on the gravel this time, but very soft, and very swift, before silence closed in again.

January bent to pick up the pitcher, then stopped. "I don't think that man bolted the door."

"You shittin' me," said Bobby.

January pushed the door.

It opened.

The trunks will still be at the hotel.

I can at least warn Rose.

This is a trap, isn't it?

January caught Bobby's arm as the young man started to rush past him into the sunlit yard. People did do stupid things, of course. Careless oversights that would get them a whipping from Deputy Rees and Tom.

But his every nerve and muscle prickled with watchfulness as he and Bobby slipped through the door, hastened across the yard and out the narrow gate to Commerce Street. . . .

"This way, boys!" A tall man in a shabby black coat was waiting for them at the corner of the alley. Rusty braids hung Indian-fashion down to his shoulders, and a faded black patch covered one eye; the other was blue and sharp under a curling fringe of brow. As he caught each of them by the sleeve, to draw them through a side-door into the shed behind an apothecary shop, January saw he wore a clerical collar.

"Thank God you had the sense to run," whispered the preacher. "There's men so cowed by fear they won't even take the blessing of freedom when the prison door swings wide!"

"Who are you?" asked Bobby in the same tone the Patriarch Abraham must have addressed the angels who came calling at his tent.

"Reverend Levi Christmas." The man shook Bobby's hand, then January's. "Of the Underground Railway."

Even in New Orleans, January had heard of what was beginning to be called the Underground Railway. In the copies of the *Liberator* that Mr. Quince had slid beneath the stateroom door he had read a good deal more. It was a loose organization of Abolitionists, Quakers, and some free blacks who worked together to smuggle runaway slaves to freedom in Canada. They passed the fugitives from one household to another, hiding them in barns and false attics and under the raised bottoms of specially-made boats and wagon-boxes, guiding them by night, sometimes hiding them for weeks at a time until chance offered an opportunity for them to slip across the river to Ohio.

Senators like John Calhoun of South Carolina stormed about the responsibility of the United States Government to protect slaveholders' property, and Democratic newspapers denounced the organizers of the Railway as fomenters of slave insurrection and heirs to Nat Turner's bloody schemes. But no politician really dared to go near, or think about—or talk about—the whispers that were rising everywhere in the nation.

"Here." From a sack in the shed's corner Christmas pulled a couple of slouch hats and two ragged jackets. "Put these on, and follow me. We can keep you hid down Under-The-Hill till the time comes to pass you along."

Bobby snatched the garments eagerly, but January drew a deep breath and stepped back. "You're going to think me insane, sir," he said. "And poor-spirited, too. But I cannot forsake my master, who was arrested with me on a false charge. He's not a well man," he added, seeing Bobby's stunned astonishment at this repudiation of every field-hand's dream. "He needs me."

An easier explanation, he reflected, than the truth.

The Reverend's single blue eye widened in surprise, then narrowed again. "You think your loyalty is going to remain in his mind the next time he needs a thousand dollars and has nothing to sell but you?" he asked. "You think his family are going to remember your loyalty when he dies, and leaves you to a nephew or a cousin, like an outworn hat? God will look after your master, as He looks after us all, son."

"You crazy, man!" added Bobby. "You can't trust them from one minute to the next!"

January shook his head. "I'm sorry," he said. "I can't abandon him."

The Reverend raised his eyebrows, making the eye-patch bob. "Son, having escaped from the jail, I don't think you understand what will wait for you in this town as a fugitive slave. They don't take kindly to runaways hereabouts."

"They whip the tar outa you, do they catch you again!"

"I'll be careful." January took up the empty sack from the floor to hold his jacket and top-hat. *It's not even noon yet,* he thought, glancing at the angle of the hot yellow splinters of light that fell through the shed's cracks. *The* Silver Moon *can't be leaving this soon. . . .*

Christmas sighed. "You're a braver man than I, son." He held out his hand, callused and hard in January's answering grip, a working-man's hand. No milk-fed seminarian, this one, January thought: here was one of the few people January had encountered who looked like he could actually take on Jubal Cain and maybe win. "But loyalty is one of God's hall-marks, and I'm not going to argue with it, even if I think it's misguided. My only request is that you mention this to no one, not even your master . . . *no one.* It's astonishing how information spreads along the river, and you know that we of the Underground Railway operate at the risk of our lives."

This was true, January knew. The slave uprisings of Nat Turner and Denmark Vesey were still fresh in the minds of those who saw black faces outnumber white wherever they turned. There were many in the slave states—and in the North as well—who regarded both the Underground Railway and the Abolitionist movement as encouragement and assistance to another slave uprising. Already there had been instances of retaliatory violence and murder.

"I'll be silent, sir." January pressed that callused hand again. "You go with God."

"And you, sir."

"You, too, Bobby."

And the young man flashed him a shy grin. "He must be one good master. But I still think you crazy."

"You change your mind, son," added Christmas, "you come down to the Stump. It's a tavern at the end of Silver Street, under the hill. They know me there—and they know how to keep their mouths shut."

January glanced through the shed door to make sure the coast was clear, then stepped out into the hot, hushed morning sunlight. As he crossed the street to make his casual and hopefully inconspicuous way back to the Imperial Hotel, he glanced back. He saw Christmas and Bobby step out and stroll away toward the road that led back down under the hill. Bobby followed behind, like a respectful servant should—the way January was careful to follow behind Hannibal. He prayed the boy would get to safety.

Nobody molested him on his way back to the hotel. Even in the shabby jacket he'd gotten from Christmas he was sufficiently respectable-looking not to cause comment, and there were plenty of other black men, slaves or free, on the streets. At least, he reflected, Weems and Fischer would be well and truly gone from the hotel by this time. He tried not to hurry his steps, but he wondered what he would do if the trunks had been taken inside already. Try to talk his way in as Mr. Weems's manservant? An employee of the steamboat company would be a better ruse. An irregularity, a mix-up of trunk lables, *We have to make sure this isn't Mrs. Johnson's that was taken off by mistake. . . .* Would they believe that? *I just need a quick look inside; Mrs. Johnson's given us a list of the things that should be there. . . .*

Then at least he could get word back to Rose about how things stood, and see how much time he had before the boat left. Surely they wouldn't leave with such respectable gentlemen as Roberson and Davis ashore having a visit with friends and family.

January turned down the side-street to the Imperial's rear yard just as a dray emerged from the gate, driven by a couple of sulky bearded men in slouched hats. As January passed it, wondering if he could manage to pick the locks on the trunk if he did find them still in the yard and unobserved, he saw, under the canvas covering thrown over the dray's load, the glint of brass trunk-corners and the dull greenish leather that was instantly recognizable.

Heading back for the boat, he thought sourly. *So the whole thing was a ruse after all, designed to smoke out pursuers. Designed, in fact, to stop us here, to lure us ashore where we could be dealt with. . . .*

But in that case, why pay to have bogus chests taken back on board?

Or are they going elsewhere? To some house or receiving-office in Natchez? Did Weems and Fischer actually intend to stay for a time, until they recognized Hannibal?

January trailed the cart down Silver Street, and into the criss-crossed mangle of alleyways that spread along the feet of the bluff. Due to the lowness of the river the streets were fairly firm, but in high water at least a quarter of the buildings, to judge by the height of the stilts on which they stood, must flood. Crazy lines of duckboards zig-zagged among the sheds and shacks, and rude stairways ascended walls or rises of the ground. Mosquitoes hummed everywhere under the shadows of the houses, where weeds grew rank in standing puddles.

The dray was definitely not going back to the boat.

January recalled Mrs. Fischer's sharply intelligent dark glance, and the cool command in her voice. *You're not touching a dime. . . .*

He could easily imagine her as at home in Natchez-Under as she was in the Ladies' Parlor, sympathizing with Mrs. Tredgold about the proper methods of disciplining children.

He hung back as far as he could behind the dray, and thanked God that the blistering heat seemed to be keeping most of the troublemakers indoors. A couple of the black whores, and one who might have been Cuban or Mexican, called out to him from their windows, but he only smiled and waved and shook his head, and tried to look as unobtrusive as possible. Toward the end of Silver Street the ground grew sodden: here the river had cut in behind the last of the buildings and the ground sloped down to a sticky morass of dessicated gray weeds and puddles teeming with crawfish and gnats. On the edge of this slough, the buildings all stood on stilts, and the farthest out—whose rickety gallery was occupied by half a dozen drinkers spitting tobacco down into the water—was reached by a crazy plank gangway that stretched from its door to terra firma. Beneath it the shore currents surged sluggishly around the pilings that held it up, and little drifts of leaves, tree-branches, and what looked like the dead body of a British sailor snagged up against them, to provide footing for legions of rats.

Before this crooked gangway the dray drew rein, and January saw next to the gangway a roughly painted sign announcing the building to be the Stump.

And the man waiting for the dray at the bottom of the gangway, with an ax and pry-bar in hand, was none other than the Reverend Levi Christmas.

EIGHT

It took the Reverend two whacks of the ax to open the trunk. He and the drivers didn't even bother to carry it indoors.

"Piss on it," said the Reverend, and drove his ax-blade into the ground so he could momentarily remove the cigar from his mouth. "Fuckin' bricks."

"Fuck me." The driver scratched his head—not in puzzlement, but with the air of a man who has good reason to do so.

From where he watched, crouched behind a tangle of weed and hackberry under the stilts of a near-by shack and up to his insteps in rank-smelling seepage—January could see that the trunk did indeed contain bricks.

A flash of pink on the gangway behind him made the Reverend whirl, and like a panther he bounded to intercept the dainty form that tried to scurry past him. He caught her by the wrist and dragged her to the dray with such violence that her stylish hat tumbled from her head, but January had already recognized the frock, with its ruffles of blond lace and its bunches of silk roses on the sleeves.

"You been diddled, you little spunk-bait! You and that toss-pot Irish boat-driver of yours!"

"Piss on you!" retorted Miss Skippen, trying to pull her wrist from the Reverend's iron grasp. "Molloy said they'd stole money and was takin' it north! He said he knew the man from seein' him at the bank! This has got to be a trick!"

"Of course it's a trick, you brainless slut! Didn't you think of that when you come here all full of how there's two trunks of money comin' ashore? My God, of all the stupid cunnies I've had to do with, you're the stupidest! But if you think this pays me off for what you owe me . . ."

January backed slowly up the alley, keeping to the cover of the snagged-up deadfalls and the rough stands of brush. At higher water one would have needed a boat to get to the back of the Stump, but now only ten or twelve yards of knee-deep brown river separated it from the muddy shore. A broken-down gallery sagged at its rear, to which a ladder led up, its feet propped in the shallows. The single window was boarded up.

It would be best, thought January, to simply return to the *Silver Moon* at once, tell Mr. Tredgold that his "master" had been falsely accused and was in the town jail, and to have the boat held until the matter was regulated. He was almost certain that Weems had no intention of pressing the charge—the object of the game was clearly to delay whoever pursued Weems ashore, not to bring up a lot of questions about why Weems would have made the charge.

That would be best. The longer he, January, lingered in the filthy and anonymous precincts of Natchez-Under, the greater his chances became of being spotted and recognized by Christmas. Or of being randomly attacked for the contents of the flour-sack he still carried, with hat and jacket.

Instead of doing what would be best, however, he glanced up and down the alleyway, satisfied himself that nearly the entire population of the Stump had assembled on the front gangplank to observe the screaming-match developing between Miss Skippen and the Reverend Christmas—and waded swiftly across to the ladder and climbed.

The door at the top was locked, but the framing was so rotted, it yielded at once to a sharp blow of his shoulder. Someone in the room beyond scrambled aside in panic. January called out hoarsely, "Bobby? It's Ben."

"Ben!" The runaway hurried to the door as January pushed it open. "You gonna come after all?" His young face shone with hope, and with delight for his new friend's change of heart.

The tiny back room contained little. A blanket, a bowl that smelled of rice and beans, a couple of bottles: whiskey and beer. The liquor colored Bobby's breath as he spoke.

"Ben, the Reverend Christmas got the beatenist scheme for gettin' me money for when I get to Canada!" Bobby caught January's hand like an eager child. "They gonna take me over the other side of the river to Feliciana Parish, where nobody know me, an' *pretend* to sell me! Then they helps me escape, an' we go a little farther an' they sell me *again*! We do that two-three times, then we splits the money fifty-fifty, an' they sends me on north!"

January walked—or rather climbed, because the angle of the floor was almost twenty degrees—over to the inner door that led to the rest of the saloon, and tried it. It was, as he'd suspected, locked.

He looked back at Bobby, infinitely weary, infinitely angry at men who'd ply a boy like this—for he was scarcely more than a boy—with liquor and lies. There were times when January truly hated white men. "You do that two-three times, then they cuts your throat, an' slits your guts so you won't blow up an' float to the surface, an' dumps you in the river. They thieves, Bobby. Thieves an' whoremasters. They out there right now, fightin' over two trunks they stole from the Imperial Hotel."

Tears flooded the young man's eyes: tears of half-drunken grief, of fractured hope. "What you tell a lie like that for, Ben?" Bobby whispered. "They gonna get me out of here. Get me to freedom."

A country boy, thought January. A village boy. Born on one plantation and sold to another, or to two or three—he'd probably seen no more than five hundred people, all-told, in his entire life, before coming to Natchez, and four hundred and fifty of those had been country-born slaves like himself.

Clinging to his dream of freedom.

"Don't believe them, Bobby," he said softly. "You run now. You follow the river north. You travel at night, and you stay away from people. If you got to leave the river, you follow the stars—you know the stars that make up the Drinkin' Gourd?" He sketched the Dipper on the dirty wall with his finger. "These two stars, they point to the North Star. You follow the Drinkin' Gourd, you'll be headin' north." He reached in his pocket—wincing, since he was almost certain he was simply handing the sum, through Bobby's agency, to the first scoundrel who happened along—and brought out thirty dollars of Hubert Granville's money.

He pressed the heavy coins into the boy's hand, closed the work-callused young fingers around it. "You got about two minutes to make up your mind," he said, "before they come back inside." With a corner of his sleeve he scuffed away the dusty ghost of the star-map from the wall. "Whatever you decide to do, you don't tell a soul it was me who warned you, or they come after me, too. All right?"

Bobby's lips formed the words *all right* without sound. Tears rolled down his cheeks—of disappointment, and of terror.

January descended the ladder, waded through the stinking tug of the Mississippi current, and back to shore.

Only the faintest wisps of smoke rose from the *Silver Moon*'s stacks when he crossed the muddy landing to the boat. The big stern wheel was still, its upper surfaces dry under the grilling noon sun. Tremendous activity surged around the engine-room door on the bow-deck, and January could hear Molloy cursing.

"I refuse to allow you to let that man speak so in your presence!" Mrs. Tredgold's strident voice soared over the hubbub. "Let alone in mine! If there is damage to one of the boilers, I refuse to continue on this boat. . . ."

"Darling, I swear to you . . ."

Coming up the landing-stage, January could see Mr. Tredgold

sweating and wringing his hands as he pleaded with his wife in the engine-room doorway.

"Every inch of the engine was checked before the voyage began! You know I would never let my family journey on an unsafe boat! Now, whoever it was who told you that one of the boilers was faulty could not possibly have known such a thing—"

"She said in her note that she was 'walking out' with one of the engineers. But her handwriting is that of a lady." Mrs. Tredgold thrust a piece of notepaper under her spouse's nose. Though not nearly close enough to study it, January felt almost certain that he would have recognized the hand.

"What happened?" he asked Mr. Lundy, who was leaning against one of the pilasters of the promenade arcade near-by.

The former pilot's lips tightened under his white-streaked mustache. "Some woman put a note under Mrs. Tredgold's door, claiming an assistant engineer had told her one of the boilers was faulty, and like to blow."

All around them the anxious chatter of the deck-passengers covered their words. The Irish and Germans were trying vainly to grasp the nature of the danger, holding their children close and glancing at Tredgold as if debating whether or not to ask for their money back and take another boat, the Kaintucks speculating about how one could tell if the boilers were about to blow and trading tales of similar catastrophes: "I was comin' downstream on a raft and we was but thirty feet from the *Queen of Sheba* when she blew, this huge spurt of fire come flamin' out frontwise from her bow, then like the whole top of the boat ripped off with boards go sailin' up a hunnert feet in the air in shoots of flame. . . .

"Now it's true the boilers on this boat are American-made, which are likelier to split than the English, owin' to poorer-quality iron," Lundy told January. "But if a boiler's faulty, nine times out of ten you can't tell by lookin' at it, unless it's a seam starting to give. Mostly you can't tell even by the sound of the steam, or by the shake of the engine, or the feel of the boat when she makes speed. But Mrs. Tredgold won't hear of goin' on until they been checked." He nodded at the stout garnet-red form that nearly filled the engine-room door. "And she's standin' there until they're all checked in front of her eyes. I reckon if a woman's got her children on board I can understand her fears, and the wife of an owner will have heard more than her share about boiler explosions."

Tredgold turned from the tugging questions of a German woman to his wife's resolute profile—Mrs. Tredgold averted her face from him and called out in a voice like a parrot's "Cissy! *Cissy,* you keep those children where I can see them! Don't you let them go ashore!"

"We won't be goin' nowhere till nearly supper-time, given how long it'll take 'em to get up steam again," added Lundy in his soft, humming voice. "Mr. Roberson and his family already went back to their visit with Colonel Quitman, and Colonel Davis has gone on to more visits, and God help Tredgold now when he tries to get his deck-hands out of the saloons . . . they'll be mostly too drunk to walk. Of course Gleet's taken his whole coffle up to the Imperial Hotel to try to drum up buyers. . . ."

Lundy glanced behind him at the men still chained to the starboard promenade, and Jubal Cain walking slowly along the rail before them, scanning the landing with his chilly amber gaze. "If it wasn't a woman's hand on the note, I'd suspect Gleet planned the whole thing, to give him time to peddle his wares in town."

"As it turns out, it's just as well, sir," said January diffidently. "My master's in trouble in town. Some gentleman"—It would be worse than useless, he knew, to set a hue and cry against Weems until he had evidence—"gave the sheriff the idea my master was a slave-stealer, and they put us both in jail. . . ."

Lundy's eyes narrowed sharply, and January went on. "A gentleman named Mr. Christmas got me out, and claimed he was with the Underground Railway. A churchman, he was. . . ."

"Churchman, my arse," said the former pilot. "And you had the brains not to go with him? Let me shake your hand, my friend. Levi Christmas is one of the worst scoundrels on the river. For years he'd hold camp revival meetings, and preach so well, not a soul in the tent noticed when his friends went out and stole every horse outside. Lately—since there's been talk of the Underground Railway—he's gone into slave-stealing, promising the poor souls he's going to raise money for them by the old sale-and-escape game, then killing them to keep their mouths shut after he's collected four or five thousand dollars with their help. I'm surprised he let you get away."

January was a bit surprised, too—and a bit disappointed. He'd have enjoyed beating the tar out of Levi Christmas. It was as he'd guessed, but the confirmation raised a wave of burning rage in him.

"I didn't know that, sir," he said when he realized how long he'd been silent, and what his expression must look like. He wished he had dragged poor young Bobby out of the Stump instead of simply giving him a choice that the boy was clearly unfit to make. He took a deep breath, trying to keep his voice from cracking. "I told him I couldn't forsake my master. He must have figured he'd need me to consent to play his game, because he pressed me, but didn't try to use force. But my master's still in jail. . . ."

"I'll take care of that." Lundy straightened up and groped for his cane. "You stay on board here, Ben. No sense taking chances on things getting any more complicated than they are. It's that weasel Rees, I bet . . . he makes a fair-enough living off bribes, he'll end up as sheriff himself one day, and God help the town then. You don't happen to know," he added with a sharp sidelong look up at January, "who accused your master of slave-stealing, or why?"

And though Lundy tried to cover it with a casual tone, January thought there was a note of deeper and more intent concern in his voice than the query seemed to warrant.

"No, sir, I don't. I thank you for taking care of it—you're sure I can't go and help you in some way?"

"Just get me a cab if you'd be so kind."

January was, in fact, glad to return to the safety of the *Silver Moon* after a brief excursion down to the landing to signal one of the hacks waiting in the shade of a warehouse. He had no desire to run into the

Reverend Christmas on shore. Even if Bobby had kept his mouth shut about January's warning, he had a feeling that Christmas would be merciless at silencing critics. He made his way down the starboard promenade, past the chained line of Cain's slaves: they were talking quietly, gathered as well as they could around 'Rodus. He felt their silence as he walked past.

At the stern end he found Rose. She was talking with Julie, so he couldn't very well catch her up in his arms and kiss her, as he wished to do, or say, *You, my nightingale, are a genius. . . .*

"Mrs. Fischer returned about half an hour ago with Mr. Weems," Rose said, turning to meet his smile. "So I suppose poor Sophie's going to be occupied for the rest of the evening. Mrs. Fischer seemed to be in a frightful mood when she called to Sophie, probably because she realized the boat wasn't going to be able to proceed until nearly dark."

"I never figured why white folks always got their hair on fire to get somewhere quick," sighed Julie, squinting in the sharp, hot sunlight as Molloy stormed out of the engine-room's rear door and up the stairs to the boiler-deck. "What's it matter if we stays here another few hours? What's so all-fired important in Vicksburg, or Memphis, that it can't wait? The boiler really gonna blow up if they runs the boat too fast?"

She looked scared, and trying to conceal it. She wasn't even, January guessed, as old as Bobby, and the recollection of Bobby stabbed him with guilt again, that he'd left the boy his own choice about escape.

Even if making your own choice was what freedom was about.

"Most accidents on steamboats are because the pilot gets careless," Rose soothed. "I think whatever else can be said of him, Mr. Molloy is a good pilot, and not likely to take foolish risks."

"Then how come they think they got to check all the boilers?" asked Julie. "They wouldn't be check 'em if there wasn't somethin' wrong."

"I can't imagine," said Rose with a sidelong glance at January. Eli, the cook, on his way back into the galley, overheard and paused long enough to shoot back.

"Hey, Julie, these is *white folks* we're talkin' about."

And all three of them laughed.

"Shit," sighed Julie. "Here she is." Across the open mud-flat of the landing, Theodora Skippen appeared out of the mouth of a scummy alley. "God, I hope she ain't drunk again." As Miss Skippen hurried toward the *Silver Moon,* her white bonnet-plumes nodding with her step, one of the stevedores said something to her that elicited an obscene gesture, quickly released as she realized there might be respectable ladies on the upper-deck promenades who might see her. She was not, January reflected, particularly bright—or else she'd had enough liquor at the Stump to blunt her animal cunning for survival.

Julie rubbed her ear, which, dark as she was, showed fresh bruising as well as the earlier nail-gash cuts, and went up the rear stair to be in Miss Skippen's stateroom when Miss Skippen returned there. Across the confusion of the wharf, January could see the Reverend Christmas leaning in the mouth of the same alleyway, watching the *Silver Moon.*

An hour later Mr. Lundy returned, with Hannibal in tow.

"*Quid non mortalia pectora cogis, auri sacra fames,*" sighed Hannibal as he slumped onto the nearest wood-pile next to the galley passway and took a sip of opium. "And now, of course, our precious friends know who we are. At least they know about you and me, Ben. Owl-eyed Athene still wears the hood of invisibility. . . ."

"Which I won't much longer," retorted Rose, "if I persist in being seen in your company."

"What, will you join the regiment of women who tell me my friendship does their reputations no good?"

"You don't think La Pécheresse will believe that you were overcome by my charms when we met on the boat?" January drew himself up in mock indignation. "I am cut to the very heart. I wish now I'd stayed a little longer hiding near the Stump, to know whether Miss Skippen escaped from the Reverend Christmas or whether he sent her back here as his spy."

"You'd only have gotten yourself killed." Hannibal followed his eyes to where the young lady in question was briefly visible, crossing the landing-stage before being swallowed up in the crowd still milling before the engine-room's bow door. "Christmas doesn't sound like a man whose suspicions take much arousing. I wonder if asking her to my cabin for a few sips of Black Drop would induce in Miss Skippen a confiding mood?"

"It would be likelier to induce a duel with Molloy," replied January grimly. "He regards the girl as his property. . . ."

"Well, everything she owns apparently is," remarked Rose uncharitably.

"And *I* have no desire to spend the next three months in a slave-jail awaiting the arrival of your putative next of kin. Or to see you killed." January spoke roughly, his anger at the Reverend Christmas, and Ned Gleet, and Miss Skippen breaking through his voice like the black limbs of trees breaking through the river's surface; Hannibal's eyes met his, for a moment reading the affection that underlay the rage.

It was the affection that Hannibal answered a moment later: "Well, I have no desire to see me killed either," he said, and rose to head for the steps back to the white purlieux of the boat. "And the thing that troubles me now is that, having seen who we are, and failed to have us detained in Natchez: what is La Pécheresse's next attempt going to consist of?"

January's mood was not improved when, later in the day, he saw Ned Gleet return with two slaves gone from his coffle, and two more added, a boy of fifteen or so and a girl so young that January suspected there'd been chicanery about her birth-date. Or maybe the law in Mississippi had never heard of the Louisiana provision that a child not be sold from her parents under the age of ten.

Of course, the law only said "where possible."

Gleet looked so pleased with himself as he chained them to the wall, rubbing his hands and chuckling, that January had to remind himself who he was and where he was, lest he stride down the promenade and drive the man's teeth through the back of his head with his fist. Even Jubal Cain, walking past, remarked sourly, "You like 'em a little short, don't you, Gleet?"

"You say what you please," chortled the other dealer, wagging his finger. "I'll get five hundred apiece for 'em in Memphis. . . . What's your name, boy?"

"Ephriam," whispered the boy.

"It's Joe now," retorted Gleet. "Damn silly name, Ephriam—you ought to re-name the lot of yours, Cain. That Fulani boy—Herodotus, what kind of name's that for a field-hand?"

"Not my damn business what a nigger's name is," returned Cain. " 'Rodus does just fine. Sometimes you make me damn sick, Gleet."

He stalked away, stopping at the end of the promenade and standing aside to let Miss Skippen pass in a flurry of pink muslin and blond lace. She hurried up to Gleet; they stood together talking for some time.

The *Silver Moon* achieved full steam and was poled off the Natchez landing just before sundown, steaming north again into the hot evening light. About an hour later, a rumor went around the galley passway that Miss Skippen had sold her slave Julie to Ned Gleet.

NINE

"He gonna sell me for a field-hand." Julie pressed her trembling hands over her lips, as if by doing so she could still the fear and grief cracking in her voice. Spray splashed from the paddle, flecking the deck-hands with wet as they moved about stowing ropes and push-poles, the women as they gathered around their friend among the wood-piles. Behind them, Natchez glowed on its high bluff in the evening light, before the gray-green wall of Marengo Bend hid it from view.

"He gonna sell me for a field-hand, an' whoever buys me'll put me with whoever they got needs a wife, to make babies whether I wants 'em or not, or whether I likes him or not." A sob shook her, and she hugged her arms around her big, firm breasts, but January saw rage as well as fear in her dark eyes.

Rose put an arm around the girl's shoulders but said nothing. January, sitting beside the four women on a crate of dishes labeled THE MYRTLES—VICKSBURG, understood that there was no room for comforting disagreement: Julie was a big girl, African-featured and dark, and without the refined speech and manners of a house servant. Gleet's jeering voice returned to him: *What the hell you need a big buck like that for a valet for, anyway? He's got field-hand written all over him.*

Remembered, too, more softly: *She's a beauty, ain't she?*

From here on up the river was cotton country. The plantations starting up on newly-ceded Indian lands needed field-hands far more than they needed half-trained ladies-maids.

"My granny that's a free woman was savin' to buy me free," Julie continued in a whisper. "But Michie Binoche, he needed money right then, 'cause of his girl gettin' sick. He wouldn't a' sold me, he said, 'cept that I'd be a ladies'-maid, an' he made Mamzelle Theodora swear she wouldn't sell me off, the dirty bitch."

"Do you know for sure she's done it?" asked Sophie, grasping at straws. Trying to push aside her own fears of what would become of her on the voyage—as well she should, January reflected. Had Mrs. Fischer put her foot down about selling off her maid rather than letting Weems lead his watchers to the trunks in the hold? "Surely she wouldn't rob herself of a maid while she's traveling?"

"She say, 'Don't be stupid,' when I ask her." Julie wiped under her nose with the back of her wrist. "An' she slap me when I ask her again. But when she leave the room I look in her bag, an' she got four hundred dollars there she didn't have before."

"I don't suppose she could have made that in Natchez," mused Rose. "Not all in one afternoon, anyway."

And the women laughed—even Sophie, who looked shocked, too—the wry, bitter laughter of those who lace corsets and wash dirty underwear and tidy away stained sheets. Then they tightened their arms around Julie again, and held the girl close among them as the hard-held tears began to flow. "What'm I gonna do?" whispered the girl, her face pressed to Rose's shoulder. "What'm I gonna *do*?"

Preparing to climb the steps to assist his "master" in getting ready for supper, January paused, his eyes drawn down the passway to the locked door of the hold. The thought rose in his mind: *Queen Régine might help.*

Help how? Poison Gleet? That would result only in Julie and the other seven men and women of Gleet's coffle spending several months in a slave-jail in Vicksburg, waiting for letters to make their patient way up and down the river in quest of his next-of-kin.

Help Julie escape? Even this close to shore, among the snags and eddies of low water, the current was strong. Julie could stay afloat on a couple of pieces of furnace-wood, but once ashore, she'd have county patrols to contend with, and almost certainly the Reverend Levi Christmas, dogging the boat like a carrion wolf.

Along the starboard promenade, the men were singing, their voices rolling out across the water:

Ai, tingwaiye, ai tingwaiye. . . .

And from the women's side of the boat, two or three voices at first, then on the next round more, replied, *"Ah waiya, ah waiya."*

African words, learned by rote from mothers who'd sung them long ago. Even those who hadn't known them before took them up, drawing comfort from the sound, from the memory of the quarters of their childhood, and the villages on the other side of the ocean, beneath the hot African moon.

Day-zah, day-zah, day koo-noo wi wi,
Day-zah, day-zah, day koo-noo wi wi. . . .

Could Queen Régine hear them, he wondered, down in the terrible dark of the hold? Was she able—he couldn't imagine how—to come out on deck, to move about silent in the night, seeking him like a vengeful ghost? *I curse you to the ruin of all you touch, and the destruction of all you hope.*

All he hoped stood a pace from ruin now, that was for certain.

January shivered, and fished in his pocket for the comforting touch of his rosary. He'd lived in Paris, and read the works of Locke and Hume, Kant and Hegel, and had listened to the talk of students in the cafés. He would no more have admitted to belief in a half-crazed old freedwoman's curse than he'd have worshipped God by cutting a lamb's throat and splashing blood on the altar. As a child he'd been told, by old Père Antoine, that the strength of God was stronger than any curse of African devils.

But he still felt safer on the upper deck, where he knew Queen Régine could not come.

After supper January again borrowed Eli's guitar, and played duets with Hannibal for dancing and gaiety in the Main Saloon. There was, he reflected, singularly little glee that night. Led by Mrs. Fischer, the women definitely and completely ostracized Theodora Skippen, who retreated a number of times out onto the promenade to comfort herself, and returned with head held high and a distinct whiff of brandy on her breath. Mr. Weems, still apparently under orders not to advertise his association with Mrs. Fischer, remained in a corner, playing cribbage with Quince and listening to the handsome young man's interminable encomia of Vegetarianism and the Thompsonian system of health through the consumption of honey and onions. Mrs. Fischer for her part kept a wary eye on January and Hannibal, and by the way Mrs. Tredgold avoided the fiddler and Mrs. Roberson drew her daughter away from him, January guessed Mrs. Fischer had been spreading a little gossip about him in the Ladies' Parlor by way of guaranteeing an upper hand.

Still, this left four ladies who consented to dance in a set with one another—Mrs. Roberson, Mrs. Tredgold, Mrs. Fischer, and sixteen-year-old Dorothea Roberson—so the gentlemen took it in turns to dance with them, though the gluttonous Dodd was beginning to demonstrate a disposition to disappear out onto the promenade every time Miss Skippen did. January only hoped the elderly Bostonian's wealth would distract the girl from her smoky glances at Hannibal, but by the way she returned from such encounters with red cheeks and angry eyes, he didn't hold out much hope.

Mr. Souter, not yet on duty, buttonholed Colonel Davis in a corner with a lengthy account of the pilot on the *Louisville Belle,* who used to navigate the bend above Poverty Point in pitch darkness by ringing the bell and listening for the barking of Rush Thompson's dog—that was Rush Thompson whose brother had run a wood-yard at Kentucky Bend, and had married a woman named Clanton who'd had an affair with Aaron Burr supposedly—the dog's name was Henry Clay. Henry Clay would always bark at the sound of a steamboat bell, and the day after Henry Clay died of being gored by Enoch Andrews's bull, Melchizadek, who had one bent horn and had been calved by this Spanish feller, Dorado's, cow Elizabeth, that was stole from him by river pirates and later he got her back—the day after Henry Clay died the pilot ran the *Louisville Belle* aground in the fog because he didn't hear the dog bark on the bank. They did manage to save the *Belle*'s engines, though, and put them on a new boat, the *Louisville Pride,* whose pilot was . . .

Mr. Byrne engaged the two black-clothed Jews who'd come on at Natchez in a game of vingt-et-un. Mr. Cain simply settled back to listen to the music, his yellow eyes half shut like a sleepy cat's and his face transformed by an expression of profound and peaceful joy.

Hannibal's fiddle floated light over the notes of the Marlborough Cotillion, the silk of skirts swishing over the straw matting on the floors.

"Tell you what I'll do, Cain," drawled Gleet's whining voice. "I'll give you seven hundred for that boy of yours, *He-ro-do-tus,* plus those two young 'uns I picked up in Natchez, Joe an' Jane." The slave-dealer spat, not even bothering to aim for the cuspidor. "Now, you can't say you been offered a fairer deal than that. I got a customer in Memphis, a steady customer, always lookin' for smart boys like that 'Rodus, an' you can't tell me he ain't trouble to you."

What Cain's reaction was to this, January didn't know, because movement in the doorway drew his eye; Thu pausing there to look back at the two slave-dealers, his thin face impassive but his eyes wary and listening. In the dim light of the overhead lanterns his face looked suddenly very African, despite its fair complexion, the narrow Fulani bone-structure thrown into sharp relief.

And January understood, as if he'd known it all along: *Herodotus and Thucydides are brothers.*

Then the steward stepped through the door and was gone.

Through the following day, as the *Silver Moon* thrashed through the endless tangle of loops, false bends, chutes, snags, and bayous that surrounded the mouth of the Arkansas River, January watched the men of Cain's coffle, and was almost certain he was right. It wasn't merely the tribal similarity of bone-structure and features. Both young men had the same gestures, the same ways of walking, the same expressions. The way Thu folded his arms and nodded when Mrs. Roberson gave long and elaborate instructions about bringing the Parlor tea-things was mirrored in the angle of 'Rodus's head when two of the boys in Gleet's coffle asked him about whether they'd be unchained if the boat snagged and sank.

Does Cain realize? January wondered, watching in fascination from behind the piled cordwood as the *Silver Moon* lay behind yet another bar while the leadsman took soundings in the skiff. Thu was passing along the starboard promenade, and stopped to trade a word with the men of Cain's coffle—*How can he not see?*

But whites, January had found, frequently had trouble distinguishing the features of blacks.

And the man might have no knowledge of ancient Greek historians. It was common, January knew, for masters to name slave children the way they named dogs, for characters in literature or the Bible, or for sets of things: Faith, Hope, and Charity for girls, Marquis and Baron and Duke for boys. There were two boys in Gleet's coffle, brothers fifteen and sixteen years old, named, of all things, Jeremiah and Lamentations, testifying to some white man who knew the names of the books of the Bible but hadn't the slightest idea what they meant.

Would it matter, he wondered, if Cain knew?

"Quarter twain!" called out the leadsman, and Molloy's voice could be heard roaring curses from the pilot-house. "Quarter less twain!" The brown water barely stirred among the black army of snags that lay between the boat and the shore, the drips from the paddle like diamonds in the burning sunlight. *"Quarter less twain!"*

Jubal Cain came walking down the promenade, glancing sharply around him; Thucydides turned at once and left, passing the white man with neither a glance nor a word.

They tied up at the Vicksburg landing at midnight; Weems and Mrs. Fischer disembarked at once. From the shadows of the boiler-deck promenade, January took note of their luggage as they had it loaded onto a dray: three trunks this time, and two heavy portmanteaux. Sophie stood back, laden down with valises. "Looks like business," murmured Hannibal, standing beside January in the darkness, and Rose replied softly, "It's supposed to."

Across the muddy flat of the landing, a gaping space now studded with boxes, bales, and deadfall debris washed up with the river's summer retreat, lanterns burned even at this late hour in the gaggle of barrooms, whorehouses, and gambling-dens that clustered at the foot of Vicksburg's tall hill. Shouts of drunken anger floated on the dark air that hummed with mosquitoes and reeked of thrown-up booze and untended privies. Since the big vigilante crackdown the previous year at Natchez, Vicksburg had, if anything, a worse reputation than the larger port.

"Well, they can't very well board again before daybreak without drawing attention to themselves." January shrugged his rough jacket straight: the sorry garment he'd gotten from Levi Christmas could pass him as either slave or a laboring freedman. He felt in his pocket again for the pass Hannibal had written him. "If they check into a hotel, I'm guessing the night porter will just store the trunk somewhere until more staff arrives in the morning. It may be another ruse, but we can't afford to assume that it is. There they go." Turning, he clasped Rose hard in his arms. As he kissed her he seemed to hear a whispering voice hiss in his ear: *Marinette-of-the-Dry-Arms will tear your woman from your arms. . . .* "Whatever you do, stay on the boat. We'll get you word as soon as we can."

As at Natchez, it was no difficult matter to follow Weems's cab up the hill. Clay Street was nearly as steep as Natchez's bluff, and the hill, though set a little farther back from the river, was just as high, one of the long line of bluffs that rose like a wall on the east side of the river.

Once away from the torchlight and clamor of the red-light district along the landing, Vicksburg, in its darkness and silence, seemed a much more American town than Natchez. Though the town was only twenty years old, it already had showy houses, pillared like Greek temples in the style favored by Americans: cotton-planters whose lands lay across the river on the flat, fertile, and smotheringly hot delta plain.

The Majestic Hotel was of this style, new and freshly-painted, with very young elm-trees planted on either side of its door. The night porter who opened for Weems and Mrs. Fischer had a gimcrack and brightly-painted air to him, too, fresh-faced and busy. From the darkness beneath the oak-trees across the street, January left Hannibal to watch the front door and followed the cab around to the rear yard. There Sophie got down, saw to it that the trunks were put in a locked shed, tipped the porter, and went inside, carrying her own modest bundle of clean apron and fresh petticoat.

There was no gate on the yard. January stepped back out of sight as the cab passed him—the single lantern above the hotel's rear door threw about as much light as a tallow candle—then slipped around back to Adams Street, where Hannibal waited under the oaks of the vacant lot.

"They've taken a room." The fiddler pointed to a curtained window now glowing with the illumination of lamplight within. "Goodness knows what name they gave. *The merchant, to secure his treasure / Conveys it in a borrowed name. . . .* Though they may in fact just spend the night playing backgammon, as they cannot, as you pointed out, get back on the boat without drawing attention to themselves until morning. Are the trunks back there?"

"In a padlocked shed."

"*Two massy keys he bore of metals twain / The golden opes, the iron shuts amain. I shall return 'ere the leviathan can swim a league. . . .* though I wonder now whether that's in low water or high. *For some must watch, while some must sleep / So runs the world away. . . .*" He darted across the street and vanished like a wayward elf into the darkness.

The lamp upstairs was still burning when Hannibal re-materialized at his side.

"*Stand, and unfold yourself,*" whispered his voice from the shadows, and quite properly January gave back the next line from the opening of Hamlet,

"Long live the king. You come most carefully upon your hour."

"Wretched newfangled patent Yankee locks on the trunks." Hannibal flexed his long fingers, and shivered, though the night was gluily warm. "But worth the effort. They're full of old books, Bible tracts and collections of sermons . . . perhaps we should reclaim them and make a present of them to Mr. Quince."

"They'll be heading back to the boat as soon as they think they're unobserved, then," said January. He glanced up at the moon, trying to gauge how many hours had passed. "Would you do me a favor? Go back to the boat and see what they've done with the engines? See whether they've let the steam down—which will mean the boat's here until noon at least—or just banked the furnaces so they can get up steam in a few minutes. You don't need to rush coming back," he added, taking a second look, by the reflected glow of the single door-lantern across the street, at his friend's rather drawn face.

"*Will ye reach there by moonlight / If your horse be good and your spurs be bright,*" said Hannibal, saluting. "I will be *bloody, bold, and resolute*. You be bloody, bold, and resolute as well, *amicus meus,* and watch your back. We may be away from the waterfront, but personally, I wouldn't trust myself anywhere in this town—or anywhere around our precious friends up in that hotel-room."

With that he departed, and January didn't begin to worry about him until cock-crow. The light burned steadily in the window until almost dawn; by four, first light began to flush the sky above the tangled morasses of cow-pastures, swamps, and willow-choked ravines that stretched out behind the town. Despite the high, breezy situation of the town and the oil of citrus January had smeared on his face and hands, mosquitoes whined around him. Hannibal, he guessed, had rested when he returned to the *Silver Moon*—it was a long walk up and down a steep hill, and though the fiddler had lost the hoarse, wet cough of consumption last year, one never really recovered from the disease.

But when the shapes of trees and houses began to emerge from the blackness of night—when, as Ayasha quoted the blessed Koran, "a white thread could be told from a black one"—January began to wonder whether his friend had made it through the noisome alleys of the district Under-The-Hill in safety. They'd passed through a little after midnight coming here, but they'd been two men together, Hannibal's whiteness protecting January from molestation and January's size protecting Hannibal. Though Hannibal wasn't visibly wealthy, January was well aware that the men who haunted such dockside establishments would kill a man for his watch and boots.

Even worse, the thought crossed his mind that Rose might have come on Hannibal resting on deck and said, "I'll go instead. . . ."

The thought brought him out in a cold sweat. Had she tried to come up here sometime during the small hours? Tried to pass through those filthy alleyways that were darker than the inside of a black cow?

He looked back at the nearest house. Servants were waking up. At certain times of the day a black man could idle unremarked, but early dawn wasn't one of them, not across the street from the best hotel in town. He moved off to loiter behind the corner of a closed-up wine-merchant's store halfway down the block.

A porter came out of the hotel and began sweeping the steps. A cab drew up, depositing the stumpy black forms of Mr. Rosenfeld and Mr. Goldblatt from the *Silver Moon,* with more luggage than January could have imagined possible. He wondered how much of their money Byrne the gambler had managed to lift.

All over town, cocks shrilled the coming morning, above a rising, insistent twitter of lesser birds. Wagons passed on the street, heading to the wharves. A burly-bearded gentleman emerged from the hotel, nearly dragging his dainty wife into the waiting cab.

The grass went from indistinct gray to clearest emerald, and a cart rattled up the street with cans of morning milk for the patrons of the hotel. Smells wafted from the hotel kitchen and that of the house across the way, first smoke, then bacon. A dog barked.

Do I go back to the boat and risk losing them? January wondered. If by some chance they weren't returning—if they'd had other trunks delivered to another location in Vicksburg, for instance . . .

Chambermaids threw open the hotel windows and hung bedding out to air.

When one did so in the room where Weems and/or Fischer had passed the night, January realized, with sinking heart, that the burning lamp had been no guarantee that the room was occupied.

He scrawled a quick penciled note in his memorandum-book—*I shall be at the American Hotel in Memphis on the 7th*, but it didn't really matter what the message was—and hastened across the street with it, entering the side door of the lobby and hurrying to the desk with the air of one who has strode fast and far. The clerk was just polishing the smooth oak counter, black instead of white and an older man than had admitted Weems and Fischer last night but just as smart-looking.

"May I help you?"

"I have a message here for Mr. Weems, that come in last night." January held up the note. "Weems may not be the name he signed under," he added as the clerk frowned over the register. "He travelin' with a lady, taller'n him. . . ."

"Must be Mr. and Mrs. Gordon," said the clerk. "They're the only ones signed in last night. Charlie, the night man, signed 'em in, and there's a note here that they have to be out early, so they paid up right then."

And slipped out the back when nobody was looking?

Damn, damn, damn. . . .

"Thank you. You didn't happen to see 'em leave?"

The clerk shook his head. "That may have been the couple that left an hour ago. I didn't recognize them, so they might have come in last night. But she wasn't taller than him."

January frowned as if puzzled, though a rush of suspicion washed over him. "That's funny, I thought that's what my master said . . . I ain't never seen 'em, myself. He said for sure they'd be carryin' green-and-black-striped portmanteaux. . . ."

"That's them," agreed the clerk promptly. "They sent the boy for a cab around four-thirty, said they had to catch an early boat."

"Thank you," said January again, cursing himself for not having looked more closely at the luggage borne behind the bearded gentleman who had emerged from the hotel, and his fluttery, veiled wife. "I reckon I'll catch 'em down by the landing."

He left through the yard and the alley, loitering a little, though he couldn't imagine that if Hannibal had returned—or if Rose had taken his place—one or the other of them wouldn't have come seeking him. In any case, neither accosted him as he circled back to Adams Street. Deeply worried now, he made his way through the quiet neighborhoods and up and down the rolling slopes of the hill, back toward Clay Street and the levee.

As he came around the corner onto Washington Street and looked down at the waterfront, he froze.

It was barely six in the morning—activity was only just beginning to stir among the boats, wood-piles, heaps of cargo along the mushy fringes of the river; the time when boats were just beginning to take on their cargoes and work up the final heads of steam.

But the *Silver Moon* was gone.

TEN

He ran down to the landing as if, contrary to reason and all evidence of his senses, the steamboat were still in view and he could overtake her.

Brown water lapped sullenly on the clayey slope where the landing-stage had rested. Gouged and trampled mud marked the coming and going of feet. His friend Abishag Shaw of the New Orleans City Guards might have been able to pick Hannibal's tracks, or Rose's, from the mess, but to January it was only a muck of slop and puddles.

Shit, he thought, and his mind wouldn't work further than that. *Shit, shit, shit.*

"When did she leave?" he asked one of the stevedores heaving wood onto the *Concord,* another stern-wheeler that had—to judge by the activity on her deck—just come in.

" 'Bout a hour ago." The man paused in his course toward the wood-piles on the landing, wiped the sweat from his face with the green bandanna that was all he wore above the waist. "They drawed out the fires and damped 'em but never let the steam go all the way down. Musta cost 'em heavy, waitin' like that most of the night, burnin' up wood. Then this couple come in a cab from town, get on board, an' away they go."

Shit.

January was, he reflected furiously, exactly where he'd spent most of the past three years trying not to be: in the middle of cotton territory, without five dollars in his pockets. Hannibal had carried money—in a fit of worry about Rose's safety, he had left his cash with her.

Shit!

None of the other vessels at the landing looked capable of overtaking the *Silver Moon*. Not upstream on a low river, among the snags and shallows around Vicksburg. If worse came to worst, he supposed he could heave wood to get himself back to New Orleans, and pick up a few dollars extra playing for passengers at night, always supposing he could find a boat where someone had a guitar. . . .

And then what? Wait for Rose and Hannibal to return? *If* they returned? When would that be?

Twenty-five hundred dollars was due to Rosario DeLaHaye for the house on Rue Esplanade on the first of September, just over sixty days away. If that wasn't paid, January would be back living in the garçonnière behind his mother's house—if she were willing to evict the boarder currently occupying the room where January had grown up. Knowing his mother, he wasn't entirely certain she would be. She'd been of the strongly-voiced opinion that he and Rose should have used their money to open a construction business, or to buy slaves to rent out to others.

The prospect of relying on his mother for the cost of a bowl of beans, much less a place for himself and Rose to live, turned his stomach.

And after that?

He took a deep breath and raised his eyes to the willow-gray line of DeSoto Point, where the river made a hairpin bend west. "Where could I catch that boat, goin' overland?" he asked.

The stevedore grinned. He was a man of about January's age, squat and ape-like with smiling eyes. "Whoever on board, you must want her pretty bad," he said.

January thought of Rose. Of the school that was her dream, and the scrabbling life that he wanted to save them both from. "I do," he said.

"Then you head on straight north up Chickasaw Bayou." He pointed along the waterfront, along the outer edge of the bend around DeSoto Point. "You cross the Yazoo River, follow it along left through the swamps till you find Steele's Bayou. That'll put you out above Miliken's Bend. It's ten, twelve miles as the crow fly, an' I guarantee you, that boat'll take so long proddin' through them bars around the islands in the bend there, you should catch 'em with time in your hand to spare. You got food? Water?"

And when January shook his head, the man only sighed, as if at a child who'd set out to run away from home with no more than a biscuit in his pocket. He wore, January saw, pinned to his belt-loop the tin badge of a slave who was rented out—who would come home every evening to his master and hand over his wages, the way January's mother wanted her son to do. Leading January to the pile of cordwood that sheltered the lunches of the dock-workers, he handed him a stoppered gourd and a bandanna bundle that smelled of cheese and fresh-baked bread.

"You watch out," said the stevedore. "They's slave-stealers in them swamps. Don't you go speak to no white man, and you look twice at the colored ones."

"I know that much," January said. "Thank you." And he gave him fifty cents he couldn't well afford, knowing the man would now have to find a lunch of his own.

"Mind how you go now. And give your pretty lady a kiss from me."

"I'll do that." *And any number of candles to the Virgin Mary,* added January silently, *if I catch up with that boat. . . .*

A mounted deputy stopped him just beyond the last few shacks up-river of the town, but seemed satisfied when January showed him the pass Hannibal had written. After that January quickened his steps along the river road. In New Orleans—and in cities on the borderline of slave states and free—there were organized rings of slave-stealers who'd keep their captives half-stupefied with opium until they were deep in the South, too far to strike out easily for their homes.

It was one thing to say *Follow the river north.* It was another to think of how many miles there were to cover between some plantation deep in Louisiana or Alabama, and the Ohio River that divided Kentucky from states where white men didn't ride nightly patrols. He remembered, too, the six-foot post in the jail-yard at Natchez, and the crack of the deputy's whip.

In New Orleans, January felt more or less safe, at least in the old French Town. But even that area of safety was steadily shrinking. He didn't go above Canal Street into the American suburbs if he could help it. Even in the French Town, he was careful to dress well and speak well, the marks of a man of wealth and position. The marks of a man who had family, people who would miss him and call in the law if he should disappear.

As he walked along the river road in the blazing Mississippi sun, he felt anger rise again in him, anger and fear. Fear that he had to push aside, daily, if he was to function at all. Anger that could scorch and wither his soul out of all possibility of love and joy, if for one instant he let it get the upper hand.

But how, he sometimes wondered, could a sane man not be angry?

How could a sane man not be afraid?

The anger and fear were a pain in him, like the pain in Hannibal's joints and lungs, a pain that never eased. He understood how men with that constant grinding ache of soul would seek out opium or alcohol, not for pleasure, but simply for relief from the knowledge that there was nothing that he could do.

A lizard eyed him from a gray deadfall tree a little ways down the slope of the batture, fixing him with a sharp black gaze before it flicked away like an eyeblink. In the brush beneath the willows of the bank something moved, a rabbit or a fox, but January's breath jerked hard in his lungs for a moment.

Somewhere behind him, and probably not very far away, the Reverend Levi Christmas would be trailing the *Silver Moon.*

Unless of course he simply got on her at Vicksburg this morning, all decked out in his black coat and pastoral collar.

That will be all I need.

But at least if that were the case it would mean that Christmas wasn't somewhere behind him, waiting to kidnap him and sell him to some cotton planter in Texas.

The mouth of Chickasaw Bayou lay three miles up-river of Vicksburg, part of the murky bottomlands that lay between the meandering Mississippi and the bluffs along the Yazoo. The air was thick with gnats there, the sunlight greenish through the motionless leaves of cypress and willow. Turtles basked on dessicated logs that rose through the glassy brown surface of the water, arranged, as usual, largest to smallest, with an occasional tiny turtle perched on its larger cousin's back.

January cut a sapling with his pen-knife—the only knife a slave might carry—and prodded the long weeds and honeysuckle that overgrew the faint trace of cow-path, twice startling sinewy rustlings in the undergrowth that spoke of copperheads or water-moccasins lying just out of sight. Once he saw an alligator in the bayou, masquerading as a floating log. Its gold eyes reminded him of Jubal Cain's, glittering just above the line of the silent water.

He was far from New Orleans, and far from the *Silver Moon,* but Queen Régine's curse seemed to be working just fine.

He moved as quietly as he could, stopping repeatedly to listen. The woods were so still that the drumming of the cicadas seemed to roar in the trees, and the squeaky mew of a catbird cut the stillness like a violin note. He wasn't sure what made him first realize he was being pursued.

It wasn't a sound—he didn't hear the strike of hooves until afterwards, nor the rustle of a man flanking the road through the underbrush. Whatever it was that lifted the hair on his nape, January didn't hesitate. He waded silently into the bayou (*Virgin Mary, please don't let there be gators*) and made for the nearest half-sunk tree, sliding almost completely under the water on its far side and keeping the slime-draped trunk between his head and the waterside path.

Still silence. *Did I really just hop in the bathtub with every gator and cottonmouth in Warren County out of sheer bad nerves?*

He stayed where he was.

And stayed.

"Where the fuck'd he go?"

Shit, was the ground dry or muddy on the edge where I went in? He couldn't recall.

Hooves, and the faint jangle of a bit-chain. The creak of saddle-leather.

"Got to gone in the woods."

"The fuck he did, Reverend, I was comin' round through the woods. He can't have gone up a tree."

The Reverend Christmas laughed, a hoarse braying. "I'd like to see a nigger that big hangin' in a tree like an old coon. We'll get him, Turk. If he's headin' for the river, we'll catch him."

"What if he ain't?"

"Where else he gonna go? They all head for the river when they run. I hear there's a regular leg of the Underground Railway runnin' up the river these days. That's where he's headed, sure."

"You think he got that boy Bobby with him?"

"I didn't see him. He coulda been waitin' for him outside town. One way or the other, if that big bastard is indeed our loyal friend, I got a score to settle with him on that boy Bobby's account. . . ."

The voices faded, swallowed up in the soughing of the trees.

So Bobby decided to run after all. Christmas and his bravos had probably counted on the *Silver Moon* laying by for a few more hours, and had been caught on the hop by her sudden departure. They had almost certainly seen him on the waterfront. At least the Reverend wasn't on board with Rose.

". . . figure we can catch 'em at Horsehead Bar."

January had just begun to reach down for footing on the murky bottom, when other voices sounded on the path. He ducked down again, praying the movement hadn't caught anyone's attention.

"That's twenty miles!"

"You ever know a boat to get off Horsehead Bar in less'n two days at low water?"

Something brushed January's leg underwater, and he fought not to flinch. By force of will he remained where he was for another ten minutes, listening. When the frogs began to croak again, eerie in the stillness, he cautiously raised his head. The path and the woods were empty. Trembling, he waded, not back to the path, but across the rest of the bayou, and plunged into the tangled undergrowth of the woods.

His benefactor at the landing had instructed him to follow Chickasaw Bayou but hadn't mentioned what other bayous might intersect it in the marshy lands within the big river's loop. Trying to keep the bayou on his left, January encountered a wider body of water. . . . Another bayou? The Yazoo River? It seemed to have a current, but bayous frequently did. In the leafy summer woods it was difficult to determine the direction of the sun, which stood nearly straight overhead now. The windless air was suffocating. January crossed the river—or bayou—and followed it to his left, but it bent back on itself, and rapidly dried to a shallow pan of reeds and dead trees fringed with ants' nests the size of flour-sacks.

When he turned back to seek the original bayou, he found himself amid trees that looked totally unfamiliar, cypress and bright-green thickets of harshly-whispering palmetto, the ground a jungle of elephant-ear underfoot. He pushed through this until, ahead of him, he smelled the whiff of smoke, the ashy pungence of a fire newly damped. He stood to listen but heard nothing. No voices, no curses, no friendly bicker of men breaking camp.

Silently, January moved back into the palmetto thickets . . .

. . . and heard a rustling away to his right.

He moved away from it as silently as he could, but something—the birds too silent, perhaps? The cicadas hushed?—turned him back farther into the woods, and after a few moments he heard the unmistakable crack of a trodden stick to his left. Among the palmettos he was at least sheltered from sight, and he moved from clump to clump, listening to the rustle of the men hunting him. And they were hunting him, two of them at least, working through the thickets on either side. Somewhere close by he heard a dog bark, and made for the sound, his steps quickening as the slashing rustle neared.

They had to have heard him, he knew, and broke into a jog, then a run. The thresh of his legs through the tangles of honeysuckle and elephant-ear drowned all sound of pursuit, but he didn't dare look back. Only strode, struggled, ran upslope, then down to a marshy little trickle of puddles that might have once been a bayou. Someone behind him yelled, "You, boy, stop!" as he broke cover at the bottom, but he plunged into the woods on the far side and cut toward his right as soon as he thought he was out of sight. The heat dazed him, beat on him, suffocated him; he smelled smoke again and heard a cock crow, and the next minute he saw open sky through the trees ahead.

A small field lay before him, corn thick and nearly head-high under a sun like molten brass. January vaulted the split-rail fence and threw himself into the green shelter of the rows, ducking low and keeping still, like a rabbit, like Compair Lapin when Bouki the Hyena prowled around. The dust-smell filled his nose. Closer the dog barked again. A cornsnake blinked at him from the dappled shade, then slid away in a little whisper of red and gold.

Through the rustling of the long, leathery leaves he thought he heard voices at the edge of the field.

Let him walk through the swamps and the hills with men hunting behind him. . . .

He remained where he was for a long time, bars of sun scorching across his back.

Then he crept along the rows, endlessly, to the other side of the field. A swaybacked dogtrot cabin stood under two trees. A smokehouse, an outhouse, a barn, a couple of cabins for slaves. On the other side of the home-place a cotton field stretched, the young plants still too small and thin to have concealed him. Far down the rows, two men were chopping at the weeds around their roots with hoes, the endless work of early summer. Their voices buzzed in song:

Farewell the ol' plantation, o,
Farewell the ol' quarters, o,
I been sold away to Georgia, o, farewell. . . .

A woman came out of one half of the dogtrot and crossed to him, the dog he'd heard—a shaggy gray monster with a lolling tongue—shambling at her heels. January stood up as she approached. She carried a baby on her hip and moved like an old woman, but when she came near he saw she was young, under thirty. Her hair, under the head-rag of a slave, lay in fine, curly wisps around her forehead, more like a white woman's hair than a black's. She was darker than white men liked, but delicate-featured and pretty. "It's all right," she said in heavily-French-accented English. "They are gone."

She shaded her eyes with her hand to look up at him—she was barely five feet tall in her faded osnaberg dress—and asked, "Are you running away?"

"I'm running away from *them,*" he replied in French, and produced his free papers from the inner pocket, where he'd kept them hidden. He didn't expect she'd be able to read them—it was against the law to teach slaves to read and write, mostly so they couldn't write up their own passes—but she took the paper and scanned it, and said, as she handed it back. "Those were not the patrols, then, M'sieu Janvier? You were right to run. There are slave-stealers all along the river. The men here stay indoors at night, and close to their work by day, for fear of them more than for any consideration of the patrols. Come into the kitchen—the master is hunting in the woods today and will not be back until night. I think one of the men here can help you get to where you are going."

Her name was Mary. "Marie-Hélène, before my master re-baptized me as a Protestant—a 'real Christian,' he calls them—and wed me to my current husband." Her voice was dry. "My marriage to Jean-Claude in New Orleans was only a Catholic one, he said—he is a minister of his own Church, my master, called to the faith, he says, by God Himself."

January glanced outside, to where Mary's husband, Amos, and Lafayette, the younger cotton-hand, were putting the mule to the wagon. Amos was a medium-sized man, impassive and heavy-muscled. Close to, in the shadows of the kitchen, January could see the dark mark of an old bruise on Mary's face, and a small fresh scar beneath her left eye. It was none of his business, he thought, and Amos was going to drive him across the river and down Steele's Bayou—neither of which was anywhere near this small bottomlands farm—almost certainly saving him from the Reverend Christmas and his boys.

Was it Amos's fault, January asked himself, that he had in him smoldering anger equal to January's own? Anger that would unleash itself on the nearest and weakest target?

He thought of Julie on the boat, rocking back and forth in Rose's arms. *What'm I gonna do?*

With a baby in arms and two more hanging on to her skirts, Mary was obviously not going to run anywhere.

How did you get here? he wanted to ask her as she laid before him a couple of ash-pones and a cup of milk, food her master might well want an accounting of at the end of the day. *What are you doing here, with your good French and your beauty and your quick movements, so unlike those of the field-hand who knows that to conclude work swiftly will only earn another task?*

But he already knew the answer to this, and the harrowing-up of details would be no joy to her. So instead he raised an eyebrow and asked, "And was this Divine communication via a burning bush, or the more modern whirlwind method?" And laughed as the young woman recounted her master's vision of the fiery letters "GPC," which had appeared to him in a dream:

"He said they must surely mean *Go Preach Christ,* though the members of the local Methodist synod who rejected his application for the ministry suggested that Our Lord more probably meant *Go Pick Cotton. . . .*"

"You have no idea," she said as she and Amos helped him into the back of the wagon and piled brush and kindling over him, "how good it is to hear good French spoken again, and to see—" She hesitated, sadness darkening her eyes. "Oh, anyone new. Anyone at all."

Her voice was wistful. The sun, already slanting over above the encircling woods of cottonwood and pine, made black squares on the bare earth around the house; the cawing of the crows seemed to emphasize rather than break the dense stillness of that solitary farm. "When you return to the city—if you return to the city—burn a candle for me to the Virgin, and tell her that I pray to her in secret every night. Yes, yes, *cher,* I am coming," she added as the toddler in the passway between the two rooms of the cabin began to scream.

"You make sure you get them sheets washed after the bread's in," grunted Amos, springing to the wagon-box and picking up the reins. "Marse gonna be sore enough when he come home, 'bout how little cotton we got hoed."

"I will tell Marse that you were overcome by the heat, and lay down until the earth stopped spinning beneath your feet," said Mary, and pulled down the last chunks of dried brush and palmetto-leaves over January's head. "Do not agitate yourself about Marse."

"Yeah," grumbled the man, "you good at lyin', woman." And he lashed the mule hard with a cotton stalk.

The wagon lurched as it pulled away down the rutted track toward the bayou. The last January saw of the young woman Mary was of her walking back toward her master's cabin, her newest baby on her hip and her shoulders bent with exhaustion.

ELEVEN

Whether or not Amos and his wagon passed the Reverend Christmas on the road, January never knew. They passed someone who called out drunken jovialities at Amos *("Hey, Sambo, bit early to be haulin' the cotton to market!")*, but January kept under the brushwood. Even when he would have gotten out to help with the ferry, the field-hand snapped, "You stay put in there," and dragged on the creaking winch himself to get the raft across the sluggish Yazoo. His mind relieved of most of his concerns about being enslaved—or murdered—himself, January had ample leisure to conjure visions, some of them completely illogical or impossible, of Rose or Hannibal being enslaved—or murdered—as one or the other of them attempted to rejoin him in the dark yard opposite the Majestic Hotel.

Now that he was no longer running, exhaustion overtook him, amplified by the stifling heat under the brushwood and the canvas stretched over it. He would have slept had the condition of either the road or the unsprung wagon-bed permitted it. As it was, his weary mind produced pictures of himself waiting on the riverbank by the mouth of Steele's Bayou for days for a boat that had gone past already, waiting until he was caught by Reverend Christmas. . . . How would he know whether the *Silver Moon* had passed or not? And how would he convince Kevin Molloy to land the boat and let him come aboard, particularly if Hannibal had been murdered (or enslaved) back in Vicksburg . . . ?

Then the jolt of a wagon-wheel in a pothole slammed him from his half-dreaming doze into painful contact with the side of the wagon, back into heat and thirst and the aching stiffness of enforced immobility.

How quickly would the *Silver Moon* negotiate the long bends of the river that lay between Vicksburg and Steele's Bayou? He felt he'd been traveling for days, but the heat beneath the kindling-wood seemed unaltered, and the wagon was jolting too badly for him to put his eye to any of the numerous cracks in the side. It was still daylight. Had God halted the sun in the Heavens, as He had for the Israelites in battle? They'd never reach the riverbank before the boat passed. . . .

"You in luck," announced Amos as if he deeply regretted the fact.

January squirmed out from beneath the brushwood and sat up.

The *Silver Moon* was visible perhaps a half-mile downstream, hung up on one of the innumerable gravel bars that dotted the wide expanse of the river's loop. Men swarmed the decks in the slanted evening light, and January could see the long iron poles, like extra masts, wavering and wobbling above the hurricane deck as the men thrust them down into the mud of the bar. The boat must be firmly stuck, he reflected, for them to be sparring that way. He could see the piles of crates and trunks on the bank under a small guard of deck-hands, with the skiff beached beside them, where they'd been off-loaded to lighten the boat's draft.

He sprang down from the wagon, held out his hand to Amos. "Thank you," he said, and handed the man one of the three dollars that remained to him. "More than I can ever say."

The field-hand said, "Huh," took the dollar, and pulled the mule's head savagely around. Whether the comment implied annoyance, envy, scorn, or shyness, January didn't know, for Amos lashed the beast's flanks with the cottonstalk whip, and drove back into the woods without another word.

Horsehead Bar—which January guessed this had to be—lay obliquely out into the channel, formed by the wash-off from a small point a half-mile or so below the bayou mouth. He couldn't imagine how even an inexperienced pilot like Mr. Souter could have missed it: trees and debris snagged on it showed clearly above the surface in four or five places. As he drew near the bar, the Mississippi planter Lockhart—who was in charge of the deck-hands around the luggage—exclaimed, "By God, just what we need, another pair of hands! You, boy . . . !"

And Colonel Davis came over from the skiff, rifle in hand, and said, "Why, it's Ben, isn't it?"

"Was last time I looked, Colonel Davis." January scraped at the dried scum that still covered his clothing from his dip in Chickasaw Bayou, additionally speckled with straw from the wagon-bed and bits of brushwood. "Though I can't tell myself who I am, under all the mud."

"There," said Davis triumphantly to Lockhart, "I told you the boy hadn't run away." Though he called him "boy," Davis was probably January's junior by a dozen years. "You treat darkies decently and they are as loyal as any man."

"Run away?" January scratched a shower of twigs from his hair. "You got to be joking, sir. Man'd have to be crazy to run away in this country." And the men around him laughed. "I nearly got stole and sold to Texas twice, and that's the truth. . . ."

"Go on out to the boat," chuckled Davis, and slapped him companionably on the shoulder. "They need every pair of hands out there. We're glad to have you back safe and sound."

The water over the bar was so low, January could walk out along it most of the way to the boat, and it was seldom more than breast-deep thereafter. Where it was over his head, the bar broke the current so effectively that the water behind lay almost still. Rose and Hannibal emerged from the engine-room doorway and ran to the railing as January drew near: Hannibal held a rifle, one of the .45-caliber Lemans that were generally locked in the purser's office.

Simple caution on this relatively isolated stretch of the river? January wondered. Had someone—Mr. Lundy, perhaps?—convinced Mr. Tredgold that Levi Christmas might attack the boat?

Or had they armed all the white men on board because both coffles of slave men had been unchained and pressed into service in raising and planting the long sparring-poles? In the blue shadows of the starboard promenade the chains hung down empty against the wall, like a horrid still-life, and he heard 'Rodus's voice call out from the hurricane deck, "Slip her down!" followed by the splash of the pole-end in the shallow water at the stern.

"What the hell happened?" January asked softly as Rose threw herself into his arms regardless of his soaked and muddy clothing and the fact that they weren't supposed to have known each other before the voyage began.

"That is, as Hamlet said, the question," replied Hannibal. He was in shirtsleeves, like all the other men on deck, and didn't look like he'd slept. Rose, too, looked haggard and ashy. "I was on my way back to join you, when I saw that wench Sophie. . . ."

"Well, I'm sure this is all very touching," chuckled Mr. Souter, emerging from the engine-room rubbing his hands. "And I'm sure your boy has some remarkable tales to tell of his odyssey—" He flung out his arms like a barker at a raree-show, "Amazing feats by land and sea! But let's save the tears of joy for after we get this god-damned boat off this god-damned bar. . . ."

So January followed Souter to the bow, and spent until nightfall in the tedious occupation of sparring the steamboat over the Horsehead Bar. This well-known local landmark below the small Horsehead Point had apparently proved too high and too gravelly to be simply rammed through, and the *Silver Moon* had hit its outer end too hard to be poled off backwards. Once the long poles were sunk upright behind the boat, every male on board, white as well as black, with the exception of the three planters standing guard and the deck-hands wooding the engine, was drafted to turn the capstan-wheels to which the upper ends of the poles were chained. The ends were levered down, and the whole weight of the boat inched gradually forward across the shallow, with the paddlewheel turning slowly to push and a leadsman crying out soundings at the bow.

Then the poles were pulled loose, re-positioned, and the whole laborious process repeated again. The manufacturer Dodd fumed and refused to join the others at the capstans, and Ned Gleet attempted to charge rent for the use of his slaves and was shrieked into submission by Mrs. Tredgold, but on the whole the process went smoothly under Mr. Souter's shouted orders from the pilot-house.

The white women—cabin and deck-passengers alike—crowded the starboard rail to watch, and Molloy came charging along the boiler-deck promenade cursing them and shouting "Trim the goddam boat! D'you want to sink us?"

Muscles aching, arms smarting, body numb with fatigue as he leaned on the capstan-bars between Jim the valet and Hannibal, January scanned the beardless faces in the twilight. He picked out Mrs. Fischer, with her thick brunette chignon and her dark eyes narrow and hard, and Theodora Skippen, turned, not toward the men around the hatch but toward the bank. Saw Sophie and Julie clinging together on the lower deck, arms around one another's waists, the sylph-like daintiness of the one emphasizing the strength of the other.

Saw Rose a little apart, the last of the daylight flashing in her spectacles, and knew that she was watching him.

Where was Queen Régine? he wondered, bending his back again to 'Rodus's rhythmical shout. How had she been able to slip out of the hold as they started unloading the luggage—if that was, indeed, her hideaway down there in the darkness? Could she be simply concealing herself by sitting among the women slaves on the portside promenade in the gathering shadows?

"If she did, I've seen no sign of her," said Hannibal when January asked, under cover of the slaves' chant as they labored. "And they've kept the luggage under guard from the moment they started moving it out, drat them."

'Rodus's voice rose in the work-chant, and the slaves took it up as they threw their weight on the capstan-bars:

Mama brought me coffee-uhn!
Mama brought me tea—uhn!
Mama brought me evvythin'
'Ceptin' the jail-house key—uhn!

On the capstan-bar before them January picked out the bent back of Jubal Cain, heavy shoulders standing out like pink-stained marble between the black and whip-scarred backs on either side. He took up the song; a moment later Mr. Byrne the gambler, heaving the bar between Quince and Weems, added his.

Turn me over easy——uhn!
Turn me over slow——uhn!
Turn me over easy, lord,
'Cause de bullets hurt me so——uhn!

Every man of Cain's coffle, January saw, was whip-scarred—most of the scars fairly fresh. 'Rodus's naked back told January everything he could have asked about a short life-time of defiance. Yet the dealer worked among them, sweating in silence, and neither the man to his left nor to his right offered challenge.

"As I said, I was halfway back to you with the news that the boat hadn't let steam down, when I recognized Sophie," said Hannibal, panting as he leaned his weight on the bar to the timing of the chant. "I followed her back to the boat, and she went straight to their stateroom. I watched to see if I could get in—they clearly hadn't abandoned it—and just as it began to get light, who should appear but the guilty pair themselves, La Pécheresse with a false beard and enough padding to hide her Junoesque curves, and Weems in a very fetching French-blue gown and veils. I was looking around the boat to see if you'd followed them back when we put out. They must have bribed Molloy to keep steam up—Tredgold was furious when he woke up about an hour later."

"The more fools they," murmured January. "Since Molloy was one of the Bank's depositors. He must have laughed when they handed him the money—probably the remainder of what Weems got from Cain. Molloy's too good a pilot for this to have been an accident—with the luggage in a shambles you couldn't get to it, but he could. I saw Weems and Fischer leave the hotel but didn't recognize them."

With solemn mischief, 'Rodus led the chant:

Massa, he an ugly man——uhn!
Missus, she a sinner——uhn!
Skin a flea for tallow an' hide
An' gimme the bones for dinner——uhn!

It was dark by the time the skiff was loaded up, and the two coffles of slaves were put to work helping the deck-hands replace the cargo in the holds under Thucydides's sharp eye. Iron cressets loaded with firewood burned on the deck and on the bank to light the work, and all the white men were given rifles and set to guarding the bank, with the exception of Mr. Quince, who declared that violence of any kind was repellent to his nature. "Milksop," said Cain impersonally, pulling on his coat and taking up a rifle—his own, a .50-caliber Henry, not one of the Lemans from the ship's store.

A belated dinner was served in the Grand Saloon, and January retired to Hannibal's stateroom, where the fiddler tipped Thu to send in a copper tub and hot water for a bath. "It's one thing there's never a shortage of on a steamboat, thank God," said Hannibal as January stripped off his mud-crusted clothing and settled in the round towel-draped tin vessel. "Rose was going to dump the boilers if you didn't show up by the time the cargo was re-loaded. With everyone on deck it wouldn't have been difficult."

January smiled. "That's my Rose."

"According to Tredgold, we should be under way by the time dinner is finished, and Mrs. Tredgold ventures to hope you and I will play after dinner, though I don't expect there will be much in the way of dancing." Hannibal knelt on the bunk—there was almost no floor-room left with the bath—and dug through his portmanteau for clean shirts for them both. "I think we can safely venture to say that neither Weems nor Fischer will abandon the boat tonight. With the luggage jumbled as it is, they probably couldn't find their own trunks, even if they had some means of transporting them elsewhere, and there's a fog rising. I doubt Molloy could see the flag on the landing of any plantation we pass, and the next town is Mayersville, fifty miles up-river. It's small. I suspect we're safe until we get to Greenville, sixty miles beyond that."

"We may not have to worry about them leaving the boat," said January softly. "But I saw Mrs. Fischer as she looked down at us turning the capstan—I saw the look in her eyes. We're not safe."

Though it would have been pleasant to linger in the bath, he was mindful of his responsibilities to friendship. He got out promptly, while the water was still hot, so that Hannibal could bathe as well. The fiddler looked haggard, as if he, too, had not slept after their shared vigil outside the Majestic Hotel the previous night; January could only be thankful that when the boat snagged up on Horsehead Bar, Hannibal hadn't attempted to look for him on shore.

Still, the fiddler took his violin with him when he went to supper, and a few minutes later a porter appeared, to lug away the bath. January supposed he should go down and scrounge his usual supper from Eli, to share with Rose. But weariness overwhelmed him. He rolled up in his blanket with one of the spare bed-pillows under his head, and slept, hearing through the black-velvet weight of exhaustion the soft clang of the *Silver Moon*'s bell, and the voices of the slaves, singing on the promenade below.

Follow the Drinkin' Gourd, follow the Drinkin' Gourd,
There's an old man 'cross the river gonna carry you to freedom,
Follow the Drinkin' Gourd.

In his dreams he saw Mary, with her child on her hip, a lonely figure walking back across that weedy field to the dogtrot cabin under the grilling sun. Saw Julie, weeping in Rose's arms—*What'm I gonna do?*—and the backs of the two slaves who'd shoved on the capstan-bar ahead of him, knotted with whip-scars as if sections of fishing-nets were embedded under the skin. In his dream he tried to explain to them, *I'm traveling on this boat to get my money back, so that I can be free.*

And in his dream a man chained to the wall of the promenade deck, a man who had his father's face with its tribal scars, said gently, *You already free, Ben.*

No, thought January, waking to gaze into the darkness of that tiny stateroom, *I am not free.*

What time it was he couldn't guess. Not very late, since Hannibal had not returned—even in pitchy dark he would have been able to hear the fiddler's breathing. The floor beneath him vibrated with the shaking of the engine; the night smelled of the wet straw matting where the bath-water had dripped on it, and of fog.

Flickers of yellow light, tiny and dim but vivid as stars in the complete dark of the stateroom, outlined the louvers of the door. The cautious rattle of metal, a minute scratching, nothing like the sound of a key. A gash of light opened vertically, the pierced glow of a shuttered dark-lantern, wreaths of fog trailing around it and everything behind it lost in blackness.

January sat up, raised a hand against the light. "Rose?"

The door slammed shut. Footfalls retreated down the promenade. January scrambled to his feet, fumbled the blanket around his waist, tripped over the portmanteau that Hannibal had left sticking out from under the bunk, and by the time he pulled open the stateroom door, there was nothing outside but utter blackness, and the smell of the river and of fog. From the bow end of the boat a voice called out, "Quarter twain! Quarter twain!" monotonous as the creak of a branch in wind.

January thought, *Not another damn bar,* and returned to the stateroom floor to sleep.

He thought again, *I am not free. Nor is Rose, nor will our children be.*

Then it was misty daylight.

And still.

ANOTHER bar? Or the same one?

Hannibal's bunk was empty, but his fiddle lay in its case on the chair, and the blankets had been rumpled. January dressed, and strode aft to look for Rose.

Half the passengers on the boat seemed to be gathered at the stern ends of both the lower and upper promenades, leaning over the rails. They seemed to be craning to look at the paddle, which hung still and glistening in the warm gray vapors that seemed to hold the boat locked. *We hit a snag,* thought January, *and damaged the paddle. . . .*

Now we'll be stuck here until Christmas and his boys arrive. . . .

Why hadn't the jolt of it waked him?

He picked Rose's white tignon from the crowd, close to the rails on the port side, talking to the Roberson ladies'-maid—who slept on her mistress's stateroom floor and almost never came downstairs—and Colonel Davis's valet, Jim Pemberton. January hurried down the stairway and made toward her—she caught sight of him and turned, reaching out. She looked shaken and sick.

At the same moment January saw behind her that what he'd originally thought was a scrap of moss snagged in the paddle was in fact a piece of green and yellow cloth, soaked with water and river mud.

A man's cravat.

"What is it?"

"Weems."

"What's he done?" So much for Hannibal's theory about what the pair of thieves were likely to do.

"He hasn't done anything," said Rose. "His body was found this morning, snagged up in the paddle."

TWELVE

"Murderer!" Diana Fischer swung around from the stern rail where she stood and stabbed a finger at January. Her rich contralto voice cut through the eager chatter of the deck-hands, deck-passengers, and servants all crowded around.

"Ask him where he was last night, and what orders his master gave him! Ask him why he followed this boat with such determination! Why he returned to re-board it, if not to accomplish his master's fell design!"

I followed this boat with such determination because I didn't want to be sold by slave-stealers in Texas, thought January, but he had better sense than to say so. He could see by the faces of the male passengers surrounding Mrs. Fischer that his sassing a white lady would not help the situation.

Instead, he assumed the most shocked and innocent expression of which he was capable, fell back a pace, and looked to Mr. Tredgold as if Mrs. Fischer did not exist. "Sir, where is my master?"

"Your master is locked up!" Mrs. Fischer stepped in front of Tredgold while the harried little man was still drawing breath to reply. "Where he belongs, and you with him, you Othello! You bloody-handed villain, with a heart as black as your hide! Oh!" She clapped her hand to her forehead and staggered back into Mr. Tredgold's arms. "Oh, that my *hope* of salvation should be rent from me by such *monsters* as these!"

Mrs. Tredgold rushed to Mrs. Fischer's side, elbowed her husband out of the way, and put her arms around the afflicted lady, who had, January noticed, had time to get her corsets and dress on—a somber confection of blue and white—but whose thick waves of raven hair still lay tumbled over her shoulders like an opera heroine's in a mad-scene. Mrs. Tredgold snapped at her husband, "Have this man locked up!"

"Now, dearest, nothing's been—"

"Thu!" bellowed Mrs. Tredgold. "Eli! Take this man and—"

"Why don't you come on up to the Saloon, where your master is?" said Mr. Lundy's buzzing monotone, and a shaky hand was laid on January's arm. "There's nothing more to see down here."

January glanced at Rose, who nodded slightly, with an expression of calm—she had been on the deck longer than he, and perceived herself in no danger. As he followed the former pilot up the steps, January glanced back at the paddle again. It was undamaged, human bone and flesh being less fibrous and tough than waterlogged tree-stumps. Beyond that it was impossible to see anything, if there was anything to see—only what was immediately obvious. That nobody could have fallen accidentally over the elbow-high railings that surrounded the entire deck.

Ned Gleet thrust past January and Lundy on the stairway to the boiler-deck, almost knocking the fragile former pilot over the rail. At the bow end of the promenade, Molloy held Theodora Skippen pressed to the wall beside the door of the Ladies' Parlor: "Sold her?" he was saying, his voice hoarse with fury. "God damn it, girl, is that all you can do with the things a man buys you? What else that I paid for have you turned into cash?"

"Darling," Miss Skippen whispered, raising her hands supplicatingly against his broad blue-clad chest, "darling, let me explain!" She gazed up into his blotchy face, her soft blond curls cascading over her shoulders—like Mrs. Fischer, she appeared to have gotten herself mostly dressed when the alarm went up at the finding of the body. "Oh, my beloved, it was a matter of most tragic urgency. . . ."

January would have been deeply interested to hear Miss Skippen's explanation for selling Julie—which Molloy appeared to have just heard of. He would have bet any amount of money that the tale of tragic urgency she was about to relate had nothing to do with large sums owed to Levi Christmas.

Hannibal sat at one of the card-tables in the saloon, drinking opium-laced sherry out of a wineglass. Without the warm glow of the oil-lamps the Saloon had the shadowy atmosphere of a cave. Nick and Thu were laying out plates and silverware on the buffet, and the scent of coffee filled the air. Colonel Davis was just dropping sugar into a cup—he glanced up as January's huge form blotted the light from the short hallway to the outside, and nodded as Lundy escorted him in.

Tredgold and Mr. Souter followed, with a red-faced and seething Molloy bringing up the rear moments later.

"Have I the court's permission to point out how ridiculous that woman's accusation is?" inquired Hannibal quietly.

"This isn't a court, Mr. Sefton." Colonel Davis returned to the card-table and sat down next to Hannibal. "You aren't being accused of anything."

"My error. I was deceived by the outstretched finger and the shrieked words *There stands the murderer.*"

"Surely you must make allowances for the poor woman's shattered state of mind," replied Souter, shocked. "I understand that she and Mr. Weems were affianced."

"She has a point, though." Molloy walked over to the bar and fished behind it for a whiskey-glass and bottle. His blue eyes sparkled still with malice and anger, but he kept his voice judicious and calm. "Your boy wouldn't have run over hill and dale to catch us up without a damn good reason to do so. Why not just turn himself over to the sheriff at Vicksburg and wait for you to come back and pick him up?"

"According to Mrs. Fischer," said Tredgold, propping his spectacles with a nervous finger, "you, Mr. Sefton, are in the employ of business enemies of her—er—intended. She says you were sent to prevent him from reaching St. Louis and consummating the purchase of ten thousand acres of Indian lands which your employers—the Bank of Louisiana—also wish to own."

"*What?*" Hannibal set his wineglass down with a clack. "Who in their right mind would hire *me* to murder anyone?" He glanced across at January, asking for instructions, though they both knew that revealing the facts of the bank theft at this point would simply spread the information up and down the river like the plague.

"Mrs. Fischer says," went on Tredgold with a hesitant cough, "that you have previously made the accusation—to the sheriff at Natchez—that her intended had stolen money from the Bank of Louisiana, and that you even had documents from one of the bank officials to back up this story."

"You keep your money in the Bank of Louisiana, don't you, Kev?" put in Souter. "Any of this make sense to you?"

Molloy's brow creased in thought, and he sipped his whiskey with the air of a man piecing together what he knows. "Well, I know the bank directors have been trying for months to close some kind of Indian land deal, but it's none of my business." He regarded the speechless Hannibal with half-shut eyes, a malicious smile curving one corner of his mouth beneath the red mustache. "I thought I recognized Mr. Sefton when he first came on board, and it might well be from the bank, now that I think of it. I seem to recall the Director has a secretary named Sefton, anyway."

Through his own shock January had to admire the cleverness of the story. *We might as well tear up Granville's letters now,* he reflected. It would take a week or more for letters to reach New Orleans, in confirmation or denial, another week for them to return. . . .

If the story of the theft hadn't broken in the meantime and collapsed the bank anyway.

If Granville hadn't fled.

"It is nevertheless a precept of American law that a man is presumed innocent until proven guilty." Colonel Davis's clear, sharp voice cut into the silence. "And I see no proof on one side or the other. Certainly there are no grounds to deprive anyone of their liberty, especially if the vessel makes no stops between here and Mayersville. I think it equally likely that the murder could have been done by that girl who disappeared. Our best course would be to proceed to Mayersville and turn this entire affair over to the Issaquena County sheriff."

"But without the fares from the plantations between here and Mayersville . . ." began Tredgold, who was completely ignored.

Molloy shrugged, and tossed down the rest of his whiskey. "If you want to trust an Orangeman, it's no skin off my behind. Now, with your permission, *Captain* . . ." He bowed ironically to Tredgold. "Colonel, I'll be after gettin' this vessel under way."

Tredgold and Davis followed Molloy to the door, where low-voiced conversation ensued. January fetched Hannibal a cup of coffee from the big porcelain urns, and a biscuit, at which the fiddler shook his head. Men were coming quietly into the Saloon, edging past the muttered convocation in the doorway and being careful not to look at Hannibal.

"What girl was he talking about?" asked January, standing at Hannibal's side as a good servant should. "What went on last night?"

"What didn't?" The fiddler glanced up at him from dark-circled eyes. "It appears Julie escaped last night. Her shoes were found on the starboard promenade deck just before you came down. Gleet went storming up to Miss Skippen's stateroom to ascertain that, no, she wasn't there . . . Miss Skippen was sound asleep still and Gleet was damn lucky not to run into Molloy in her stateroom. Molloy had come down to get breakfast before going on watch at six, and was—according to Rose, anyway—on the stairs from the boiler-deck down to the kitchen when Jim started shouting."

"Jim was the first one to see the body, then?"

Hannibal nodded. "He sleeps closest to the paddle, and got up before rosy-fingered Aurora even started *thinking* about spreading the light of dawn o'er meadow and lea. I suppose goddesses have to get their beauty-sleep sometime. It was still foggy then, and Jim thought the body might have been a clump of branches or debris; then he realized what it was and gave the alarm."

"And when did you get down there?"

"Almost at once. Following the usual after-supper card game I wasn't sleepy, but didn't want to wake you by lighting a candle and reading—an unnecessary precaution, as it turned out, since you never stirred when Jim raised the alarm. I don't think you moved all night."

"I did," said January. "Or at least I think I did. . . ." It flashed across his mind that his nocturnal visitor might have been a dream, but he shook the thought away immediately. Rose might dream about waking up in the same room she'd gone to sleep in, but January knew himself better than that. "I'll tell you later."

"*Nisi Dominus custodierit civitatem,* as the Psalmist says, *frustra vigilat qui custodit eam.* In any case I settled myself on a quiet corner of the bow-deck and played—in spite of the fog it was a relatively warm night. Later I came to bed, but I don't think I slept more than an hour or so before the alarm was raised. Do you think Weems might have encountered Julie as she was going overside, and Julie struck him to prevent him from giving the alarm?"

"She certainly could have," said January thoughtfully. "She's a big girl—taller than Weems, and heavier. If she shoved or thrust him, he might have struck his head on a stanchion. Did the boat go over a bar at some time during the night?"

"Around eleven." Hannibal glanced up at the clerestory windows that ranged around the top of the Saloon; the light dimmed and faded in them, warning of gathering clouds. Thunder muttered in the distance. "They barely scraped over. Does that make a difference?"

"Only that Weems must have gone overside sometime after that, or else his body would have been scraped off entirely. Where have they put the body?"

Hannibal, who had entirely too much imagination for his own

good, looked slightly green at the image this conjured up, and said a little faintly, "In his stateroom." He poured himself some more sherry. "Though whether Tredgold will let you have a look at it is . . ."

"Mr. Sefton." Colonel Davis withdrew a morocco-leather memorandum-book from his pocket as he approached. "I understand you claim to have been playing the violin on deck after you left the Saloon?"

"At the time I hoped I wouldn't waken anyone," sighed Hannibal. "Now I wish that I had. My man Benjamin has pointed out that Weems probably went overboard after we crossed over that bar at eleven—providing us with a *terminus ad quem,* anyway."

"More than that." The young planter consulted his notes, a nervous tic pulling sharply at the left side of his face. "According to Mr. Souter, the rudder was dragging and pulling shortly before midnight, as it does when it's picked up a branch. Mr. Molloy was just getting ready to come off watch when it happened, and cursed at it, Mr. Souter says. When Souter took over the wheel, he felt it, and whatever it was, it pulled loose in about an hour."

January shivered. The man might well have ruined him—and hundreds of other investors—walking away without a thought to the lives he was wrecking. . . . But it was still a horrible way to die. Even in the deserts of Algeria, a thief would lose a hand, not his life.

"Mr. Weems left supper early," Davis went on, glancing at Hannibal, whether for reaction or confirmation January could not guess. "Almost as soon as dessert was served . . ."

"And I stayed on," pointed out Hannibal, "to entertain the company as usual after supper was over—not wishing to play the despot, I did not demand Ben accompany me after the day he'd had. If you recall, I was continuously in the Saloon from supper until well after midnight, engaged with either music or cards."

"Yes," agreed Davis, "yes, of course. As for where Mr. Weems was . . ."

"Begging your pardon, sir." Thucydides turned from preparation of a pot of tea for the ladies breakfasting in the Parlor, setting the enormous japanned tray down. "I don't know where Mr. Weems was the whole of that time, sir, but I met him on the upper starboard promenade, outside the gentlemen's staterooms, just after ten o'clock. He was standing outside a stateroom, trying to unlock the door, I thought. I spoke to him, not meaning disrespect, but thinking he'd mistaken the room, for his stateroom is the first one at the bow end of the boat, and he was trying to unlock one down at the stern end. But he turned away fast and went off down the promenade to the stern without speaking."

"You're sure it was he?"

The steward nodded gravely. "I saw his face clear in the light of the lantern he carried, though it was black foggy."

Davis frowned. "Now, why would he have mistaken which end of the boat his stateroom was on? Unless he was intoxicated, and I have never seen him so—though of course if he was, it might explain his falling accidentally over the rail."

"A man would have to be more intoxicated than liquor could make him," mused January, "to go over the railings of either the upper deck or the lower . . . sir," he remembered to add, hoping Davis wasn't a stickler for servants not speaking unless and until spoken to. And when the planter only furrowed his brow inquiringly, he went on. "Those railings are nearly elbow-high, and the upper-deck promenades are narrow—three feet, I think, from the wall to the railing. A man falling backwards against the rail *might* flip over it if he hit it with sufficient force, but his feet would almost certainly strike the wall and catch him.

"And the fact is, sir, though I don't know why Weems was trying to get into one of the staterooms at the stern end of the promenade, I think he tried to get into more than one." And he recounted the attempted intrusion into Hannibal's stateroom, ending with: "That was just about at eleven, because I heard the leadsmen calling out as the boat was coming up to the bar."

Davis glanced sharply at Thucydides—who very properly kept his eyes lowered from the white man's gaze—then at January. "And where is your master's stateroom in relation to the stern end of the promenade?"

"Third from the end," said January. "Sir."

"The last four are Mr. Lundy's, Mr. Sefton's, Mr. Cain's, and Mr. Molloy's, sir," provided Thu.

"I expect the lock-faces would bear some sign of it," said Hannibal as the steward left the Saloon with his enormous tea-tray in hand, "if the locks of those staterooms had been picked or forced, unless Mr. Weems was extremely adept at what he was doing." With considerable deliberation he poured the rest of his sherry-and-laudanum back into the flask and worked the cork back in. "Even if my protestations of innocence are out of order—and I do bear letters from Vice-President Hubert Granville of the Bank of Louisiana on the subject of Mr. Weems's theft of quite a substantial sum of the Bank's specie—I wonder if perhaps my man here could take a look at the body? He used to work for a surgeon—I think he's probably the best-trained medical observer on board."

"Is he, indeed?" The Colonel's pale gaze raked up and down January as if comparing his height and size with his hands—which did not have the knotted tendons and swollen joints of a field-worker's—and his air of calm self-confidence. Then, "So you do admit to being sent by the Bank of Louisiana?"

"I was, yes, sir," replied Hannibal. "To recover the Bank's specie—which I have no proof whatsoever that Weems took. But Weems's actions—and those of the woman he's been pretending not to know for the past week and who now claims herself as his fiancée—aren't those of a man with a clear conscience."

"No. But they may be those of a man who knows himself to be unjustly persecuted. Mr. Tredgold?" Davis turned to beckon the *Silver Moon*'s owner. Tredgold had returned to the card-table and was pouring a shot of brandy into his coffee with the air of a man who really needs it. "Will you accompany us to view the body?"

"Er . . . please," replied Tredgold, fumbling a key-ring from his coat-pocket and selecting from it a stateroom key. He looked pale around the mouth beneath his drooping mustache. "I leave the matter entirely in your hands."

With a gratified air young Colonel Davis strode from the Saloon, January and Hannibal trailing at his heels.

The door to Weems's stateroom was closed, but when Davis fitted the key into the lock, January heard sharp movement inside, followed at once by Diana Fischer's unmistakable voice. "Who's there . . . ?"

Davis opened the door to reveal the woman kneeling beside the bunk. The soaked bedclothes were dragged back and the thin mattress wrenched awry. Weems's body lay on the floor in the corner, bundled awkwardly on one side with its unbuttoned clothing half pulled off it.

Mrs. Fischer scrambled to her feet, her face first pale, then flushing red. "What is the meaning of this outrage?" She strode toward Davis like an avenging harpy, and seized him by his lapels. "I come here to pay a final farewell, to sit for a time beside my poor beloved's body, to look once more into his poor face. . . ."

Her voice caught in a sob, though her eyes bore no sign of either tears or swelling and her nose was decidedly un-red. "And what do I find? Those animals, those vile murderers have been in here! Look at what they have done!" She released Davis's lapel long enough to sweep her hand at Hannibal, and at January, who was taking note of the fact that the front of her dress was splotched with dampness across the hips, where she would have levered a sodden body off the bed.

"I'm afraid you must hold us excused, m'am." Hannibal politely removed his hat. "Since your affianced husband was brought here, my man and I were either in the presence of Colonel Davis, or that of some of the deck-passengers—"

"That yellow hussy?" She spat the words in her contempt.

Davis said nothing.

"Then there is more happening aboard this accursed vessel than meets the eye!" She pressed the back of her hand to her forehead, with the appearance of a woman about to crumple in a faint. "For when I came into this room it was as you see it, *desecrated*! Well might you imagine my horror, my outrage . . ."

While she trumpted her horror and outrage, January looked around the tiny stateroom. Under Weems's half-stripped body the straw matting of the floor was rumpled and twisted, as if it, too, had been taken hastily up, section by section. The dead bank manager's portmanteau and valise were open and their contents hastily jammed back or lying strewn around. Davis's eyes narrowed and his tic twitched again. "The room has been searched," he said.

With that grasp of the obvious, thought January, *you'll go far in politics. Sir.*

With some difficulty they persuaded Mrs. Fischer to leave, Hannibal going to fetch Sophie and returning, not only with the young maid—her face streaked with tears of sympathy for a grief her mistress clearly was far from feeling—but with January's small surgical kit. Outside, the thunder clouds of a summer storm were gathering and the water was growing choppy; when Sophie helped Mrs. Fischer from the room, Davis lit both lamps and brought them close to the bed.

"Did Mrs. Fischer have a key to the stateroom?" asked Hannibal, going to the corpse.

"Thu would know. Sir." January held up his hand, and instead of going at once to lift Weems back onto the bunk, he knelt, and examined the seams of the mattress, thoroughly fingered the wet pillow for anomalous lumps or shapes, and held one of the lamps low to get a close look at every crack and crevice of the wooden frame. That done—and nothing discovered—he handed the lamp back to Colonel Davis and helped Hannibal manhandle the body onto the bed.

Most of Oliver Weems's bones had been broken by the action of the rudder and the paddle in which his body had been entangled—his left arm, when January gently disentangled the shirt and coat from the torso, proved to have been almost torn off. Because of its long submersion there was very little blood left in the veins. The head and neck were board-stiff, but it was impossible to tell how many of the other joints would have been so had the body lain undisturbed.

"Which doesn't tell us anything, really," he said, glancing back over his shoulder at Davis as he gently probed at the joints. "Rigor can set in as soon as three hours after death if the body's undisturbed and warm, but in water it would be delayed."

There were at least four places where the skull gave sickeningly to pressure. January supposed he should be grateful that the head hadn't been torn entirely off. There were no gashes or stabs, and the hands were unmarked by defensive wounds.

As his hands turned the mud-sodden cloth of coat, shirt, trouser-band, January noticed how some of the buttons had been nearly ripped from their holes, while others were whole, as if neatly unfastened by searching fingers. But why search? he wondered. Anything in his pockets she could have easily claimed.

Trunk-key? Notes . . . to what?

Had she suspected her confederate of holding something out on her?

Weems's long-tailed coat contained a wallet and about a hundred and fifty dollars, part in Mexican silver, part in notes: Merchants' Consolidated Bank of New Orleans, Forrest's—a private bank in Baton Rouge—Bank of Natchez, and Bank of New Orleans. No Bank of Louisiana.

"So he was not robbed," observed Davis, standing behind January's shoulder with the lamp.

In one pocket January found a pen-knife, the stateroom door-key, and a waterlogged copy of the *Liberator*. Another contained a little tangle of long, stiff shanks like very slender keys, each with a single metal tooth at the end. "Pick-locks," he explained, seeing Davis's baffled face. "Burglars' tools."

"Not surprising," commented Hannibal, leaning in the open doorway of the stateroom and watching the first spits of rain slant down onto the river. "On my quest for Sophie just now I paused long enough to look at the doors of the other staterooms on this side. All of them were scratched around the keyholes, not just the last four. Fresh scratches, since the last time they were polished."

Before lifting Weems onto the bunk, January and Hannibal had pulled off the bedding, laying the body instead on the pulled-up sections of the floor's straw matting. Now January opened his surgical kit, and with Davis hunkering near to watch in businesslike fascination—and Hannibal keeping his face averted as he held the lamps close—January made an incision under the curve of Weems's ribs and gently detached and drew out the dead man's right lung. There was no water to be found in the rubbery pink mass of rough-textured globules; no mud, and no sand.

"He didn't drown, then," he said, and handed Davis his magnifying lens so that he could look for himself. "He was dead when he went in, almost certainly from one of those skull fractures."

"But nothing to indicate how long he was in the water?"

January shook his head. "But in addition to Mr. Souter's testimony about the rudder, both the newspaper and the money from his pocket look like they've been submerged for closer to eight hours than four."

Since Weems's jaw and neck muscles were frozen into immobility, January had to cut into the esophagus rather than probe down it with a swab. There was neither water nor sand there, though there was both mud and sand in the nostrils.

He replaced the organ in the body and bound the incision with knotted handkerchiefs taken from one of the rifled drawers, then washed his hands in the dresser ewer, and even remembered to walk out onto the promenade and dump the water overside himself rather than hand it to Hannibal to do. Though Davis was clearly a man who respected his slaves and treated them well, January wasn't sure how the Colonel would react to the news that a man he'd been initially told was a slave was in fact a free black surgeon, or how discreet the man would be with such information. With the slave revolts of the past five years still burning in memory, and with the rise of both the *Liberator* and the Underground Railway, more and more men in the South were coming to distrust free blacks as fomenters of rebellion—if not actively, then by the very difference between their state and that of the slaves around them.

And slavery, January had found—as any number of ancient Roman comic playwrights had found before him—was a camouflage that caused men to act and speak with less guardedness than if they thought themselves in the presence of an equal.

When he came back into the stateroom, Davis had covered Weems's body to the neck, and was folding up the wet and muddy garments. Hannibal sat crosslegged with Weems's portmanteau in his lap, its contents heaped beside him on the floor while he probed and felt around the lining for either a hidden pocket or the ripped-open remains of one.

The Colonel set down the clothes and said, "It sounds as though Mr. Weems died shortly before midnight. Or shortly after."

"I'd say so." January knelt by the bunk and tucked Weems's protruding hand back under the sheet, pausing as he did so to feel the joints of the fingers. On the right hand they were stiff down to the wrist. On the left, the arm that had been caught in something, the joints of all but the smallest had been broken. That smallest finger was also locked in rigor.

"Then perhaps we had best find out," said Colonel Davis, still turning the pick-locks over in his hands, "where Mr. Weems's enemies—whoever they might have been—were at that time."

THIRTEEN

Immediately upon their return to the Saloon, Davis sent for Mr. Souter from the pilot-house. "It's next to useless dealing with that arrogant boor Molloy," remarked the Colonel, and January wondered if Molloy had seen Miss Skippen's attempts to claim the young widower's attention with dropped handkerchiefs and worshipful gazes.

By this time rain was hammering down in earnest, churning the brown water with fluttering white-edged waves. All the male cabin passengers had sought shelter in the long, gloomy room, drinking coffee or whiskey as their natures dictated, and playing cards. The sole exception was Mr. Quince. He as usual remained as a guest in the Ladies' Parlor, entertaining them—if the word could be used—with his views on Vegetarianism and the organization of the spiritual hierarchies.

Passing the open door of that small chamber, January felt a pang of sympathy for Miss Skippen, who sat in a corner by the window, gazing bleakly out at the rain, clearly bored to sobs. Mr. Quince, finding the company of his own sex unbearable and vice versa, had the option of ingratiating himself with Mrs. Tredgold and being invited to hold court among the ladies. For a woman to spend the day in the

Main Saloon chatting with the men would have marked her as inerasably as if she'd sewn a scarlet A on her dress.

At least she had a dry room to sit in, thought January. Most of his pity went to Rose, sheltering among the wood-piles, and to the chained slaves and to the immigrant women huddled with their children in the doubtful cover of the bow. It did not, of course, occur to Mrs. Tredgold or anyone else to extend an invitation to them to come up and stay dry.

Nick the barkeep lit the whale-oil lamps in the Saloon, and the men pretended to talk or play cards. But the planters Roberson and Lockhart, the two slave-dealers, and the New Englander Dodd all kept glancing up from their cards or their newspapers at the corner table where Davis established his headquarters.

At least, reflected January, they'd all be in one place to be questioned.

"Molloy cursed somethin' wonderful," asserted the junior pilot in response to Davis's question. "Went on for five minutes about unprintable expletive-deleted branches from trees that'd grown out of the Devil's toenails—although *toenails* might not have been the word he used—snaggin' up his rudder, and how if he had his way he'd turn crews of niggers loose on the banks to shave 'em to the ground five miles on either side, and him pullin' and wrestlin' with the wheel all the time, with the smoke of his cigar rollin' around his head like Satan's own breath."

The young man chuckled, fresh-faced, long-jawed, and rather plump, with big dark eyes under long lashes, a bit like a friendly cow. "Not much trash in the river when she's low like she was last night, but now and then you'll get branches and leaves caught up on a snag. When I took over the wheel I could see what he meant, and it was a struggle, keeping to the center of the channel and easing off 'round the bends where she gets strong. . . . Even in low water she can be strong around Magna Vista Point. And it was blind foggy. Couldn't see hardly down to the nose of the boat."

"When did the rudder snag, do you know?" asked Davis. "How soon before Molloy went off at midnight?"

"Fairly soon. I came in maybe fifteen, twenty minutes of midnight, just as we come opposite Ulee's wood-yard, and it was maybe five-ten minutes after that."

"If it was blind foggy," asked Davis, curious, "how do you know you were opposite Mr. Ulee's wood-yard?"

"Oh, there's an eddy backs under the point just below the yard," replied Souter. "Even in low water you can feel her."

"Surely there are other eddies along the shore?"

" 'Course there are! But they all feel a tad different—you can tell the voices of one of your niggers from another in the dark, can't you? Well, I can feel the difference in the way she pulls, between that little eddy under Ulee's yard and, for instance, that cantankersome bull-bitch you got under Dead Man's Bend, for God's sake. Besides, where else would I be, that time of night? I'd just heard old Fergusson's dogs barking when we passed his place, we'd made the crossing over Magna Vista, so where the hell else would I be gettin' a little eddy 'cept opposite Ulee's?"

Lightning flared, a white explosion in all the high clerestories of the Saloon; thunder cracked like the sky splitting. Souter listened, then nodded approvingly. "About time we got a rise. Be a hell of a lot of trash in the stream, but the rise'll be a help."

"Did you hear anything?" asked Davis. "You say you heard dogs barking on the bank. . . ."

" 'Bout a mile and a half the other side of the levee, actually," corrected Souter. "Fergusson has this mastiff bitch, you see, name of Penelope. . . ."

"If you heard dogs barking a mile and a half away," persisted Davis, "it must have been a very still night. Did you hear voices on the deck? Or the sound of argument?"

Souter frowned, then shook his head. "Oh, I heard those deck-passengers, laughin' and tellin' jokes as they played cards as I came up the stairs, and a nigger gal singin' to her pickaninny. . . . Say, it's been twenty years since I heard 'House Carpenter.' My Grandma used to play it on her cheeks, slappin' her own face and making mouths to change the pitch. . . ."

"When did Weems leave dinner?" asked January softly, leaning down to where Hannibal sat at the other side of the table.

"Almost before the pudding was served." The fiddler scratched a corner of his gray-flecked mustache. "And he was fidgeting throughout it like a fly in a tar-box. Mrs. Fischer was most insistent that I stay and play for them—one would almost think she'd forgotten about swearing out a warrant for my arrest in Natchez. She was overpoweringly gracious, and exerted her charms on every man at table, I think, to get them to stay on as well. I didn't think much of it at the time—well, in fact I suspected she'd had a falling-out with Weems—but now I realize she must have been trying to keep as many people as possible in the Saloon while Weems searched their staterooms."

"That's what it sounds like." January turned his head at the drawling whine of Ned Gleet's voice.

"I was here till about two, weren't we, Jubal?" The two slave-dealers had taken Souter's place in front of Davis's table. "Us and Byrne . . ." Gleet nodded in the direction of the gambler, who was dealing a game of whist for Roberson, Lockhart, and Dodd, none of whom had apparently learned his lesson yet about playing with the so-called "dry-goods importer," who invariably seemed to win.

"Davis played until one," supplied Hannibal in an undervoice. "Gleet proposed the game—he usually does—and as usual insisted that I play. As usual I dumped most of the liquor he plied me with into the spittoon. After several hours heaving at a capstan, I assure you it was not easy, but the last thing you'd need after the day you had yesterday was to wake up this morning and be told I'd lost you to Gleet at vingt-et-un."

"Thank you," said January dryly.

"They played vingt-et-un, all-fours, short whist and ecarte, turn and turn about—Byrne won most of the money but not so much as to be pointed at. *Si possis recte, si non, quicumque modo rem.* Gleet and Cain left together twice to check on their slaves, and were together the whole of that time. The rest of us played short whist in their absence. Roberson, Lockhart, and Davis left once apiece, to piss over the side—at least that's what they said they were going to do, and they were back quickly enough to have done no more unless they were very speedy murderers indeed. Molloy came in about twelve-thirty for a drink and a hand of whist, then left, presumably, for the perfumed delights of Miss Skippen's bower—that was just before one. Davis played another hand and left just after one, and I left just after that."

A tremendous flash of lightning illuminated the windows; rain pounded down as if the *Silver Moon* were passing under a waterfall. In the door of the Saloon Souter rubbed his hands together and reported, "Plenty of water now!" in a pleased voice, and trotted down the hall and outside, presumably to observe the effects of the rise on every sand-bar and point within view.

"What I'm curious about," went on Hannibal, "is what Weems was searching for in everyone's staterooms. A hundred thousand dollars in gold—not to mention Bank of Pennsylvania notes and all the rest of it—isn't something you tuck in the back of your glove drawer. Even if the trunks that contained it were stolen and hidden somewhere during the upheaval with the luggage, surely a glance through the stateroom window would have sufficed to tell him whether they were in the room or not. None of those bunks is big enough to conceal a hatbox under, let alone a trunk."

"Which means the specie was taken out of the trunk," said January. "Was there time for that?"

"Oh, I think so." The fiddler's eyes narrowed as he mentally reviewed the events of the previous afternoon. "But probably only just. When the boat hung up on Horsehead Bar, there was about an hour of driving and heaving as Molloy tried to bull through, when anyone on board could see that we were going to have to unload and spar over. Afterwards Molloy turned the pilot-house over to poor Souter, and directed the deck-hands to start unloading. But he had plenty of time to come and go from the hold, pretty much unobserved in the confusion. I'm not sure how much gold he could have emptied from trunks, but it could have been transferred to sacks—God knows there are plenty of pillow-cases in the linen-room and flour-sacks in the galley—and stowed to be moved later, or simply transferred to a crate or box with his own labels on it. Molloy's certainly the only one who could have done it unobserved."

January grunted thoughtfully. "I wonder if Weems knew that."

At Davis's table, Kyle Outliver—even more verminous and bedraggled-looking than when he'd tried to lift Sophie's skirts a week earlier—was explaining that most of his fellow deck-passengers had been awake playing cards. . . . No, they didn't know what time they'd quit, but it was before the boat had gone over the bar. No, all the boys wasn't together playing all that time. Some of 'em crawled off to sleep behind the crates, or to have a smoke or take a piss or whatever—it wasn't his look-out what they did. Who'd played? Him and Sam Pawk and Cupid and Billy Earthquake most of the time. . . . No, they hadn't heard nuthin', 'cept Johnny Funk's snorin'. . . .

"An' you fartin' ever' time Cupid took money off you," retorted Johnny Funk, a bear-like man with one ear bitten off.

"Either Weems didn't figure it out," said Hannibal quietly, "or he had some information that we don't."

Leaving Hannibal to follow the proceedings as Davis systematically questioned the deck-passengers—who seemed to have mostly gotten drunk and fallen asleep before midnight, as usual—January descended to the lower promenade to look for Rose. He found the niches among the sheltered wood-piles empty—niches considerably enlarged now because of the amount of wood burned at Vicksburg and Horsehead Bar—for all the inhabitants of the stern were bunched along the starboard rail among the male slaves, watching while Mr. Molloy rowed the skiff away toward what looked like a murky, bubbling tributary stream that broke the wall of trees.

"He ain't really gonna try and take this boat through there, is he,

'Rodus?" asked a boy in Gleet's coffle of the tall, slim Fulani who stood at his side.

" 'S'a matter, Lam?" joked an older man to whom the boy was chained. "You ain't anxious to get to Memphis?"

"We could probably do it." 'Rodus narrowed his eyes to watch the skiff maneuver through the sluicing curtains of rain. "See what he got there, that rope with the markers on it? That's a lead-line, to measure how deep the water is back there."

"That's the thing he didn't use yesterday tryin' to run over that bar," added Mr. Roberson's white-haired valet Winslow, and everybody laughed.

"What's goin' on up there, Michie Ben?" asked 'Rodus as January moved along the rail to search for Rose among the spectators. "They figure out anythin' yet about that poor buckra that went overside?"

And January heard in the young man's voice the false note of assumed casualness. Well hidden, of course—*blankittes* were always complaining that slaves were habitual liars, not seeming to make the connection between the necessity to tell whites what they wanted to hear and the fact that whites could flog or sell the speaker if they didn't like what they heard. As a child, January, with his open and innocent face, had been the champion liar on Bellefleur—something that hadn't saved him when old Michie Simon went on a tear with the rawhide.

Now he scanned the faces of the men chained along the wall, and he saw in all of them a wary and desperate interest.

He said quite quietly, "Colonel Davis askin' questions. I think he means to question everybody on board, probably you included."

"Us?" The boy Lam looked scared, and put a protective arm around the younger brother chained at his side. "Why us?"

"What would a dressed-up buckra like Weems be doin' down here that time of night?" asked 'Rodus in a tone of such complete calm naturalness that January would have bet money they'd seen something, knew something.

And with an almost audible click, like the sound of a key in a lock, he heard Souter's voice again: *a nigger gal singin' to her pickaninny . . .*

Every night, the voices of the male slaves had risen in song. Desultory, sometimes, or joyful; sometimes the familiar call and response of work songs. He'd heard them himself as he slid into sleep last night. . . .

So why not at midnight, when Souter had gone up to the pilothouse?

Why had the men on the starboard side fallen silent, while the women continued to sing?

But he only shook his head. "They know he was dead when he went in the water," he replied, and saw the glance go back and forth among the men. "Somebody smashed him over the head."

The men around were silent. In the to-and-fro of their eyes he could almost hear the words: *How'd they know? How much do they know? What's it gonna mean for us?*

"He tell 'em?" asked 'Rodus mildly, but before January could answer, Mr. Lundy appeared at the bow end of the promenade and flourished his cane at the cluster of servants and deck-hands watching Molloy in the skiff.

"God damn the lot of you, trim the boat! What do you think you're looking at? Trim the damn boat before we get in more trouble—how do you expect a body to steer with all the weight on one side? Haven't you anything better to do than gape?"

"Oh, 'scuse me, sir," murmured 'Rodus too low for the former pilot to hear. "I'll just move on upstairs into the Saloon for a few hands of ecarte." And the men on either side of him, including January, snickered. The servants moved obediently on their way, some of them as usual pointedly ignoring the slaves chained along the wall—as if they themselves couldn't just as easily end up in the same situation next week—and others exchanging nods with them. January wondered how much the valets might have heard, or guessed, of what had happened on the other side of the piled cordwood, and whether he could ask questions without engendering suspicion.

"Man's an idiot." Lundy tottered over to January's side. "Claims we can cut half a day off our time by going through Hitchins' Chute—high water be damned, you couldn't drown a cat in that chute!" The former pilot looked exhausted, hollow-eyed with strain as he glared out across the threshing water with its floating masses of downed trees, broken lumber, and torn-off branches.

Across the narrow stretch January could see Molloy standing in the skiff, dropping the lead-line overboard, then pulling it back. What he found must have satisfied him, for he rowed on a ways, almost invisible now between the rain and the intervening boughs.

"Looks deep enough to me, sir," commented January, folding his arms. The thunder had ceased, save for ever more distant rumblings over the Mississippi bluffs. "Why's he in such a hurry all of a sudden?"

"Well, we lost most of a day yesterday." Lundy's mouth twisted sourly. "More hurry, less speed, I say. River's gonna fall the minute the rain lets up and we'll be stuck in the chute waiting for Levi Christmas and his boys to show up. Molloy threatened to cane me when I told him what that girl of his had been up to in Natchez—like I couldn't have taken on that Gaelic drunkard with one hand behind me, before the palsy caught up with me! But the first thing he did when we got ourselves stuck good was to get every man-jack armed and on the deck, watching the shore. He knows." Lundy shook his head, and unslung his spyglass from his side.

After a moment of silent scanning he offered it to January, who took it and followed the far-off figure in the skiff until it disappeared behind the trees. Down at the stern the paddle was turning slowly, more to keep water in the boilers than anything else. With the strength of the storm-fed current the *Silver Moon* was almost literally standing where she was in the water.

"How did the boat get hung up on Horsehead Bar to begin with, sir?" January folded up and returned the glass. "Souter seems to know his business better than that."

"Souter?" Lundy sniffed. "If Molloy told Souter to stand on his head bare-naked in the Saloon, he'd do it. Mind you, anyone can run on a bar—in high water they build up fast. But it wasn't high water. The boy knew damn well there was a bar below Steele's Bayou, but Molloy told him to shave the bank close and shave it he did, and everyone on board got to rassle spars until nightfall because of it."

"Is that what happened?"

"It's what Souter says. He was near in tears about it when I talked to him on the bow that afternoon and asked him what the hell he meant by shaving the bank that close. Molloy came down the stairs and slapped him on the shoulder and says, *'You shouldn't go believin' everythin' you're told, boy. . . .'* " Despite the crippled soft monotone of his voice, Lundy captured the Irishman's speech with blistering scorn. "It's my opinion Molloy did it just to break the boy's spirit a little and keep him under his thumb."

The white triangular sail of the skiff winked from among the trees, tacking before the brisk gusts back toward the *Silver Moon*. Molloy's oilskin coat and wide-brimmed hat were running with rain, but he looked cheerful and stood up in the skiff to shout, "Plenty of water in the chute, laddies!"

"Oh, the hell there is!" Lundy limped over to the pilot as the deckhands crowded forward to draw the skiff close to the bow and help Molloy spring aboard. January saw the older man gesture furiously, pointing toward the gap in the trees as the *Silver Moon* came slowly around and pointed her nose to the chute.

Because of the palsy, Lundy's buzzing, timbreless voice was inaudible over the rain and the paddle's splashing, but Molloy's reply boomed out arrogantly.

"What's the matter, man? You can't run a boat in ten feet of water? I thought you were the one with the hard-on to get to Lexington—in a manner of speaking," he added, and strode on up the stair with a jeering laugh.

Lundy clung for a moment to the stanchion as if all strength had deserted him. But as January came forward to help him, the former pilot pushed himself away and moved, with surprising agility, up the stair as well.

"What causes it?" asked Rose's voice softly behind him. January turned to see her looking after the old pilot with compassionate eyes. "Palsy, I mean."

"They don't know." January went to take her in his arms, to press her to the thin boards of the wall through which the throb of the engines beat like a heart. To press his lips over hers, as the touch of her, the scent of her—even after a week unwashed in the heat on a steamboat's deck—aroused in him the desire to pull her behind the woodpiles and crates and have her on the bare deck like a savage, a Kaintuck, a rapist.

I feared I would never see you again.

He realized how often this was his fear when something separated them, when something went wrong.

"We wouldn't have left you, you know," Rose said after that long, wordless time of silent rocking in one another's arms. Of silent thanks to God and the Virgin that in spite of Queen Régine's curse and every effort by the world in general to the contrary, the ultimate thing was still all right. She was still with him.

"I don't think I've ever felt so relieved in my life as when I saw you coming down the bank," she went on. "Hannibal and I were watching for you, of course—Mr. Lundy told us Steele's Bayou was the likeliest place you'd make for."

His lips brushed the feather-soft curls that emerged from beneath the edge of her tignon. "Don't tell me you were the one who actually got poor Souter to run the boat up on the bar."

"Nonsense." Her smile was a quick sunflash, quickly tucked away. "If we hadn't run aground on that bar, Hannibal was going to light a small fire in the cordwood near the engine-door just as we came within sight of Steele's Bayou so that I could slip in and dump the boilers in the confusion."

January sighed. "It's good to know I have ingenious friends. Where was Lundy last night, by the way? I'll have to ask Hannibal what time he left the Saloon after dinner."

"You don't suspect poor Mr. Lundy of heaving Weems overboard, do you? Why would he? I'd say it would be Mr. Molloy, if anybody. Or that cold savage, Cain."

"Except that Molloy was in the pilot-house when it happened," said January. "And Cain appears to have been continuously in the company of others—either the other card-players or Gleet—between nine-thirty and one. And I suppose," he added thoughtfully, "if I were being suspicious, I'd find that in itself suspicious . . . because as far as I've seen, Cain can't stand Gleet. But it doesn't alter the fact that he couldn't have hit Weems over the head and dumped his body overboard at eleven-thirty—which is what seems to have happened."

And he recounted to her, briefly, the results of his makeshift autopsy, and Hannibal's account of events in the Saloon the previous night. "Which makes nonsense of Mrs. Fischer's accusation, of Hannibal at least," he concluded. "In fact with both Molloy and Cain accounted for, the murder could have been committed by anyone on board, including Mrs. Fischer herself. She's certainly tall enough and strong enough to have killed a man with a sharp blow over the head, especially one who had no reason to be wary of her. And in fact, we know almost nothing about anyone on board, including such ostensible innocents as Lundy and Quince."

While he spoke, the *Silver Moon* had drawn closer to the fast-racing waters of Hitchins' Chute. Seven or eight deck-hands clambered down into the skiff, rowing across to the steep clay banks among the willows. Four sprang ashore on one side of the chute's mouth; the rest took the skiff across the fifty or sixty feet of water to the other. There they waited, with the long poles they'd brought with them in hand, for the steamboat to approach and be nudged into the narrow passageway.

Meantime the rain was lightening, till by the time the *Silver Moon* was fairly into the chute it was barely a patter. Though the current of the main river still surged with trees, limbs, scraps of sawn lumber or dead animals, the force of the stream was noticeably lessened. January could see where the wash-line on the banks already stood several feet above the surface.

Overhanging boughs swept the arcades of the boiler-deck above, and slapped at the stanchions only feet from where January and Rose stood by the passway. The male slaves pointed and commented about the suddenly-close scenery—the boys Lam and Jeremiah moved out to the end of their chains to lean over, to catch at the dripping leaves that whipped in under the arcades, and overhead January heard Melissa Tredgold scream, "I want to see! *I want to see!*"

No doubt while she tried to drag the unwilling Cissy over to the edge to let her do the same.

"No, you're right." Rose leaned against January's side, rested her head on his shoulder. With his palm on her back he felt the tension in her slender body ease. "We don't know a thing about anyone on board except what they've told us. My guess is that Lundy was in bed. Sufferers from his ailment don't have much stamina. He told me once he has to lie down every few hours. He was the *Silver Moon*'s original pilot, the one Molloy undercut. He took on the job because he has to get to Lexington, Kentucky—Tredgold is a friend of his and agreed to let him work, since he desperately needs the money. Because Tredgold reneged and hired Molloy, he's letting Lundy ride for free—though to my mind it's a high price, to put up with Molloy's abuse. There's evidently a professor at the medical school there who can help nervous disorders of this kind."

"Did he say what his name is?" January felt a twinge of chagrin, like a twist in the muscle beneath his breastbone, at the reflection that it had been months since he'd had time to read the issues of *The Lancet* so dutifully stacking up in the small study at the back of the new house. He'd been conscious, as he'd examined Weems's body, of how long it had been since he'd done any serious medical work at all. Though the circumstances had appalled him—and though he felt pity for that sly, weasely little man—he had also felt all his old delight and wonderment at the tiny structures of the human body, the sense of probing into some of God's more mysterious and beautiful secrets.

"Burnham? Barham?" Rose shook her head. "I can't recall exactly."

"The name isn't familiar. I'll have to ask. But one thing I do know.

Whoever did the murder, I'd be willing to bet—if I had any money of my own to bet with—that it took place either on the starboard promenade of the boiler-deck, or more probably on the starboard promenade of the main deck. And that dark as it was, at least some of the slaves saw it."

FOURTEEN

"Herodotus." Colonel Davis's sharp voice sounded calm and firm, and as January and Rose looked around the corner of the 'tween-decks, the young Fulani rose to meet the tall, black-clothed planter.

"Yes, sir."

Behind Davis, Cain watched with folded arms and Gleet spat tobacco onto the deck. In the presence of the dealers the men chained along the wall moved together as much as they could.

One never knew, with *les blankittes,* thought January.

Even if one hadn't—almost certainly—witnessed murder last night.

"Tell me about last night."

'Rodus sighed. "I wish I could, sir. Believe me, I asked among the boys here if they heard anything. That poor buckra's got to gone in the water someplace. But I swear to you last night was quiet. We tells stories some, like we always does—I thought I'd split laughin' over one old guy told 'bout the three mice in the barroom—an' sang some, just to keep our spirits up in the dark. Sound carries funny in the fog, as you'll know, sir. We heard voices now an' then from above, when folks went along to their cabins, but we didn't hear no shoutin' nor angry voices. Not like there'd been a fight or nuthin'."

"You lyin' nigger." Gleet's rawhide riding-crop lashed out like a lizard's tongue, striking 'Rodus on the muscle of his bare arm. The slave flinched, his dark eyes going to Cain for an instant, then back to the deck, where all good slaves' eyes belonged. "Colonel Davis talked to every man on the bow-deck an' to his own man that was sleepin' just aft of you lot, an' they saw nor heard shit. So it got to be one of you that did it—one of you, or one of the bitches over the other side of the boat. Now, you tell what you saw or I'll thrash the skin off every one of you."

"You treat your own niggers as you please, Ned." Cain removed his cigar from his mouth and blew a thread of smoke like an unspoken line of scorn. "Myself, I ain't fixin' to try and explain no hashed-up backs to buyers in Memphis. What the hell would Weems be doin' down here, anyway? He was your milk-and-water Abolitionist: he'd cry big tears about niggers bein' treated bad, but he didn't want to be around 'em."

At the threat of beating, January had watched the faces of the men, especially the two boys Lam and Jeremiah. He saw not only the fear there, but the way they'd all, even the members of Gleet's coffle, turned toward 'Rodus, as if for some sign. As if last night—January could almost see it in his mind—'Rodus had said, *You all keep silent, and leave the talking to me.*

Davis, of course, had looked back to Cain and Gleet during the altercation. As white men, they were the ones who had the power to do or change things. It was their words that mattered. Turning back to 'Rodus, he said, "As you say, 'Rodus, Mr. Weems has to have gone into the water somewhere. If he fell—or was thrown—from the promenade deck overhead, he would have made a considerable splash."

"It's what I thought myself, sir," agreed the slave. "But here with the engine-room so close, an' the paddle threshin' so loud, you don't hear much and that's a fact."

"I thought I'd heard smooth customers teaching girls' school," remarked Rose softly as Thu came past them from the stern stairway and made his way along to the three white men. "But I think he takes the biscuit for butter not melting in his mouth."

Whatever Thu told them, in a voice too quiet to carry, Gleet, Cain, and Davis turned and headed for the bow. The steward lingered for a moment to exchange a word with 'Rodus before coming back along the promenade to the stairway at the stern, and January saw again, in the rainy grayness, the steward's narrow, almost girlish face settle into age and strength when relaxed from its habitual cheerful smile. Face-to-face there was no mistaking the resemblance.

January glanced down at Rose, and met her eyes, which had followed his gaze. She raised her eyebrows: "Is that my imagination?" she asked, and January shook his head. "Do you think Cain knows?"

"He'd have to be a fool not to notice how alike they look," answered January. "And whatever else he is, Jubal Cain isn't a fool. Any other white man, it's even odds whether they'd see it or not—their color's so different, and it always shocks me how little *blankittes* notice. But it might explain why, on a dark and foggy night, Cain made sure he wasn't alone when he came down to see that his slaves were fed."

"*Could* a slave kill a white man walking by?" asked Rose as they retreated through the passway to the port-side promenade. The rain had stopped entirely; the paddle was moving slowly as the banks closed in around the *Silver Moon,* overhanging boughs of oak and tupelo scraping hard on the sides. As January had feared, closed in by the trees the damp heat was ghastly, and away from the main channel of the river the air swarmed with mosquitoes and gnats. "Those chains aren't very long—they have to turn around and lean out to the extent of their arms to relieve their bowels over the river. And that iron must be extremely heavy."

Rose, January realized, had never worn chains.

"You'd be surprised what you can do," he said softly, "if you're really frightened, or really angry."

"But would any of them have been that frightened of—or angry at—Weems? He was a thief, and a blackmailer, but not, as far as I've ever heard, a man of violence. I can't imagine anyone wasting his time trying to blackmail a slave. Not one who has no useful information about a current master, like these. Weems was an Abolitionist, too, at least a milk-and-water one. Why would any of the slaves have attacked him?"

January shook his head. "But they saw something. And two things happened last night: Weems's murder, and Julie's escape."

"Julie." Rose's mouth hardened into a thin line of anger.

"Did you see her go?"

"No," From the bow January could hear the leadsman's shouts: *"Half one! Half one! Quarter less twain . . ."* And hoped that Levi Christmas and his boys had passed them in the night and were at present somewhere on the other side of Hitchins' Point. Looking up, he saw the planter Lockhart at the stern rail of the boiler-deck, rifle in the crook of his arm, silhouetted against the hot summer sky.

"It was dark as Egypt, as they say—you know how fog seems to drink up light, and there wasn't any too much from the deck lantern to begin with. Sophie and Julie came down to share supper with me, after they got their respective mistresses ready for dinner—Julie was just shaking over the prospect of being sold to Gleet."

She ducked as a willow-branch swept over the deck, spattering her with leftover rain. Behind them the paddle slowed, water slithering from its bucket-boards, and the monotonous voice of the leadsman chanted, *"Quarter one . . . quarter one . . ."*

The thick trees seemed to absorb the sound.

"Mark one."

"I don't think she's stopped crying since we left Vicksburg," Rose went on. "And that nasty little hussy Skippen boxed her ears for it. Julie spoke of running away, but was terrified—naturally—of being beaten if she were caught and brought back: she has no concept of where Canada is, or even Ohio, nor which states forbid slavery and which permit it. She wasn't even terribly clear which direction north was, only that slaves running away follow the river. She'd been born and raised within five miles of New Orleans: she knows only upstream and down, toward the river or toward the swamp. Not unlike," she added with sudden asperity, "some of the damsels whose mothers bring them to my school. We're stopped."

The paddle hung still. Gleet came down the stern stair, cursing, his whip in one hand and a rifle in the other. Without a glance at them he went through the passway to the starboard promenade where the men were chained. A few moments later deck-hands appeared, unfastening the long boat-poles from the sides of the 'tween-decks.

Mr. Lundy, reflected January, had evidently been right about the chute. "How late in the evening was the last time you saw her?"

"Then," said Rose. "Just before, and during dinner. Cissy came down, too, with the leftover tea-leaves from the children's tea; she got Eli to give us some hot water for a second run. All three of the girls went up together when the waiters came down the stairs from clearing away supper. That meant Mesdames Fischer and Roberson, and Miss Skippen, would be coming out soon, and might need someone to re-pin their hair before they spent the evening listening to music and dancing in the Saloon."

There was a dry note in Rose's voice that made January flinch, though he knew she wasn't angry at him. And he felt again the slow, hot fury, that Mrs. Fischer's scheme should oblige Rose—a woman born in freedom, the daughter of a planter on Grand Isle—to sleep on the bare deck, live on the scraps of white folks' meals, and relieve herself over the side in full view of any stranger passing on the river road or sailing downstream in a flatboat.

No, he thought. *No, we are not free. Having money will help—having a house will help. But it will not make us free.*

She went on. "By then it was foggy and pitch black. Julie usually sleeps with me, and Sophie, when Mrs. Fischer is entertaining Weems—Julie generally comes down at eleven, after getting Miss Skippen ready for bed, but if either of those so-called ladies comes back from the dancing early, she wants her maid waiting right there when she comes in. I heard the leadsmen start calling out as we were coming up on the bar, and Mr. Molloy cursing them from the pilot-house. Just after we crossed over the bar Sophie came down with a blanket, and lay down beside me. I asked, *Is Julie all right?* And she said, *I don't know. I'll tell you in the morning.* I heard her crying a little before she went to sleep."

"And in the morning, of course, the first thing anyone saw was Weems's body. So I take it you haven't had a chance to talk to her?"

Rose shook her head. "Jim saw the body first, and called out, *Dear God, it's a man caught up there!* Sophie was the one who recognized him, and screamed. Simon—he's the head engineer—was sleeping on deck and ran at once into the engine-room to have the engines stopped, and Sophie clutched on to the wood-pile, sobbing. She got herself in hand quickly, though, and said, *Madame! Oh my poor Madame!* and went running up the steps. That's the last I saw of her."

"Julie had better be moving fast," January said. "If the patrols catch her, they'll take her straight to Mayersville. She may, of course, have actually killed Weems—if he caught her going over the rail, for instance, and tried to stop her, though I can't imagine why he would have or what he'd have been doing down on the lower deck at that hour."

"I can't either," agreed Rose. "And I'll still take oath she got off the boat as we were going over the bar. The starboard promenade would be the logical place for her to go into the water unobserved. Her escape may be all they're hiding, you know."

"It may," agreed January. "I can understand Gleet's gang being terrified, but it's harder to believe Cain's gang would be that scared over the accusation of not reporting a runaway."

"If I know Mrs. Fischer, I'll have the perfect opportunity to question Sophie, but at such appalling cost to myself that I hesitate—"

"Benjamin."

January turned, to see Colonel Davis coming down the stern steps. The young planter wore a look of rather grim puzzlement, and the glint in his pale eyes told January instantly that there was trouble.

"Would you mind coming back with me to the Saloon? There are a few questions I need to ask you about where you were last night."

• • •

The Saloon was hot and dim, and nearly empty, now that the rain had stopped and there was activity on shore worth staring at. As he followed Davis up the steps, January saw the deck-hands, and both coffles of male slaves, spreading out along the soaked muddy banks of the chute, shoving with their poles at the sides of the boat in an attempt to back her out before the water sank too far. In the engine-room they'd be drawing the fires out of the furnaces yet again.

Why no one had ever thought to disconnect the water-pumps from the engines and arrange for them to operate independently, January couldn't imagine. He'd suggested it to Rose, and she'd said, "My guess is the owners won't pay for a second engine. You have no idea how cheaply steamboats are built."

Which, to January, sounded exactly like the sort of logic the *blankittes* lived by.

Whatever the reason, Mr. Molloy was pacing the Saloon like a caged tiger, a whiskey-glass in hand and face crimson with anger and impatience. "Where was he?" he demanded as Davis and January came out of the hallway into the Saloon. "Down with his yellow bitch? Any money she'll tell you he was with *her* last night."

January opened his mouth to say, *My wife isn't in the habit of lying,* then closed it again, and made himself look at the floor.

There was something about, *she'll tell you he was with her last night* that brought the hair up on his nape.

As opposed to where?

He glanced across at Hannibal, still sitting at the card-table, and he saw the fiddler was both angry and scared.

Davis said, "Earlier today you told me you were in your master's stateroom all last night, sleeping, except that you woke once when you heard someone trying to force the door. Is that the truth?"

"Yes, sir." January tried to keep the anger out of his own voice. "Maybe I should have gone after the man, but I didn't. It was pitch dark on the promenade and I was dead tired."

"Yet you said you saw him when he opened the door."

"He had a dark lantern, sir, shuttered. I could see there was someone there, but nothing of his face."

"According to Mr. Molloy," said Davis slowly, "when he returned to his stateroom at twelve-thirty, he saw that the door of Mr. Sefton's was ajar. Opening it—concerned lest there be a robbery in progress—he struck a match and found the room empty, though he says he saw your blankets on the floor."

January opened his mouth, and closed it, fury rising like slow combustion through his chest to scald his face. Molloy lounged back against the bar, eyes on January's face, daring him to speak. Daring him to call a white man a liar in the presence of other white men.

Carefully, January said, "I don't know what to say to that, sir. I was in the room, and I was asleep. It wasn't you I saw unless you were out of the pilot-house at eleven, because I heard the leadsmen calling. In any case, the man I saw was small. He didn't fill the door, as you would, sir. Beyond that . . ."

"You telling me that ain't what I saw," asked Molloy, with deadly softness, "boy?"

January took a deep breath and remained silent.

Hannibal said quietly, "Since my bondsman has better manners and more sense than to contradict a white man in this benighted country, *I* am telling you that wasn't what you saw, sir."

Like a pouncing lion, Molloy crossed the distance between the bar and the card-table, dragged Hannibal from his chair by the front of his coat, and drove his fist hard into the fiddler's stomach. Davis was taken by surprise at this sudden violence, so it was January who caught Molloy first, the enraged pilot flinging Hannibal to the floor like a rag and whirling to smash January in the jaw. January staggered—Molloy was nearly his own height and twenty pounds heavier—and checked his own returning blow, braced himself as a second blow took him in the stomach.

Then Davis was pulling Molloy back, and January, gasping a little and with blood trickling from his nose, went to Hannibal's side.

"You're a lyin' goddam Orangeman and a whoremaster!" yelled Molloy, yanking against Davis's grip. "And no nigger lays a hand on me or on any white man while I'm in the room. You tell me I'm not a liar, Sefton, or before God I'll—"

"Mr. Molloy!" shouted Davis with the command in his voice that men achieve when they've governed troops in war. "This is not a barroom, nor is this a question of anyone's honor. This is an investigation of the facts leading to a man's death."

"You know damn-all about it, you pusillanimous little pup! As a son of Ireland I'm not going to sit still for it when a nigger and a pimp of an Orangeman tell the world I didn't see what I saw!" bawled Molloy. "And if there's another word for that besides *liar,* I'd like to hear what it is."

"*Mistaken,* I believe is the word I was groping for." Hannibal struggled to sit up, clinging to January's sleeve and cutting off Davis's furious rejoinder. "I apologize to you profoundly for the anger of the moment in which I spoke. It was my own mistake and I most humbly beg your forgiveness."

Molloy hadn't expected this, and his eyes narrowed with suspicion, but in the face of an apology there wasn't really much he could say.

"In fact," Hannibal went on as January helped him to his feet, "in the near-absolute darkness of the promenade, it isn't surprising you might have made an error in which door you saw ajar. I believe Mr. Cain's stateroom lies next to mine, or Mr. Quince's. . . ."

"Are you after telling me I don't know every foot of my own boat?" Molloy bristled again, like a boar hog about to gore. "It's my goddam business to know every goddam foot of this river by heart, every point and bar and chute of her, and I know which door is which—"

"Of course you would, sir," interrupted Hannibal smoothly, "and without the smallest error, on a vessel you had piloted for more than a single week. All men are liable to error, as the philosopher Locke quite reasonably points out; no man's knowledge may go beyond his experience. But since someone appears to have been trying to force their way into various staterooms along that side of the vessel last night . . ."

"That's your story," retorted Molloy, and turned to Davis. "Sir, you need to remember—and so I'll tell the sheriff at Mayersville—that this man had instructions from his banking board to stop Weems, by whatever means he could, before he could reach the land office in Louisville. Now, I'm not saying they deliberately set out to murder him, but like Mr. Sefton says"—his voice twisted sarcastically over the words—"men are liable to error, specially if you get a big brute like Sefton's boy takin' hold of a runty little specimen like poor Weems."

"I agree absolutely," said Hannibal with such earnestness that Molloy blinked. *"Spurius es, blennus, vervexque et pila foeda."* He turned from the pilot to Davis, who was slack-jawed with shock at what the fiddler had just called Molloy to his face. "It seems to me that matters hinge on Weems's own intentions. It was *his* story, after all, that I was sent by the Bank to stop him from reaching Louisville, and I fear that if Weems *was* a thief, he may also have been a shameless deceiver, hoodwinking even so intelligent and honest a woman as his loyal fiancée into believing his story."

January smiled inwardly—Hannibal seldom missed a stitch in his fabrications. Molloy was turning red with genuine annoyance—as opposed to the manufactured rage by which he'd clearly been trying to provoke Hannibal into challenging him to a duel—but Davis was listening as the fiddler went on.

"Perhaps the best thing to do would be to establish, once and for all, who Mr. Weems was and what he was doing on this vessel. For that, I would suggest that all the trunks on board, regardless of their putative ownership, be examined. If one is found to contain a large quantity of assorted specie, we will at least have advanced our knowledge to that degree."

The enterprise of removing all the trunks and crates to the bow-deck had to wait until the *Silver Moon* had been backed from Hitchins' Chute. This lengthy procedure occupied the whole of the noon and early afternoon, so that the deck-hands—tired already from shoving and poking the steamboat out of the narrow and sinking water-course—went directly from that to bringing on deck every trunk and crate in the hold.

In this enterprise January, Jim, and the other valets were pressed into service, while the deck-passengers stood around and gaped at the possessions of their betters, the white men grumbled and snarled, and Mrs. Tredgold protested vociferously that no one was going to violate the sanctity of *her* baggage. Hannibal—the only white man to actually assist with moving the luggage—explained to them that it was believed that Weems might have abstracted something from one of the pieces of luggage on board, and Davis—who seemed to have taken over the investigation by sheer force of will—ended the discussion by announcing, "Justice must be served."

A man definitely destined for politics, thought January.

Molloy, clearly baffled at how his attempt to rid the boat of both Hannibal and January had failed, kept to the pilot-house during the proceedings.

Mrs. Fischer did not even emerge from her stateroom.

January was one of the men working the crane at the bow hatch, so he was able to watch the little clumps of passengers along the upper-deck railing, as well as the lantern-lit square of the dark hold below. Thucydides coordinated the shifting of the trunks in the hold, as deck-hands brought them to the crane, lifted them out to be checked, then lowered them to be replaced; he was assisted by 'Rodus and two other slaves of Cain's coffle, Marcus and Guy. On the deck itself, Mr. Tredgold was in charge. Davis chalked a line and appointed Nick the barkeep to make sure nobody crossed it except the owner of the trunk—it was Sophie who brought Mrs. Fischer's luggage keys.

"The specie was taken out of the trunks, all right," murmured January as he, Hannibal, and Jim paused to lean on the still-netted load of the Roberson trunks. "All of it, apparently."

"It must have been scattered among dozens, you know," panted the fiddler. "We haven't seen an empty trunk yet. Yes, Molloy had time to get at the luggage while it was being off-loaded at Horsehead Bar—

when all the men were out of the way—but he'd have to have known *exactly* which trunks to open, and even at that would have to have worked *very* fast."

"If he had an accomplice—or more than one—it would have gone quicker," responded January thoughtfully. "But that theory brings its own problems." He nodded back up toward the pilot-house, visible above the arcade that shaded the wide upper-deck apron at the top of the stairs. "However Molloy managed it, he isn't worried about the trunks. He's worried about *us*—about trying to get us off the boat. But not the trunks. And as you notice, Mrs. Fischer isn't, either."

"And that worries *me*." Hannibal yanked the netting back, helped January and Jim skid two green canvas trunks with brass corners, an old wooden trunk with iron strapping, and a crate that proved to contain dishes onto the deck, where Mr. Roberson waited with the keys. "Do we need to concern ourselves with a second gang under Molloy's command as well as Christmas's boys, or is there something here we're not seeing?"

January only shook his head. Down in the hold, he saw Thu and 'Rodus pause in their work and trade a low-voiced joke, and laugh; then Thu went back to his notebook and his list. From the upper deck, Mrs. Roberson called down, "Mr. Roberson, you need not trouble yourself with that and with mounting guard, too. I can deal with the keys."

Roberson shaded his eyes against the afternoon sun and called back up, "It's quite all right, Mrs. Roberson," and handed his rifle to Davis—Lockhart, Byrne, Dodd (who was likelier to accidentally shoot one of the deck-hands than an attacking river-pirate), and Cain stood with rifles, surveying the green, silent bank. Considering the startling cache of pornographic prints that Davis unearthed from Roberson's trunk a moment later, the Kentucky planter's attitude was understandable.

Davis's mouth thinned to a needle-scratch of disapproval, and his tic twitched the side of his face a number of times, but he said nothing. Tucked among the shirts, coats, and stockings were also a number of packets of cheap glass jewelry so garish that it could not possibly be intended for the subdued and elegant Mrs. Roberson: some of the housemaids on Mimosa Plantation, January reflected cynically, were going to get new earbobs when Marse got home.

Turning to say as much to Jim, January thought he glimpsed—but wasn't sure—the movement of a skirt down in the shadows of the hold. It was only on the edge of the darkness, and gone like the flicker one sometimes sees at the corner of one's eye. . . .

January thought, *She's there.*

Queen Régine.

And what did SHE see last night? What does she know?

As January had guessed, Mrs. Fischer's numerous trunks contained nothing but clothes and jewelry—extremely opulent, vividly colorful, and completely at odds with her ladylike and withdrawn exterior—and a number of books printed in Paris or Amsterdam, with titles like *The Flogging-Block, Confessions of a Lady of Leisure,* and *The Lustful Turk.* None of the trunks bearing her name seemed disordered or incompletely packed. Sophie turned her shoulder away from Hannibal when he spoke to her, and as she returned up the stair hesitated to greet Rose. . . .

"God knows what La Pécheresse has been telling her about the three of us," remarked Hannibal under his breath. "Or told her cronies in the Parlor, for that matter. Look how La Tredgold has been watching every move I make."

Sophie and Rose stepped aside as Molloy swaggered down the stair and over to Davis. "When the hell you going to be done playing about here and let me get my deck-hands back to their work? We can't stay here keepin' the fires drawn for all the night!"

"We shall remain," retorted Davis, glaring coldly down his nose at the pilot, "as long as it takes to ascertain once and for all who is lying and who is speaking the truth."

"*What is truth,* asked Pilate, and washed his hands." Hannibal went forward to start hauling the trunks back to be lowered into the hold again, and replaced by others. "I have my pick-locks on hand for those items addressed to people not on the boat, though I'm sure that will clinch what remains of my reputation. All I can say is, we'd better find *some*thing in one of these trunks, or I suspect we're both going to hear about it from the sheriff at Mayersville."

Mr. Quince's single trunk contained numerous identical sets of shirts and underclothing, innumerable Swedenborgian tracts, fifty back issues of the *Liberator,* a dozen bottles of "Vegetarian Tonic," and a dozen more of Kendal Black Drop, a quadruple-strength opium tincture.

Theodora Skippen's held enormous quantities of frilled night-dresses, silk stockings, fifteen gold watches, twenty-seven men's gold signet-rings, four gold and seven silver cigar cases (two with cigars), no two of anything engraved with the same initials.

Kelsey Lundy's yielded, among a few shirts and a spare pair of boots, two Bibles, several Abolitionist pamphlets, four copies of the *Liberator,* three bottles of laudanum, and a packet of sulfate of zinc, which January recognized as a powerful emetic.

No trunk, crate, or box examined held either banknotes, the packets of securities Granville had spoken of, or gold.

FIFTEEN

"La Pécheresse couldn't possibly have managed to *spend* four million dollars all in one afternoon before she left New Orleans, could she?"

Hannibal trailed January down the starboard promenade as Thucydides locked up the hold door and the hatch under Davis's watchful eye. The two coffles of slaves, having spent the forenoon poling the *Silver Moon* out of the chute and the mid-afternoon dragging luggage around, were now being ordered to assist in the task of helping the exhausted deck-hands lug wood to the furnaces to get steam up again, a process that would take until nearly dawn.

Climbing overboard in sightless night and fog and swimming for an unknown shore in the dark was beginning to make more and more sense.

"Even if she'd bought all those clothes and Weems had paid cash for three plantations and the slaves to run them," January replied wearily, "it wouldn't have gone unnoticed. No, the money was on board and Molloy did something with it—or with some important portion of it. For that matter, Fischer and Weems had several days to remove the loot from their trunks themselves. We've been able to keep an eye on the stern doorway down into the hold, but they—or Molloy—could slip in at the bow end. . . ."

"And the deck-hands wouldn't have gossiped about it?"

January spread his hands helplessly. "It wouldn't take much for them to disguise themselves as German or Irish deck-passengers. Gold and securities could be brought up a little at a time and concealed under his stateroom floor between the joists. The same applies to the flooring of the hold."

And, when Hannibal looked startled, he added, "We did that all the time at Bellefleur—the adult slaves did, I was too young. They'd steal things—food, mostly, or things that could be sold to the river-traders for food—and bury them under the cabin floors. That's why most planters build slave cabins up off the ground, no matter what they like to say about proper air circulation. It's to make it harder for the slaves to bury things under the floor."

"The things I missed by not being born an American." Hannibal eased himself down stiffly between the wood-piles. "Dear gods, I'm tired. I have the distressing suspicion I would not have made a particularly good slave." And he unstoppered his flask for a quick drink.

Privately suppressing his certainty that as a slave his friend would have died of overwork and consumption long before the age of forty, January said bracingly, "Of course you would have. You'd have been promoted to butler and be running the plantation. The way you turned Molloy's attempt to push you into a duel into an opportunity to *finally* search the trunks—"

"Which got us exactly nothing."

"Nonsense. It was a Socratic exercise in finding out what we do not know, clearing the way to look for Truth."

Under his graying mustache, the fiddler's mouth twitched in a smile.

"Weems must have suspected some kind of jiggery-pokery with the luggage the moment it started being off-loaded to spar over Horsehead Bar," went on January. "He ran to check it the moment he could get himself clear of the work-gang. If he found a substantial portion of the gold or securities gone, of course he'd begin searching staterooms the moment it grew dark—"

"At which activity Molloy surprised him and threw him overboard while miraculously making it appear that he was in the pilot-house with Mr. Souter," finished Hannibal. "Unless Souter was lying, but I can't for the life of me see why he would be."

He shut his eyes, and leaned his head back against the wall of the 'tween-decks. The sun was nearly down, long shadows reaching out over the water and bringing a merciful degree of coolness. With the clanging of its bell softened by distance, the *Wellington* appeared around the bend, heading down-river in mid-channel. Voices shouted across the water—the wood-detail was forgotten as deck-hands hastened to lower the skiff and row out to exchange New Orleans newspapers for those of Memphis, St. Louis, and Louisville. January watched the small *Wellington* idly, blithe in its disregard even for low water, barreling southward with the rest of the torn-off branches and floating debris.

"That may be," he told Hannibal, "only because we don't know much about Souter. Or Lundy. Or Byrne. Or Davis, for that matter—if Weems was blackmailing one man on this boat to get bribe-money to have pursuers shaken off his tail, there may have been others. If we can . . ."

A flash of blue and pink skirts appeared on the stair over their heads, and a moment later Rose came around the wood-piles. "La Pécheresse has gone to the Ladies' Parlor to slander Hannibal until dinner," she reported cheerfully. "Having spent the entire morning doing so to Sophie, who now believes him to be the Devil incarnate."

"Just what I needed to complete my happiness." The fiddler opened his eyes. "I shall give her my mother's address so they can correspond on the subject."

"I've promised I'll help her—Sophie, I mean. Mrs. Roberson's elder daughter, Emily, is still in mourning for her husband, and offered to lend her some blacks until the boat reaches Memphis. . . ."

"Emily, who's all of four feet tall and as big around as my arm?" asked Hannibal interestedly, getting painfully to his feet. *"You dwarf, you minimus . . . you bead, you acorn . . ."*

"Even the very same. Sophie has been cutting and fitting most of the afternoon, as Mrs. Fischer wants to be properly in mourning for dinner. I've offered to help her—a measure of my dedication to the purposes of justice, as I cannot sew a stitch and detest the exercise."

"Then let me strengthen your fingers by an invigorating kiss." January took her hand and pressed his lips gently to every long, slender finger. "Am I included in the incarnation of evil? Or would you ladies like a little gallant company while you gossip?"

She gave him her quickflash smile. "I came out for that very reason. Only remember you're as puzzled by Hannibal's infamous conduct as anyone—you have *no* idea whether he's telling the truth or not."

"I'll just run along, shall I?" suggested Hannibal. "Perhaps before supper I can catch the Tredgold children and tear out and devour their hearts."

Rose said, "You do that and Cissy will be forever your friend."

As Hannibal turned to go, and Rose disappeared up the stair once more, January laid a staying hand on the fiddler's frayed sleeve. "I hesitate to keep you from slaughtering the Tredgold children," he said, "but if you're not too tired, you might idle your way up to the pilothouse instead and have a chat with Mr. Souter. I have no reason to think Mr. Lundy would have killed Weems—or that he *could* have, for that matter—but with both Fischer and Molloy trying to get us off the boat dead or alive, I think it's time we started checking on everyone aboard who wasn't somewhere at midnight last night."

Sophie glanced up quickly as January's tall form blotted the last twilight from the open door. January creased his brow in a look of deepest concern and said, "Miss Rose, I'm glad I found you—good evenin', Miss Sophie. Miss Rose, what in the name of Heaven's goin' on around here? Michie Hannibal givin' me a tongue-lashin', that gold he's been talkin' about since we left New Orleans not bein' where he said it was. . . ." He shook his head in helpless bafflement. "An' now they're talkin' accusin' *me* of harmin' Mr. Weems. I swear"—he turned to Sophie appealingly—"I didn't know nuthin' about the man, 'cept what Michie Hannibal said. 'Cept I don't think anybody can be as sly an' sneaky as Michie Hannibal says he was."

"Well, Mr. Weems was no saint with a halo on his head," said Sophie primly, her needle flying in the neat, tight stitches that Ayasha would have approved of and that Rose couldn't have produced at gunpoint. "And I know that what he and Madame did was wrong. But her husband used her cruelly. . . ."

January realized that Sophie was referring to the Seventh Commandment, not the Eighth.

". . . forcing her to flee from his house one night in a rainstorm, taking nothing but the clothes on her back and her jewelry. Surely she can be forgiven for running from such a man as that. How she has suffered! And poor Mr. Weems was very good to me, giving me a little extra money—for my inconvenience, he said, wasn't that sweet?—every time I had to sleep on the deck, and making sure that I had a good blanket, and fruit from dinner. I had only known him three months—since I came into Mrs. Fischer's house—but he was always so kind. Oh, how could you have done what you did, Ben? Cut him up, like a . . . like an animal? My poor mistress wept and wept. . . ."

"It cut up my heart to do it, M'am," January assured her. "Just as bad as it cut up him. But he's dead, and felt nuthin'. An' my old master, that was a doctor, he taught me how to tell if a man'd been murdered. Without me doin' what I did, no one would have known, and Mr. Weems would have gone to his grave cryin' out to be avenged, an' no one knowing."

Sophie sniffed, and wiped those immense brown eyes. "And to think that the murderer might be your own master!"

"I don't see how it could, M'am," said January earnestly. "Michie Hannibal, he was playin' cards all that night in the Saloon."

"Mrs. Fischer says he's sly, and dangerous, and clever," replied Sophie, her voice sinking dramatically. "He could surely have slipped away to do the awful deed, while the others were engrossed in their game. She even thinks *you* might have done it, but if you had, why would you have cut up his body, to prove the murder? No." She shook her head decidedly. "It was your master, in the pay of Mr. Fischer, seeking revenge upon Madame, and after she and poor Mr. Weems had tried so hard to achieve happiness. Oh, my poor Madame!"

A tear fell on the pieced-together crape of the black dress in her lap, and left its stain, like a sad echo, on the slave-woman's gray skirt beneath.

Refraining from taking issue with this unlikely scenario, Rose asked, "Were they together at all on that last night? I know you came down to the deck to sleep, after you helped poor Julie. . . ."

"Oh, poor Julie!" Sophie shook her head, and pressed a delicate hand to her brow. "I feel so guilty for having helped her instead of waiting for Mr. Weems! I might have been able to do something, to say something. . . ."

"But Mrs. Fischer sent you away," pointed out Rose, "didn't she?"

"Yes." Sophie sighed tragically and removed her hand, the stains from the crape on her fingers leaving a long, sooty smudge beneath the edge of her pink tignon. "Yes, she did. There was nothing, really, that I could have done. But I should have been able to. I brushed out her hair for her, and folded up her clothes and locked up her jewelry. She settled down in her wrapper to wait for . . . for Mr. Weems. . . ." A blush suffused the girl's ivory cheeks. "I'd made up a bundle, you see, for Julie, while I was waiting for Mrs. Fischer to come back from dinner. Some food, and a dress Mrs. Fischer had given me, which didn't fit me, and shoes. I took it out of the stateroom with me just as Julie came out of Miss Skippen's stateroom crying. I put my arms around her and tried to comfort her, and it was then that the boat ran on the bar. We clung to each other—I was afraid the boat would sink . . . !"

January blinked for a moment at this concept—by running onto the bar the boat had in effect touched the bottom of the river, and *couldn't* sink—but Sophie went on breathlessly.

"Then Julie said, 'I'm going now! We must be near shore, and the water shallow, to run on a bar. I can get to shore, I *know* it!' Oh, poor Julie! I only hope she made it to shore!"

Eleven o'clock, then, thought January, *unless something delayed her . . . But what would have delayed Julie for the hour that it took to walk the boat over the bar?*

Which left, unfortunately, only one other black culprit with reason to wish Weems harm, and without an alibi.

Benjamin January.

"Do you know if Mr. Weems came to see your mistress at all?" asked Rose sympathetically.

Sophie shook her head tragically. "I know he didn't. She lay awake far into the night, waiting for him—when I came up in the morning to tell her of that . . . that horrible sight, that horrible thing Jim saw . . . all the lamp-oil was burned away. When I opened the door the first thing she said was, *Run to Mr. Weems's stateroom, and learn why he did not come last night.*"

"She did not go look herself, earlier in the night, then?"

Sophie recoiled in shock at the suggestion. "She was not dressed! She was so much the lady, she would not have ventured about the boat only in her wrapper and her nightgown! Oh, if only I had been there, I could have gone and searched in the night myself! Perhaps, if I had found him, I could have prevented his terrible death!"

"And when you told her . . . ?" prompted Rose gently.

"My poor Madame," whispered Sophie. "The shock of it . . . all she could do was sit up in bed and say, *What?* Just like that . . . as if she could not believe. Then she said, *Good Christ,* and got out of bed without another word, and dressed. No tears," she whispered, "though she has been weeping all the afternoon in the Parlor, with the other ladies about her. . . ."

I'll bet she has, thought January. *After breaking into Weems's stateroom and searching . . . for what?*

"It is a most tragic story. And I am the more grieved for hurting her, after all she has suffered already," he said gently. "It might indeed have been my master who killed Mr. Weems." He spoke reluctantly, like one convinced against his will. "But there are other evil people on this boat who might also have done this terrible thing. Not all of them," he added, lowering his voice to a whisper, "men."

Sophie's beautiful eyes widened and her lips parted with understanding and shock, and she glanced automatically to her left, the direction in which Miss Skippen's stateroom lay. Rose, taking her cue, produced a perfectly-judged little gasp and breathed, "*Miss Skippen?*"

January raised his eyebrows: like Hamlet's friends, *We could an if we would,* and, *If we list to speak . . .*

Rose prompted, "But surely Julie was with her?"

"Not after we ran onto the bar," answered Sophie. "And Miss Skippen didn't undress as Mrs. Fischer did—Julie told me. In fact, she said Miss Skippen . . ."

At the forward end of the promenade Thucydides appeared, carrying a tray of lemonade. As he passed January and Rose in Mrs. Fischer's stateroom doorway, he said quietly, "Mrs. Fischer's coming," then walked on by without breaking stride. January and Rose followed him immediately, without even a word to Sophie, who for her part instantly bowed her head over her sewing so that she would be stitching away industriously when her mistress rounded the corner.

It wasn't until dinnertime that January heard what Miss Skippen had done on the night of Weems's death. He spent the twilight hour with Rose, huddled next to the galley passway beside a makeshift smudge of lemongrass and gun-powder that Eli had rigged to give some relief from the mosquitoes that swarmed in the dead water under Hitchins' Point. Around them, deck-hands beat a steady trail into the engine-room with wood, to Eli's loudly-voiced annoyance. In the cobalt gloom the passway, and the engine-room door, looked like the furnace-gate of Hell.

"You want maybe to sit here all day tomorrow, with all those passengers eating their heads off?" roared Molloy's voice. "Settle in, maybe, set up camp on the shore? This is a steamboat, by God, and what we need is *steam*!"

The pilot came stamping out of the engine-room and swung himself around the newel-post and up the stair. January glanced across at Rose and raised his brows: "Any ideas on how we might be able to get into his stateroom for a look at the floorboards?"

"Thucydides has spare keys to every stateroom on the boat," she replied quietly. "If he was good enough to warn us about Mrs. Fischer . . ."

January shook his head. "Any slave would do that for any other slave." And when Rose—a freewoman born and bred—looked inquiring, he explained, "You ever heard field-hands singing, and they'll change their song when the overseer rides by, or when a party of whites rides along the road? They'll sing something like, "*Chink, pink, honey o lula, 'way down in the bayou . . . go wade in the bayou.*" His deep, velvety baritone shaped one of the earliest field-songs he knew. "I was five or six, before I understood what it meant when they'd sing it. . . . That they'd heard rumor someone had run, and they were singing warning, if the runaway was resting near, to get into the bayou so the dogs couldn't sniff him out."

"My mama used to sing that song when she'd cook," added Roberson's valet, old Winslow, coming over at the sound of January's singing. "She was from bayou country, but we didn't have bayous in Virginia where I was born. They'd sing in the tobacco-fields,

Oh hide me in the rock,
Oh Lord, oh Lord,
Oh hide me in the rock. . . .

His voice lifted in the rolling rhythm, echoing out over the dark water. "Then they'd go on, '*Oh hide me in the tree, Oh hide me in the earth, Oh hide me in the sea. . . .*' We children would all know it was somebody who'd run, though I don't recall anyone ever tellin' us so." He smiled reminiscently, looking back from a lifetime of clean, comfortable house-service, then shook his head. "One fella—from the plantation next to ours—he ran off, and hid out in our mule-barn for three weeks. Everybody on the place knew he was there, while the patrollers hunted clear up to Fairfax County. He finally got out in a wagon of hay."

Molloy came down the steps again, strode past Rose and January to where Cain was just coming from checking the spancels on his slaves. As he swaggered past the dealer, the pilot said something quietly—impossible to hear, but the angle of his head, the crowding jostle of his shoulder, were like a shove.

Torchlight shone on Cain's pockmarked, impassive face as the bigger man jostled by. Winslow murmured, "Molloy better watch how he mess with that man. That's a hard man, an' no mistake."

"They both strike me as hard men," remarked Rose.

The gray-haired valet shook his head. "Molloy, he a loud man, an' he no gentleman, but he's not hard. Not hard like that Cain. A bully'll crowd a weaker man, or a nigger, someone who can't fight back, but he like a barkin' cur-dog. He think Cain ain't gonna push back, 'cause of that letter he's got—"

"Who's got?" asked January. "Molloy?"

Winslow nodded. "This mornin', when it start to rain so bad, I went to the stateroom to fetch Mr. Roberson's umbrella for Mrs. Roberson. Our stateroom's next to Mr. Weems's, and I heard someone movin' around in there. An' I stay still, wonderin' if it's Thu makin' Mr. Weems decent, or Mr. Weems himself . . . Mr. Roberson gives lectures about history at the University in Lexington, an' he's always tellin' me how there ain't no such thing as the dead walkin' or whisperin' or bleedin' when their murderer comes near, but I don't know about that. I seen some damn strange things in my life."

He watched as Molloy moved on away toward the bow. In the darkness the end of Cain's cigar glowed briefly brighter, like the Devil's eye when Satan speculates evil in Hell.

"So I hears the door open an' I figures it got to be Thu, 'cause whatever I hear of haunts, they don't bother openin' no doors. But next minute I hear Mr. Molloy say, from out on the promenade, *It's no good lookin'—I got it.*"

"Got what?" asked January in his most fascinated voice. And indeed he was—he traded a sidelong glance with Rose, and returned his gaze to Winslow's face.

"Got no idea," replied the valet, shaking his head. "But Mr. Cain say from in Weems's stateroom, *I don't know what you're talkin' about,* an' Mr. Molloy said, *Have it your way—BREDON. But if you don't want to see it printed in the* Mayersville Gazette, *you and I better come to an understandin'.* Then he walked away—I heard his boots goin' off along the promenade—and Cain must have stood there in Mr. Weems's stateroom for two minutes 'thout movin', for I didn't hear a sound. Then he walks off, too, fast."

"*Printed in the* Mayersville Gazette," repeated Rose, and propped her spectacles on her nose.

"So I think it got to be a letter," concluded Winslow. "A letter Weems had that Molloy got hold of somehow. You mark my words, whatever they sayin' about your master"—he jabbed a finger at January—"it was either Mr. Molloy or Mr. Cain that pushed poor Mr. Weems overboard. You just mark my words."

And he turned away to greet Andy and Jim as the two valets came down the steps, shaking their heads over the lateness of supper and the fact that the *Silver Moon* was likely to be sitting still until after midnight.

"Your words are definitely marked." January watched as the three servants greeted one another and displayed tidbits abstracted from the galley or stateroom trays. "But unfortunately they won't do us much good until we can figure out a way Cain could have murdered Weems without Gleet becoming aware of it, or Molloy could have done so while he was in the pilot-house with Souter."

"Molloy might not have been there constantly once Souter came on," pointed out Rose. "I can easily see him leaving his replacement for a few minutes, saying he's going to check on the paddle after thrashing loose from the bar. . . ."

"And what?" asked January. "For him to have been gone any substantial length of time would rouse comment from Souter. And if

Molloy had been on watch since six, he wouldn't have known where Weems was or what he was doing. It's not a big boat, but it would take time to search it. Still, we can ask."

Sophie appeared a few minutes later, silent and a little standoffish—it was clear Mrs. Fischer had re-indoctrinated her in the villainy of January and Hannibal. It took twenty minutes of Rose's patient gossip and sympathy to return to the interrupted account of Theodora Skippen's nocturnal habits, with the only result being the information that Miss Skippen was in the habit of remaining dressed after she retired for the night when she was waiting for Mr. Molloy.

"If he didn't come straight there from the pilot-house at midnight, she would sometimes go up looking for him, or tap on the windows of the Saloon. But why would she have wished harm to poor Mr. Weems?"

"Perhaps she knew him earlier, in Natchez," suggested Rose.

"No, I don't think so," Sophie said. "Julie once spoke of Miss Skippen saying, when she was drunk, that Mr. Weems had a secret: *You'd hardly think it of that silly little man, but that's what Mr. Molloy tells me.* She meant that he was keeping Mrs. Fischer, but I think if she'd known him, she'd have said so. Julie says Miss Skippen isn't very discreet when she's had a few brandies."

It was well and truly dark now, and the mosquitoes hummed thick as the trees on the bank faded to a sable wall. Close enough, January thought, for Levi Christmas and his boys to easily swim. But the *Silver Moon* couldn't go farther into the river, for fear of being caught by the current and swept down toward New Orleans again, and the hands came and went on the deck, carrying wood into the insatiable furnace maws. Every time January had walked along the starboard promenade he'd seen flies by the hundreds swarming around the shut door of Weems's stateroom, and latterly he had begun to smell the unmistakable sweet sickliness of the corpse inside. It was nearly fifty miles to Mayersville. Unless they caught up on a bar they should reach it by noon.

It would still make an unpleasant task for the undertaker.

And a worse one, he thought, for himself and Hannibal, to explain to the Issaquena County sheriff why they could not leave the *Silver Moon.*

Both Mrs. Fischer and Molloy knew that Rose was friend to Hannibal and him. Even if she remained with the boat, God knew what would happen to her, between Mayersville and Memphis, if she made it that far.

Winslow was right, he thought, looking sidelong at Rose's angular profile as she chatted with Sophie. He would lay money on Molloy or Cain having done the murder, despite having explanations for their whereabouts at more or less the moment of the crime, with a side-bet on Mrs. Fischer, night-dress and all.

And none of the three would hesitate even a moment to dispose of Rose the instant he and Hannibal were off the boat.

Looking up, he saw the fiddler descending the steps, though by January's estimation supper had barely started. "You're quite correct," agreed Hannibal, perching himself on the rail and producing his bottle of opium-laced sherry. "After this afternoon's events I am completely *persona non grata.* Every lady on the boat, including little Melissa Tredgold, gave me the cut direct and dragged their menfolks away as if I had the Black Death. God knows what Mrs. Fischer told them in the Ladies' Parlor—she was there, by the way, decked out in complete black. Your handiwork is much to be congratulated," he added, taking the flustered Sophie's hand, bowing deeply, and kissing her fingers.

"According to Souter, Molloy was in the pilot-house continuously from the time they walked the boat over the bar until he went down to the Saloon at twelve-thirty. After Molloy left last night, Lundy came up—he often does, Souter says, for he doesn't sleep well on account of his illness."

Hannibal shivered as if at some terrible memory, and drank a quick sip of sherry to chase it away. "And on the subject of Mr. Lundy's illness, Souter was . . . comprehensive. He related every symptom and theory concerning the palsy, illustrated with anecdotes from Souter's own experience or the experience of literally hundreds of people he's talked to, is related to, or has heard about from second-cousins twice removed, ad infinitum. . . . The man makes Polonius look like a Spartan. If I could have escaped the pilot-house by cutting off my own foot, I'd have done it.

"I was also treated to Lundy's complete biography, with speculative side-trips into the histories of the various boats Lundy—and three other fellows from whom Souter never could tell Lundy apart—ever piloted, plus what Henry Clay said when Lundy—or one of the other three fellows—accidentally swung the *Aetna* around a little too sharply coming away from the wharf in New Orleans and put the paddlewheel through the dining-room wall of the *Desdemona*."

"What did he say?" asked Rose curiously, for she, like January, was a great admirer of the Kentucky politician.

"Something along the lines of 'Get that thing out of here, we haven't had our coffee yet.' Souter's tales are definitely of the *Parturient montes* variety, though at the end of the birthing, one is lucky even to get a mouse." Hannibal sighed, and sipped more sherry with a shaky hand. "On the other hand, I now know that Kelsey Lundy is fifty-one years old, that he was born in Kennebec, Maine—what appalling names Americans give their towns—where his three daughters, Elsie, Mary, and Margaret, still live with their assorted progeny, whose names I will spare you; that he goes to see them nearly every summer; that he came to New Orleans with Jackson's troops and that the first boat he piloted was the *Volcano,* to Louisville, in 1815. He is a teetotaler and an outspoken Abolitionist and once engaged in a duel with a man in New Orleans who was beating a slave in the street, a circumstance which gave him such a disgust for the town that after that, apparently, he seldom went ashore in New Orleans at all. Cutting to almost nil," he added regretfully, "the occasions upon which he might have met Mr. Weems, unless they encountered one another by chance at an Abolitionist meeting in Boston."

"Curious," mused January, "that as badly advanced as Lundy's palsy is, he would still be in New Orleans at all, instead of returning to Maine and his daughters."

"He returned to New Orleans the week before last, on the *Sprite,*" said Hannibal. "For his health, he said. . . ."

"In the *summertime*?" Rose and January spoke almost in chorus, and January added, "Nobody in his right mind goes to New Orleans in the summer for his health."

"Regarding Mr. Lundy's mental condition, I have no data. And if you ask me to question Souter further on that or any other subject whatsoever, I shall throw myself overboard." He capped the bottle regretfully and tucked it into his coat pocket.

"The *Sprite* came into New Orleans a week ago Saturday," said Rose. "I saw the men still unloading the last of her cargo as we waited for you in the market. That means Lundy came into New Orleans—presumably to see a doctor—with the expectation of immediately turning around and piloting a boat up the river, in low water, in order to see another doctor in Lexington. . . . It doesn't make sense."

"It makes sense," said January grimly. "It's only we who can't see the rest of the pieces of the puzzle. Winslow," he called, and the valet, who was just heading for the stair to be in his master's stateroom when Mr. Roberson returned from supper, turned back with an expression of friendly inquiry.

"We were just talking about poor Mr. Lundy here on board. . . ."

"The poor gentleman with the palsy?"

January nodded. "Now, my old master, who was a surgeon, spoke of a doctor at Transylvania University in Lexington who's done work with the palsy—who's had some remarkable cures—but for the life of me I can't remember his name. Since Mr. Roberson is at the University, too . . ."

Winslow's honest face creased for a moment with thought. Then he shook his head. "Your master musta heard wrong, Ben, or else you got it crossed up with some other university. I know most of the gentlemen in the medical faculty that come out to Mimosa to dinner with Mr. Roberson and there's none of 'em that's worked on the palsy."

"Hmm." January shook his head with mild regret. "I coulda sworn, but you're right, I might have heard wrong—Michie Simon always did get one university mixed up with another. Sorry I troubled you."

"No trouble at all."

"Angels and ministers of grace defend us," said Hannibal thoughtfully. "Definite indications that something is rotten in the state of Denmark. But if you can think of a way poor Lundy could have heaved even so minor a specimen as Weems overboard by main strength, I'll give you a sweet. And speaking of sweets . . ."

He fished in a pocket of his too-large silk vest and produced a folded piece of notepaper. The scent of it—a sickly reek of cheap geranium—hit January like a slap in the face with a slightly wilted bouquet. He didn't even need to ask who had sent it.

I must see you alone! ran the delicate, if rather unformed, writing, the exclamation point a frenzied balloon and the tails of the long letters tortured into girlish curlicues. *I beg you wait for me in your room at ten I have inportant news to ~~inpu~~ ~~inper~~ tell. Theodora.*

SIXTEEN

Being no fool, and not trusting Theodora Skippen farther than he could throw January's piano, Hannibal arranged for January to loiter unobtrusively on the wide bow apron of the upper deck, to be on hand should the young lady either produce a weapon or scream rape. "Not that your testimony would be of the slightest use in a court of law in this country," added Hannibal, setting a large japanned tin tray—pilfered from the galley—on the foot of the bed and balancing on it three tin cups and half a dozen pieces of silverware from the same source. "But Colonel Davis may be disposed to listen to you informally, and draw his own conclusions. I suppose it's the best we can do."

It being only eight o'clock, and most of the cabin passengers still at dinner, January and Hannibal then descended to the lower deck, where Rose was seated beside the smudge-pot, talking to Cissy. The nursemaid looked harried as usual as she devoured her bowl of rice and beans: ". . . pretendin' to be asleep good as gold, but the fuss they both put up I know it's just pretend . . ."

The end portion of the promenade was otherwise deserted, for the piles of cordwood separating the servants from the chained slaves were nearly gone. The whole line of Gleet's coffle, and Cain's, were visible now, wolfing down their beans and rice from gourd bowls or passing tin cups of water along the line. Stepping back into the passway, January glanced through the engine-room door. As he'd suspected, the hands were bringing in the smaller quantities of wood from the bow.

Supper over, Eli's voice could be heard through the passway from the women's side of the boat, chatting with his old mother and with a young woman of Cain's coffle as he played with her child.

The narrow door that led down to the hold, thick with shadow, seemed to beckon like Aladdin's Cave.

"You got your pick-locks?"

Hannibal produced them without a word.

The profound stillness within the bowels of the ship seemed to breathe, a velvet-black abyss beyond the feeble rectangle of torchlight falling down the ladder from the passway. For fear of drawing attention, January carried no light—the most he'd have been able to provide was the candle-end he habitually carried in one pocket—and beyond the first few jumbled outlines of trunks and crates, stacked any-old-how where the deck-hands had left them, it was as if the universe itself fell away to nothing. Overhead, men's footfalls creaked in the engine-room, masking whatever tiny noises another human's presence might have produced, but January smelled the very faint whisper of habitation, of a latrine-bucket hidden somewhere in the darkness.

She was there, all right. Or someone was.

He drew a deep breath, then said, "It's me. I know you're there. Please, speak with me."

Silence. He remembered the wrinkled, furious face in the torchlight of Congo Square, the rotting rooster-head Rose had brought to him, still covered with specks of down from the pillow it had been sewn up in. The rasping whisper in the darkness of the cemetery: *I curse you to the ruin of all you touch, and the destruction of all you hope. . . .*

He had never in his life expected the extent of jeopardy that he now stood in, with the money vanished, and the near-certainty of arrest and detention—and possible hanging—facing him when the boat reached Mayersville.

"Régine," he said, his voice carrying softly in the darkness, "I beg your pardon. I lost my temper, and spoke to you as I shouldn't have. I was only trying to help a young girl under my protection. I was afraid, and angry. I need to speak to you. I need your help. Please speak to me and I swear my oath I'll tell no one you are here."

Go ahead and tell the world I'm here, piano-player, if you think it'll do you any good. No one will find me.

Thu had to know she was here by this time, even if he had not on that first day when he'd called out, *Who's there?* January could swear—almost—that Thu had been near the hatch above when he had glimpsed the movement of skirts in the shadow. The steward had always impressed January as a sharply intelligent young man, but intelligence didn't mean a man wouldn't be cowed by a voodoo.

January's own luck since Queen Régine had spit in his face had certainly not been anything to boast about.

And there were other ways of buying Thucydides's assistance than superstitious awe. Voodooiennes were artists in secrets and information, buying, selling, trading knowledge and the power that knowledge gave. The presence of Thu's brother in chains on the vessel qualified as a lever whichever way you looked at it.

And, voodooiennes were never above paying top price for what they needed, whether that was protection, information, or hands to do work in places where they themselves could not go.

Good God, he wondered suddenly, *did Queen Régine invest her money in the Bank of Louisiana as well? Did she get on the boat, not in pursuit of me, but in pursuit of Weems?*

She'd been in a position to see everything that went on, over the past week. Could Thucydides be working for her, or at least supplying her with information . . . ?

In which case he, January, wasn't safe anywhere on the boat.

"Your Majesty," he whispered desperately, "please . . ."

But watching silence was his only reply. A moment later Hannibal's musical whistle sounded in the passway above: *Oh hide me in the rock, O Lord, O Lord. . . .*

Since there was no way of knowing whether the approaching company was black or white, someone who could be talked around or someone potentially genuinely dangerous, January backed hastily out the door and closed it behind him, and crouched, waiting, in the dark of the narrow stairwell. "My dear Gleet," said Hannibal's voice from the passway, with just enough trace of drunken slur to it to convince January that his friend was as sober as a judge—or as sober as Hannibal ever got. "Just the man I've been looking for."

"Damn shame," groused Gleet heavily. "Damn shame, to hang a well-set-up boy like yours. Complete waste . . ."

"Particularly," said Hannibal, "since Ben actually *was* asleep in my stateroom the whole time and never laid a finger on Weems."

"Oh, of course, of course!" Gleet hastened to agree. "But a white man, you know . . . I'm afraid once the sheriff gets hold of it, there'll be no way around hanging him. *Do* you really work for the Bank of Louisiana?"

"In a manner of speaking," said Hannibal. January snapped the padlock shut, and stole up the steps like a shadow just as Hannibal maneuvered Gleet out of the passway and onto the promenade beyond. "But in nothing like the capacity our friend Mr. Molloy seems to quite sincerely believe. You and Cain were out that night, two or three times—you heard nothing? Saw nothing?"

As January looked around the corner, Gleet shook his head, and spat a long stream of tobacco juice onto the deck, so close that it fouled Cissy's skirt. If looks could maim, there would have been blood on the deck as well as tobacco juice, but the nursemaid said nothing, and Gleet either didn't see her glare or didn't care.

"Like I told the Colonel, it was quiet as tombs. Even the niggers were quiet—seems like the fog hushed 'em down. Lookin' for ghostses an' ha'nts,' I expect." Gleet laughed with jovial contempt at anyone who would believe in a spirit world. "I looked over the wenches first, then the bucks, and Cain walked along with me, civil for once—

touchy bastard." He laughed again, an obnoxious haw-haw. "Maybe he thinks there's ghostses an' ha'nts in the dark, too."

From behind the corner January watched the burly slave-dealer put a brotherly arm around Hannibal's shoulders. "What'd he offer for your boy?"

Hannibal shook his head sadly. "Not a thing—not a red cent."

January expelled his indrawn breath and whispered a prayer of thanks that Hannibal had decided on the truth rather than a fabrication, which, though it might open new avenues for information, might also be checked.

"Cheap bastard," Hannibal added as if the thought had just occurred to him. "Stuck-up, too."

Gleet nodded, and spat again. Cissy and Rose moved the boxes on which they sat back away from the smudge-pot, into the soft, gnat-filled gloom closer to the silent paddle.

"Gets his niggers to mind him, though," Gleet told Hannibal. "They's so scared of him, if he told the lot of 'em to turn somersaults on the deck, they'd do it. Look at him like whip dogs, even that stuck-up boy 'Rodus—who I told him'll make him trouble, just see if I'm not right. And it is a stupid name, like I said. People don't want to buy a boy named Herodotus. Give 'em a boy name of Jim or Joe or Pete. . . . That boy Pete I got, you know what his name originally was?"

"Then you don't think Cain was staying close to you last night because he was worried about his own gang attacking him?"

"Attack him how?" demanded the dealer sharply. "They's chained to the wall, just long enough so's they can piss over the side. If any of 'em was so stupid as to take a swing at him, like tryin' to get the key away from him, all he'd have to do was sing out and get half a dozen deck-hands from the engine-room." He shrugged, anger in his movement. January wondered if Gleet guessed Hannibal's real meaning. Not, *Was Cain afraid of being thrown overboard by his own gang on so black a night,* but, *Was it physically possible for them to have thrown Weems over the side?*

The last thing either Gleet or Cain would welcome, he reflected, was an accusation against any member of either of their gangs . . . which would automatically lose them over a thousand dollars, if the sheriff in Mayersville decided that that was what had happened. Far better to push off the blame onto someone else's slave.

"Though now you speak of it," Gleet went on thoughtfully, "he might have been twitchy about somethin' at that. Cain, I mean. When I started around to see the bucks after we fed up the wenches, he did scamper some to catch me up, and most times he don't have the time of day to give me."

"Does it sound to you," asked January after Gleet had gone into the galley for the pail of rice and beans that would be dished out to the men of his coffle, "as if *Cain* was the one who expected to be attacked last night, and not Weems?"

"You could look at it that way," agreed Rose, settling her box again beside the smudge. "Provided you can come up with some way Weems—or anyone on the boat for that matter—could have taken on Cain and done any damage. The night was pitch black and foggy, but it would need a blind man to mistake Weems for Cain."

"Cain go armed with a pistol in his boot and a knife in his belt," provided Cissy, washing her hands with a bandanna dampened in the rain-barrel after her hasty meal. "Even when he go in to dinner, he got a knuckle-duster in his pocket, Mr. Tredgold says."

They fell silent as Gleet came out of the galley, and walked down the promenade checking his property for the night. On the other side of the boat, the women's voices rose in a gentle crooning, a lullaby over the stillness of the water and the muffled grunts and curses from the boiler-room.

The women weren't worried. The men were.

Because they'd seen Julie slip over the side there last night?

Or because they'd seen something else?

"One more thing," he asked Cissy. "You spend most of the day in the Ladies' Parlor looking after those br—those charming Tredgold children. You must hear every piece of gossip on the boat."

She grinned. "Don't I just."

"What can you tell me about Jack Quince? Other than that he's out to reform the world."

Cissy laughed indulgently as at a child. "Lord, the way he preaches . . . and don't those ladies in the Parlor eat it up, though? One day it's how nobody should eat meat 'cause it pollutes the blood—let him grow up gettin' nuthin' but pulses an' corn, an' see how pure *his* blood gets!—an' another it's about how many circles an' levels Heaven has, like he been there. Last night he sat in the corner of the Saloon tellin' the ladies about how nobody was dancin' right—since the reels an' waltzes Mr. Sefton was playin' weren't how the Ancient Greeks would have done it—an' just this evenin', when I left the children up in the Parlor to come down here for dinner, he was on about how all the troubles in the United States just now date from movin' the capital to Washington City instead of leavin' it in Philadelphia, where it belongs."

"From Philadelphia, is he?" asked January.

"Lord, yes. You ever hear a man say 'ah' for 'o' like that who wasn't? He clerks for a firm that brokers sugar, cotton, an' tobacco in Cincinnati, makes two-three trips a year on the river, which is how he knows Mr. Tredgold—Mrs. Tredgold can't get enough of him. Myself, pretty as he is, I'd think a lot more of him if he did somethin' about slavery besides just goin' around sayin' how bad it is. I already *know* that."

An innocuous and well-known personage, then, thought January, following the nurse as she climbed the stairs in a rustle of petticoats to resume her position at the bedside of her wretched little charges. The door of the Saloon stood open, throwing light out into the humid darkness. Someone—Thu, probably—went into the Ladies' Parlor and lit a single oil-lamp there, anticipating that even had Hannibal not been in disgrace with the rest of the passengers, there would be no after-supper dancing.

Rifle on his arm, Mr. Roberson walked along the upper promenade, peering at the matte-black cut-out of the shore. Looking up at the hurricane deck above, January glimpsed a black shape that had to be Lockhart, silhouetted against the stars.

Quince came from Philadelphia.

Co-incidence?

January shook his head. A lot of people presumably came from Philadelphia, and because that city was one of the business centers of the United States, it wasn't odd that they'd find their way to New Orleans.

Still . . .

Molloy's voice bawled an order, on the bow-deck by the sound of it. He was on watch till midnight, and probably longer, since the *Silver Moon* would be getting under way again at about that time. Just as well, thought January. The last thing they needed was for Molloy to glimpse Miss Skippen making her way along to Hannibal's room.

I have important news to impart.

A trick? An excuse to get into Hannibal's room so she could throw herself into his all-too-susceptible arms?

Some variation of the badger game?

Voices floated down after him as he descended again to the galley. The ladies emerged from the Saloon, chatting softly as one and then another disappeared into the ladies' toilet: "Dearest, would you like a little company in your stateroom?" trumpeted Mrs. Tredgold in a voice that she probably thought was gentle and confidential. "I can come sit with you—I have some of the finest China green tea, *much* better than the horrid stuff they use in the galley—I've told Tredgold and told him. . . ."

January leaned against the corner of the passway and took Rose's hand.

Hannibal tactfully faded into the darkness.

"Don't I know you from somewhere, sir?" asked Rose diffidently, and January settled down on the box at her side.

"My face is familiar," sighed January, "but I can't quite place my name."

"It looks like it should be Joe, or Jim, or maybe Pete. . . ."

And the two of them dissolved into giggles.

An hour or so later, January took his place on the wide bow apron of the upper deck. The lamp in the Ladies' Parlor had been put out, but a few still burned in the Saloon, where Quince and Lundy played cribbage. January caught the names of William Lloyd Garrison, and Henry Clay, and of the Colonization Society. He glanced down the promenade toward Hannibal's stateroom, wondering if Miss Skippen would approach from the bow end or the stern, and whether, if she passed him here on the bow, he could remain unobtrusive by simply standing away from the lanterns. At six feet three he was not the most unobtrusive of men. . . .

"Benjamin."

Colonel Davis emerged from the door of the Saloon. January inclined his head respectfully, and after a moment's hesitation, the young planter came to his side.

"Benjamin, I regret to say I have been making inquiries pursuant to your case—" The corner of January's mouth twisted a little at the way it had become *his* case, and not Hannibal's—

"—and I must say I am becoming extremely troubled."

YOU are becoming troubled??? Sir.

"I have inquired of the whereabouts of every person on this boat, and you are one of very few who cannot account for his movements at or about midnight last night. Now, I don't say this to worry you," the Colonel added, raising a preemptory hand although January had made no attempt to interrupt. "I am much inclined to believe that you were where you say you were, in spite of Mr. Molloy's insinuations to the contrary. The man is a blackguard, a braggart, and a scoundrel . . . but a scoundrel who was in the presence of a witness when Mr. Weems met his end. And of those who have no alibi for the material time, you are the only one who seems to have had a connection with Mr. Weems."

"I'm the only one whose connection can be proven so far, sir," replied January slowly. "And you're right in that a man of my race will always be blamed before a man of yours—you know that's the way of the world." *At least it is in this country,* he wanted to add but didn't. But he saw in Davis's eyes the acknowledgment of his tribute to the planter's worldliness.

Davis said, a little to January's surprise, "I won't desert you. Whomever else the sheriff decides to detain in Mayersville for his investigation, I plan to leave the boat and remain as a witness, to make sure that justice is served."

"Thank you, sir," said January, and wondered how much further into his confidence he could take this stiff-necked and arrogant young man, and whether Colonel Davis might be prevailed upon, instead, to remain on the boat as some kind of assistance for Rose. "I've been asking questions, too. . . . Were you aware that Mr. Quince, who also lacks an alibi, comes, like Weems, from Philadelphia?"

Davis looked surprised. "Where heard you that?"

"I understand it was spoken of in the Ladies' Parlor as common knowledge. Since both Weems and Mr. Quince dabbled in Abolitionist circles, it isn't impossible that they knew one another there. I understand also—though this is only hearsay and I'm sure he will deny it—that Mr. Lundy went to considerable trouble to come up-river on this particular boat, and appears to have been less than truthful about his reasons for doing so: the doctor he claims to be going to see in Lexington doesn't exist. And I'm not sure if you know that Mr. Weems was blackmailing Mr. Cain."

"Blackmailing?" Davis's sparse, jutting eyebrows flicked upward, and the side of his face twitched. "That is a very serious charge to make on hearsay."

"It isn't hearsay, sir. I heard Weems threaten Cain with exposure of some secret, the night Cain came on board at Donaldsonville."

Davis was silent, stroking his wispy beard for a time. Then he glanced up at January. "That may be true—I have no way of knowing—but Mr. Cain was with Mr. Gleet the entire night."

"Doesn't that in itself strike you as a little odd, sir?" asked January diffidently. "Considering that Cain generally avoids Gleet?"

"Everyone avoids Gleet," agreed Davis. "The man is an excrescence, and I won't permit him on my place, for all he comes around two or three times a year trying to buy slaves or sell them—pah! A human mollusk." His sharp voice was shrill with distaste. "The worst of a bad class, of whom even the so-called best suffer by comparison to the average hound dog."

"Do you know why Cain detests Gleet the way he seems to?"

"I can't imagine any gentleman of taste who wouldn't." Davis frowned, as if realizing that Cain by definition did not fall into that category. "As for Cain, I don't know him or anything about him—he's new on the river. But it's curious that he would have paid Weems money at the threat of exposure, being already, as it were, the most despicable form of life known to man. Unless . . ." A look of momentary enlightenment flickered across the sharp features, then passed into a look of calculation, and the idea he'd scouted—almost certainly, January guessed, the possibility that Cain might himself be part African—was dropped.

It was a concern—and a cause for blackmail—everywhere in the South, where a man ran the risk of ostracism and possible enslavement if proven to bear even the smallest proportion of African blood in his veins: more than one murder had been committed in New Orleans to conceal just such information.

But a more Saxon product than the hawk-nosed Jubal Cain was hard to picture. The supposition was simply absurd.

Which left them where?

Bredon, Weems had called Cain.

Printed in the Mayersville Gazette.

What possible social consequences would threaten a man who was already a slave-dealer?

Striding footfalls shook the stairs that led down from the pilothouse. January whipped around as Molloy shoved past him, a pistol in his hand. He nearly ran down the promenade, January pelting at his heels, cursing himself for not finding a way to watch Hannibal's door during his talk with Davis—January and Davis had not quite caught up with the infuriated pilot when he reached Hannibal's door, yanked it open . . .

The lamplight within showed them all Theodora Skippen leaning against Hannibal and grasping his lapels, while Hannibal, backed to the wall, attempted to disengage her grip.

As the door was ripped open, Theodora whirled, mouth and eyes widening to a series of perfectly round O's; Hannibal began, "Sir, it isn't—"

"God damn you, if it isn't what it looks like, what is it, then?" bellowed Molloy, grabbed Hannibal by the front of his coat, hauled him from the room, and showed every sign of heaving him over the rail and into the river had not January and Davis both intervened.

Molloy thrashed against their grip, shouting curses—when Hannibal, with a sad lack of gallantry, dragged Theodora's note from his coat pocket and held it out, the pilot simply crushed it in his fist and hurled it overboard: "You don't think I don't know the bitch can't write? Nor read—she had to get someone to read her this. . . ."

He slashed Hannibal across the face with a sheet of notepaper and, when Hannibal took it, followed up the blow with the back of his hand. "And don't you be pretending you don't know what's there," snarled Molloy. "Now, sir, it's insulted me you have and done murder on my boat, and this time I will have satisfaction! You name your friends if you've got any!"

Hannibal probably could have gotten out of it with another abject apology—January had seen him wriggle out of worse—but Colonel Davis, face jerking with his tic, stepped forward and snapped, "You, sir, are a boor and a commoner, and I take it as an honor to stand as Mr. Sefton's friend."

"*Non tali auxilio nec defensoribus istis tempus eget,*" said Hannibal sadly, and Davis, ignoring him, went on.

"I take it that it shall be pistols at dawn?"

"It shall, and here the boat shall stand until we've had this out once and for all," shouted Molloy. "And you, surgeon—or surgeon's nigger"—he jabbed a finger at January—"you'd better be ready to take a bullet out of your master's thieving Ulsterman heart."

Curious, January bent down as Molloy seized Theodora by the wrist and went storming off toward the bow, Theodora gasping, "Oh, how I am undone! He deceived me, drew me into the room with lies. . . ."

The note said:

Beloved,

I have tried to put you from my heart, but I have failed. I can no longer live without your kisses. Please, please, come to my stateroom at ten.

Your own,
Hannibal

January could tell the difference, but the handwriting was an excellent facsimile of Hannibal's own.

SEVENTEEN

So eager was Colonel Davis that *someone* should stand up and take a shot at Kevin Molloy that he was very little use as a second. "The man is a boor and a swine," he announced decisively at the War Council that took place in Hannibal's stateroom minutes after Molloy's departure with Theodora in tow. "You're a gentleman, Sefton. You should be able to out-shoot him with ease."

"Ah." Hannibal took a long, shaky swig of opium-laced sherry. "A fact which entirely slipped my mind in the excitement of the moment . . ."

"Brace up, man! Surely you aren't thinking of backing out?"

"I have the feeling that I backed *in*. . . . As challenged, mine is the choice of weapons, I believe? And conditions?"

The door opened without the smallest vestige of a knock. It was Gleet.

"Molloy asks, what'll you have?"

Davis's sensitive nostrils flared like a spurred thoroughbred's at this display of arrogance from a man he despised. "Pistols at twenty paces!" he snapped before Hannibal could open his mouth to suggest shuttlecocks at a hundred yards. "And you can tell that bog-Irish blackguard that he should consider himself fortunate that gentlemen of blood would consider going out with him at all!" He turned back to Hannibal as Gleet left in an offended huff. "I applaud your chivalry of heart, sir, in trying to help the young lady, but I fear she is scarcely worth a gentleman's assistance."

"I actually deduced that some time ago," responded Hannibal, taking another drink only to have Davis remove the flask from his grip. "I didn't write that note."

"The minx wrote it herself, then," said Davis serenely. "She's doubtless lying herself to perdition at this moment. . . ."

"*I'm* the one who's going to end up being lied to perdition. . . ."

"Nonsense, man," said Davis. "Buck up! No rabble can shoot straight. You'll do splendidly."

"Who do you think did it?" asked Hannibal after Davis strode off, a-bristle with righteousness, to further confer with Gleet and locate pistols. The fiddler's hands were shaking as he uncapped his laudanum-bottle. Then he glanced at it and re-capped it, and thrust it at January. "Don't let me have that again." He took it back, took one last quick drink, and pressed it into January's hand. "My money's on La Pécheresse. I'll bet she's got a pretty skill at forgery, and she'd welcome the chance to have me laid out on the floor next to her dear departed."

"You aren't going to go through with it?"

"Do you think I'd get far ashore? You and I go over the side, they'll have posses after us for the murder before you can say *Issaquena County*. . . . And where does that leave Rose? Here on the boat alone? Or announcing her complicity by fleeing with us?"

"Where does that leave Rose—or myself—if you get killed and Davis hands me over to the sheriff at Mayersville . . . if I make it to Mayersville, with jackals like Gleet and Cain aboard? Completely aside from the loss of your friendship . . ."

"I'm sure there are plenty of other drunken wastrels in the world for you to choose from if you really miss my company," retorted Hannibal bitterly.

"None that play the fiddle as well as you, though." Rose stepped through the stateroom door and shut it behind her, and, putting her arms around Hannibal's neck from behind, kissed the bare scalp in one of the long fjords of his hairline. "And if you were killed, with whom would I make jokes about the *Dialogues* of Plato? Run for it. Both of you. I can at least stay long enough to see what La Pécheresse does next. . . ."

"I'm not leaving you alone on the same boat with Gleet," said January at the same moment Hannibal said, "And I will not condemn the pair of you to the sort of poverty I've been living in since I washed up on these shores."

"All right," agreed Rose readily. "But please review for me the part about how both of you being dead will help my situation?"

"Either we all run or we all stay," said Hannibal firmly. "Who knows? I may actually shoot the man. Twenty paces isn't *that* far."

"As you say." Rose's voice was grim as she turned the implication around. The light of the single oil-lamp transformed her spectacle lenses into ovals of gold as she folded her arms. "Have you ever handled a pistol?"

"It's been many years," admitted the fiddler. "And I was never very good at it. The one duel I fought when I was up at Oxford was with a dear friend, and we were both so drunk, it's astonishing we didn't kill our seconds while trying to delope."

"Sounds promising," said Rose. "Was the woman you fought over properly appreciative of the occasion?"

"How did you know it was a woman?" asked Hannibal, genuinely surprised, and Rose rolled her eyes.

"This is serious," said January quietly. "Someone is trying to murder both of us using Molloy's temper—and his marksmanship—as the weapon. Without Hannibal's protection and testimony I stand a very good chance of being hanged once the boat reaches Mayersville. Even with it, it's going to be a closer call than I like."

"They really have nothing on you except Molloy's testimony," pointed out Rose reasonably. "And as Hannibal showed, that can easily be explained as a mistake. There's an even chance that the case against you will fall apart in the face of any kind of defense at all, particularly when all the facts come out."

"Facts like me being a depositor in the bank that Weems robbed?"

"Absolutely," said Rose. "For all you knew at the time, Weems was your only link with your money. We may even be able to convince the sheriff to hold the *Silver Moon* for a proper search . . . though I imagine Molloy will put up a fight about it."

"And the demand by a single woman, and a woman of color to boot, would not carry much weight with the average county sheriff, would it?" asked Hannibal quietly. "Whereas even my death would convince Colonel Davis that I am a man of honor, and hence my cause is worthy of his taking up arms in its—and your—defense."

"I am not," said January grimly, "going to stand by and let you get killed in the cause of convincing Colonel Davis of our honor. It's all of us run or none of us—hanged or acquitted, our detention in Mayersville is going to lose us the money. I think it may be time for all of us to go over the side and swim for shore."

He reached under the narrow bed as he spoke, and pulled out Hannibal's meager valise. Outside, footfalls hastened back and forth along the promenade, and confused voices proclaimed the general uproar on the boat as the tale of seduction, discovery, and challenge spread. January could only imagine the comments flying about the engine-room as Molloy announced that the *Silver Moon* would remain in place until dawn—that the fires had to be drawn again, the steam dumped off.

In the confusion, he supposed, it would be an easy matter to slip over the rail, though he didn't look forward to trying to navigate the woods in the darkness, with or without the added complication of Levi Christmas and Company. At least, he reflected, it would be some time before their disappearance was confirmed, and they could probably make it down to Vicksburg again and take a boat for New Orleans. . . .

Hannibal settled back in his chair and folded his arms, watching

January with a stony dark gaze that eventually stilled January in his tracks.

The two friends regarded one another in silence. Then January said, "I won't have you die for the sake of my money."

"He might not kill me," said Hannibal.

"Pigs might fly," added Rose in a tone of helpful sarcasm. "If you do not flee with us now, we shall be obliged to drag you into the river by force, you know."

"I shall cling to the rail and scream," replied Hannibal.

Rose started to speak, then closed her mouth with a whisper of released breath. January set the valise down on the bunk. Outside on the promenade, Dorothea Roberson's voice pleaded tearfully, ". . . Surely they cannot delay us further! We have nothing to do with this terrible muddle. . . ."

"You two have saved my life more than once," said Hannibal into the cicada-ridden quiet that followed. "And I have been able to do nothing—literally nothing—except express my undying gratitude, entertaining as far as it goes but of as little use as anything else I've managed to produce in the course of my misspent life. Our flight—and the concomitant relinquishment of the chase—is almost certainly the intent of this little badger-game, whether it was La Pécheresse who forged those notes or Molloy himself. And I rather resent the automatic assumption," he added, "that I will turn tail."

"I'm not going to be like the lady in the ballad," said January, "who throws her glove into the lion's den simply to see if her suitor loves her enough to fetch it out. *No love, quoth he, but vanity / Sets love a task like that.*"

"He may not kill me," repeated Hannibal. "Depending on the sheriff's views on dueling, Molloy runs the risk of being taken off the *Silver Moon* himself if he does—*Is* dueling illegal in Mississippi? Or anywhere in the South? All he has to do is miss once—then even if I miss *my* shot, which I almost certainly will, it is up to me, not him, to demand a second round. But I won't let you lose all that you've worked for because I haven't the courage to stand still for one shot which may not even hit me."

A brisk knock: to Hannibal's *"Ine!"* Davis appeared, followed by Gleet, both of whom stopped on the threshold in surprise to see not only January, but Rose in the stateroom. In the thin line of Davis's lips—and the twitch in his face—January read disapproval. A man's valet is one thing, but the presence of that valet's sweetheart as well bordered on willing fraternization with people of color that ill became the gentleman Hannibal was striving to personate.

"Mr. Byrne was able to provide us with a pair of pistols," said Davis as Rose departed with a curtsy and a smile. "Do these meet with your approval?" He held out a rosewood case containing a pair of silver-mounted Mantons—from somewhere on the promenade little Neil Tredgold's voice whooped triumphantly, "Bang! You're dead!"

Hannibal's mouth flinched under his mustache, but he said steadily, "They do, thank you."

"The encounter itself will take place on the bank of the river," continued Davis. "There is a clearing there about thirty yards in length, just this side of Hitchins' Chute. The ground is level and the surrounding trees are thick enough to prevent the sun from giving especial advantage to one or the other. However, the encounter will take place as soon as it is light enough to see, so direct sunlight itself should be no issue. Ben, will you accompany the shore party as surgeon?"

January inclined his head. Gleet objected, "Mr. Molloy's not gonna want no nigger pokin' around, if Sefton should happen to wing him," and Davis regarded him with cold blue eyes and demanded, "You have an alternative candidate?"

Gleet didn't, but retired nevertheless to consult his principal on the subject, and Hannibal spent most of the remainder of the night writing out a true account of Weems's theft, Granville's instructions, and the status of January and Rose, both legally and vis-à-vis the Bank of Louisiana, "in case worse comes to worst." January, descending to the galley in quest of coffee, found, as he had suspected, the rest of the boat in a state of milling excitement, the deck-passengers already staking out positions along the rail of the upper-deck promenade to watch, and laying bets as to the outcome. Even the deck-hands were betting—one of them asked January what Hannibal's experience of dueling had been and he was hard-pressed not to throw the man overboard. As he passed the engine-room door he heard the crew cursing as they dumped steam and probed the glowing amber maws of the furnaces to draw out the fires once again.

"That Molloy, he come down to the engine-room for a couple planks to make hisself a target," said Eli as he poured out coffee for January from the pot on the iron spider above the flames in the box of sand. "He say he gonna shoot at playin' cards, to put his eye in." And even as he spoke, from overhead came the bellow of a pistol.

January felt in his coat for Hannibal's flask—not that the fiddler didn't almost certainly have a spare in his luggage somewhere. He only hoped Hannibal's nerves were sufficient to get him through the night without recourse to an anodyne that wouldn't help his aim any the following morning.

"According to Jim," said Rose when January encountered her on the promenade outside, "a note saying, *You are betrayed—Miss S has gone to Sefton's room* was tucked under the coffee-cup that Thucydides carried up to Molloy in the pilot-house at ten. I haven't located Thu to check this, but I've certainly seen the note, which Jim retrieved from the pilot-house floor. The paper looks like that in the writing-desks of both the Saloon and the Ladies' Parlor, and the ink seems identical to that of the note purporting to be from Hannibal to Theodora. Cissy brought the blotting-paper from the Ladies' Parlor for me just now, and there's nothing on it that matches. . . ."

"Which means only that Mrs. Fischer—or Molloy, or whoever arranged this trap—worked in his or her room." January set the small tray of coffee-cup and miniature pot down on top of one of the crates that had been left on the deck after the great Investigation that morning: it was labeled Triple-Refined Sugar and destined for Giron's

Confectionery in Lexington, Kentucky. "I wonder if Sophie could be prevailed upon to check Mrs. Fischer's waste-basket? How often does Thu empty them? I wonder."

"Daily, but it's been a most confused day." She flinched at another pistol-shot from the Saloon. "The one in Hannibal's stateroom hadn't been emptied. I'll see if I can get Sophie to check. Mrs. Fischer has returned to the Parlor, with the other ladies, to discuss the fate of That Man. . . ."

"Are they laying bets?" asked January with savage irony, and Rose laid a hand on his arm.

He sighed, hearing the rage in his own voice, and shook his head.

"Evidence of a trap won't help Hannibal tomorrow . . . good Heavens, this morning, I should say. . . ." Rose glanced through the window of the galley beside her, at the big box-clock that hung on the wall in the corner. "But whatever we find will strengthen our case when we get to Mayersville."

"If we get there." January took her hand gratefully, then scrubbed a weary palm over his unshaven face. "It feels like we've been stalled on this particular bend of the river for days." And it felt like weeks, he thought, since he'd swum out along the shallow waters over Horsehead Bar, to be hauled up onto the *Silver Moon* again, battered and exhausted by his cross-country jaunt from Vicksburg. Yet it had been only Sunday, the day before yesterday.

Strange, he thought, that so little time had passed since the most complicated matter in his life had been to simply stay with the boat and watch Oliver Weems. Since the solution to the problem had been merely one of finding which trunks the stolen gold and securities were in, and proving the crime on Weems.

And now even the retrieval of the money, if it could be accomplished, began to seem like a tawdry and trivial goal compared to all the greater things he could not do. Compared to the image of the woman Mary walking back to the isolated prison of her slavery, to the thought of Julie weeping on Rose's shoulder, terrified of a fate to which she'd been betrayed . . .

Compared to the voices of the chained men along the starboard promenade, singing to keep up their spirits in the night, and the ropy cross-hatch of scars on 'Rodus's back.

And those things filled him with a helpless aching, like those dreams of trying to rescue Rose from some terrible fate. But this was the world into which he woke from dreams.

There was nothing that he could do, he knew. Not even vote for men who might change what the Founding Fathers of the United States had decreed should be.

The thought of simply taking his money—if he could find it—and using it to make himself, and Rose, and their future children as safe as he could make them, now felt to him as dirty and mean as if he were leaping into a rowboat from a sinking ship, leaving 'Rodus and Jim, Julie and Sophie, and all the rest chained on board to die.

The sense of helplessness was worse than his earlier anger, his earlier fear.

Another shot cracked out, and he cursed, thinking of Hannibal back in his cabin, patiently writing out instructions to be opened in the event of his death. Rose slid her arms around him, comforting or seeking comfort; he pressed his cheek to the soft white folds of her tignon, the scent of her, as always, dissolving the pain inside.

He couldn't do a thing to save Mary back in Mississippi, or Julie hiding in the woods along the river, or the men and women chained along the sides of the 'tween-decks fifteen feet away from him. . . . He couldn't do a thing to save Hannibal, short of murdering Molloy himself, and even that might not work. . . .

He couldn't even accomplish what he'd set out to do on the *Silver Moon*, namely, find where the Bank of Louisiana funds were and pin the crime on Fischer and Weems. Somewhere out there in the deepening blackness of the Mississippi woods, he thought, Baron Cemetery and the Grand Zombi and Guédé-Five-Days-Unhappy were all laughing—and down in the hold, Queen Régine was laughing, too.

And waiting.

Had the Bank of Louisiana collapsed during the course of this past week? Would Hubert Granville even be in New Orleans still, to back up January's assertions when the sheriff at Mayersville would, inevitably, write for clarification?

And what would happen if Granville had absconded as well?

To distract his mind from this question, he followed Rose over to the lantern that hung in the galley passway, where Winslow, Andy, and most of the deck-hands were clustered around Jim, gaping at the Fatal Note. A comparison under his magnifying lens showed January that the two notes, though the handwriting was disguised, had been written with the same pen, or at least with two pens cut at precisely the same angle, almost certainly by the same hand, though whether that hand had been a man's or a woman's he couldn't tell. Thucydides still could not be located to tell how the Fatal Note had come to be under the Fatal Coffee-Cup, but Eli, when asked, said he put up the tray for the pilot on the counter near the door, for either Thu or one of the lesser stewards to carry up at ten. Anyone could have gotten to it.

And given the absolute darkness that reigned once you got three steps away from the light of the passway, January supposed that even a statuesque matron could have managed it, particularly one in the inky black of full mourning.

As he climbed the steps to the boiler-deck and Hannibal's stateroom once again, January heard, along the misty blackness of the banks, the first birdsong of the early-breaking summer dawn, and his heart flinched in his chest like a beached trout dying in air.

Due to Molloy's objection to a "nigger doctor" "poking" him, January was at the last minute dropped from the shore party in favor of Mr. Quince, who claimed expertise in both the mystical healing of the long-vanished Egyptians, and the "vegetarian mathematics" of the Thompsonian system of medicine. "If you see me go down, come over to the shore if you have to swim," said Hannibal as he put on his frayed coat and the darkest and plainest of his rather tattered collection of waistcoats.

"Is there anyone we should notify if you're badly hurt?" asked Rose tactfully, and handed the fiddler a black velvet ribbon to tie his hair.

Hannibal cocked an ironic eye back at her, knowing that she really meant "killed." Since he'd appeared in New Orleans four and a half years ago, he had never spoken to January—or to anyone January knew—of his former life, though he was clearly a man of breeding and education. He would speak sometimes of being up at Oxford, or of the family estates in County Mayo or their town-house in London. But why he had left them, and how he had fetched up in New Orleans a penniless consumptive opium-eater with a hundred-guinea Italian violin, January could only guess. Somewhere in London, or in the English-held estates of western Ireland, there was undoubtedly a family Bible with a name that probably wasn't Hannibal Sefton, with a date of birth and also a date of death. January wondered how long ago that second date had been filled in.

"I think everyone who cares anything about me is here." Hannibal kissed Rose's hand, then clasped January's. "And I must say you're displaying a woeful lack of confidence in my abilities at both shooting and dodging," he added, pulling on his shabby gloves. "At least that idiot Davis didn't demand bowie-knives, though I'd have been able to hold my own with a sword, or I did back in the days when I had any wind to speak of. I shall be all right." He looked as white as a sheet—and stone-cold sober—in the grimy glow.

January followed him down to the skiff, then made his way back to the servants' end of the promenade to watch. Even the deck-hands, and the male slaves, had paused in their work, and clustered the rail like ravens on a fence, watching the skiff pull to shore. On the hurricane deck, Roberson and Lockhart set down their rifles and turned their attention from vigilance to observation: "You'd think it was a public hanging," muttered January as he and Rose edged their way to the rail among the other servants. The engineer's curses to trim the boat might just as well have been the whistling of the birds.

Over the past twenty-four hours the river had fallen still farther. It was going to take some tricky maneuvering to come away from the vicinity of Hitchins' Chute: the glassy brown surface was broken by a hundred splinters and daggers of black snags barely showing above the water, and by a hundred more deadly arrowheads of ripple that marked others still hidden. Davis and Gleet, rowing the skiff, had to back or push a number of times to keep the little craft from tangling itself in the floating branches, and Mr. Quince, sitting stiffly amidships with a satchel full of bandages and medicines, winced visibly every time the boat so much as rocked.

As Davis had said, there was a clear space of thirty or forty feet on the bank, perhaps twenty feet above the muddy water and ooze of the river's brim. Behind it the trees formed a misty wall, which curved inward on both ends toward the river. At the downstream end the land rose into a higher bank above the chute, where the trees grew thicker near the now-invisible water. At the upstream end a tangle of willows and cottonwoods hovered over the jumble of leafy trash that the retreating water had left. The final shadows of night seemed to linger beneath the trees.

Behind January a slave dropped an armload of wood, and Cain shouted, "You black bastard, I've seen trained donkeys at the circus less clumsy than you!"

Nervous? January wondered as Mr. Tredgold—at the bellowed command of his wife—hurried to admonish the slave-dealer for cursing in the presence of the ladies crowding the rail above. It wasn't like the imperturbable dealer to shout at his slaves.

The skiff scraped the mud bank just west of the chute, and Molloy leaped ashore, as if impatient to kill his man and be done with it and on his way. Hannibal fished a flask from his pocket, then put it back unsipped. He looked very small and thin stepping ashore among the tangle of deadfalls, jetsam, and matted leaves.

The seconds conferred for a few minutes, then loaded both Mr. Byrne's pistols and held them out to their principals to choose.

Twenty yards, when paced off, looked appallingly short.

Rose's hand closed around January's.

A raven burst, squawking, from the stand of oaks that marked the entrance to Hitchins' Chute, like a vengeful ghost in the gray dawn-light.

Davis held up his handkerchief, and let it drop. The roar of the shots ringing out together was like a cannon.

Molloy spun like a kicked rag-doll, arms flung out, blood spraying from his head. His knees buckled and he dropped.

Hannibal stood for what seemed like nearly a minute as Gleet and Davis strode to the body; Mr. Quince sat down very suddenly on the nearest deadfall tree and put his head between his knees. In the gray morning mists, the pistol still in his hand, Hannibal looked absolutely alone as he lowered the weapon, then let it slip from his fingers. He turned, and walked as shakily as a drunken man to the edge of the river, where he fell to his knees and was violently sick.

EIGHTEEN

"Get your tools, boy." A rough hand gripped January's arm. "The man needs a real doctor, not that quack." The next moment Jubal Cain leaned over the rail and bellowed, "Send the skiff back, damn you!" to the men on shore.

Davis pressed a hand to the chest of the man at whose side he knelt, glanced across at the obviously useless Quince, and said something to Gleet. The slave-dealer grunted a reply but went to the skiff and began to row, while Davis got to his feet and walked over to Hannibal. From the engine-room, January could hear shouting beginning—including a whoop of joy from old Winslow, who was apparently the only man with faith in Hannibal's aim or luck. Mr. Souter came running down the steps in a panic, and January heard Tredgold gabbling, "What are we going to do . . . ?"

"Idiot," grunted Cain, thrusting January along ahead of him to the bow-deck. His yellow fox-eyes glinted under the white slant of brows and his pockmarked face was grim. "Should have thought of that. . . . Guy! Marcus! Zack! Gonna need hands to carry that paddy bastard's corpse . . . Porter! Clay! And the rest of you trim the boat, god damn you! Nothing more on shore to see."

The men of his coffle promptly retreated. Nobody else did.

"What the hell they gonna do for a pilot now?" demanded Gleet as he maneuvered the little boat against the rails. "We're losin' money every day, feedin' these damn niggers—"

"What the hell you think?" snarled Cain. "Man doesn't need to have nerves to guide a boat. Just brains enough not to get himself killed over yellow-headed bitches that aren't any better than they should be. Get in the boat, god damn you," he added, half throwing his remaining men down into the skiff. As he climbed down after them, January saw Mrs. Fischer thrust her way through the little gathering of women at the promenade rail, staring out across the water at Molloy's body lying on the weedy bank.

January was the first ashore when the skiff scraped mud a few feet from the corpse. "Mr. Sefton is unwounded," said Davis, who had returned to Molloy's side, probably to discourage the attentions of the ravens and buzzards that had already begun to circle overhead. "But deeply shaken, as any man of sensitive nature would be . . ."

Quince was crouched beside Hannibal, still rather greenish himself, proffering a bottle and spoon at which Hannibal was shaking his head with weary nausea. "I assure you," Quince was saying, "that a decoction of boiled lettuce-root and honey is a sovereign remedy for complaints of the stomach."

"Pray do not corrupt me with pallid brews and weak elixirs," whispered Hannibal as January came near. "And the problem is not my stomach but my nerves . . . and probably my heart. Nothing will do for it but laudanum, and lots of it. . . ."

"Are you all right?" The fiddler was still shaking all over, as if with deathly cold despite the humid heat already thick in the air.

Hannibal responded with a cracked laugh. "As all right as any man is who has slain his first man.

Will all green Neptune's ocean
Wash this blood clean from my hand?
No, this my hand will rather the multitudinous seas incarnadine,
Making the green one red. . . ."

"He would have killed you!" said Quince in considerable surprise.

"Ah, that makes it all right, then."

"It does," said January firmly, pulling Hannibal to his feet. In a lower voice, he added, "God knows what kind of mess it's going to make of Mrs. Fischer's plans to get her treasure back without anyone knowing. . . ." And was rewarded by his friend's sudden wan grin.

"Good God, I'd forgotten it was Molloy who knows where the money is. What do you bet she's searching his cabin even as we speak?" He tried to take a step and caught January's arm; his hand, when January felt it, was like ice, his face still gray and clammy with sweat. "Did you bet on me?"

"No!" said January, anger flaring in the aftermath of shock. "I didn't bet at all."

"Pity. It might have made your search for your four thousand dollars superrogatory." Hannibal shivered violently, clearly struggling to stay on his feet. He would have been easier to carry bodily—he weighed barely more than a hundred pounds—but he shook off January's offer to do so.

Cain, in the meantime, had gone with his little gang of slaves to the woods to cut saplings for a litter for the dead man, leaving, again, Davis alone beside the corpse. January bestowed Hannibal in the skiff and went back to kneel beside the Colonel in the mud.

"It was a splendid shot for a pistol." Davis nodded down at the handkerchief he'd laid over Molloy's head. January lifted the big square of red-blotched white linen, looked down at the gaping crimson hole just beside the left eye. "In a similar situation I don't think I'd have had the resolution to aim for the head. It's far too easy to miss, even at twenty paces. Your master is a remarkable man."

"He is indeed," said January, thinking of what it had cost Hannibal, to stand out there and let an experienced marksman aim at him with a loaded gun.

"To be honest—if you will forgive my saying so—I did not think he had it in him." Davis edged aside as January examined the wound. "I have commanded men, and am something of a judge of them. Mr.

Sefton is not one I would have chosen for a mission requiring desperation or resolution."

"He fools many people," agreed January, sitting back a little on his heels. Then he leaned forward again, and with as matter-of-fact an air as he could muster, went on to press his hands to Molloy's chest and sides beneath his blue pea-jacket, to listen to Molloy's chest, and to extract the contents of Molloy's pockets. "Had Mr. Molloy near kin?" he asked, spreading out the temperance tract and rumpled copy of the *Liberator* that Molloy had clearly been tearing up for cigar-spills, and laying upon them the cigar-case, match-box, stateroom key, and thirty dollars in assorted coin and Bank of Louisiana banknotes that the pockets had yielded.

"Mr. Tredgold would know," replied Davis, wrapping the items in the tracts and folding them together carefully. "He certainly never spoke of family, though of course I was not intimate with a person such as that."

January felt around Molloy's waist and drew out a money-belt containing another five hundred dollars, a hundred of which was in the form of gold Spanish or Portuguese dollars. These were common currency on the river, of course . . . as were banknotes from the Bank of Louisiana, which was one of the largest establishments in New Orleans and was, of course, Molloy's own Bank. There was nothing else in the belt, nor in Molloy's pockets: no nails, no unexplained keys, no letters.

"There will be an inquiry, of course, in Mayersville." Davis unfolded his lean form as Cain and his gang returned from the woods and began to lash together a makeshift bier. Interestingly—to January at any rate—violence and death seemed to have calmed the young Colonel's tic rather than exacerbated it. "I think there is ample evidence that it was Molloy who provoked the quarrel; perhaps sufficient reason to believe that had your master not accepted the challenge, Molloy might have resorted to less formal violence. You will not lose many days on your journey, and I assure you, I will debark also to testify to all that I have seen."

"Sir," said January, glancing across the water at the *Silver Moon,* "I appreciate that, and I thank you for all the help you have been. But I am almost certain now that the quarrel was engineered by others—by someone who sent messages to both Hannibal—my master," he corrected himself quickly, "—to Miss Skippen, and to Mr. Molloy, with the intention of forcing a duel in order to get us, and Molloy, off the boat."

"Surely you're not still claiming that Weems's ill-gotten goods are hidden somewhere aboard? Every trunk and crate was searched. . . ."

"Every trunk and crate was on that boat for days—long enough for Molloy, I am almost certain, to transfer the bulk of the gold and stock certificates to another hiding-place on board," said January. "I think that's what Weems was looking for when he was killed. If this boat continues on without us, we lose all chance of finding the loot—and incidentally any chance of identifying once and for all Weems's murderer."

Davis was silent, one finger curling around the ends of his wispy beard, studying January's face with thoughtful eyes. Beside them, Guy and 'Rodus gently lifted Molloy's body onto the bier, and the other slaves clustered around to load it into the skiff. January glanced back toward the *Silver Moon,* and saw Mrs. Fischer on the bow end of the boiler-deck, engaged in what looked like a furious three-way argument with Theodora Skippen and Thucydides.

The Colonel said slowly, "Well, I admit that there is something very strange going on aboard the *Silver Moon*—something that has so far cost two men their lives. I believe that a great number of people are lying about what happened the night before last, and about why you and your master came aboard the vessel in the first place. But as for delaying the entire boat so that it can be taken apart piece by piece . . ."

"I suspect there's something in Mr. Molloy's stateroom that may help us," said January desperately. "When we get back to the boat, with your permission, and in your presence, I'd like to have a look through the room. . . ."

"I think that's a good idea. I am most curious myself as to what we might find there."

"And if I might be so bold as to make the suggestion, it might be a good idea to lock and seal the door until the room can be examined."

Davis looked a little surprised. "Aren't you coming back to the boat with us now?"

"I'll return in a few minutes. Half an hour at the latest. There's something I want to look at here on shore—or look *for*. Could you speak to Mr. Tredgold about holding the boat until I come back, sir?"

The Colonel nodded, evidently perfectly comfortable with the thought of a trusted slave being permitted to poke about on shore unsupervised. With Hannibal huddled in the bow, and Quince clinging queasily to the stern gunwale and trying not to touch the corpse, the skiff set out over the water, leaving January alone on the bank under the watchful rifles of two deck-hands and Mr. Lockhart on the hurricane deck.

Even with such guardians, January had qualms about remaining on shore alone, though on balance he judged that Davis's authority—self-assumed though it might be—would be better used in making sure Mrs. Fischer didn't ransack Molloy's stateroom, than in witnessing whatever he himself might find here. He first paced off the dueling-ground, finding in the damp mud of the bank the marks of Hannibal's battered old boots, and, twenty paces away, the rucked-up, bloodied earth where Molloy had stood.

Putting his feet in the heel-gouges left by the pilot's first rocked-back shock, he sighted along his own outstretched arm to where Hannibal had stood . . . then turned his head just slightly to the left.

He was looking straight at the little rise of ground covered with oak trees, from which the raven had flown, shrieking, a moment before Davis had given the signal to fire.

But when he reached the grove itself, January gave a groan of frustration, for it was here that Cain's slaves had cut the saplings for Molloy's litter. Bare feet, ragged knees, had left their marks everywhere. Saplings had been pulled up, branches broken . . . any of those forked sticks lying snapped on the ground could have been used to rest the barrel of a rifle on. If the still, damp air here had ever held the smell of powder smoke, it was gone now, shaken away by the stir of activity.

January could only kneel in the soft earth behind a bank of hackberry brambles, where a break in the foliage gave a clear view of the dueling-ground, and of the place where a few minutes before he—and earlier Molloy—had stood. But whatever tracks might have been left there, by whoever it was who frightened the raven from its perch, had been obliterated.

He returned to the upstream edge of the dueling-ground, and for nearly half an hour searched the straggling willows and cottonwoods without finding a lodged pistol-ball that would have borne out his theory of what had actually taken place on the shore. By the time Thu called out to him that Mr. Souter wanted to get under way—that Simon in the engine-room had threatened to cut his own throat before he drew out the fires one more time—January had still found nothing.

One of the deck-hands rowed across in the skiff, and brought him back.

"What were you looking for?" asked Rose, waiting for him on the promenade.

"Hannibal's pistol-ball," said January. "Did you see Molloy when they brought him aboard?"

She shook her head.

"He was shot through the left temple, just in back of the zygomatic bone—the outer rim of the eye socket."

"How could Hannibal have shot him there?" asked Rose immediately. "If he was looking straight at Hannibal to fire . . ."

"Exactly. The hole is huge, and the path of the bullet—as far as I could see, and I'll probe it when I see the body again to make sure—seems to go diagonally through the head, cracking the right occipital bone in the back. When Davis dropped the handkerchief as a signal to fire, did you see anything strange? Anything out of the ordinary?"

"Other than two grown men shooting at one another because one of them didn't like the fact that the other had spoken to a woman he claimed was 'his own'? I was watching Hannibal," she added in a gentler voice. "Hoping against hope he'd be all right."

"*Is* he all right?"

Rose sighed. "He's probably unconscious with laudanum by this time, and who can blame him? He looked deathly sick when he came aboard, and went straight to his stateroom. That Skippen hussy came tearing down the stair and tried to throw herself into his arms and he thrust her aside, but he couldn't speak. She's knocked at the door of his stateroom three times since, and tried to open it—I was keeping watch at the end of the promenade—but it's locked from the inside. What did you see?"

"Two grown men shooting at one another," replied January with a wry grin. Then he sobered. "I was watching Hannibal, too. But when I saw the wound in Molloy's head I remembered how that raven flew up, just before the signal to fire, and it came to me that the *whole thing* might have been set up. That the intended victim wasn't Hannibal and myself, but Molloy. I think Molloy was shot with a rifle from that little oak grove at the head of the chute."

"By whom?" asked Rose, startled. "Mrs. Fischer was on the promenade with Mrs. Tredgold and Mrs. Roberson—I saw her. And Mr. Cain was on the deck below."

"Levi Christmas, maybe? Or one of his men?"

"But that would imply communication between him and someone on board—either Theodora or one of those awful deck-passengers. Since we've been stopped, there hasn't been a moment when there wasn't a guard of some kind on the hurricane deck. I don't think they could even have signaled without being seen."

"I know," said January. "I didn't say this was something I could prove, or even explain. But one thing I can and will do is have a look at the bullet lodged in Molloy's skull. And if it's a ball from a Manton dueling pistol, I'll eat it."

While they'd been speaking, the great stern paddle had begun to turn, slowly driving the *Silver Moon* out into the channel of the river from the dead water behind the point. The river had fallen to its former low level, and the boat was surrounded by a veritable forest of snags that scraped at the hull and caught in the paddle, forcing the vessel to stop repeatedly while the deck-hands clambered here and there with poles to thrust off. January could hear Mr. Souter's voice yelling down from the hurricane deck, and unbidden to his mind rose the thought of what it must be like to be hidden in the damp, smelly darkness of the hold, listening to the grate of dead wood on the thin walls and knowing how much water lay immediately outside.

The thought made him shudder. He might fear Queen Régine, waiting like a spider down there in the darkness—holding whatever secret it was that she held about Weems's death—but he pitied her, too. She was a woman half-crazy and without fear, but there were limits even to craziness and courage.

January wasn't certain he could have stayed down there and listened to that horrible scraping sound.

When he and Rose reached the upper deck, almost the first thing they encountered was a knot of people grouped at the corner of the 'tween-decks near the door of Molloy's stateroom. Colonel Davis stood by the door, looking as if he wished he could simply call a sergeant and order everyone back to their quarters. Mrs. Fischer, her handsome face flushed behind the black veils she'd assumed, was shouting at him, "The man was a thief and a scoundrel, and I know that it was he who stole poor Mr. Weems's money! Mr. Weems told me himself, that on Saturday, when the boat ran aground on the bar above Vicksburg, and all the men were pressed into service in that *disgraceful* manner, he came back to find his stateroom door open and his money gone. . . ."

"And you just *know* it was poor Kevin, do you?" Miss Skippen lashed at her shrilly. "You just *saw* in his face that he was evil, because he didn't play up to you and tell you you were beautiful, is that it?" She turned to Davis, clutching at his sleeve. "Oh, what am I to do? Mr. Davis, I *must* get into that cabin! I left some things—my money—

with Kevin—with Mr. Molloy—for safekeeping, and I must get them back! Oh, to be left this way without my fiancé's protection . . ."

"Fiancé?" Mrs. Tredgold sniffed. "A fine way to treat your *fiancé,* to make up to other men and send him to his grave, not that I believe for a *moment* that he offered to marry such a piece of work as yourself. . . ."

"Ladies," pleaded Mr. Tredgold faintly.

"You see here." Mrs. Tredgold stabbed a thick finger at Davis. "I've heard the rumor that you plan to tell the sheriff at Mayersville to hold the entire boat for investigation of these absurd stories about Weems having a fortune in stolen gold aboard. . . . What I have to say is, I'd like to see that fortune! You order us about, ransack every piece of luggage on board, delay us needlessly, run up a fortune in wood-charges that we'll have to pay and soon, if we're to make it to Mayersville at all. . . ."

"And where do you think you're going?" Mrs. Fischer rounded on January as he tried to speak quietly to Davis. Without waiting for a reply she went on. "You forbid me to enter the stateroom of a man who robbed my fiancé, yet you're going to let a thieving black Negro in—"

"As a surgeon, Madame," interposed January, "I need to make an examination of the body—"

"For what purpose? We all know he's dead."

Theodora cried, "Oh!" and sagged against the rail of the stair up to the hurricane deck. Nobody paid any attention.

"All you want to do is search the room for anything you can get that you think will help your master prove my poor Oliver was a thief! Well, if *he* can enter, then so can *I*!"

"Madame, you will do nothing of the sort," retorted Davis, blotches of color staining his pale cheekbones. "I will accompany this boy and no one else—"

"Who are you to treat us like you were a policeman and we were all criminals?" interrupted Mrs. Fischer, shoving her face inches from the planter's. "You paid your passage on this boat like everyone else!"

"Tredgold," said Mrs. Tredgold sharply, "it's for you to take charge here. Now, you go into that stateroom and look for Mr. Weems's money for poor Mrs. Fischer!"

Davis stared at her, speechless with indignation, and from above Souter shouted, "Mr. Lundy says, if you're all gonna argue, argue someplace else! He can't hear the leadsman and he can't hardly hear himself think, he says!"

"You be quiet!" yelled Mrs. Tredgold back. "This is my husband's boat and we'll say what we want, where we want to!"

"Dearest . . ."

Mr. Souter came hesitantly halfway down the steps from the deck above. The *Silver Moon* had begun to move, the breeze flowing down the river as they rounded Hitchins' Point riffling his thinning black hair. "Er—then Mr. Lundy says your husband can pilot the boat wherever he wants it to go."

Geranium-red with fury, Mrs. Tredgold stormed up the steps, nearly shoving Mr. Souter over the rail. Davis and January darted at once to the stateroom door, to which Davis bent with a key, probably obtained from Thu. Mrs Fischer strode in their wake like a black-sailed ship fully rigged for a race and Theodora Skippen brought up the rear, not a tear on her face and the only redness visible being her rouge. From the hurricane deck voices drifted down, mostly Mrs. Tredgold's.

"That's just what we need," muttered January as Davis unlocked Molloy's cabin door. "Lundy quitting on us . . . because there isn't a pilot under the sun who'll put up with being told what to do. . . . Ladies," he added, turning in the doorway as the two bereaved caught up with them. "It is my intention simply to make a medical examination of Mr. Molloy's body—"

"And cut him up," demanded Theodora shrilly, "as you did poor Mr. Weems? How *dare* you? How can you permit . . . ?"

To Mrs. Fischer—ignoring the younger woman's tirade—he continued. "Mr. Davis here will vouch for it that I do nothing else while in the room. Perhaps, Madame, if you could give Mr. Davis a description of what you are looking for, he could locate it without the unseemliness of ransacking the room, as Mr. Weems's was ransacked?"

The woman stood for a moment, staring up into January's face. Her dark eyes were like an animal's, that calculates its opponent's strength, a crimson flush of anger rising under the sallow skin of her cheeks. Though no black man was supposed to meet a white woman's eyes January did so, quietly challenging her, and he was interested to see that she didn't react like a woman born to command slaves. She met his eyes as an equal, an opponent.

Then she turned to Davis and snapped, "I never thought I would live to see the day when a Southern gentleman would stand by and let a lady be insulted by an impertinent Negro!"

And without waiting for Davis to reply, she turned, and strode toward her own stateroom. Miss Skippen wavered, clearly not up to challenging both January and Davis. January wondered whether she would faint. Instead she burst into somewhat artificial-sounding sobs, and hastened away in the same direction with her handkerchief pressed to her face.

"And *I*," panted Davis as he locked the stateroom door despite the suffocating heat, "never thought *I* would live to see the day when a woman—*not* a Southerner, I perceive—would so unsex herself . . ."

"There's a great deal of money at stake, sir," said January. "Men speak a great deal about women being worse than men, if they decide to take to crime, but I suspect that's because crime is one of the few ways a woman *can* get her own money, and need not rely on a man. But it's curious, isn't it, that both ladies are acting as if what they're looking for is small enough to be easily palmed, or concealed in a pocket—either mine or hers. So Miss Skippen doesn't seem to think there's six hundred pounds of gold, or several trunks full of securities, hidden in here."

He knelt beside Molloy's body on the narrow bunk, turned the head gently, and withdrew a bullet-probe from his small medical kit. The pilot's closed eyes had begun to settle back into his head; blood and brain matter leaking from the wound had soaked the pillow, and in spite of the closed door the room was droning with flies. January inserted first the probe, then a pair of long-nosed bullet forceps into the channel cut by the bullet, which had cracked the skull on the other side.

Davis, after a rapid search of Molloy's portmanteau and the few drawers in the tiny dresser, came over to January's side, looking down over his shoulder as he withdrew the bullet from the wound. "That's no pistol-ball," he said at once. "I loaded those pistols. That ball wouldn't have gone down the barrel."

"I'm glad to hear you say it, sir." January dropped the bullet into the nearest vessel, in this case the saucer under an empty coffee-cup that had been on the cabin's single chair. "In fact, I didn't expect it to be. You can tell from the angle of the wound that it wasn't made from the front, but from about twenty degrees to Molloy's left—that is, from the little rise at the head of the chute. The only thing Hannibal had to do with Molloy's death was to unknowingly lure him out on the riverbank, where someone could take a clear shot at him . . . and blame the death on Hannibal."

"Well . . . I'll be dipped," murmured Colonel Davis. "Who would have done such a thing?"

"I can think of four, right off-hand." January covered the dead man's face with the sheet, then went to the washstand and poured water to wash his hands and the probe and forceps. "Unfortunately, three of them were within sight of half a dozen people at the moment of the shooting . . . and the fourth, as far as I can figure out, had no way of knowing that Molloy would be on the bank, involved in a duel, at dawn today." He fetched the bullet and washed it in the basin as well, then held it up.

It was a .45-caliber, the same as the Leman rifles handed out to the guards.

"Anything in the drawers, sir?" He remembered to modify his tone into one of humble inquiry.

Behind them the door rattled peremptorily. Mrs. Fischer demanded, "Open this immediately!" and Mrs. Tredgold and Miss Skippen chimed in as a sort of operatic chorus, mezzo, contralto, and soprano.

Davis shook his head.

"In the portmanteau? A letter? Or tools of some kind—hammer, nails, pry-bar?"

"Nothing. Only a couple of empty tins."

"Tins, sir?"

"Such as they sell candy in." Davis held one up—English, gaudy reds and golds, flat and square and slightly larger than January's enormous palm.

"Open this door immediately!" shouted Mrs. Tredgold. If her tone of voice was any indication of her attitude in dealing with Mr. Lundy, January despaired of ever getting to Memphis.

"I will go to the purser's office," Davis said, "and ascertain if any of the rifles is missing, or if one has been fired recently."

"Missing is more likely," said January as Davis unlocked the door and the two men stepped out, letting the three women push past them into the small cabin. "It could simply have been thrown in the chute afterward—it's what I'd do." Behind them in the cabin three shrill voices rose, quarreling already over who had the right to be there.

"But if the man who pulled the trigger came off this boat," said Davis worriedly, "how did he come back on? While you were ashore, Mr. Tredgold and Thucydides counted most assiduously to make sure that no one was inadvertently left behind. Every deck-hand and passenger is accounted for, even to the slaves who went ashore with Mr. Cain. And if the man who pulled the trigger *didn't* come off this boat, why would his accomplice on the vessel need to smuggle him a rifle? Surely such a man as that would have his own weapons? And why in any case would they wish to kill Mr. Molloy, who is, as far as we know, the only one who knew where Weems had hidden his loot . . . if indeed the loot exists at all?"

January shook his head, and glanced up to see Souter coming

down the steps from the hurricane deck. Tredgold followed him: January caught a snatch of their speculation about where the nearest wood-yard was and whether the *Silver Moon* could make it there or would have to stop yet again for the deck-hands—and the hard-worked slaves—to cut enough trees to keep the fires going.

Down below, the half-submerged forest of snags and towheads closer to the bank was finally being left behind. So Lundy had apparently agreed to stay, when any other pilot would have stomped down to the Saloon and left poor old Tredgold at the wheel himself.

Any other pilot who didn't have such an overwhelming desire to be on the *Silver Moon* . . . To *pilot* the *Silver Moon.*

There's a pattern here somewhere, thought January as he walked along the promenade to Hannibal's room, the rifle-ball in his hand. At least, he thought, his friend would be grateful to learn that he hadn't killed a man, even a man he despised and who was trying to take his life.

Or he'd be grateful when he woke out of the opiated stupor into which he'd almost certainly drunk himself in reaction to the thought that he was a murderer.

Will all great Neptune's ocean
Wash this blood clean from my hand . . . ?

And anger burned up in him at the thought that someone would have used an innocent and morbidly sensitive soul like Hannibal as their cat's-paw.

The stateroom door stood open. Coming closer, even above the faint, terrible reek from Weems's closed room, he could smell vomit.

He sighed, not much surprised. Hannibal no longer got blazing drunk several times a week, and had nearly killed himself trying to get opium out of his system. January had encountered men who were able to cut down their drinking in the face of necessity, but had never found one who could break free of opium.

And even those who turned away from alcohol often turned back.

He'd been waiting to see if Hannibal was one of them.

Rose was kneeling beside the bed where Hannibal lay—Thucydides was just mopping up the floor with a towel. The fiddler looked ghastly, worse than any drunk January had ever seen, shut eyes sunken and lips gray as he gasped for breath. Horrified, January dropped down beside Rose and felt for the racing, thready pulse.

"Good God, how much did he drink?" How much *could* he have drunk, in the . . . what? An hour, at most, since he'd returned to the boat?

Rose glanced at him, her eyes warning—she reached into her pocket and took out her red bandanna, with which she wiped their friend's face.

January fell silent. Like the songs about wading in the bayou, a red bandanna had long been a signal of danger between them.

Only when Thucydides had left did she whisper, "About half an ounce, as far as I could tell . . ." She nodded to the flask of opium and sherry on the floor beside the bed, the only bottle in the room. "The door was locked—I had to get Thu to force it. He isn't drunk, Ben. And he doesn't have a fever, he's like ice. I think he was poisoned."

NINETEEN

January dabbed some of the liquor from the flask onto his finger and tasted it, but the bitterness of the opium and the heavy sweet of Malaga sherry drowned any hint of whatever had been added to the brew. Still, he had no doubt that the poison, whatever it was, had been put into the flask. Taking a drink from it would have been the first thing Hannibal did upon entering the room.

And the second thing would have been to lock the door against Theodora Skippen, who was apparently determined—not to say desperate—to find a new protector for herself. No wonder Rose had had to get Thucydides to open it.

Since Hannibal seemed to have vomited everything in him, there seemed little point in a further purge. "See if you can get some water and a little salt beef from the galley," January said, and dug in his medical kit for a paper twist of dried foxglove. Hannibal's hands and face were icy, but sweat stood out on his forehead and cheeks. When January lifted back his eyelids, he found the pupils dilated rather than constricted, as opium would have left them. His breathing was sunken to a thread—January watched closely the rise and fall of his chest, but though he seemed deep in a stupor he was having no obvious trouble or spasms.

"Why on earth would anyone have wanted to poison Hannibal?" demanded Rose, returning with a pitcher.

January mixed the tiniest pinch of foxglove with the water, and gently raised his friend and spooned some of it into his mouth. Hannibal swallowed, but didn't open his eyes.

"For exactly the reason we thought he—or she—had provoked the duel," replied January grimly. "To get us off the boat. To get *me* off the boat . . . since, if I'm supposed to be Hannibal's slave, I *must* remain in Mayersville with him even if I didn't do so out of sheer humanity. If he died—"

Rose's eyes widened and filled with tears, and January shook his head reassuringly.

"His heartbeat seems to be steadying. And his breathing isn't weakening, so I suspect our poisoner miscalculated the dose. But if he had died, I'd be held by the local authorities pending arrival of next of kin. . . ."

"Or Gleet would produce a bill of sale and a story about how Hannibal signed you over to him to pay a gambling debt." Rose's voice had an edge like chipped flint.

January raised his eyebrows in agreement, but said nothing for a time. For a long while the only sounds in the room were the droning of the flies—which infested this side of the boat—and the dull throb of the engine and the splashing of the paddle as the *Silver Moon* picked up speed, and the slow, sobbing whisper of Hannibal's breath.

"Yet it was *Molloy* they killed." Rose picked up the rifle-bullet January had laid on the dresser and turned it over in her fingers. "They could have shot Hannibal at the same time. It is 'they,' isn't it? Not 'he or she'?"

"I think so. And the more I look at it, the less I'm inclined to believe that Molloy's death has anything to do with Weems's theft of money from the Bank of Louisiana."

"You mean if Weems was blackmailing Cain—and had a letter or whatever it was in his stateroom that Molloy later took—he could have had something that implicated someone else on board? Mr.

Lundy, for instance? Except we know where Lundy was when Molloy was shot as well." Rose edged around January and began to pull off Hannibal's boots.

"I'll get that," January offered, making to put down the medicine, but Rose shook her head,

"I'm no good with nursing, and I've had plenty of practice at yanking off Hannibal's boots."

January grimaced agreement and ran an affectionate hand along his unconscious friend's arm. "I'm afraid most of his friends have," he said. Rose looked exhausted, and no wonder, thought January. The night of stress and fear for her friend had been followed by the terrible shock of finding him still in peril . . . and there was still the decision looming of what they'd do when they reached Mayersville and the sheriff took January and Hannibal into custody.

A decision, thought January, glancing at the brightening daylight through the louver-slits of the door, that he—and she—would have to make probably within the hour.

"You don't think it was Queen Régine who poisoned him, do you?" she asked. "You said there were poisons in the bundle we found. If he'd seen her accidentally, for instance . . ."

"If Queen Régine wanted to poison anyone," said January, "it would be me. . . . And I've been very careful not to eat or drink anything that's stood unwatched in this stateroom. And Queen Régine knows perfectly well that *I* know—and therefore, that you and Hannibal know—that she's on this boat, and nobody's been able to see her yet, except one glimpse of a skirt. *If* that was her. If she'd wanted to poison Hannibal, for whatever reason, he'd be dead now."

"I suppose so." Rose sank down onto the bed, rubbing her forehead. "But even if someone got off the boat under cover of darkness, to hide in the trees—which could have been done fairly easily—I still don't see how they could have gotten back on after the duel, when it was daylight. We watched everyone go over and come back: Gleet came back, Cain and his slaves went over, and Cain was with the slaves the whole time. They came back with Molloy's body, then later a deck-hand rowed over and got you."

"Yes." January came around behind her and laid his big hands on her shoulders—the muscles of her neck felt like wood under his fingers. "Cain and his slaves. There are unanswered questions concerning Cain and his slaves on the night of Weems's death, too, aren't there?"

Rose opened her mouth to say something, then closed it. Then she said, "Cain . . . is using his slaves as agents? That's terribly risky, isn't it? He's a slave-dealer. . . ."

"He *says* he's a slave-dealer," said January softly. "But we've been on this boat for over a week and I have yet to see him even *try* to sell a single slave."

Outside, the pilot-house bell clanged as the *Silver Moon* approached the landing of Brock's Wood-Yard. Souter's voice trumpeted orders to the deck-hands to cast lines and bring her in. A shadow darkened the doorway of the stateroom, and Quince said, "Much as I abhor intemperance of any variety, might I offer your master a sovereign remedy for the inevitable fruits of such behavior? In this particular instance I am inclined to hold him guiltless—it is clear to me that the quarrel was forced upon him by that . . . that *abominable* hussy, and Mr. Molloy got no more than he asked for."

"That's very kind of you," said January as Rose moved aside to let the young man into the already crowded stateroom. "As it happens, I suspect my master is ill rather than drunk. There was no liquor in the stateroom, and, as you can see, no smell of it." He took the bottle proffered and sniffed the cork. "What's in it?"

"A distilled vegetable elixir known to the ancient sages of Persia and India," replied Quince helpfully.

"Known to the Old Man of the Mountains, anyway," remarked Rose, taking a sniff of the cork, but she spoke in Latin and January—who had also detected the unmistakable pong, not of the Old Man of the Mountains' legendary hashish but of more modern laudanum—carefully schooled his face not to laugh.

The vibration in the deck was easing as the engine stopped. Gleet yelled, "You bucks get that wood on deck fast as you can, hear?" and footfalls thudded dimly down below.

"As if one can smell anything," added Quince, his handsome face set in a grimace, "over the stench of poor Weems. It is absolutely disgraceful that we were so long delayed in taking his body to Mayersville. I cannot think what state it will be in, to be returned to Philadelphia for burial. I have asked to be moved—it will serve Mr. Tredgold right if no one is able to occupy that chamber ever again. All Molloy's fault, and Tredgold's, for letting a pilot ride roughshod over him in that fashion. I have taken it on myself to write to Weems's family. . . ."

"Did you know Weems?" asked January. "Before last Monday, that is?"

Rose raised her eyebrows at the question, but Quince replied without hesitation, "Not well. I saw him, of course, at the meetings at Brotherhood Hall—the Philosophical Antislavery League. But I suspect he was only a dabbler. He ceased to come, oh, four or five years ago. I was not surprised," he added primly, "to learn that he had submerged his principles in his quest for pecuniary advancement in the slaveholding states."

"But he did go to Abolitionist meetings in Philadelphia?"

"Oh, yes. It's funny—well, not really funny—but queer, in connection with those meetings . . ." Jack Quince laughed self-consciously, and ran a hand through his smooth black hair, rendering his face suddenly boyish. "I could have sworn there was another old acquaintance from them here on this boat, and I was much chagrined to discover how wrong I was. What curious tricks the Deity plays upon humankind to be sure!"

"What was that?" asked January, leaning his elbow on the side of the bunk and looking absorbed in fascination.

"Well, when I first saw that dreadful Mr. Cain, I could have sworn that he was one of the speakers at those Brotherhood Hall meetings. In fact, I mentioned the matter to Weems, and asked him if Cain didn't look exactly like Judas Bredon, except for the beard. Imagine my embarrassment when I discovered that not only was Cain *not* an Abolitionist, but that he was actually a slave-dealer, a trafficker in—"

From somewhere close—down on the bow-deck, January thought—came the unmistakable crack of a pistol, followed by a woman's scream.

An instant later Souter's voice rose in panic. "Pirates! In the wood-yard—" and was cut off mid-sentence by the bark of another gun. Then all hell broke loose.

A fusillade of gunfire crackled from the bow-deck. A man howled in agony, a woman screamed something in German, and the whole vessel shuddered and heaved.

January said, "Stay here," grabbed Hannibal's pistol from the floor beside the bunk, and darted from the stateroom, whose door was promptly slammed behind him—he heard Quince's wailing protest, "But he told us to stay here!" as he raced along the promenade. Other men jostled him, running toward the bow, too, Roberson and Lockhart pelting from their cabins coatless and in stocking feet. A bearded ruffian with a pistol in either hand came around the front corner and started to yell something to them—Lockhart whipped a pistol from his pocket and fired.

January dropped to the deck—the ruffian fired both weapons at once and missed with both, then turned and fled as the two planters, both completely unscathed, tore after him, whipping from their belts the bowie-knives that Southern manhood rarely went without.

Underfoot the *Silver Moon* lurched and heaved, the paddle driving forward and someone in the pilot-house—almost certainly Lundy—veering the flat-bottomed craft over the shallow mud of the shelving shore by the wood-yard and back to deeper water. Reaching the bow, January got a glimpse of one-eyed Levi Christmas down on the main deck below, crouching behind a crate with half a dozen ruffians while two or three more—including several of the rougher deck passengers—struggled with the deck-hands.

They were waiting at the wood-lot, thought January. A wave of self-disgust rolled over him that it hadn't occurred to him, after all the delays around Hitchins' Chute, that the wood-yard was the single place where the outlaws knew the boat would *have* to put in.

January wondered if Hannibal's pistol was even loaded. A moment later a bearded scoundrel in a faded shirt swung himself up over the promenade rail with a knife in his teeth and ran straight for the bow stair to the main deck, to take its defenders Davis, Gleet, and Cain from behind. The scoundrel had three pistols slung around his neck on ribbons, the way pirates of old used to carry them—he was reaching for one to shoot Davis in the back, when January shot him from a distance of less than eight feet.

Hannibal's gun was indeed loaded.

Davis whirled as the bandit fell, his own pistol at the ready. January ripped free both the bandit's unfired pistols and the powder-horn. He tossed one gun down to the young planter, and the next second Christmas and his ruffians emerged from cover and made a run for the stair, firing as they came.

Davis flattened behind a stanchion as a bullet tore a hunk of wood inches from his face. Cain fell back against the rail, clutching the spreading crimson stain on his chest, then pitched forward off the stairway to the deck. He was still trying to get up, when two of the attackers seized his arms and threw him overboard, one of them following him immediately, shot through the head by Davis. Gleet turned tail and charged up the stair, nearly colliding with January as half a dozen deck-hands rallied around Davis, armed with logs of firewood, push-poles, and an assortment of artillery that was illegal for any black man to possess.

"They'll try to take the engine-room and the pilot-house," January yelled down the steps. "Anyone at the back of the boat?"

"Eli in the galley!" a deck-hand yelled back, so January dashed to the steps that ran down to the stern by the galley passway. No one was guarding either stern flight, nor the rear door of the engine-room in the passway. At the moment the only occupants of the deck were

Sophie and Mrs. Fischer, in the midst of hauling the work-table out of the galley and dragging it to the rail as an improvised raft.

"Hold it steady, you imbecile girl!" Fischer screamed at her weeping maid.

"Don't do it!" January yelled, and both women whirled. Sophie was ashy with shock, but Mrs. Fischer raised the pistol she held to fix unwaveringly at January's heart. January halted, let his own pistol fall, and held up both hands. "You'll be safer on board," he told her.

"Under the protection of this parcel of dolts?" Mrs. Fischer stepped close enough to scoop up the weapon.

"Madame, he's right, I told you! Please . . ."

Fischer didn't even glance at her servant, her eyes on January. "Get on the raft, you stupid wench, and don't argue with me!"

"Madame," said January, "all you'll do by jumping ship is make yourself a target. . . ." As if to prove his words, a bullet tore the deck near his feet.

"And I suppose if I remain, Mr. Christmas is going to content himself with inquiring politely about the gold?" Her hat and veils gone, her black hair tumbled thick about her shoulders, Mrs. Fischer had an air of grim gypsy wildness, as if she had finally thrown aside her disguises and revealed the woman beneath. "No, thank you . . . I'm sure that bitch Theodora will be as quick to point you out, and your drunken master, as the ones who know something about it, as she will to point her dirty little finger at me. Now, get that table under the rail!" She reached back to grab Sophie's arm and thrust the girl at the flimsy craft balanced on the edge of the deck.

But Sophie sobbed, "No!" and pulled back. As another bullet ripped the deck, Mrs. Fischer shoved the girl aside and kicked the table down into the river, gathering her black skirts above her knees to slither under the rails and down to its work-smoothed surface. The shouting in the promenades was getting louder as the deck-hands, armed with sticks of firewood, clustered among the slaves—somewhere Levi Christmas's booming bass voice yelled, "Don't shoot the goddam niggers, they're worth a thousand dollars apiece! Go over the stairs to the back!"

The thunder of boots on the upper-deck promenades seemed to decide Mrs. Fischer. She pushed off the side of the boat, crouched almost flat on the stained oak, and began to paddle with a broad-bladed fire-shovel toward the shore. Her black clothing stood out against the muddy yellow of the river, the blinding glare of the morning sun.

"Get up to the pilot-house," January ordered Sophie, who seemed frozen by the sight of her mistress paddling away. When the girl only raised tear-soaked, terrified eyes to him, he shook her, and thrust her in the direction of the stair. "Hurry! They'll be back here in a minute . . . !"

She fled as if all the devils of Hell were snapping at her skirts, and January plunged into the starboard promenade, where the deck-hands and the chained slaves clustered tight.

January strode straight to 'Rodus and said, "Cain was shot, thrown overboard. You'll have to use your key."

The slave looked at him steadily for a moment—"You crazy, man?" demanded a deck-hand near-by.

Someone on the deck above screamed and fell with a crash that shook the arcade overhead. Slowly 'Rodus reached into the filthy juju-bag tied around his waist under the band of his ragged trousers, and pulled out the manacle key.

"Keep them from getting in the engine-room or the pilot-house," said January. "Guard the stairs and the passway. Will this key work for Gleet's women?"

'Rodus shook his head. "He got padlocks on 'em." He'd already unlocked his own manacles and passed the key to the next man, all the deck-hands—and Gleet's male slaves, who'd been unchained to help with the wooding—staring in disbelief. "I'll get a pry-bar from the engine-room, if I can get in there. . . ."

At that moment the engine-room door flew open and Thu sprang out, pry-bar in hand. He skidded to a stop at the sight of January. Recovering quickly, he threw the bar to Guy, who was next beside

'Rodus in the line, and said, "You go get the women." Fishing in his pocket, he produced another key; this he handed to Guy—when the man and three of Gleet's slaves had ducked into the passway to cross through to unchain the women on the other side, the steward turned back to January, unconsciously moving shoulder to shoulder with his brother.

"Cain is gone," said 'Rodus to Thu. "An' Ben here seems to know all about him."

"Only what I could guess," said January. "That you and he were taking these runaways"—he nodded toward the others of Cain's gang—"to Ohio. You didn't need to poison Hannibal," he added quietly. "We wouldn't have betrayed you."

"A court trial would have held us up," returned the steward calmly. "I didn't put enough snakeroot in that liquor of his to kill him. Just enough that they'd see he was too sick to try. They'd lock him up someplace to get better and let the boat go . . . damn!" He turned sharply as a small skiff emerged from the mouth of an overgrown bayou behind Brock's Point, the dozen men aboard hauling hard on the oars.

"Reinforcements," said January grimly as the men on board began to shout and wave to the outlaws on the *Silver Moon*.

Caught between the steamboat and the smaller vessel on her makeshift raft, Mrs. Fischer half sat up, dark hair flying in the wind, and looked back toward the steamboat. Before she could make up her mind to turn back, one of the men on the skiff whooped and brought his rifle around. There was a puff of smoke. Mrs. Fischer sank slowly down, holding her side. A moment later she rolled from her fragile square of boards into the opaque flood.

There was a flash of black, a ribbon of red unreeling into the water, and she was gone.

TWENTY

"Get in the engine-room!" Thu waved to the newly-released slaves and the deck-hands clustered in the promenade. "Get the women in there. . . ."

"Hold the doors as long as you can," panted January. "They'll try to take the pilot-house and run the boat to shore. . . ."

"There's guns in the purser's office," said Thu. "I can break in the case—Tredgold's got the key. We've got only a few minutes before they figure it's worth it to shoot a nigger or two."

'Rodus grinned, a slash of white in his dark face. "Never thought bein' worth a thousand dollars to some white man would come in handy."

"You gonna see how handy it is when you end up bein' sold in Texas, brother," snapped Thu, not unaffectionately, and loped off to unlock the office door.

January sprang up the steps and along the upper promenade, going first to the Ladies' Parlor—where he found every woman and child on the boat, with the exception of Rose, huddled together under the protection of Jim, Andy, and Winslow. He yelled, "Get to the pilot-house!" and raced down to Hannibal's stateroom. Rose, Hannibal, and Quince had already gone. Rose, like January, had guessed that the outlaws had to take either the engine-room or the pilot-house, and when January mounted to the hurricane deck, he found them already in the little cupola, Hannibal stretched out on the lazy-bench only barely conscious and Rose trying to get the other women—including one Irish and two German deck-passengers and their children—to be quiet and stay still. The room was tiny, and with twenty extra people jammed into it, there was barely room for Mr. Lundy to cling to the wheel.

"Blame you, what the hell you have to send 'em all up here for?" The pilot's buzzing voice sharpened with annoyance, though January guessed he actually knew perfectly well. He was barely to be heard over the screaming of the Irishwoman's baby and Melissa Tredgold.

"Too hard to defend three places," January answered. "They killed Cain and three deck-hands and threw them overboard like dead dogs. Any captive's going to end up a hostage."

Mrs. Tredgold slapped her daughter with a blow like a gunshot, and the girl screamed even louder.

"I'll give 'em a list of who they can have with my compliments. . . ."

Jim—clustered with the little group of men outside the door—shouted, "Here they come!"

January yelled, "Let's go!" Their ammunition was gone, so the little gang of men who'd gone up—January, the three valets, Byrne the gambler, Mr. Tredgold, blanched and shaky with shock, and even Mr. Quince—caught up logs and canes and threw themselves across the dozen feet or so to the top of the stair, to stop the attackers before they swarmed onto the hurricane deck itself. Those who followed unquestioningly—and January had one terrible moment of fear that nobody would—soon realized the strategy he didn't have time to explain: that bunched together on the narrow stair, it was almost impossible for the attackers to fire or, if they did, to aim, whereas if they were able to fan out over the hurricane deck, they'd be in a position to rip the pilot-house itself apart with cross-fire.

Swinging his makeshift club of firewood, January dodged to one side as Levi Christmas fired on him almost point-blank. The stinging heat of the ball whiffed his arm, then he fell on the outlaw before Christmas could unsling another pistol from around his neck. January grabbed the stringy outlaw by the throat, his hands tangling in a mess of filthy beard, and twisted his hip to protect his groin from a jabbing knee. With his other hand he caught the Reverend's wrist as the older man brought up a pistol—they clung to each other, rocking and swaying at the top of the stair with the other outlaws massed below, unable to fire, trying to shove past and being beaten back by the defenders on deck.

Christmas pulled a knife from his belt with his free hand, and January had to twist aside to keep from being eviscerated. His grip on the Reverend's throat broke, and as the outlaw brought up his pistol, January kicked him backwards, down onto the men on the stair.

"Don't let them go!" he yelled, and plunged down after them, crowding them to keep them from shooting. But this time no one followed. Jim and the others were already falling back to the perceived safety of the pilot-house, not understanding how fatal it was to give ground, and January felt a knife rip into the muscles of his back. Then he was falling backwards, down off the stair, clutching and grabbing and then hitting the back of the deck hard.

A fury of shouting and pounding came dimly to him from below as he lay on the boards of the deck, stunned and trying to breathe. Every whisper of air brought stabbing pain in his side—a rib broken, he thought, the pain wasn't where he'd been stabbed and though he felt weak and lightheaded, it was the long burning pain of a slash. Opening his eyes, he saw the last of Christmas's men piling up the stair onto the hurricane deck, surrounding the pilot-house.

Head swimming, January rolled over, tried to get up. Two of the last men up the stairs halted, turned back, and climbed down to him. They had pistols, but spent smoke poured from the barrels—January let himself fall back onto the boards of the deck, and both men stuck their knives into their belts.

"Big bastard," said one of them, bending to grab January's wrists. The other took his ankles to drag him to the rail, so the kick January delivered to his groin was unexpected, perfectly positioned, and murderous. The man at his wrists dropped them and fumbled for his knife—Mr. Ankles being doubled up on the deck screaming—and January didn't even bother going for a weapon, just pistoned his feet down to the deck and drove his elbow up under Mr. Wrists' chin with a force that smacked him hard against the arcade support.

January heaved first the one, then the other overboard, and was scrambling up the stair to the hurricane deck before either of them hit the water.

From above him he heard Levi Christmas yell. "You might as well give up in there, old man, 'fore we shoot the pilot-house to pieces!"

There were a dozen outlaws, ranged in a circle around the flimsy board structure. From inside, January could hear Theodora Skippen screaming, "Levi, no! Levi, it's me, Dora . . . !"

Oh, that will certainly get him to throw down his guns. . . .

January yelled, "Christmas, the money isn't on the boat!" and all the outlaws turned.

There was momentary stillness. Levi Christmas brought up his pistol to bear on January; then, when January remained unmoving, the Reverend walked toward him on the blood-splattered decking. When he got within two yards of January, he said in a calm voice, "We been followin' this boat since Natchez, and we had a look at every trunk that's been took off it. We ain't seen no gold yet."

"That gold never left New Orleans," January told him. "If you've been watching this boat, you'll have seen that every trunk and box in the hold was searched the day before yesterday, and all we found was a lot of underwear and shoes."

"All that means is that Irish bastard hid it," replied Christmas evenly. "Wasn't that why he tried to shoot your master? You and that master of yours wouldn't still be on board if the money wasn't here. It's a good try," he added with a broken-toothed grin. "But that money's here, and I'm gonna find it, if I gotta heat up some irons and toast the titties of every woman on board to get somebody to break loose with a little—"

The whole deck lurched underfoot as the *Silver Moon* staggered like a drunkard on a spree. January covered the six feet between himself and Christmas with a single leap and wrenched the pistol from the Reverend's hand—when Christmas grabbed for another of the several around his neck, January brought the pistol-butt against his verminous temple with crushing force. A chorus of screams rose from the pilot-house and above them rode Jim's shout,

"We hit a snag! We goin' *down*!"

The boat was already beginning to list.

January was nearly trampled by Christmas's men as they pelted for the stairway down to the lower decks. Not one of them so much as paused to scoop their stunned and unconscious boss from the deck. Even as January reached the door of the pilot-house it flew open and the women streamed out, Mrs. Tredgold screaming at her husband, "This is all your fault!" and Melissa Tredgold simply screaming.

January tossed his pistol to Rose and dragged Hannibal onto his shoulder like a sack of flour; Rose put her shoulder under Mr. Lundy's to help him along, last of them all, down the steps to the deck. "What happened?" panted January. "Did you hit it deliberately?"

"Hell, no," buzzed the pilot. "With all the windows but the visor-board shut, I couldn't see, and the river's stiff with towheads . . . it had to happen. You think I was gonna wreck the boat this far from the free states, with all those folks still on board?"

"So you were part of it?"

" 'Course I was part of it!" snorted Lundy. He clutched at Rose's shoulder and the stair-rail as they carefully negotiated the steps first down to the boiler-deck, then to the main deck below. "Why the hell else would a spavined old wreck like me be still rasslin' around this river, if it wasn't to help get a flock of runaways north to Canada?"

By the time they reached the main deck, Christmas's men had already taken both the *Silver Moon*'s skiff and their own and cast off. At the bow the decks were almost awash—Thu and Davis were coolly directing the deck-hands in the ripping-out of doors and bull-rails to provide spars to swim to shore. Water slopped over into the hatchway as they pulled the cover clear for a raft, and January froze.

He said, "Shit."

"What?" Rose tucked the pistol into her waistband, was preparing to ease Hannibal onto a hatch-cover to paddle to shore.

"Get him ashore," said January. "I'll be back."

And he sprang down the ladder-like stair to the door of the hold.

It was still padlocked, but since there was no longer need for secrecy of any kind, January knocked it in with two kicks. Away from the wan light of the hatch the hold was pitch black, waist-deep in water at the bow end already, bobbing with crates and boxes floating about in the darkness like ambulatory islands. More crates were slithering down as the deck slowly tilted. Rats clung to them, climbed on January's back and arms—he thrashed them off and they went scrabbling for the steps.

"Régine!" he bellowed into the darkness. "Régine, here! This way!"

A woman's voice called back out of the abyss, frantic with terror. "Here! Oh, God, I'm caught! Help me!"

January plunged in the direction of the stern. Water heaved and sloshed around his hips, then his thighs, but he could hear it rushing behind him where the tear in the hull was. Ahead of him in the blackness the woman's voice sobbed, "Here, I'm here, oh God please don't leave me . . . !"

The boat lurched as the weight of water in the head dragged it farther down. The deck-boards slithered under January's feet, and something big and square-edged slipped down and struck his shoulder a glancing blow in the darkness, the sudden jab of his broken rib and the wound on his back bringing on a wave of nauseated faintness.

"I'm caught, oh God, somethin' fell on me, I can't move it, I can't push it. . . ."

The shadows showed him nothing, only outlined the edges of the shifting crates. Darkness suffocating, like a wet nightmare of slanting deck-boards and huge things like pyramid-blocks slithering and bumping as they slid, further adding to the weight at the boat's nose. "I'm here," he called out, "I'll get you. . . ."

Her voice had been quite close to him. Hands groped for his.

Big hands, not Queen Régine's tiny, childlike fists.

He didn't ask, only felt along the folds of a dress, found where crates and trunks had fallen on her with the boat's first reeling lurch. "Hold still." He dug in his pocket for matches. In the sudden flare of yellow light he saw, not the bitter little voodooienne he'd expected to find, but the slave-girl Julie. "Hold these. You know how to light a match? Scratch it in the paper, like this. . . . Is there someone else down here? Another woman?"

"No." Her eyes were huge in the tiny flare of light, following his movements as he hauled and threw the trunks from the top of the pile that pinned her legs. The pain of his rib went through his vitals like a sword. "Thu said I could stay here," Julie gabbled as if the words themselves fought back panic. "I was gonna swim for the shore when we caught on the bar, but 'Rodus stopped me, came up, and caught my hand. He wasn't chained—you know Thu's part of the Underground Railway? Him and 'Rodus? They're brothers—'Rodus had a key to the chains—they was takin' folks north, disguised as a slave-gang. He said Thu had blankets hid down here, and food, in case somethin' went wrong an' somebody had to hide out. They had poisons here, too—I know they's poisons, 'cause my granny knows about them things . . . oh, God . . ." she gasped as the boat lurched again and water slopped up around January's ankles. "Oh, God, we're gonna drown. . . ."

Moving the crate on top of the trunk that actually pinned her legs was like trying to move a house. January grunted, feeling his muscles crack and strain, panic icy in his heart. " 'Rodus brought you down here?"

"No, we had to wait for Thu. And 'Rodus told me, *Be quiet or we're all of us dead,* and pushed me far back in the gang when Thu came down. Thu had Mr. Weems with him, tellin' him how he'd found somethin' strange hid in the hold. I didn't see much—it was plenty dark—but 'Rodus had a stick of firewood in his hand, big around as your arm. I don't think Mr. Weems ever saw what hit him. Oh!"

The matches had burned down to her fingers; she fumbled with the scratch-paper, and with a hiss everything fell into the water as the boat lurched again. January pulled the last trunk out of the way and felt for Julie's hands in the darkness, wondering in despair how they were ever going to find the open door. The deck was at an angle of over forty-five degrees underfoot and there was a constant slipping and scraping in the darkness as trunks slithered down.

The door at the stern end, thought January. It opened inward, padlocked on the outside—was there enough purchase to kick it open, with the deck tilted, always supposing he could find it in total darkness . . . ?

Light. A rectangle of daylight, above and behind as the stern door opened, and Rose's voice, "Ben! Ben, are you there?"

"Here!" He grabbed Julie's arm, half dragged the limping girl up the slippery slant of boards. Rose, Thu, and 'Rodus reached down, clinging to the slant of the steps; dragged Julie up, then January, as the *Silver Moon*'s boards groaned and snapped with the weight of water in her head. January blinked in the daylight, half-blinded, seeing the water all around the vessel full of spars and planks, doors and shutters, each bit of wood bearing a paddling figure, heading toward the shore. Some, he saw, had already reached safety, and were wading out into the water to haul others in.

"Hannibal . . . ?"

"Is safe, Davis and Jim took him over." Rose removed her spectacles and tucked them into her skirt pocket. "When the vessel started going down, I realized you couldn't get out of the hold the way you'd gone in. . . ."

The two Fulani brothers had rounded up several doors on the stern promenade. The *Silver Moon* lurched over sideways, dripping paddle still turning wildly in the air—"Better get out of here before the weight brings her over," warned Thu as he helped Julie down onto a door, then dropped into the water to seize the end of the door and kick toward the shore. 'Rodus took a plank—January and Rose, another door, with January holding and kicking in the same fashion, and feeling like his cracked rib was going to work its way out of his body at every kick. Tomorrow, he knew, he'd pay for the surge of desperate energy that kept him going now.

Thucydides, he noticed, was letting the current carry him farther down, toward a point of land separated from the others, where Julie could get ashore without being noticed. Mindful of the number of outlaws still roving around the woods, January followed.

Water splashed in his mouth and his eyes, and under the surface nameless things—branches, rotting trees, what felt like tangles of submerged rope—tore and grabbed at his ankles. Even in low water the tug of the current was like a giant's hand. Rose pulled her skirts and petticoat up around her waist and slipped the lower part of her body into the water, kicking, too.

They were both breathless and numb when the door finally grated on sand.

Then all they could do was lie on the muddy bank among the dead trees and mats of leaves, feet in the water, gasping for breath and staring up at the cloud-puffed blue of the sky. It wasn't even noon.

That morning before dawn, Hannibal had been rowed over to the bank to shoot and be shot at by Kevin Molloy, now sunk, with Oliver Weems, and Levi Christmas, in the wood and iron coffin of the *Silver Moon.*

The duel seemed weeks ago. January tried to calculate when he'd last slept and realized it had been on the floor of Hannibal's stateroom the night before last, the night that Weems had been murdered by the conductors of the Underground Railway because he'd tried to blackmail the wrong man.

"I suppose all the sheriff of Issaquena County is going to have to do is bring a posse out here on the first moonlit night," mused Rose, rolling painfully over. She'd lost her tignon in the river, and her long brown hair hung down soaked over her shoulders like seaweed. She fished her spectacles from her skirt pocket, put them on again, and looked back at the river, where smoke still poured from the tall stacks of the *Silver Moon,* still visible above the surface of the water. Mr. Souter would have to warn other pilots of it as they came bowling down the river to Brock's Wood-Yard.

She went on. "He'll be able to round up most of Christmas's men when they go diving to try to find the gold in the wreck. . . . Did you mean it when you said the gold wasn't even on the boat?"

"I think so." January heaved himself shakily to his feet and took Rose's hand, led her up the muddy bank. All around them rats were scrambling up out of the water, shaking their brown coats and trotting purposefully off into the woods. *They probably have relatives in the neighborhood.*

Forty or fifty yards upstream, he could see the door Thu and Julie had used for a life-preserver, lying near a tangle of beached snags. Movement caught his eye and he saw 'Rodus limping down the bank, then turning aside into the tangle.

Hand in hand with Rose, January made for the place, walking slowly and stumbling every now and then into potholes in the bank.

"Molloy stole *something* from Weems's stateroom," he told her. "Something that could be easily pocketed, and could be taken all at once, not like six hundred pounds of gold or even a couple of valises of securities and Bank of Pennsylvania notes. Something that was hidden with the same copy of the *Liberator* that mentioned Judas Bredon's speeches and involvement with, not only Abolitionism, but with the Underground Railway. It was something that Weems thought he could retrieve easily, too—hence his searching the staterooms of everyone on board whom he thought might have had reason to steal it. It would have been easy enough for Thucydides to tell him that some member of the slave-gang had seen Molloy hide something somewhere, to get him to go down to the promenade deck at midnight."

"It sounds like a key," said Rose. "But Molloy didn't have a key on him when he was killed, and you didn't find any such thing in his stateroom, did you?"

January shook his head. "That's because he knew La Pécheresse would find some way to search," he said, and crossed himself at her name, seeing again in his mind the red streak of her blood in the river. "Or maybe he guessed after Weems's murder that Davis would be asking more questions, and would probably search as well. Molloy was a canny bird—he got rid of it as soon as he could, got it off the boat entirely, so that nothing could be proven against him. But I have a good guess where."

"Even if you do," said Rose, "a key does us little good unless we know where the gold is actually hidden. If she and Weems left it behind in New Orleans, I'm not sure we'd ever find it."

January nodded, a wave of weariness passing over him at the thought of the long search yet to come. And in the meantime, what? Payment was due on their house in two months—sixty days—and in summer there wasn't even work as a musician.

They reached the gray and twisted oak-trees, which formed a sort of crescent in whose center sat the two Fulani brothers and Julie. 'Rodus was holding Julie's hand and laughing, pointing out at the smoke-stacks. He'd taken off his shirt, and water glistened over the scars on his naked back, the marks of a lifetime of defiance. Thu, sitting beside them, wore a look of weariness as he gazed at the river, as if already calculating what to do next.

Julie, January saw now, had gotten rid of the plain gray dress she'd worn as Theodora Skippen's servant—probably because it could be easily described in an advertisement for a runaway. Instead she wore a dark green gown, rumpled and wet from her immersion in the river and grubby from the dirt of the hold, but visibly tabbied with clusters of white and rust-colored flowers.

A gown, January realized, that he had seen before.

By lantern-light, he thought.

In the cemetery of St. Louis.

Before a tomb.

"Was that the gown Sophie gave you?" he asked, and Julie, a little startled at the question, nodded.

"It was Mrs. Fischer's," she said. "She gave it to Sophie, but Sophie's such a little slip of a thing, it didn't fit, so when I said I was going to run, Sophie passed it on to me. You like it?"

"Yes," said January with a contented smile. "I like it very much."

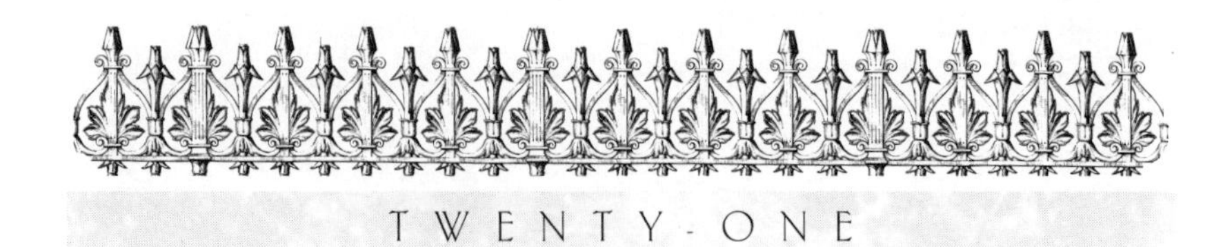

TWENTY-ONE

The sheriff of Issaquena County turned out to be an enormously fat Englishman named Lear, who arrived in a broken-down shay shortly after Roberson and Byrne set out along the river road for Mayersville. Lear immediately sent his single deputy back to town to organize men to search the river banks as far down as Hitchins' Point for castaways, and accompanied the main body of them—including January, Davis, and Rose, with Hannibal and Lundy riding in the shay—back to Mayersville's single boarding establishment, the Montague House.

Shortly after dinner Lear returned, and listened to the combined accounts of Davis, Lundy, and January with narrowed eyes, as if he detected such obvious lacunae as, *How could someone have thrown Weems overboard—much less overpowered and murdered the man—without the slaves chained on the starboard promenade having heard it,* and, *how could anyone have stolen and hidden close to six hundred pounds of gold quickly and secretly on a steamboat?*

"The bleedin' thing is," Lear said, mopping the wide brick-red moon of his face with a handkerchief the size of a tablecloth—for even with evening darkening the windows, the parlor of the Montague House was suffocatingly hot—"that the only ones truly on the spot at the time of the murder are hidin' in the woods. They're not like to be found."

"Surely the patrols in this county . . ." protested Davis.

"The patrols in this county couldn't find their own arses with a survey map and a Chickasaw guide," responded Lear mildly. "Every one of those darkies disappeared the minute they stepped ashore, and your friend Gleet's like to give birth over it, not that I blame him. . . . That poor chap Cain didn't really give Gleet title to his darkies, to sell 'em in Memphis and send the money on to Cain's family, did he?"

"Good Heavens, no!" said Davis, startled. "As far as I know, the two men couldn't abide one another."

"Not to mention a man would have to be feeble in the head to give Gleet title to anything he ever wanted to see again," added Lundy, sunk in the depths of the landlady's best blue plush armchair. "He tell you that?"

"He did indeed."

"I understand Mr. Tredgold is going on to Memphis with his family with the next northbound boat," said Lundy, and Lear leaned close and cupped his ear to hear him. The pilot looked like a dead man, draped over the chair like a pillow-case filled with broken stalks of cane, but his eyes burned sharp and green. "Not feeling so pert myself, I was fixed to stay on here a few days, so if you'd like, I'll take responsibility for any of the runaways that your patrols do find, until I can get in touch with Tredgold again and find out who Cain's heirs and assigns were."

"That was neatly done," murmured January as he helped the feeble old man up the stairs to the attic room he shared with Hannibal, January, and Thucydides. The Montague House generally had rooms enough for any steamboat's passengers to board ashore if they wished, but with another boat in port—the *Wild Heart,* down from St. Louis—and with all the *Silver Moon*'s officers to put up as well, there was a certain amount of doubling up.

Lundy had announced himself quite willing to share quarters with

Mr. Sefton and his "valet," and the steward had offered his services to the pilot. Rose and Cissy shared a room in the basement, Sophie having elected to spend the night with Julie and the rest of the two slave-gangs in the woods. Most of the other white men were doubled up three and four to a bed in the other chambers.

"Hell," said the pilot as they paused on the landing, "no county sheriff's got more than a man or two at his disposal at the best of times. Lear would have given that job to any white man who asked." He clung to the bannister, panting, as January tapped at the door of the attic room, a chamber usually reserved for the servants of guests. "Thu an' that brother of his'll have their work cut out for 'em, gettin' those folks past Memphis and on up through Tennessee and Kentucky. 'Specially now, with Gleet's folks to be led, too."

Thucydides opened the door. Past him, January could see Hannibal propped up in the room's solitary bed with Rose holding a cup of tisane for him. The fiddler looked like he was coming out of his stupor, but his hands were trembling badly—at a guess, out of need for opium as much as anything else.

Seeing the direction of January's glance, the steward said quietly, "He'll be well enough to travel in two or three days. I gather Julie must have told you that whenever my brother and I conduct cargoes north—and this was our fifth—I bring a little snakeroot, or Indian tobacco, in case someone starts getting suspicious and needs to be gotten out of the way. It removes their interference without permanent harm. Most people attribute the effects to sickness, and traveling in summertime. He was never in any danger, you know. We simply couldn't let the boat be held up—which the sheriff would not have done if the most likely suspect were too ill to be questioned anytime soon."

"No, I understand," said January. "And I understand your killing Weems. . . . You must have been watching Fischer like a hawk."

"I was," agreed Thu. "But I don't think Weems told her what hold he had over Bredon. He didn't entirely trust her."

"No sane man would." January recalled the hardness of those dark, intelligent eyes. "Would you have killed her? If you'd learned she knew?"

Thu hesitated, his face troubled. Then he let out his breath in a sigh. "I'd like to say something comfortable and respectable like 'I don't know' or 'I'd have found a way not to. . . .' But in fact, yes, if she'd showed signs of knowing—or telling—I'd have killed her. They lynch conductors of the Railway, Mr. January. In Virginia they were trying to put through a law allowing black conductors to be burned alive, as fomenters of rebellion and discontent. We can afford to trust no one. We can afford no mistakes."

The young man glanced back at Hannibal, who had sunk back on the bed and closed his eyes again, then returned his gaze to January. "I know you care a great deal about your master, and I know you trust him . . . but I never met a slave-holder who could be completely trusted. Not even the ones who claim they 'understand.' If they 'understood' so well, why do they still own other men?"

January grinned wryly, and produced his much-battered freedom papers from the inner pocket of his jacket. "It's a question that's always bothered me," he said. "As much as the question of why a slave can come and go on the upper deck—in service to his 'master'—but a free man can't. But I've given up trying to figure out how *les blankittes* think. My friend could still have been killed in the duel, and that would have been no kindness, completely aside from landing me in a lot of trouble."

Thucydides shook his head. "Believe me, my brother is too good a shot to have let your master—your friend," he amended, handing the freedom papers back with his slight smile, "—be killed. Our father had a rifle that he hid in the rafters of our cabin. He taught us to hunt whenever our master was away from the farm. Later, after we escaped, we lived in the Wisconsin Territory, where it was only a short walk from our mother's house to the woods. We would shoot game to eat, and for Mama to sell to the loggers. It was how we survived. 'Rodus can take the head off a finch at a hundred yards, before it lifts off a branch. I promise you, your friend was never in any danger."

"But you were," said January, and after a moment, Thu nodded. "And two people falling over the side would have been a little . . . obvious."

"Specially with *you* twitterin' around the boat askin' questions," put in Lundy, and Thu smiled again, and began to help the old man off with his coat and cravat.

To January, the steward said, "Weems had the issue of the *Liberator* that contained, not only one of Bredon's speeches, but a description of him. That was before he began running cargoes for the Underground Railway. The article spoke of his eyes, which are—were," he corrected himself, "—were an uncommon color, and of the pockmarks on his skin."

He was silent a moment, the muscles of his jaw standing out in hard relief under the fine-grained skin. Then he shook his head and went on. "Weems used that article to get money out of Bredon, after your friend and Byrne cleaned him out at whist . . . and don't think some of us didn't see what was going on in that game. I searched Weems's stateroom as soon as 'Rodus and I pitched his body overboard, but Molloy had been there that afternoon, when all the men were on deck setting the spars. The paper was gone. I don't know how Molloy even knew it was there. . . ."

"He didn't," said January. "He was looking for something else. Weems probably kept them in the same place."

"How did you know?" Thu helped Lundy to sit on the bed, then went to the small china veilleuse on the dresser, where Rose had put on a small amount of tisane to keep warm. " 'Rodus tells me you said to him, 'Give me the key,' as if you knew Cain wasn't a dealer, and 'Rodus wasn't a slave. How did you figure it out? If you don't mind telling me," he added, suddenly a little shy. "We do need to know where we went wrong, so it won't happen again."

"I don't think it will happen again." January pulled off Lundy's boots, settled the old man back on the pillows. "You were both very good. I don't think a white man would have suspected. But I was a slave once myself. Since Hannibal and I were doing the same thing—and had to watch out for the same things—it was clear to me that 'Rodus and Bredon were acting like partners, not like slave and master . . . and certainly not like slave and slave-dealer."

Thu nodded. "They worked together well," he agreed. " 'Rodus had helped Bredon with five cargoes. They tried to keep up the act of hate and mistrust, but sometimes there simply wasn't time to go through the . . . the dialogue."

"Make time," advised January. "Trust and cooperation show. It was clear to me by the way the men's gang was acting that Weems had been murdered in their presence. The fact that they all denied seeing or hearing anything told me the culprit had to be someone they considered one of themselves. The fact that you and 'Rodus are clearly brothers pointed out a strong probability that you had something to do with it."

The steward chuckled. "That's something whites just don't see, you know. Because 'Rodus is darker than me, not a single white man has ever asked if we're related. It's as if men of dark skin are all invisible to them—they don't look at our faces."

"Which Bredon was counting on," said January quietly, "when he took that big a gang across in the skiff to pick up Molloy's body after the duel. I take it 'Rodus swam across sometime during the night, and stationed himself on the high ground?"

Thu nodded. "He had one of the rifles from the purser's office wrapped in oilskin, and pushed it in front of him on a plank."

"That's what the final clue was, you know. After Molloy was shot, I came across in the skiff with Bredon and the slave-gang, and I didn't think 'Rodus was among them. If I hadn't been so worried about Hannibal, I'd have thought more about it. When the group of them came back from the trees on the knoll, and there was 'Rodus with the others, I simply thought I'd been mistaken. I don't think a single soul on the boat gave the matter an instant's thought. 'There goes Cain with a gang of slaves. . . . Here comes Cain with a gang of slaves.' As if that 'gang of slaves' was one single entity, and not six—or seven—individuals, each with his own face, his own fears, his own heart."

"If any whites thought like that," said Rose, looking up from the bed where she had sat in silence, "they couldn't hold slaves, could they?"

"Don't you believe it, Madame." Thu's mouth twisted as if he'd bitten into something spoiled. "Trust me, I've dealt with white men who went on for *hours* about what is best to be done with 'poor Negroes' but who wouldn't share a tin cup with me, let alone a hotel room. I underestimated your friend," he added, looking down at Hannibal. "I owe him an apology."

"For many things, I think," said Rose.

Thu glanced over at January with a lift of one eyebrow. "I wondered if anyone had noticed that 'Rodus was missing that morning until the detail came back from the shore. Bredon kept the men busy about the boat, so no one would comment that he was gone—they would assume he was simply somewhere else."

"It worked well," agreed January. "Except that it was one thing too many. Any single one of those circumstances: Bredon making sure that Gleet was with him on the night of the murder; Bredon keeping the slaves busy on the morning of the duel so no one would know quite where 'Rodus was; 'Rodus re-appearing with the gang . . . any of those might have been co-incidence by itself. Taken together, it was clear to me, at least, that Cain—Bredon—was using 'Rodus as his agent. And that, therefore, the relationship between them was not what it seemed. And given the social position of the average slave-dealer," added January wryly, "just about the only thing worse that one *could* accuse him of being was . . . an Abolitionist."

"Oddly enough," said Rose, "I never quite accepted Cain as a slave-dealer. And I realize now what troubled me about him. On the first day he came on board at Donaldsonville, he came onto the promenade to look at the women, and he encountered me there. And he stepped back out of my way, to let me pass. The way any gentleman would, for any lady. Any white lady." Her green eyes were wry behind her spectacles. "And he looked at me, for one instant, politely, as if I were indeed any common lady in the street, and not something to be raped or worked to death with indifference. Mr. Bredon was," she concluded softly, "an exceptional man."

Thu nodded, and briefly closed his eyes. "He was that," he murmured "I only wish—" He stopped himself, and shook his head again. "What was it that Molloy was looking for in Weems's stateroom, when he found the paper?" he asked. "The gold that Weems was supposed to have stolen?"

"Not the gold exactly," said January. "And that brings me, Mr. Lundy"—he turned to the old pilot—"to a great favor I would like to ask of you."

The following day, while Rose remained with the still-groggy Hannibal, January and Lundy borrowed Sheriff Lear's shay and drove down the river road to Hitchins' Chute. Davis, Jim, and Thucydides went along as armed and mounted escorts in case Levi Christmas's surviving bravos still lurked in the woods, but they encountered no trouble. As they passed under the mottled shade of willows and sycamores, January would hear, now and then, the far-off drift of voices from some hoe-gang or wood-cutting detail, singing as they worked under an overseer's eye:

Ana-que, anobia,
Bia tail-la, Que-re-que,
Nal-le oua, Au-Monde,
Au-tap-o-te, Aupe-to-te,
Au-que-re-que,
Bo.

Or sometimes it was,

Run to the rock, rock will you hide me?
Run to the rock, rock will you hide me?

And he'd see Thu turn his head, listening, a look of calculation in his eyes.

As if he flew high above the land in a dream, January saw in his mind the cautious figures slipping from rock to rock, from brush-thicket to brush-thicket, working their way toward whatever point along the river they had heard was a meeting-place. And 'Rodus—and others—were out there somewhere, gathering them in, patiently, like the Good Shepherd going back into the stormy night when he realized one lamb was unaccounted for. . . .

Once Jim turned his head at the sound of the singing, and January thought the old valet caught Thucydides's eye. Knowledge passed between them; Jim shook his head slightly, and smiled.

And Colonel Davis of course, riding importantly ahead with a rifle on his arm, saw nothing.

January slipped his hand into his pocket to touch the rosary of blue beads, the cheap steel crucifix. *Holy Virgin, Mother of God, get them safe north. Cover them with your mantle of invisibility, your mantle as blue as the sky. Lead their feet, and guide them when they get there.*

Guide me, too.

As they neared Hitchins' Chute, January, who was driving the shay, said quietly to the pilot, "The more I thought about it, the less likely it seemed to me that Weems—and Mrs. Fischer, no doubt the brains of the outfit—ever took the money out of New Orleans at all. Six hundred pounds of gold, and God knows how many cubic feet of banknotes and securities, would be both heavy enough and bulky enough to call attention to itself, even split up among many trunks and crates.

"But gold, even more than banknotes, is anonymous. Once they convinced their pursuers, by their rather ostentatious flight, that the gold had been taken *out* of New Orleans—once they'd scattered the pursuit—how much easier to leave the gold in New Orleans itself, in some safe place to which they could return in a year, or two, and slip it out of the country a little at a time."

"Given that wildcat Fischer's nerve," muttered Lundy, "I wouldn't put it past her to open her own bank in New Orleans."

January laughed, "She might have, at that. By the places she and Weems were searching on the boat, it became fairly obvious to me that what they were looking for was not gold and banknotes, but a key—the key to wherever they'd hidden the gold. It was easy for Molloy to steal that key, but Molloy knew it was easy for someone else to take it back, either Fischer or Theodora Skippen. . . ."

"Who folded her tents and vanished during the night," put in Lundy. "Without paying the landlady, I might add—and helped herself to the jewelry of Mrs. Roberson's daughters, whose room and bed she was sharing. I'm guessing Miss Skippen went south on the *Wild Heart* this morning. There's no other way out of town."

"Minx," said Davis, who had dropped back to ride beside the shay. The side of his face twitched convulsively.

"If she shows up in Natchez again," said Lundy comfortably, "she'll get what she deserves."

And just what did a girl deserve, wondered January, *who was born poor and recognized at least that marrying a stevedore and bearing a child a year—the only options open to a poor girl—was not what she wanted?*

What had Mrs. Fischer deserved? To end as no more than a streak of blood in the river's muddy stream?

"So you think Molloy disposed of the key the same way Weems disposed of the gold?" Thu, riding on the other side, glanced down at January. "Why not keep the key on his person? Around his neck, or in a pocket?"

"Because it was a big key, an old key, wrought-iron and heavy. . . ."

"How do you know that?" demanded Davis.

January smiled. "Because I know now what it opens," he said. "And yes, I think the first thing Molloy did, when he got the key, was to look for a way of getting it off the boat entirely, so that he could come back for it after he'd gotten rid of pursuit. Once Molloy had the key, I'm not sure that either Weems, or Fischer, would have finished the voyage"—his glance crossed Thu's—"no matter what else went on."

There were at least three places behind Hitchins' Point where water would break through to form a chute on a high river. As January suspected, it took a pilot to recognize which of the low sloughs behind the tree-covered rise had been the chute through which Molloy had attempted to take the *Silver Moon*—January would never have believed that a steamboat, even a small stern-wheeler, could have maneuvered down that swampy aisle of mud and trees.

But Lundy found the place without trouble. Moreover, once January and Davis had helped him hobble along the bank from where they left Jim with the shay, Lundy guessed exactly which tree it was likeliest Molloy had concealed the key in. "Lord, everybody uses that big black oak that overhangs the chute in high water. It's got a box on it that pilots use to drop messages off to one another." The old pilot pointed ahead of them, to the oak on the muddy rise of ground, far above the few nasty pools that were all that remained of the chute. The tree was the largest on the bank and shaped distinctively, bending forward like a beggar-woman, with two limbs that reached out like arms.

"So he wouldn't have used it to hide the key in," remarked January. "But as a marker."

Lundy winked at him. "You're getting good, son. So which tree would we find your key in?"

"That sweet gum next to it. It's a little lower down the bank. Molloy could have reached it easily without getting out of the skiff. The whole left side of it's dead; look at how the branches are leafless. It has to be hollow inside."

Having learned painful details about hollow trees as a child, January threw a couple of rocks at the sweet gum from a safe distance, to satisfy himself that bees had not taken up residence in the hollow. Then he clambered up the mess of deadfalls and graying dry debris to the old tree's side.

The key was in a hollow in the tree's trunk, tucked in a tin candy-box only slightly larger than the one he'd found in Molloy's cabin. There were two keys, one of them small and modern, the other four or five inches long, and made of heavy wrought iron—too big to be hidden easily around the neck or in a pocket.

An old key.

The key, in fact, to the grillework that surrounded the crumbling tomb in the St. Louis Cemetery, where January had seen a small man whom he'd taken for an undertaker, and a tall woman in a green dress figured with rust and cream, bestowing what he had thought to be the coffin of a child by night.

The following day the *Gloria Zicree* put in at Mayersville, and January, Rose, and Hannibal took passage south for New Orleans. Hannibal slept for nearly twenty-four hours in his stateroom—with January again acting as "valet," this time simply to make sure he was all right—before he was himself again.

Thu had calculated well, thought January. Mrs. Tredgold, manipulated by Mrs. Fischer, would never have consented to holding the *Silver Moon* in port long enough for the fiddler to recover sufficiently to be questioned. Sheriff Lear, though both intelligent and kind, was at heart a lazy man, and January had no doubt that he'd have yielded to pressure and let the boat go on, simply taking everyone's depositions and holding the most likely suspect.

And Rose would have been on her way to Memphis alone.

"You don't think I could have dealt with Mrs. Fischer on my own?" Rose teased as she and January sat on the lower promenade deck somewhere between Vicksburg and Natchez, listening to Hannibal and two of the several servants play an impromptu trio on Stradivarius and spoons.

"I think you could have," said January, "had the playing-field been a level one. But it wasn't. I think the minute Hannibal and I were out of the way, Mrs. Fischer would have done something—forged papers, or sworn out an affidavit that she'd seen you owned by someone in some other town—that would have ended up with you being taken as a slave by Gleet. Then God knows where you would have ended up."

Rose thought about it, her face growing still. Then she glanced at the promenades along both sides of the engine-room of the *Gloria*'s main deck, where lines of slaves were chained, going to market in New Orleans. "I think you may be right, Ben. There are some things that we simply cannot fight." She closed her hand around his as clouds of ash and paddle-spray drifted over them and, along the banks, vociferous bullfrogs croaked in the gathering darkness.

They reached New Orleans on the third of July, in hot darkness with palmetto bugs roaring around the cressets that illuminated the levee. January half expected, with all that had gone wrong on the river, to find their home reduced to a pile of ashes. But his sister Olympe's son, fourteen-year-old Gabriel, greeted him at the door with the news that he and his father had been trading off sleeping there at night—that Cosette Gardinier was just fine at her grandmère's out at the lake, and that no, there wasn't much sickness in town except a little bit of fever and no, the house was fine except for the fire in the kitchen and that hadn't burned up too much. . . .

January sent a note via Gabriel that night, to Hubert Granville, and though it was past two in the morning, he, Rose, and Hannibal walked along Rue des Ramparts in the cicada-sounding darkness, to the cemetery of St. Louis. In the thick summer heat the town was silent, except for the far-off clamor of the gambling dens along Gallatin Street and the quieter din of the more respectable gaming parlors on Rue Orleans. Had the Four Horsemen of the Apocalypse ridden their steeds into those establishments, January didn't think the play there would even pause.

Somewhere in one of the dark houses, a man and a woman sang an aria from a popular opera to the light, tinny music of a piano. It was a lilt of joy against the leaden hum of mosquitoes above the gutters.

Congo Square was empty, whispering with the scent of ash and burned flesh. On one of the plane-trees there, January glimpsed the ant-creeping corpse of a snake, nailed to the wood with a rolled-up paper in its mouth. January helped Hannibal—and Rose, who was dressed in a pair of Hannibal's trousers and a calico shirt—to clamber over the wall, the resurrection fern that grew atop it flicking like ghost fingers at his flesh as he followed them over.

He found the DuFresne tomb, near which he'd waited for Queen Régine, and the statue of the sleeping child. Close to it, after a little search, he found the crumbling nameless tomb where he'd seen Mrs.

Fischer in her green and cream-colored dress, with Weems pushing a barrow behind, a little coffin resting upon it.

It must have been the final load of several, January thought. The two of them couldn't have lifted any box containing all the gold at once. The big lock on the wrought-iron grille that surrounded the tomb gave silently, recently oiled.

Rose's eye met his with a glint of triumph as they grasped the iron ring and, with a shrill scraping of iron on marble, opened the door of the tomb itself.

There were five little coffins there, all crowded into the cramped brick space that whispered with insects and rats.

January unlocked the padlock of the top one's lid, and took the lantern from Hannibal to hold it close as he untied one of the sacks within.

"It's six hundred pounds of vegetarian tracts," he said in a disappointed voice.

But both his friends saw the dancing light of triumph in his eyes, even before he gave himself the lie and held up the handful of glittering gold.

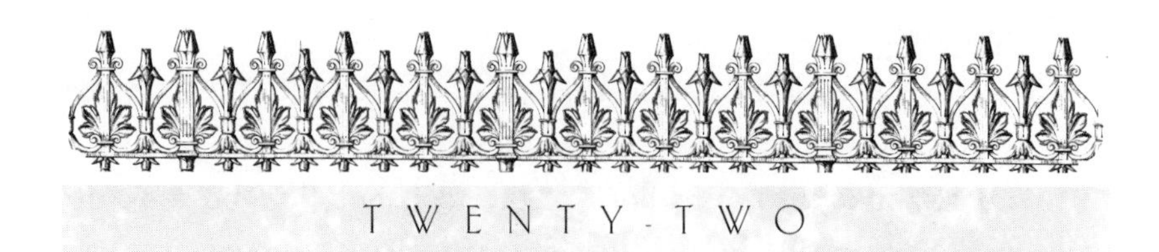

TWENTY-TWO

Hubert Granville expressed great doubt and disappointment when January withdrew all but two hundred dollars of his money to pay off the house free and clear. "You're leaving yourself nothing to live on," the banker warned, which January knew was true. "It takes time for a school to establish itself. You'll be in debt head over ears before you know it."

"We can deal with that," January replied.

Rose added, "At least we'll be sure of a roof over our heads while we starve."

Granville shook his head, and drew close the branch of candles to illuminate the draft to be paid to Rosario DeLaHaye. It was again evening, as hot as it had been a month before, when he'd sat there last at the big oak table in the dining-room, to tell January that the coffers of the Bank of Louisiana were empty, and his money gone.

"At least invest it in something worth your while," snapped January's mother, the elegant Widow Levesque. She had joined the banker in visiting the Januarys that night, a week after Granville and several unobtrusively armed bank officials had transferred the five little coffins from the cemetery back to the bank itself. Granville, January thought, had visibly lost weight during the past month, and looked like a man who had not slept much or well. His red-gold hair and beard seemed faded, and there were smudges of weariness under his piggy hazel eyes. He shook January's hand over and over again, repeatedly assuring him that if there was anything he ever could do . . .

January wondered how well that assurance would hold in times of real financial distress.

"A school will get you nothing," declared the Widow Levesque, folding her lace-gloved hands over the ivory handle of her parasol. His mother was slim and still beautiful, and there was something in the shape and setting of her eyes that reminded January, in the candlelight, of his sister Olympe. "Even the four best schools in the parish return no more than twenty percent, and I don't think there's a school in town that returns more than five percent its first five years . . . if you can keep it open at all. If you must invest, invest in slaves, as I told you before. If you feed them on rice and beans, and sausage only once a week, it costs you only . . ."

To hear her, January thought, one would never think she'd been a slave herself. He wondered if she'd ever been chained to the side of a steamboat, if she'd been fed from a bucket and had to hang out at the end of her chains to relieve herself over the side.

It was not something he could ask her. Not if he ever wanted her to speak to him again.

"Maman," he said gently, "Rose and I have talked this over at length, and we think a school is best."

One couldn't really say to one's mother, *We believe in educating the young, rather than putting chains on the innocent.*

"Besides," said Rose, who had learned in the past six months a great deal about handling her mother-in-law, "who knows when the State Legislature might not forbid people of color to hold slaves? They could, you know."

Livia Levesque stared at her in horror, the first time January had ever seen anyone break his mother's armor of self-satisfaction. "They most certainly could *not*! We pay our taxes . . . we support their businesses. . . ."

They will do to people of color, thought January, *whatever they wish. And there is nothing we can do about it, except leave.*

If there is anywhere for us to go. From what he'd heard from Dodd the manufacturer, and from some of the deck-hands who'd tried to make a living in Cincinnati and Alton, the North didn't sound like any paradise either.

"The least you could do is teach people who'll pay you decently," the Widow Levesque went on as Rose refreshed her coffee-cup and offered her a plate of pralines. "Nobody's going to pay more than fifty dollars a year to educate a colored girl . . . these are stale, by the way. Did you get them from that Vignée woman on Rue Royale? I thought so. . . . Hire a white teacher and make it into a boys' school; they pay the best. You could even get that worthless fiddler to teach Greek, if you can keep him sober. I don't expect *he'd* cost much. . . ."

"Dearest," sighed Rose as January returned from seeing Granville and his mother out the door, "it breaks my heart to have to tell you this, but you're so good to me, you really ought to be warned about it: one of these days I am going to murder your mother."

"Let me know when you're getting ready to do it so I can dig a grave for her under the house." January slumped back into the chair and poured himself the remains of the coffee. "You shouldn't have to do everything around the school." He added in a voice of mock horror, "Why, this coffee's *Mexican* rather than Ethiopian! And the plate the pralines was on isn't Sèvres."

"The plate the pralines was on is going to be in pieces over your head, sir." Rose settled herself comfortably on his thigh, and took the cup from his hand to take a sip herself. "I think the part I liked best was when she went around the room pinching out the candles," she added thoughtfully, and January laughed—his mother was always lecturing them about the cost of candles, though she also expressed scorn that they burned tallow rather than beeswax. Only a single branch of them had been left burning on the table after the Widow Levesque's parting lecture on economy. It made mellow pools of light on the worn oak, leaving the corners of the dining-room and the simply-furnished cavern of the parlor in darkness.

It was after ten, and the street outside was quiet. The shutters were closed against the mosquitoes that hummed in the darkness.

But with the signing of the draft that Granville would deliver to DeLaHaye the following morning, the house was theirs.

"Mr. Granville is right, you know," Rose added quietly. "It is going to be hard to make ends meet for a time. I'd hoped you wouldn't have to keep on with music lessons. That you'd have time to write music of your own . . ."

January shook his head. "I can teach them around the classes here," he said. "And playing balls and the opera is really only from Christmas to Mardi Gras. And I do my best writing late at night anyway. We'll manage. . . . Now, who's that?" He looked up at the sound of knocking on the door.

It wasn't Hannibal's usual brisk long-short-short-long rap, more like the knock of a walking-stick.

January lit a candle on one of the extinguished sticks and carried it to the door.

It was Jubal Cain.

Judas Bredon.

For a moment all January could do was stand staring at him in shock. He was far too well-dressed to be a ghost, and as far as January had ever heard, ghosts walked around with their wounds still gaping and, when possible, dripping spectral blood. Bredon's left arm was in a sling, and there was a half-healed cut on his right temple as he removed his hat. The yellow glint of his eyes in the candlelight was unmistakable.

He said, "Mr. January?"

January stepped back. "Mr. Cain," he said. And then, recollecting himself, "Mr. Bredon. Please come in. It's an honor to have you in our home, sir."

Bredon smiled. It changed his whole face. "You've been talking to

Thu," he said. "I'm the one who's honored, Mr. January—considering the amount of money they pay for the recovery of runaway slaves."

January nodded with mock consideration: "And thirty pieces of silver times twenty-five is how much?"

"Enough to set a man up in business," replied Bredon. When he stepped across the threshold, January could see that he walked haltingly, limping on a stick. "Or to buy him property for his family. However you slice it, I'm in your debt."

"Did they make it to the North all right?" asked Rose, rising from the table. "Will you have coffee, by the way, sir? It's no trouble."

"It may bring you more trouble than you know, M'am—but yes, to answer your question, 'Rodus managed to locate every one of those two gangs, mine and Gleet's, along with those two girls, Julie and Sophie. And they picked up another runaway, too, a boy named Bobby who'd been following the river from Natchez. He said he knew you. . . ."

January grinned, as if a weight had been lifted from his shoulders, delighted that Bobby had made it that far. "He does," he said. "He does indeed."

"Gleet's keeping a lookout along the river," said Bredon, "so they're moving inland through Tennessee and Kentucky. It'll be a slow trek for such a large group, and they'll have to split up to cross the Ohio in ones and twos. But I think they'll make it." He nodded consideringly, and repeated, as if to himself, "I think they'll make it."

January brought him a chair. Bredon hesitated, then shook his head. "Not just yet. You did us all a great service, for which, as I said, I—and all of us—are in your debt. And though I realize it's the worst kind of bad manners to impose on a man who has helped you, I'm going to."

"Anyone on the *Silver Moon,*" replied Rose with a smile, "would tell us that that's exactly what one could expect of an Abolitionist, sir."

And Bredon smiled back, relaxing as he understood the acceptance behind her jest.

"Will you help us?" he asked as simply as a starving man asks for bread. "Oh, not tonight," he added as January's eyes widened in alarm. "Nor this week, or this month. But we need help. There's a lot of runners crossing along the borders, where the slave states lie alongside the free. Slaves in Kentucky and Tennessee, or in Virginia and Maryland—it isn't so far for them to travel, and there are enough people from New England and Pennsylvania and New York who've moved down into those states and who don't like what they see there, who're willing to let runaways sleep in their cellars, or who will put out food. In Kentucky and Missouri things aren't the same as they are deeper south. I know a lot of slaves, instead of trying to get north, will come to New Orleans and make their living as free men. . . ."

"As men who're free to be paid pennies because they don't dare ask for dollars," said January. "Free to live in shacks on the outskirts of town because nobody will pay them much attention there. But yes, I guess it is easier than trying to make it all the way to Ohio."

"More and more are trying it," said Bredon. "As more and more laws are passed to control freedmen, to limit what free people of color can do. More and more rich men who make their living from slaves are getting scared. They keep pretending that once they get everything nailed down and set, things will go on as they have, with slaves in the slave states doing the heavy work and living like animals, and ignorant as animals, kept that way by men who don't dare let them learn to read." His deep voice was level and quiet, but anger burned in the yellow wolf eyes.

"But things won't stay the way they are, no matter how hard the slave-holders try to make them. Thu tells me you were once a slave, sir."

"As a child, yes," said January. "My mother was bought by a wealthy sugar-broker who made her his mistress—that is the custom here. And as the custom is here, he freed me and my sister."

"Then you don't remember slavery clearly?"

January said, "I remember it."

There was silence then, in the deep shadows, silence like the hush of a Mississippi farm on a hot afternoon, like the dark stinking shadows of a slave-jail in Natchez.

"We need hideouts," said Bredon at last. "We need places where runaways can come, until they can be taken north. We need places where they can sleep for a night, or two, or three. We need men—and women—who are willing to guide runaways on to the next stage; who are willing to take food to a hiding-place, or give clothing to help an escape.

"I watched you on the boat, Mr. January. I know you were pretending to be Sefton's valet, but it was clear to me who was doing the thinking. I watched you trailing that scoundrel Weems and Mrs. Fischer, and I watched you searching for the money Weems was supposed to have stolen. . . . Did you ever recover it? Thu tells me you found a key."

"We recovered it," said January. "And returned it to the Bank from which it had been stolen."

Bredon nodded. "Good," he said. "I'm glad you retrieved what was your own. I'm asking you to put your lives in danger. They hang white men for assisting runaways—slave-stealing, they call it—and for men of your own race it's worse. I'm asking you to put in danger the futures that you're trying to build for yourselves—the school Thu tells me you're opening for girls, the music that made for just about the only pleasure I had on that truly god-forsaken boat.

"But we need people with brains. We need people who are honest. . . . And we need people with houses."

He gestured at the deep velvety dimness of the parlor, the gentle shadows thick in all the rooms where next winter—please God, thought January—a few more soft-eyed young ladies would study Latin and mathematics and history, would learn that there were other dreams in life than being beautiful and submissive so that they could become white men's mistresses.

"I won't ask for your answer right away," said Bredon quietly. "I'm staying at the Verandah Hotel on St. Louis Street. There are others in the city I'll try and speak to as well. But think about it. You're some of the lucky ones, the ones who were given your freedom. One day, God willing, we will be able to strike down slavery root and branch, and eliminate it from this country. Until that time, we're trying to save those we can, one by one, soul by soul."

He bowed over Rose's hand and extended his hand to January. January kept his own hand at his side and looked across at his wife.

The wife he had worked so hard to protect. The woman with whom he hoped to build as safe a life as they could make.

Rose's eyes met his, calm and gray-green, with the points of candle-fire multiplied infinitely in her spectacles.

This could ruin all we have. Take from us even what little we've fought to achieve.

She looked a question at him, and, after a moment, January nodded.

Then she smiled at Bredon, and said, "Are you sure you don't want to sit and have coffee? If . . ." She looked at January again, and again he nodded, more strongly now. "If we are going to be friends?"

After Bredon left, January found it hard to sleep. Beside him, Rose dropped off as usual within seconds of their final kiss—it was a source of never-ending wonder and annoyance to him that she could sleep with the uncaring ease of a cat, while he lay awake looking at the glowing shapes thrown by the night-light in its red glass bubble, listening to the mosquitoes whine beyond the cloudy gauze of the bar. Hearing, beyond that, the croak of frogs in the gutters outside, the unceasing throb of the cicadas in the trees.

Wondering just what the hell he'd let himself—and Rose—in for.

Five years ago Nat Turner had risen in revolt against the whites in Virginia: he and his followers had been captured, tortured, hanged. Since that time the merest whisper of revolt was punished, brutally for whites, and for blacks with the animal fury of terrors that the slaveholders would not even admit they felt.

Judas Bredon had risked his life to smuggle his fifteen runaways up-river to Memphis. At the time he'd realized what was going on, January had not even been certain he'd have the courage to do the same.

And now he was being asked to.

And had, God help him, agreed.

God help me, he thought again, groping out to the nightstand to touch through the mosquito-bar the blue beads of his rosary. *Dear God, what have I done?*

As if in answer to the question he slept, and dreamed of the *Silver Moon* again, and of young Mr. Purlie getting on the boat. Of Gleet's gloating voice saying, *She's a beauty, ain't she?* as he dragged the girl forward and tore open her dress. *She's yours for a thousand dollars. . . . Go ahead, feel of her. . . .*

In his dream January saw again the young girl weeping with shame, and the handsome and ineffectual Mr. Quince, his hands full of copies of the *Liberator,* standing by shaking in fury.

But Quince is more a man than I, thought January. *At least he went around the boat speaking out against what he saw. And not letting mockery stop him.*

His dream changed. He was with Rose, walking along the banks of a bayou deep in the Barataria country, in the old pirate-haunted lands where Jean Lafitte and his men had roved and hidden out thirty years before. Rose, in boy's garb, had been speaking cheerfully of what her neighbors in that country, former pirates themselves, had told her about the logistics of hiding treasure—and January, and the half-dozen slaves who'd gone along with them—knelt by the side of the bayou, just where January had deduced they should, and from the water drew the old iron ship's cannon, plugged with tar, from the hiding-place where one of Lafitte's captains had left it.

In his dream he saw again the glitter of the gold in the new sun, and Rose with a necklace of blazing topazes strung around her hat.

That gold had been taken away from them—and given back.

On the other side of the bayou in his dream, January saw the woman he'd seen in other dreams: a flicker of blue robe, the gentle face that watches over the world. A halo of insubstantial stars.

She asked him, *Did you think the gold was given to you to use for yourself alone?*

And he knew then that God never gives anyone gold to use for themselves alone.

Then he was back in the parlor, as he had been earlier that evening, with Judas Bredon saying, . . . *we're looking for people with houses.*

And in the shadows, like a ghost in an aureole of ghostly stars, God's Mother winked at January and smiled. He saw that under her blue veil she wore Mrs. Fischer's green–and–cream–colored dress.

He woke and knew it was very early, not daylight, not even the early-rising summer dawn. He wondered what had waked him. The smell of smoke from the kitchen of the house next door, as their slave-woman built up the hearth-fire that would be her personal hell for another sweltering day? The clanging bell of a steamboat, far down the Rue Esplanade?

Then he heard again, from the yard below their window, a stealthy scratching, the scraping whisper of a basket laid down on the bricks.

Silent, January slipped from beneath the mosquito-bar, and by touch in the dark—for the night-lamp had long gone out—crossed the bedroom and gathered his shirt from the single chair. Slipping the garment on, he moved through the parlor on naked feet, past the pantry with its scents of candlewax and last night's coffee. He kept close to the wall, where the floor would not creak, and as he did so he heard the rustle of someone on the rear gallery.

He remembered the kitchen fire that had burst out while they were gone, started, Gabriel had said, no one knew how. . . . They were lucky the house had not burned down.

Guédé-Five-Days-Unhappy, tear the roof away from over his head. . . .

January shot back the bolt and threw the door open in time to see Queen Régine gather up her basket, preparing to leave.

The old woman whirled as January stepped out of the door and put himself between her and the stair down to the yard. In the gray fore-light of not-yet-day her black eyes glittered like a startled beast's, and she raised one skinny hand. Then she lowered it and looked down, and following her eyes, January saw, almost under his feet, a cross written in brick-dust, and the scribbled loops of a vévé in water that smelled of verbena.

He had been brother to a voodooienne long enough to know those signs meant life, not death, and his eyes went to the Queen's in questioning wonder.

She said, "You save my child."

"What?"

"I take the cross off you," said the old woman, "an' put blessin' on this house. You save my child. I seen you in a dream—dark, an' shoutin', an' guns firin' off. Water rushin' in, an' great black weights movin' around in that dark. You went back in that dark to save my child, and brought her up out to the light."

My granny knows about them things. . . .

"Julie is your granddaughter?" he asked, knowing even before she nodded that it was true.

"She has the Knowin' in her," said Queen Régine. "Since she was a little thing, she an' me, we shared the Power. But her mama take her to Church, so she don't think about Power no more, and don't want it. But between us, between her an' me, it's still alive."

January said, "That's why you went down to see the *Silver Moon* off? To say good-by?"

"To kiss her," said the Queen. "An' to put my Word on her, though she don't believe it no more; just to see her once more. Her master, he sell her to that Irish as a maid for his *popotte,* and they all promise, *we won't sell her, we make her a good maidservant. . . .* But she's afraid. And I'm afraid. I know I'll never see her again, not in the flesh. Sometimes I felt her scared so bad, scared one night. . . . But that mornin', as I was cookin' in the kitchen, her fear came on me so strong, I near fainted. And I put my head down on the table an' I see her in the dark, trapped an' scared, with things fallin' on her an' the water comin' in. . . . An' I see you. And I thought . . ."

Her few white teeth shone in a wry crone's grin.

". . . I thought, *Lord Baron Cemetery, don't let that hex take hold on him now!* You went back for her," she finished with tears swimming silver in her eyes. "You went back and you didn't have to, you didn't even know for sure she was there. But my girl, she's alive now 'cause of you. She's walkin' to freedom 'cause of you. So I put blessin' on your house, blessin' wherever you walk. Blessin' to guard you, whatever you do."

January said softly, "Thank you, Your Majesty."

And the little old woman winked at him, and he stepped aside to let her totter down the stair.

To himself he reflected, as she hobbled away into the half-lights and whispers of the warm, still dawn, that if he was going to start working with the Underground Railway, he was certainly going to need all the blessings he could get.

He turned, and went back into the dim sanctuary of his home.

STEAMBOATS

The steam-driven packet-boats that plied the waterways of America in the 1830s were hardly the "floating palaces" of the post–Civil War era; they, and the craft of steamboating, differed even from those of the late 1850s immortalized in Mark Twain's *Life on the Mississippi.* At the time of my story, the era of fancy wooden gingerbread trimmings, gilded antlers on the smokestacks, plush cabin furnishings, and calliopes lay a decade or two in the future. Even the steam whistle had yet to be invented.

Before the post-War era of the railroads, steamboats were the workaday backbone of commerce and transportation. They were plain, generally only two decks high (only later was the "hurricane" deck surmounted by the topmost "texas" deck), and resembled barns set on rafts. If they were primarily white, like later steamboats, it was only because whitewash was cheap. Staterooms were minuscule, and in the high-water periods of the cotton and sugar harvests, every square foot of deck-space was likely to be taken up with cargo: freight was given priority, and passengers came in a poor second. During the high-water months most commerce was done by the side-wheelers—larger, more powerful, and more maneuverable. Only in low water—or in shallower waters of lesser rivers and bayous—did the smaller stern-wheelers like the *Silver Moon* come into their own.

I have tried to describe what steamboat travel must have been like in the 1830s, when the Mississippi River was innocent of locks, flood control, uniform levees, or any variety of snag-clearance (or safety regulations for steamboat passengers). Even before the Civil War, railroads had begun to undercut the steamboats' monopoly on freight and to disrupt uninhibited navigation with bridges.

COLONEL DAVIS

In the summer of 1836, when *Dead Water* takes place, Jefferson Davis was twenty-eight years old and just embarking on a career as a planter at Brierfield on Davis's Bend of the Mississippi. He had been widowed less than a year before by the death of his young bride of three months, Sarah Knox Taylor (called Knox), the daughter of his former commanding officer—and future President—Zachary Taylor. Davis had already commanded troops in the Black Hawk War, though as far as anyone has ever been able to prove, he never encountered militia Captain Abraham Lincoln during that conflict.

In the mid-1840s Davis entered politics and re-married, to a young lady named Varina Howell. When the Mexican War broke out in 1846, he accepted a commission as Colonel and went on to become a war hero, a Senator, and Secretary of War to President Franklin Pierce, a career that culminated in his five-year term as the only President of the Confederate States of America.

James Pemberton became the overseer at Brierfield in Davis's absence, a position he held until his death in 1850.

Davis is universally described as a fair and kind master to his slaves.

ABOUT THE AUTHOR

BARBARA HAMBLY lives in Los Angeles, where she is at work on a novel about Mary Todd Lincoln, *The Emancipator's Wife,* which Bantam will publish in 2005.